The 1815 season is well under way, and while one would think that all talk would be of Wellington and Waterloo, in truth there is little change from the conversations of 1814, which centered around that most eternal of society topics—marriage.

As usual, the matrimonial hopes among the debutante set center upon the Bridgerton family, most specifically the eldest of the available brothers, Benedict. He might not possess a title, but his handsome face, pleasing form, and heavy purse appear to have made up for that lack handily. Indeed, This Author has heard, on more than one occasion, an Ambitious Mama saying of her daughter: "She'll marry a duke . . . or a Bridgerton."

For his part, Mr. Bridgerton seems most uninterested in the young ladies who frequent society events. He attends almost every party, yet he does nothing but watch the doors, presumably waiting for some special person.

Perhaps . . .

A potential bride?

LADY WHISTLEDOWN'S SOCIETY PAPERS, 12 JULY 1815

By Julia Quinn

The Bridgerton Series
The Duke and I
The Viscount Who Loved Me
An Offer From a Gentleman
Romancing Mister Bridgerton
To Sir Phillip, With Love
When He Was Wicked
It's In His Kiss
On the Way to the Wedding
The Bridgertons: Happily Ever After

The Smythe-Smith Quartet
Just Like Heaven
A Night Like This
The Sum of All Kisses
The Secrets of Sir Richard Kenworthy

The Bevelstoke Series
The Secret Diaries of Miss Miranda Cheever
What Happens in London
Ten Things I Love About You

The Two Dukes of Wyndham
THE LOST DUKE OF WYNDHAM
MR. CAVENDISH, I PRESUME

Agents of the Crown
TO CATCH AN HEIRESS
HOW TO MARRY A MARQUIS

The Lyndon Sisters
EVERYTHING AND THE MOON
BRIGHTER THAN THE SUN

The Splendid Trilogy
SPLENDID
DANCING AT MIDNIGHT
MINX

Julia Quinn

An Offer from a Gentleman

An Imprint of HarperCollins*Publishers*

This is a work of fiction. Names, characters, places, and incidents are products of the author's imagination or are used fictitiously and are not to be construed as real. Any resemblance to actual events, locales, organizations, or persons, living or dead, is entirely coincidental.

"An Offer From a Gentleman: The 2nd Epilogue" was originally published as an e-book.

AVON BOOKS
An Imprint of HarperCollins*Publishers*
195 Broadway
New York, New York 10007

ISBN 978-0-06-235365-8
www.avonromance.com

First Avon Books mass market printing: September 2015

Printed in the U.S.A.

13

For Cheyenne,
and the memory of a Frappucino summer.

And also for Paul,
even though he doesn't see anything wrong
with watching open heart surgery on TV
while we're eating spaghetti.

An Offer from a Gentleman

Prologue

Everyone knew that Sophie Beckett was a bastard.

The servants all knew it. But they loved little Sophie, had loved her since she'd arrived at Penwood Park at the age of three, a small bundle wrapped in a too-big coat, left on the doorstep on a rainy July night. And because they loved her, they pretended that she was exactly what the sixth Earl of Penwood said she was—the orphaned daughter of an old friend. Never mind that Sophie's moss green eyes and dark blond hair matched the earl's precisely. Never mind that the shape of her face looked remarkably like that of the earl's recently deceased mother, or that her smile was an exact replica of the earl's sister's. No one wanted to hurt Sophie's feelings—or risk their livelihoods—by pointing that out.

The earl, one Richard Gunningworth, never discussed Sophie or her origins, but he must have known she was his bastard. No one knew what had been in the letter the housekeeper had fished from Sophie's pocket when she'd been discovered that rainy midnight; the earl had burned the missive mere seconds after reading it. He'd watched the paper shrivel and curl in the flames, then ordered a room made up for Sophie near the nursery. She'd remained there ever since. He called her Sophia, and she called him "my lord," and they saw each other a few times a year, whenever the earl returned home from London, which wasn't very often.

But perhaps most importantly, Sophie knew she was a bastard. She wasn't entirely certain how she knew it, just that she did, and probably had her entire life. She had few memories of her life before her arrival at Penwood Park, but she could remember a long coach journey across England, and she could remember her grandmother, coughing and wheezing and looking terribly thin, telling her she was going to live with her father. And most of all, she could remember standing on the doorstep in the rain, knowing that her grandmother was hiding in the bushes, waiting to see if Sophie was taken inside.

The earl had touched his fingers to the little girl's chin, tipped her face up to the light, and in that moment they both knew the truth.

Everyone knew Sophie was a bastard, and no one talked about it, and they were all quite happy with this arrangement.

Until the earl decided to marry.

Sophie had been quite pleased when she'd heard the news. The housekeeper had said that the butler had said that the earl's secretary had said that the earl planned to spend more time at Penwood Park now that he would be a family man. And while Sophie didn't exactly miss the earl when he was gone—it was hard to miss someone who didn't pay her much attention even when he was there—she rather thought she *might* miss him if she got to know him better, and if she got to know him better, maybe he wouldn't go away so often. Plus, the upstairs maid had said that the housekeeper had said that the neighbors' butler had said that the earl's intended wife already had two daughters, and they were near in age to Sophie.

After seven years alone in the nursery, Sophie was delighted. Unlike the other children in the district, she was never invited to local parties and events. No one actually came out and called her a bastard—to do so was tantamount to calling the earl, who had made one declaration that Sophie was his ward and then never revisited the subject, a liar.

But at the same time, the earl never made any great attempt to force Sophie's acceptance. And so at the age of ten, Sophie's best friends were maids and footmen, and her parents might as well have been the housekeeper and butler.

But now she was getting sisters for real.

Oh, she knew she could not call them her sisters. She knew that she would be introduced as Sophia Maria Beckett, the earl's ward, but they would *feel* like sisters. And that was what really mattered.

And so, one February afternoon, Sophie found herself waiting in the great hall along with the assembled servants, watching out the window for the earl's carriage to pull up the drive, carrying in it the new countess and her two daughters. And, of course, the earl.

"Do you think she'll like me?" Sophie whispered to Mrs. Gibbons, the housekeeper. "The earl's wife, I mean."

"Of course she'll like you, dearling," Mrs. Gibbons whispered back. But her eyes hadn't been as certain as her tone. The new countess might not take kindly to the presence of her husband's by-blow.

"And I'll take lessons with her daughters?"

"No point in having you take your lessons separately."

Sophie nodded thoughtfully, then started to squirm when she saw the carriage rolling up the drive. "They're here!" she whispered.

Mrs. Gibbons reached out to pat her on the head, but Sophie had already dashed off to the window, practically pressing her face up to the glass.

The earl stepped down first, then reached in and helped down two young girls. They were dressed in matching black coats. One wore a pink ribbon in her hair; the other yellow. Then, as the two girls stepped aside, the earl reached up to help one last person from the carriage.

Sophie's breath caught in her throat as she waited for the new countess to emerge. Her little fingers crossed and a single, "Please," whispered over her lips.

Please let her love me.

Maybe if the countess loved her, then the earl would love her as well, and maybe, even if he didn't actually call her daughter, he'd treat her as one, and they'd be a family truly.

As Sophie watched through the window, the new countess stepped down from the carriage, her every movement so graceful and pure that Sophie was reminded of the delicate lark that occasionally came to splash in the birdbath in the garden. Even the countess's hat was adorned by a long feather, its turquoise plume glittering in the hard winter sun.

"She's beautiful," Sophie whispered. She darted a quick look back at Mrs. Gibbons to gauge her reaction, but the housekeeper was standing at strict attention, eyes straight ahead, waiting for the earl to bring his new family inside for introductions.

Sophie gulped, not exactly certain where she was meant to stand. Everyone else seemed to have a designated place. The servants were lined up according to rank, from the butler right down to the lowliest scullery maid. Even the dogs were sitting dutifully in the corner, their leads held tight by the Keeper of the Hounds.

But Sophie was rootless. If she were truly the daughter of the house, she'd be standing with her governess, awaiting the new countess. If she were truly the earl's ward, she'd be in much the same place. But Miss Timmons had caught a head cold and refused to leave the nursery and come downstairs. None of the servants believed for a second that the governess was truly ill. She'd been fine the night before, but no one blamed her for the deception. Sophie was, after all, the earl's bastard, and no one wanted to be the one to offer potential insult to the new countess by introducing her to her husband's by-blow.

And the countess would have to be blind, stupid, or both not to realize in an instant that Sophie was something more than the earl's ward.

Suddenly overcome with shyness, Sophie shrank into a corner as two footmen threw open the front doors with a flourish. The two girls entered first, then stepped to the side as the earl led the countess in. The earl introduced the countess and her daughters to the butler, and the butler introduced them to the servants.

And Sophie waited.

The butler presented the footmen, the chef, the housekeeper, the grooms.

And Sophie waited.

He presented the kitchen maids, the upstairs maids, the scullery maids.

And Sophie waited.

And then finally the butler—Rumsey was his name—presented the lowliest of the lowest of maids, a scullery girl named Dulcie who had been hired a mere week earlier. The earl nodded and murmured his thanks, and Sophie was still waiting, completely unsure of what to do.

So she cleared her throat and stepped forward, a nervous smile on her face. She didn't spend much time with the earl, but she was trotted out before him whenever he visited Penwood Park, and he always gave her a few minutes of his time, asking about her lessons before shooing her back up to the nursery.

Surely he'd still want to know how her studies were progressing, even now that he'd married. Surely he'd want to know that she'd mastered the science of multiplying fractions, and that Miss Timmons had recently declared her French accent, "perfection."

But he was busy saying something to the countess's daughters, and he didn't hear her. Sophie cleared her throat again, this time more loudly, and said, "My lord?" in a voice that came out a bit more squeaky than she'd intended.

The earl turned around. "Ah, Sophia," he murmured, "I didn't realize you were in the hall."

Sophie beamed. He hadn't been ignoring her, after all.

"And who might this be?" the countess asked, stepping forward to get a better look.

"My ward," the earl replied. "Miss Sophia Beckett."

The countess speared Sophie with an assessing look, then her eyes narrowed.

And narrowed.

And narrowed some more.

"I see," she said.

And everyone in the room knew instantly that she *did* see.

"Rosamund," the countess said, turning to her two girls, "Posy, come with me."

The girls moved immediately to their mother's side. Sophie hazarded a smile in their direction. The smaller one smiled back, but the older one, whose hair was the color of spun gold, took her cue from her mother, pointed her nose in the air, and looked firmly away.

Sophie gulped and smiled again at the friendly girl, but this time the little girl chewed on her lower lip in indecision, then cast her eyes toward the floor.

The countess turned her back on Sophie and said to the earl, "I assume you have had rooms prepared for Rosamund and Posy."

He nodded. "Near the nursery. Right next to Sophie."

There was a long silence, and then the countess must have decided that certain battles should not be conducted before the servants, because all she said was, "I would like to go upstairs now."

And she left, taking the earl and her daughters along with her.

Sophie watched the new family walk up the stairs, and then, as they disappeared onto the landing, she turned to Mrs. Gibbons and asked, "Do you think I should go up to help? I could show the girls the nursery."

Mrs. Gibbons shook her head. "They looked tired," she lied. "I'm sure they'll be needing a nap."

Sophie frowned. She'd been told that Rosamund was eleven and Posy was ten. Surely that was a bit old for taking naps.

Mrs. Gibbons patted her on the back. "Why don't you come with me? I could use a bit of company, and Cook told me that she just made a fresh batch of shortbread. I think it's still warm."

Sophie nodded and followed her out of the hall. She'd have plenty of time that evening to get to know the two girls. She'd show them the nursery, and then they'd become friends, and before long they'd be as sisters.

Sophie smiled. It would be glorious to have sisters.

As it happened, Sophie did not encounter Rosamund and Posy—or the earl and countess, for that matter—until the next day. When Sophie entered the nursery to take her supper, she noticed that the table had been set for two, not four, and Miss Timmons (who had miraculously recovered from her ailment) said that the new countess had told her that Rosamund and Posy were too tired from their travels to eat that evening.

But the girls had to have their lessons, and so the next morning they arrived in the nursery, trailing the countess by one step each. Sophie had been working at her lessons for an hour already, and she looked up from her arithmetic with great interest. She didn't smile at the girls this time. Somehow it seemed best not to.

"Miss Timmons," the countess said.

Miss Timmons bobbed a curtsy, murmuring, "My lady."

"The earl tells me you will teach my daughters."

"I will do my best, my lady."

The countess motioned to the older girl, the one with golden hair and cornflower eyes. She looked, Sophie thought, as pretty as the porcelain doll the earl had sent up from London for her seventh birthday.

"This," the countess said, "is Rosamund. She is eleven.

And this"—she then motioned to the other girl, who had not taken her eyes off of her shoes—"is Posy. She is ten."

Sophie looked at Posy with great interest. Unlike her mother and sister, her hair and eyes were quite dark, and her cheeks were a bit pudgy.

"Sophie is also ten," Miss Timmons replied.

The countess's lips thinned. "I would like you to show the girls around the house and garden."

Miss Timmons nodded. "Very well. Sophie, put your slate down. We can return to arithmetic—"

"Just *my* girls," the countess interrupted, her voice somehow hot and cold at the same time. "I will speak with Sophie alone."

Sophie gulped and tried to bring her eyes to the countess's, but she only made it as far as her chin. As Miss Timmons ushered Rosamund and Posy out of the room she stood up, awaiting further direction from her father's new wife.

"I know who you are," the countess said the moment the door clicked shut.

"M-my lady?"

"You're his bastard, and don't try to deny it."

Sophie said nothing. It was the truth, of course, but no one had ever said it aloud. At least not to her face.

The countess grabbed her chin and squeezed and pulled until Sophie was forced to look her in the eye. "You listen to me," she said in a menacing voice. "You might live here at Penwood Park, and you might share lessons with my daughters, but you are nothing but a bastard, and that is all you will ever be. Don't you ever, *ever* make the mistake of thinking you are as good as the rest of us."

Sophie let out a little moan. The countess's fingernails were biting into the underside of her chin.

"My husband," the countess continued, "feels some sort of misguided duty to you. It's admirable of him to see to his mistakes, but it is an insult to me to have you in my home—fed, clothed, and educated as if you were his real daughter."

But she *was* his real daughter. And it had been her home much longer than the countess's.

Abruptly, the countess let go of her chin. "I don't want to see you," she hissed. "You are never to speak to me, and you shall endeavor never to be in my company. Furthermore, you are not to speak to Rosamund and Posy except during lessons. They are the daughters of the house now, and should not have to associate with the likes of *you*. Do you have any questions?"

Sophie shook her head.

"Good."

And with that, she swept out of the room, leaving Sophie with wobbly legs and a quivering lip.

And an awful lot of tears.

In time, Sophie learned a bit more about her precarious position in the house. The servants always knew everything, and it all reached Sophie's ears eventually.

The countess, whose given name was Araminta, had insisted that very first day that Sophie be removed from the house. The earl had refused. Araminta didn't have to love Sophie, he'd said coolly. She didn't even have to like her. But she had to put up with her. He had owned up to his responsibility to the girl for seven years, and he wasn't going to stop now.

Rosamund and Posy took their cues from Araminta and treated Sophie with hostility and disdain, although Posy's heart clearly wasn't into torture and cruelty in the way Rosamund's was. Rosamund liked nothing better than to pinch and twist the skin on the back of Sophie's hand when Miss Timmons wasn't looking. Sophie never said anything; she rather doubted that Miss Timmons would have the courage to reprimand Rosamund (who would surely run to Araminta with a false tale), and if anyone noticed that Sophie's hands were perpetually black-and-blue, no one ever said so.

Posy showed her the occasional kindness, although more often than not she just sighed, and said, "My mummy says I'm not to be nice to you."

As for the earl, he never intervened.

Sophie's life continued in this vein for four years, until the earl surprised everyone by clutching his hand to his chest while taking tea in the rose garden, letting out one ragged gasp, and falling facefirst to the stone cobbles.

He never regained consciousness.

Everyone was quite shocked. The earl was only forty years old. Who could have known that his heart would give out at such a young age? No one was more stunned than Araminta, who had been trying quite desperately since her wedding night to conceive the all-important heir.

"I might be with child!" she hastened to tell the earl's solicitors. "You can't give the title over to some distant cousin. I could very well be with child."

But she wasn't with child, and when the earl's will was read one month later (the solicitors had wanted to be sure to give the countess enough time to know for sure if she was pregnant) Araminta was forced to sit next to the new earl, a rather dissolute young man who was more often drunk than not.

Most of the earl's wishes were standard fare. He left bequests to loyal servants. He settled funds on Rosamund, Posy, and even Sophie, ensuring that all three girls would have respectable dowries.

And then the solicitor reached Araminta's name.

To my wife, Araminta Gunningworth, Countess of Penwood, I leave a yearly income of two thousand pounds—

"That's all?" Araminta cried out.

—unless she agrees to shelter and care for my ward, Miss Sophia Maria Beckett, until the latter reaches the age of twenty, in which case her yearly income shall be trebled to six thousand pounds.

"I don't want her," Araminta whispered.

"You don't have to take her," the solicitor reminded her. "You can—"

"Live on a measly two thousand a year?" she snapped. "I don't think so."

The solicitor, who lived on considerably less than two thousand a year, said nothing.

The new earl, who'd been drinking steadily throughout the meeting, just shrugged.

Araminta stood.

"What is your decision?" the solicitor asked.

"I'll take her," she said in a low voice.

"Shall I find the girl and tell her?"

Araminta shook her head. "I'll tell her myself."

But when Araminta found Sophie, she left out a few important facts . . .

Part One

Chapter 1

This year's most sought-after invitation must surely be that of the Bridgerton masquerade ball, to be held Monday next. Indeed, one cannot take two steps without being forced to listen to some society mama speculating on who will attend, and perhaps more importantly, who will wear what.

Neither of the aforementioned topics, however, are nearly as interesting as that of the two unmarried Bridgerton brothers, Benedict and Colin. (Before anyone points out that there is a third unmarried Bridgerton brother, let This Author assure you that she is fully aware of the existence of Gregory Bridgerton. He is, however, fourteen years of age, and therefore not pertinent to this particular column, which concerns, as This Author's columns often do, that most sacred of sports: husband-hunting.)

Although the Misters Bridgerton are just that—merely Misters—they are still considered two of the prime catches of the season. It is a well-known fact that both are possessed of respectable fortunes, and it does not require perfect sight to know that they also possess, as do all eight of the Bridgerton offspring, the Bridgerton good looks.

Will some fortunate young lady use the mystery of a masquerade night to snare one of the eligible bachelors?

This Author isn't even going to attempt to speculate.

LADY WHISTLEDOWN'S SOCIETY PAPERS, 31 MAY 1815

"Sophie! Sophieeeeeeeeeeeeeee!"

As screeches went, it was enough to shatter glass. Or at least an eardrum.

"Coming, Rosamund! I'm coming!" Sophie hitched up the hem of her coarse woolen skirts and hurried up the stairs, slipping on the fourth step and only just barely managing to grab the bannister before landing on her bottom. She should have remembered that the stairs would be slick; she'd helped the downstairs maid wax them just that morning.

Skidding to a halt in the doorway to Rosamund's bedroom and still catching her breath, Sophie said, "Yes?"

"My tea is cold."

What Sophie wanted to say was, "It was warm when I brought it an hour ago, you lazy fiend."

What she did say was, "I'll get you another pot."

Rosamund sniffed. "See that you do."

Sophie stretched her lips into what the nearly blind might call a smile and picked up the tea service. "Shall I leave the biscuits?" she asked.

Rosamund gave her pretty head a shake. "I want fresh ones."

Shoulders slightly stooped from the weight of the overloaded tea service, Sophie exited the room, careful not to start grumbling until she'd safely reached the hall. Rosamund was forever ordering tea, then not bothering to drink it until an hour passed. By then, of course, it was cold, so she had to order a fresh pot.

Which meant Sophie was forever running up and down the stairs, up and down, up and down. Sometimes it seemed that was all she did with her life.

Up and down, up and down.

And of course the mending, the pressing, the hairdressing, the shoe polishing, the darning, the bedmaking . . .

"Sophie!"

Sophie turned around to see Posy heading toward her.

"Sophie, I've been meaning to ask you, do you think this color is becoming on me?"

Sophie assessed Posy's mermaid costume. The cut wasn't quite right for Posy, who had never lost all of her baby fat, but the color did indeed bring out the best in her complexion. "It is a lovely shade of green," Sophie replied quite honestly. "It makes your cheeks very rosy."

"Oh, good. I'm so glad you like it. You do have such a knack for picking out my clothing." Posy smiled as she reached out and plucked a sugared biscuit from the tray. "Mother has been an absolute bear all week about the masquerade ball, and I know I shall never hear the end of it if I do not look my best. Or"—Posy's face twisted into a grimace—"if she *thinks* I do not look my best. She is determined that one of us snare one of the remaining Bridgerton brothers, you know."

"I know."

"And to make matters worse, that Whistledown woman has been writing about them again. It only"—Posy finished chewing and paused while she swallowed—"whets her appetite."

"Was the column very good this morning?" Sophie asked, shifting the tray to rest on her hip. "I haven't had a chance to read it yet."

"Oh, the usual stuff," Posy said with a wave of her hand. "Really, it can be quite humdrum, you know."

Sophie tried to smile and failed. She'd like nothing more than to live a day of Posy's humdrum life. Well, perhaps she wouldn't want Araminta for a mother, but she wouldn't mind a life of parties, routs, and musicales.

"Let's see," Posy mused. "There was a review of Lady Worth's recent ball, a bit about Viscount Guelph, who seems rather smitten with some girl from Scotland, and then a longish piece on the upcoming Bridgerton masquerade."

Sophie sighed. She'd been reading about the upcoming masquerade for weeks, and even though she was nothing but a lady's maid (and occasionally a housemaid as well, whenever Araminta decided she wasn't working hard enough) she couldn't help but wish that she could attend the ball.

"I for one will be thrilled if that Guelph viscount gets himself engaged," Posy remarked, reaching for another biscuit. "It will mean one fewer bachelor for Mother to go on and on about as a potential husband. It's not as if I have any hope of attracting his attention anyway." She took a bite of the biscuit; it crunched loudly in her mouth. "I do hope Lady Whistledown is right about him."

"She probably is," Sophie answered. She had been reading *Lady Whistledown's Society Papers* since it had debuted in 1813, and the gossip columnist was almost always correct when it came to matters of the Marriage Mart.

Not, of course, that Sophie had ever had the chance to see the Marriage Mart for herself. But if one read *Whistledown* often enough, one could almost feel a part of London Society without actually attending any balls.

In fact, reading *Whistledown* was really Sophie's one true enjoyable pastime. She'd already read all of the novels in the library, and as neither Araminta, Rosamund, nor Posy was particularly enamored of reading, Sophie couldn't look forward to a new book entering the house.

But *Whistledown* was great fun. No one actually knew the columnist's true identity. When the single-sheet newspaper had debuted two years earlier, speculation had been rampant. Even now, whenever Lady Whistledown reported a particularly juicy bit of gossip, people starting talking and guessing anew, wondering who on earth was able to report with such speed and accuracy.

And for Sophie, *Whistledown* was a tantalizing glimpse into the world that might have been hers, had her parents actually made their union legal. She would have been an earl's daughter, not an earl's bastard; her name Gunningworth instead of Beckett.

Just once, she'd like to be the one stepping into the coach and attending the ball.

Instead, she was the one dressing others for their nights on the town, cinching Posy's corset or dressing Rosamund's hair or polishing a pair of Araminta's shoes.

But she could not—or at least should not—complain. She might have to serve as maid to Araminta and her daughters, but at least she had a home. Which was more than most girls in her position had.

When her father had died, he'd left her nothing. Well, nothing but a roof over her head. His will had ensured that she could not be turned out until she was twenty. There was no way that Araminta would forfeit four thousand pounds a year by giving Sophie the boot.

But that four thousand pounds was Araminta's, not Sophie's, and Sophie hadn't ever seen a penny of it. Gone were the fine clothes she'd used to wear, replaced by the coarse wool of the servants. And she ate what the rest of the maids ate—whatever Araminta, Rosamund, and Posy chose to leave behind.

Sophie's twentieth birthday, however, had come and gone almost a year earlier, and here she was, still living at Penwood House, still waiting on Araminta hand and foot. For some unknown reason—probably because she didn't want to train (or pay) a new maid—Araminta had allowed Sophie to remain in her household.

And Sophie had stayed. If Araminta was the devil she knew, then the rest of the world was the devil she didn't. And Sophie had no idea which would be worse.

"Isn't that tray getting heavy?"

Sophie blinked her way out of her reverie and focused on Posy, who was reaching for the last biscuit on the tray. Drat. She'd been hoping to snitch it for herself. "Yes," she murmured. "Yes, it is quite. I should really be getting to the kitchen with it."

Posy smiled. "I won't keep you any longer, but when you're done with that, could you press my pink gown? I'm going to wear it tonight. Oh, and I suppose the matching shoes should be readied as well. I got a bit of dirt on them last time I wore them, and you know how Mother is about shoes. Never mind that you can't even see them under my skirt. She'll notice the tiniest speck of dirt the instant I lift my hem to climb a step."

Sophie nodded, mentally adding Posy's requests to her daily list of chores.

"I'll see you later, then!" Biting down on that last biscuit, Posy turned and disappeared into her bedchamber.

And Sophie trudged down to the kitchen.

A few days later, Sophie was on her knees, pins clamped between her teeth as she made last-minute alterations on Araminta's masquerade costume. The Queen Elizabeth gown had, of course, been delivered from the dressmaker as a perfect fit, but Araminta insisted that it was now a quarter inch too large in the waist.

"How is that?" Sophie asked, speaking through her teeth so the pins wouldn't fall.

"Too tight."

Sophie adjusted a few pins. "What about that?"

"Too loose."

Sophie pulled out a pin and stuck it back in precisely the same spot. "There. How does that feel?"

Araminta twisted this way and that, then finally declared, "It'll do."

Sophie smiled to herself as she stood to help Araminta out of the gown.

"I'll need it done in an hour if we're to get to the ball on time," Araminta said.

"Of course," Sophie murmured. She'd found it easiest just to say "of course" on a regular basis in conversations with Araminta.

"This ball is very important," Araminta said sharply. "Rosamund must make an advantageous match this year. The new earl—" She shuddered with distaste; she still considered the new earl an interloper, never mind that he was the old earl's closest living male relative. "Well, he has told me that this is the last year we may use Penwood House in London. The nerve of the man. I am the dowager countess, after all, and Rosamund and Posy are the earl's daughters."

Stepdaughters, Sophie silently corrected.

"We have every right to use Penwood House for the season. What he plans to do with the house, I'll never know."

"Perhaps he wishes to attend the season and look for a wife," Sophie suggested. "He'll be wanting an heir, I'm sure."

Araminta scowled. "If Rosamund doesn't marry into money, I don't know what we'll do. It is so difficult to find a proper house to rent. And so expensive as well."

Sophie forbore to point out that at least Araminta didn't have to pay for a lady's maid. In fact, until Sophie had turned twenty, she'd received four thousand pounds per year, just for *having* a lady's maid.

Araminta snapped her fingers. "Don't forget that Rosamund will need her hair powdered."

Rosamund was attending dressed as Marie Antoinette. Sophie had asked if she was planning to put a ring of faux blood around her neck. Rosamund had not been amused.

Araminta pulled on her dressing gown, cinching the sash with swift, tight movements. "And Posy—" Her nose wrinkled. "Well, Posy will need your help in some manner or other, I'm sure."

"I'm always glad to help Posy," Sophie replied.

Araminta narrowed her eyes as she tried to figure out if Sophie was being insolent. "Just see that you do," she finally said, her syllables clipped. She stalked off to the washroom.

Sophie saluted as the door closed behind her.

"Ah, there you are, Sophie," Rosamund said as she bustled into the room. "I need your help immediately."

"I'm afraid it'll have to wait until—"

"I said immediately!" Rosamund snapped.

Sophie squared her shoulders and gave Rosamund a steely look. "Your mother wants me to alter her gown."

"Just pull the pins out and tell her you pulled it in. She'll never notice the difference."

Sophie had been considering the very same thing, and she groaned. If she did as Rosamund asked, Rosamund would tattle on her the very next day, and then Araminta would rant and rage for a week. Now she would definitely have to do the alteration.

"What do you need, Rosamund?"

"There is a tear at the hem of my costume. I have no idea how it happened."

"Perhaps when you tried it on—"

"Don't be impertinent!"

Sophie clamped her mouth shut. It was far more difficult to take orders from Rosamund than from Araminta, probably because they'd once been equals, sharing the same schoolroom and governess.

"It must be repaired immediately," Rosamund said with an affected sniff.

Sophie sighed. "Just bring it in. I'll do it right after I finish with your mother's. I promise you'll have it in plenty of time."

"I won't be late for this ball," Rosamund warned. "If I am, I shall have *your* head on a platter."

"You won't be late," Sophie promised.

Rosamund made a rather huffy sound, then hurried out the door to retrieve her costume.

"Ooof!"

Sophie looked up to see Rosamund crashing into Posy, who was barreling through the door.

"Watch where you're going, Posy!" Rosamund snapped.

"You could watch where you're going, too," Posy pointed out.

"I *was* watching. It's impossible to get out of *your* way, you big oaf."

Posy's cheeks stained red, and she stepped aside.

"Did you need something, Posy?" Sophie asked, as soon as Rosamund had disappeared.

Posy nodded. "Could you set aside a little extra time to dress my hair tonight? I found some green ribbons that look a little like seaweed."

Sophie let out a long breath. The dark green ribbons weren't likely to show up very well against Posy's dark hair, but she didn't have the heart to point that out. "I'll try, Posy, but I have to mend Rosamund's dress and alter your mother's."

"Oh." Posy looked crestfallen. It nearly broke Sophie's heart. Posy was the only person who was even halfway nice to her in Araminta's household, save for the servants. "Don't worry," she assured her. "I'll make sure your hair is lovely no matter how much time we have."

"Oh, thank you, Sophie! I—"

"Haven't you gotten started on my gown yet?" Araminta thundered as she returned from the washroom.

Sophie gulped. "I was talking with Rosamund and Posy. Rosamund tore her gown and—"

"Just get to work!"

"I will. Immediately." Sophie plopped down on the settee and turned the gown inside out so that she could take in the waist. "Faster than immediately," she muttered. "Faster than a hummingbird's wings. Faster than—"

"What are you chattering about?" Araminta demanded.

"Nothing."

"Well, cease your prattle immediately. I find the sound of your voice particularly grating."

Sophie ground her teeth together.

"Mama," Posy said, "Sophie is going to dress my hair tonight like—"

"Of course she's going to dress your hair. Quit your dilly-dallying this minute and go put compresses on your eyes so they don't look so puffy."

Posy's face fell. "My eyes are puffy?"

Sophie shook her head on the off chance that Posy decided to look down at her.

"Your eyes are always puffy," Araminta replied. "Don't you think so, Rosamund?"

Posy and Sophie both turned toward the door. Rosamund had just entered, carrying her Marie Antoinette gown. "Always," she agreed. "But a compress will help, I'm sure."

"You look stunning tonight," Araminta told Rosamund. "And you haven't even started getting ready. That gold in your gown is an exquisite match to your hair."

Sophie shot a sympathetic look at the dark-haired Posy, who never received such compliments from her mother.

"You shall snare one of those Bridgerton brothers," Araminta continued. "I'm sure of it."

Rosamund looked down demurely. It was an expression she'd perfected, and Sophie had to admit it looked lovely on her. But then again, most everything looked lovely on Rosamund. Her golden hair and blue eyes were all the rage that year, and thanks to the generous dowry settled upon her by the late earl, it was widely assumed that she would make a brilliant match before the season was through.

Sophie glanced back over at Posy, who was staring at her mother with a sad, wistful expression. "You look lovely, too, Posy," Sophie said impulsively.

Posy's eyes lit up. "Do you think so?"

"Absolutely. And your gown is terribly original. I'm sure there won't be any other mermaids."

"How would you know, Sophie?" Rosamund asked with a laugh. "It's not as if you've ever been out in society."

"I'm sure you'll have a lovely time, Posy," Sophie said

pointedly, ignoring Rosamund's jibe. "I'm terribly jealous. I do wish I could go."

Sophie's little sigh and wish was met with absolute silence . . . followed by the raucous laughter of both Araminta and Rosamund. Even Posy giggled a bit.

"Oh, that's rich," Araminta said, barely able to catch her breath. "Little Sophie at the Bridgerton ball. They don't allow bastards out in society, you know."

"I didn't say I expected to go," Sophie said defensively, "just that I wish I *could*."

"Well, you shouldn't even bother doing that," Rosamund chimed in. "If you wish for things you can't possibly hope for, you're only going to be disappointed."

But Sophie didn't hear what she had to say, because in that moment, the oddest thing happened. As she was turning her head toward Rosamund, she caught sight of the housekeeper standing in the doorway. It was Mrs. Gibbons, who had come up from Penwood Park in the country when the town housekeeper had passed away. And when Sophie's eyes met hers, she winked.

Winked!

Sophie didn't think she'd ever seen Mrs. Gibbons wink.

"Sophie! Sophie! Are you listening to me?"

Sophie turned a distracted eye toward Araminta. "I'm sorry," she murmured. "You were saying?"

"I was saying," Araminta said in a nasty voice, "that you had better get to work on my gown this instant. If we are late for the ball, *you* will answer for it tomorrow."

"Yes, of course," Sophie said quickly. She jabbed her needle into the fabric and started sewing but her mind was still on Mrs. Gibbons.

A wink?

Why on earth would she wink?

Three hours later, Sophie was standing on the front steps of Penwood House, watching first Araminta, then Rosamund, then Posy each take the footman's hand and climb up into the carriage. Sophie waved at Posy, who waved back, then watched the carriage roll down the street and disappear around the corner. It was barely six blocks to Bridgerton House, where the masquerade was to be held, but Araminta would have insisted upon the carriage if they'd lived right next door.

It was important to make a grand entrance, after all.

With a sigh, Sophie turned around and made her way back up the steps. At least Araminta had, in the excitement of the moment, forgotten to leave her with a list of tasks to complete while she was gone. A free evening was a luxury indeed. Perhaps she'd reread a novel. Or maybe she could find today's edition of *Whistledown*. She'd thought she'd seen Rosamund take it into her room earlier that afternoon.

But as Sophie stepped through the front door of Penwood House, Mrs. Gibbons materialized as if from nowhere and grabbed her arm. "There's no time to lose!" the housekeeper said.

Sophie looked at her as if she'd lost her mind. "I beg your pardon?"

Mrs. Gibbons tugged at her elbow. "Come with me."

Sophie allowed herself to be led up the three flights of stairs to her room, a tiny little chamber tucked under the eaves. Mrs. Gibbons was acting in a most peculiar manner, but Sophie humored her and followed along. The housekeeper had always treated her with exceptional kindness, even when it was clear that Araminta disapproved.

"You'll need to get undressed," Mrs. Gibbons said as she grasped the doorknob.

"What?"

"We really must rush."

"Mrs. Gibbons, you . . ." Sophie's mouth fell open, and her words trailed off as she took in the scene in her bedroom. A steaming tub of water lay right in the center, and all three housemaids were bustling about. One was pouring a pitcher of water into the tub, another was fiddling with the lock on a rather mysterious-looking trunk, and the third was holding a towel and saying, "Hurry! Hurry!"

Sophie cast bewildered eyes at the lot of them. "What is going on?"

Mrs. Gibbons turned to her and beamed. "You, Miss Sophia Maria Beckett, are going to the masquerade!"

One hour later, Sophie was transformed. The trunk had held dresses belonging to the late earl's mother. They were all fifty years out of date, but that was no matter. The ball was a masquerade; no one expected the gowns to be of the latest styles.

At the very bottom of the trunk they'd found an exquisite creation of shimmering silver, with a tight, pearl-encrusted bodice and the flared skirts that had been so popular during the previous century. Sophie felt like a princess just touching it. It was a bit musty from its years in the trunk, and one of the maids quickly took it outside to dab a bit of rosewater on the fabric and air it out.

She'd been bathed and perfumed, her hair had been dressed, and one of the housemaids had even applied a touch of rouge to her lips. "Don't tell Miss Rosamund," the maid had whispered. "I nicked it from her collection."

"Ooooh, look," Mrs. Gibbons said. "I found matching gloves."

Sophie looked up to see the housekeeper holding up a pair of long, elbow-length gloves. "Look," she said, taking one from Mrs. Gibbons and examining it. "The Penwood crest. And it's monogrammed. Right at the hem."

Mrs. Gibbons turned over the one in her hand. "SLG. Sarah Louisa Gunningworth. Your grandmother."

Sophie looked at her in surprise. Mrs. Gibbons had never referred to the earl as her father. No one at Penwood Park had ever verbally acknowledged Sophie's blood ties to the Gunningworth family.

"Well, she *is* your grandmother," Mrs. Gibbons declared. "We've all danced around the issue long enough. It's a crime the way Rosamund and Posy are treated like daughters of the house, and you, the earl's true blood, must sweep and serve like a maid!"

The three housemaids nodded in agreement.

"Just once," Mrs. Gibbons said, "for just one night, *you* will be the belle of the ball." With a smile on her face, she slowly turned Sophie around until she was facing the mirror.

Sophie's breath caught. "Is that me?"

Mrs. Gibbons nodded, her eyes suspiciously bright. "You look lovely, dearling," she whispered.

Sophie's hand moved slowly up to her hair.

"Don't muss it!" one of the maids yelped.

"I won't," Sophie promised, her smile wobbling a bit as she fought back a tear. A touch of shimmery powder had been sprinkled onto her hair, so that she sparkled like a fairy princess. Her dark blond curls had been swept atop her head in a loose topknot, with one thick lock allowed to slide down the length of her neck. And her eyes, normally moss green, shone like emeralds.

Although Sophie suspected that might have had more to do with her unshed tears than anything else.

"Here is your mask," Mrs. Gibbons said briskly. It was a demi-mask, the sort that tied at the back so that Sophie would not have to use one of her hands to hold it up. "Now all we need are shoes."

Sophie glanced ruefully at her serviceable and ugly work shoes that sat in the corner. "I have nothing suitable for such finery, I'm afraid."

The housemaid who had rouged Sophie's lips held up a pair of white slippers. "From Rosamund's closet," she said.

Sophie slid her right foot into one of the slippers and just as quickly slid it back out. "It's much too big," she said, glancing up at Mrs. Gibbons. "I'll never be able to walk in them."

Mrs. Gibbons turned to the maid. "Fetch a pair from Posy's closet."

"Hers are even bigger," Sophie said. "I know. I've cleaned enough scuff marks from them."

Mrs. Gibbons let out a long sigh. "There's nothing for it, then. We shall have to raid Araminta's collection."

Sophie shuddered. The thought of walking anywhere in Araminta's shoes was somewhat creepy. But it was either that or go without, and she didn't think that bare feet would be acceptable at a fancy London masquerade.

A few minutes later the maid returned with a pair of white satin slippers, stitched in silver and adorned with exquisite faux-diamond rosettes.

Sophie was still apprehensive about wearing Araminta's shoes, but she slipped one of her feet in, anyway. It fit perfectly.

"And they match, too," one of the maids said, pointing to the silver stitching. "As if they were made for the dress."

"We don't have time for admiring shoes," Mrs. Gibbons suddenly said. "Now listen to these instructions very carefully. The coachman has returned from taking the countess and her girls, and he will take you to Bridgerton House. But he has to be waiting outside when they wish to depart, which means you must leave by midnight and not a second later. Do you understand?"

Sophie nodded and looked at the clock on the wall. It was a bit after nine, which meant she'd have more than two hours at the masquerade. "Thank you," she whispered. "Oh, thank you so much."

Mrs. Gibbons dabbed her eyes with a handkerchief. "You just have a good time, dearling. That's all the thanks I need."

Sophie looked again at the clock. Two hours.

Two hours that she'd have to make last a lifetime.

Chapter 2

The Bridgertons are truly a unique family. Surely there cannot be anyone in London who does not know that they all look remarkably alike, or that they are famously named in alphabetical order: Anthony, Benedict, Colin, Daphne, Eloise, Francesca, Gregory, and Hyacinth.

It does make one wonder what the late viscount and (still very-much alive) dowager viscountess would have named their next child had their offspring numbered nine. Imogen? Inigo?

Perhaps it is best they stopped at eight.

LADY WHISTLEDOWN'S SOCIETY PAPERS, 2 JUNE 1815

Benedict Bridgerton was the second of eight children, but sometimes it felt more like a hundred.

This ball his mother had insisted upon hosting was supposed to be a masquerade, and Benedict had dutifully donned a black demi-mask, but everyone knew who he was. Or rather, they all *almost* knew.

"A Bridgerton!" they would exclaim, clapping their hands together with glee.

"You must be a Bridgerton!"

"A Bridgerton! I can spot a Bridgerton anywhere."

Benedict was a Bridgerton, and while there was no family to which he'd rather belong, he sometimes wished he were considered a little less a Bridgerton and a little more himself.

Just then, a woman of somewhat indeterminate age dressed as a shepherdess sauntered over. "A Bridgerton!" she trilled. "I'd recognize that chestnut hair anywhere. Which are you? No, don't say. Let me guess. You're not the viscount, because I just saw him. You must be Number Two or Number Three."

Benedict eyed her coolly.

"Which one? Number Two or Number Three?"

"Two," he bit off.

She clapped her hands together. "That's what I thought! Oh, I must find Portia. I told her you were Number Two—"

Benedict, he nearly growled.

"—but she said, no, he's the younger one, but I—"

Benedict suddenly had to get away. It was either that or kill the twittering ninnyhammer, and with so many witnesses, he didn't think he could get away with it. "If you'll excuse me," he said smoothly. "I see someone with whom I must speak."

It was a lie, but he didn't much care. With a curt nod toward the overage shepherdess, he made a beeline toward the ballroom's side door, eager to escape the throng and sneak into his brother's study, where he might find some blessed peace and quiet and perhaps a glass of fine brandy.

"Benedict!"

Damn. He'd nearly made a clean escape. He looked up to see his mother hurrying toward him. She was dressed in some sort of Elizabethan costume. He supposed she was meant to be a character in one of Shakespeare's plays, but for the life of him, he had no idea which.

"What can I do for you, Mother?" he asked. "And don't say 'Dance with Hermione Smythe-Smith.' Last time I did that I nearly lost three toes in the process."

"I wasn't going to ask anything of the sort," Violet replied. "I was going to ask you to dance with Prudence Featherington."

"Have mercy, Mother," he moaned. "She's even worse."

"I'm not asking you to marry the chit," she said. "Just dance with her."

Benedict fought a groan. Prudence Featherington, while essentially a nice person, had a brain the size of a pea and a laugh so grating he'd seen grown men flee with their hands over their ears. "I'll tell you what," he wheedled. "I'll dance with Penelope Featherington if you keep Prudence at bay."

"That'll do," his mother said with a satisfied nod, leaving Benedict with the sinking sensation that she'd wanted him to dance with Penelope all along.

"She's over there by the lemonade table," Violet said, "dressed as a leprechaun, poor thing. The color is good for her, but someone really must take her mother in hand next time they venture out to the dressmaker. A more unfortunate costume, I can't imagine."

"You obviously haven't seen the mermaid," Benedict murmured.

She swatted him lightly on the arm. "No poking fun at the guests."

"But they make it so easy."

She shot him a look of warning before saying, "I'm off to find your sister."

"Which one?"

"One of the ones who isn't married," Violet said pertly. "Viscount Guelph might be interested in that Scottish girl, but they aren't betrothed yet."

Benedict silently wished Guelph luck. The poor bloke was going to need it.

"And thank you for dancing with Penelope," Violet said pointedly.

He gave her a rather ironic half smile. They both knew that her words were meant as a reminder, not as thanks.

His arms crossed in a somewhat forbidding stance, he watched his mother depart before drawing a long breath and turning to make his way to the lemonade table. He adored his mother to distraction, but she did tend to err on the side of meddlesome when it came to the social lives of her children. And if there was one thing that bothered her even more than Benedict's unmarried state, it was the sight of a young girl's glum face when no one asked her to dance. As a result, Benedict spent a lot of time on the ballroom floor, sometimes with girls she wanted him to marry, but more often with the overlooked wallflowers.

Of the two, he rather thought he preferred the wallflowers. The popular girls tended to be shallow and, to be frank, just a little bit dull.

His mother had always had a particular soft spot for Penelope Featherington, who was on her . . . Benedict frowned. On her *third* season? It must be her third. And with no marriage prospects in sight. Ah, well. He might as well do his duty. Penelope was a nice enough girl, with a decent wit and personality. Someday she'd find herself a husband. It wouldn't be *him*, of course, and in all honesty it probably wouldn't be anyone he even knew, but surely she'd find *some*one.

With a sigh, Benedict started to make his way toward the lemonade table. He could practically taste that brandy, smooth and mellow in his mouth, but he supposed that a glass of lemonade would tide him over for a few minutes.

"Miss Featherington!" he called out, trying not to shudder when three Miss Featheringtons turned around. With what he knew could not possibly be anything but the weakest of smiles, he added, "Er, Penelope, that is."

From about ten feet away, Penelope beamed at him, and Benedict was reminded that he actually *liked* Penelope Featherington. Truly, she wouldn't be considered so antidotal if she weren't always lumped together with her unfortunate sisters, who could easily make a grown man wish himself aboard a ship to Australia.

He'd nearly closed the gap between them when he heard a low rumble of whispers rippling across the ballroom behind him. He knew he ought to keep going and get this duty-dance over with, but God help him, his curiosity got the best of him and he turned around.

And found himself facing what had to be the most breathtaking woman he'd ever seen.

He couldn't even tell if she was beautiful. Her hair was a rather ordinary dark blond, and with her mask tied securely around her head he couldn't even see half of her face.

But there was something about her that held him mesmerized. It was her smile, the shape of her eyes, the way she held herself and looked about the ballroom as if she'd never seen a more glorious sight than the silly members of the *ton* all dressed up in ridiculous costumes.

Her beauty came from within.

She shimmered. She glowed.

She was utterly radiant, and Benedict suddenly realized that it was because she looked so damned *happy*. Happy to be where she was, happy to be *who* she was.

Happy in a way Benedict could barely remember. His was a good life, it was true, maybe even a great life. He had seven wonderful siblings, a loving mother, and scores of friends. But this woman—

This woman knew joy.

And Benedict had to know *her*.

Penelope forgotten, he pushed his way through the crowd until he was but a few steps from her side. Three other gentlemen had beaten him to his destination and were presently showering her with flattery and praise. Benedict watched her with interest; she did not react as any woman of his acquaintance might.

She did not act coy. Nor did she act as if she expected their compliments as her due. Nor was she shy, or tittering, or arch, or ironic, or any of those things one might expect from a woman.

She just smiled. Beamed, actually. Benedict supposed that compliments were meant to bring a measure of happiness to the receiver, but never had he seen a woman react with such pure, unadulterated joy.

He stepped forward. He wanted that joy for himself.

"Excuse me, gentlemen, but the lady has already promised this dance to me," he lied.

Her mask's eye-holes were cut a bit large, and he could see that her eyes widened considerably, then crinkled with amusement. He held out his hand to her, silently daring her to call his bluff.

But she just smiled at him, a wide, radiant grin that pierced his skin and traveled straight to his soul. She put her hand in his, and it was only then that Benedict realized he'd been holding his breath.

"Have you permission to dance the waltz?" he murmured once they reached the dance floor.

She shook her head. "I do not dance."

"You jest."

"I'm afraid I do not. The truth is—" She leaned forward and with a glimmer of a smile said, "I don't know how."

He looked at her with surprise. She moved with an inborn grace, and furthermore, what gently bred lady could reach her age without learning how to dance? "There is only one thing to do, then," he murmured. "I shall teach you."

Her eyes widened, then her lips parted, and a surprised laugh burst forth.

"What," he asked, trying to sound serious, "is so funny?"

She grinned at him—the sort of grin one expects from an old school chum, not a debutante at a ball. Still smiling, she said, "Even I know that one does not conduct dancing lessons at a ball."

"What does that mean, I wonder," he murmured, *"even you?"*

She said nothing.

"I shall have to take the upper hand, then," he said, "and force you to do my bidding."

"Force me?"

But she was smiling as she said it, so he knew she took no offense, and he said, "It would be ungentlemanly of me to allow this sorrowful state of affairs to continue."

"Sorrowful, you say?"

He shrugged. "A beautiful lady who cannot dance. It seems a crime against nature."

"If I allow you to teach me . . ."

"*When* you allow me to teach you."

"*If* I allow you to teach me, where shall you conduct the lesson?"

Benedict lifted his chin and scanned the room. It wasn't difficult to see over the heads of most of the partygoers; at an inch above six feet, he was one of the tallest men in the room. "We shall have to retire to the terrace," he said finally.

"The terrace?" she echoed. "Won't it be terribly crowded? It's a warm night, after all."

He leaned forward. "Not the *private* terrace."

"The private terrace, you say?" she asked, amusement in her voice. "And how, pray tell, would you know of a private terrace?"

Benedict stared at her in shock. Could she possibly not know who he was? It wasn't that he held such a high opinion of himself that he expected all of London to be aware of his identity. It was just that he was a Bridgerton, and if a person met one Bridgerton, that generally meant he could recognize another. And as there was no one in London who had not crossed paths with one Bridgerton or another, Benedict was generally recognized everywhere. Even, he thought ruefully, when that recognition was simply as "Number Two."

"You did not answer my question," his mystery lady reminded him.

"About the private terrace?" Benedict raised her hand to his lips and kissed the fine silk of her glove. "Let us just say that I have my ways."

She appeared undecided, and so he tugged at her fingers, pulling her closer—only by an inch, but somehow it seemed she was only a kiss away. "Come," he said. "Dance with me."

She took a step forward, and he knew his life had been changed forever.

Sophie hadn't seen him when she'd first walked into the room, but she'd felt magic in the air, and when he'd appeared before her, like some charming prince from a children's tale, she somehow knew that *he* was the reason she'd stolen into the ball.

He was tall, and what she could see of his face was very handsome, with lips that hinted of irony and smiles, and skin that was just barely touched by the beginnings of a beard. His hair was a dark, rich brown, and the flickering candlelight lent it a faint reddish cast.

People seemed to know who he was, as well. Sophie noticed that when he moved, the other partygoers stepped out of his path. And when he'd lied so brazenly and claimed her for a dance, the other men had deferred and stepped away.

He was handsome and he was strong, and for this one night, he was hers.

When the clock struck midnight, she'd be back to her life of drudgery, of mending and washing, and attending to Araminta's every wish. Was she so wrong to want this one heady night of magic and love?

She felt like a princess—a reckless princess—and so when he asked her to dance, she put her hand in his. And even though she knew that this entire evening was a lie, that she was a nobleman's bastard and a countess's maid, that her dress was borrowed and her shoes practically stolen—none of that seemed to matter as their fingers twined.

For a few hours, at least, Sophie could pretend that this

gentleman could be *her* gentleman, and that from this moment on, her life would be changed forever.

It was nothing but a dream, but it had been so terribly long since she'd let herself dream.

Banishing all caution, she allowed him to lead her out of the ballroom. He walked quickly, even as he wove through the pulsing crowd, and she found herself laughing as she tripped along after him.

"Why is it," he said, halting for a moment when they reached the hall outside the ballroom, "that you always seem to be laughing at me?"

She laughed again; she couldn't help it. "I'm happy," she said with a helpless shrug. "I'm just so happy to be here."

"And why is that? A ball such as this must be routine for one such as yourself."

Sophie grinned. If he thought she was a member of the *ton*, an alumna of dozens of balls and parties, then she must be playing her role to perfection.

He touched the corner of her mouth. "You keep smiling," he murmured.

"I like to smile."

His hand found her waist, and he pulled her toward him. The distance between their bodies remained respectable, but the increasing nearness robbed her of breath.

"I like to watch you smile," he said. His words were low and seductive, but there was something oddly hoarse about his voice, and Sophie could almost let herself believe that he really meant it, that she wasn't merely that evening's conquest.

But before she could respond, an accusing voice from down the hall suddenly called out, "There you are!"

Sophie's stomach lurched well into her throat. She'd been found out. She'd be thrown into the street, and tomorrow probably into jail for stealing Araminta's shoes, and—

And the man who'd called out had reached her side and was saying to her mysterious gentleman, "Mother has been looking all over for you. You weaseled out of your dance with Penelope, and *I* had to take your place."

"So sorry," her gentleman murmured.

That didn't seem to be enough of an apology for the newcomer, because he scowled mightily as he said, "If you flee the party and leave me to that pack of she-devil debutantes, I swear I shall exact revenge to my dying day."

"A chance I'm willing to take," her gentleman said.

"Well, I covered up for you with Penelope," the other man grumbled. "You're just lucky that I happened to be standing by. The poor girl's heart looked broken when you turned away."

Sophie's gentleman had the grace to blush. "Some things are unavoidable, I'm afraid."

Sophie looked from one man to the other. Even under their demi-masks, it was more than obvious that they were brothers, and she realized in a blinding flash that they must be the Bridgerton brothers, and this must be their house, and—

Oh, good Lord, had she made a total and utter fool of herself by asking him how he knew of a private terrace?

But which brother was he? Benedict. He had to be Benedict. Sophie sent a silent thank-you to Lady Whistledown, who'd once written a column completely devoted to the task of telling the Bridgerton siblings apart. Benedict, she recalled, had been singled out as the tallest.

The man who made her heart flip in triple time stood a good inch above his brother—

—who Sophie suddenly realized was looking at her quite intently.

"I see why you departed," Colin said (for he must be Colin; he certainly wasn't Gregory, who was only fourteen, and Anthony was married, so he wouldn't care if Benedict fled the party and left him to fend off the debutantes by himself.) He looked at Benedict with a sly expression. "Might I request an introduction?"

Benedict raised a brow. "You can try your best, but I

doubt you'll meet with success. I haven't learned her name yet myself."

"You haven't asked," Sophie could not help pointing out.

"And would you tell me if I did?"

"I'd tell you *some*thing," she returned.

"But not the truth."

She shook her head. "This isn't a night for truth."

"My favorite kind of night," Colin said in a jaunty voice.

"Don't you have somewhere to *be*?" Benedict asked.

Colin shook his head. "I'm sure Mother would prefer that I *be* in the ballroom, but it's not exactly a requirement."

"*I* require it," Benedict returned.

Sophie felt a giggle bubbling in her throat.

"Very well," Colin sighed. "I shall take myself off."

"Excellent," Benedict said.

"All alone, to face the ravenous wolves . . ."

"Wolves?" Sophie queried.

"Eligible young ladies," Colin clarified. "A pack of ravenous wolves, the lot of them. Present company excluded, of course."

Sophie thought it best not to point out that she was not an "eligible young lady" at all.

"My mother—" Colin began.

Benedict groaned.

"—would like nothing better than to see my dear elder brother married off." He paused and pondered his words. "Except, perhaps, to see *me* married off."

"If only to get you out of the house," Benedict said dryly.

This time Sophie *did* giggle.

"But then again, he's considerably more ancient," Colin continued, "so perhaps we should send him to the gallows— er, altar first."

"Do you have a *point*?" Benedict growled.

"None whatsoever," Colin admitted. "But then again, I rarely do."

Benedict turned to Sophie. "He speaks the truth."

"So then," Colin said to Sophie with a grand flourish of his arm, "will you take pity on my poor, long-suffering mother and chase my dear brother up the aisle?"

"Well, he hasn't asked," Sophie said, trying to join the humor of the moment.

"How much have you had to drink?" Benedict grumbled.

"Me?" Sophie queried.

"Him."

"Nothing at all," Colin said jovially, "but I'm thinking quite seriously of remedying that. In fact, it might be the only thing that will make this eve bearable."

"If the procurement of drink removes you from my presence," Benedict said, "then it will certainly be the only thing that will make *my* night bearable as well."

Colin grinned, gave a jaunty salute, and was gone.

"It's nice to see two siblings who love each other so well," Sophie murmured.

Benedict, who had been staring somewhat menacingly at the doorway through which his brother had just disappeared, snapped his attention back to her. "You call *that* love?"

Sophie thought of Rosamund and Posy, who were forever sniping at each other, and not in jest. "I do," she said firmly. "It's obvious you would lay your life down for him. And vice versa."

"I suppose you're right." Benedict let out a beleaguered sigh, then ruined the effect by smiling. "Much as it pains me to admit it." He leaned against the wall, crossing his arms and looking terribly sophisticated and urbane. "So tell me," he said, "have you any siblings?"

Sophie pondered that question for a moment, then gave a decisive, "No."

One of his brows rose into a curiously arrogant arch. He cocked his head very slightly to the side as he said, "I find myself rather curious as to why it took you so long to determine the answer to that question. One would think the answer would be an easy one to reach."

Sophie looked away for a moment, not wanting him to see the pain that she knew must show in her eyes. She had always wanted a family. In fact, there was nothing in life she had ever wanted more. Her father had never recognized her as his daughter, even in private, and her mother had died at her birth. Araminta treated her like the plague, and Rosamund and Posy had certainly never been sisters to her. Posy had occasionally been a friend, but even she spent most of the day asking Sophie to mend her dress, or style her hair, or polish her shoes . . .

And in all truth, even though Posy asked rather than ordered, as her sister and mother did, Sophie didn't exactly have the option of saying no.

"I am an only child," Sophie finally said.

"And that is all you're going to say on the subject," Benedict murmured.

"And that is all I'm going to say on the subject," she agreed.

"Very well." He smiled, a lazy masculine sort of smile. "What, then, am I permitted to ask you?"

"Nothing, really."

"Nothing at all?"

"I suppose I might be induced to tell you that my favorite color is green, but beyond that I shall leave you with no clues to my identity."

"Why so many secrets?"

"If I answered that," Sophie said with an enigmatic smile, truly warming to her role as a mysterious stranger, "then that would be the end of my secrets, wouldn't it?"

He leaned forward ever so slightly. "You could always develop new secrets."

Sophie backed up a step. His gaze had grown hot, and she had heard enough talk in the servants' quarters to know what that meant. Thrilling as that was, she was not quite as daring as she pretended to be. "This entire night," she said, "is secret enough."

"Then ask me a question," he said. "I have no secrets."

Her eyes widened. "None? Truly? Doesn't everyone have secrets?"

"Not I. My life is hopelessly banal."

"*That* I find difficult to believe."

"It's true," he said with a shrug. "I've never seduced an innocent, or even a married lady, I have no gambling debts, and my parents were completely faithful to one another."

Meaning he wasn't a bastard. Somehow the thought brought an ache to Sophie's throat. Not, of course, because he was legitimate, but rather because she knew he would never pursue her—at least not in an honorable fashion—if he knew that she wasn't.

"You haven't asked me a question," he reminded her.

Sophie blinked in surprise. She hadn't thought he'd been serious. "A-all right," she half stammered, caught off guard. "What, then, is your favorite color?"

He grinned. "You're going to waste your question on that?"

"I only get one question?"

"More than fair, considering you're granting me none." Benedict leaned forward, his dark eyes glinting. "And the answer is blue."

"Why?"

"Why?" he echoed.

"Yes, why? Is it because of the ocean? Or the sky? Or perhaps just because you like it?"

Benedict eyed her curiously. It seemed such an odd question—*why* his favorite color was blue. Everyone else would have taken blue for an answer and left it at that. But this woman—whose name he still didn't even know—went deeper, beyond the whats and into the whys.

"Are you a painter?" he queried.

She shook her head. "Just curious."

"Why is your favorite color green?"

She sighed, and her eyes grew nostalgic. "The grass, I

suppose, and maybe the leaves. But mostly the grass. The way it feels when one runs barefoot in the summer. The smell of it after the gardeners have gone through with their scythes and trimmed it even."

"What does the feel and smell of grass have to do with the color?"

"Nothing, I suppose. And maybe everything. I used to live in the country, you see . . ." She caught herself. She hadn't meant to tell him even that much, but there didn't seem to be harm in his knowing such an innocent fact.

"And you were happier there?" he asked quietly.

She nodded, a faint rush of awareness shivering across her skin. Lady Whistledown must never have had a conversation with Benedict Bridgerton beyond the superficial, because she'd never written that he was quite the most perceptive man in London. When he looked into her eyes, Sophie had the oddest sense that he could see straight into her soul.

"You must enjoy walking in the park, then," he said.

"Yes," Sophie lied. She never had time to go to the park. Araminta didn't even give her a day off like the other servants received.

"We shall have to take a stroll together," Benedict said.

Sophie avoided a reply by reminding him, "You never did tell me why your favorite color is blue."

His head cocked slightly to the side, and his eyes narrowed just enough so that Sophie knew that he had noticed her evasion. But he simply said, "I don't know. Perhaps, like you, I'm reminded of something I miss. There is a lake at Aubrey Hall—that is where I grew up, in Kent—but the water always seemed more gray than blue."

"It probably reflects the sky," Sophie commented.

"Which is, more often than not, more gray than blue," Benedict said with a laugh. "Perhaps that is what I miss—blue skies and sunshine."

"If it weren't raining," Sophie said with a smile, "this wouldn't be England."

"I went to Italy once," Benedict said. "The sun shone constantly."

"It sounds like heaven."

"You'd think," he said. "But I found myself missing the rain."

"I can't believe it," she said with a laugh. "I feel like I spend half my life staring out the window and grumbling at the rain."

"If it were gone, you'd miss it."

Sophie grew pensive. Were there things in her life she'd miss if they were gone? She wouldn't miss Araminta, that was for certain, and she wouldn't miss Rosamund. She'd probably miss Posy, and she'd definitely miss the way the sun shone through the window in her attic room in the mornings. She'd miss the way the servants laughed and joked and occasionally included her in their fun, even though they all knew she was the late earl's bastard.

But she wasn't going to miss these things—she wouldn't even have the opportunity to miss them—because she wasn't going anywhere. After this evening—this one amazing, wonderful, magical evening—it would be back to life as usual.

She supposed that if she were stronger, braver, she'd have left Penwood House years ago. But would that have really made much difference? She might not like living with Araminta, but she wasn't likely to improve her lot in life by leaving. She might have liked to have been a governess, and she was certainly well qualified for the position, but jobs were scarce for those without references, and Araminta certainly wasn't going to give her one.

"You're very quiet," Benedict said softly.

"I was just thinking."

"About?"

"About what I'd miss—and what I wouldn't miss—should my life drastically change."

His eyes grew intense. "And do you expect it to drastically change?"

She shook her head and tried to keep the sadness out of her voice when she answered, "No."

His voice grew so quiet it was almost a whisper. "Do you want it to change?"

"Yes," she sighed, before she could stop herself. "Oh, *yes*."

He took her hands and brought them to his lips, gently kissing each one in turn. "Then we shall begin right now," he vowed. "And tomorrow you shall be transformed."

"Tonight I am transformed," she whispered. "Tomorrow I shall disappear."

Benedict drew her close and dropped the softest, most fleeting of kisses onto her brow. "Then we must pack a lifetime into this very night."

Chapter 3

This Author waits with bated breath to see what costumes the ton will choose for the Bridgerton masquerade. It is rumored that Eloise Bridgerton plans to dress as Joan of Arc, and Penelope Featherington, out for her third season and recently returned from a visit with Irish cousins, will don the costume of a leprechaun. Miss Posy Reiling, stepdaughter to the late Earl of Penwood, plans a costume of mermaid, which This Author personally cannot wait to behold, but her elder sister, Miss Rosamund Reiling, has been very close-lipped about her own attire.

As for the men, if previous masquerade balls are any indication, the portly will dress as Henry VIII, the more fit as Alexander the Great or perhaps the devil, and the bored (the eligible Bridgerton brothers sure to be among these ranks) as themselves—basic black evening kit, with only a demi-mask as a nod to the occasion.

LADY WHISTLEDOWN'S SOCIETY PAPERS, 5 JUNE 1815

"Dance with me," Sophie said impulsively.

His smile was amused, but his fingers twined tightly with hers as he murmured, "I thought you didn't know how."

"You said you would teach me."

He stared at her for a long moment, his eyes boring into hers, then he tugged on her hand and said, "Come with me."

Pulling her along behind him, they slipped down a hallway, climbed a flight of stairs, and then rounded a corner, emerging in front of a pair of French doors. Benedict jiggled the wrought-iron handles and swung the doors open, revealing a small private terrace, adorned with potted plants and two chaise lounges.

"Where are we?" Sophie asked, looking around.

"Right above the ballroom terrace." He shut the doors behind them. "Can't you hear the music?"

Mostly, what Sophie could hear was the low rumble of endless conversation, but if she strained her ears, she could hear the faint lilt of the orchestra. "Handel," she said with a delighted smile. "My governess had a music box with this very tune."

"You loved your governess very much," he said quietly.

Her eyes had been closed as she hummed along with the music, but when she heard his words, she opened them in a startled fashion. "How did you know?"

"The same way I knew you were happier in the country." Benedict reached out and touched her cheek, one gloved finger trailing slowly along her skin until it reached the line of her jaw. "I can see it in your face."

She held silent for a few moments, then pulled away, saying, "Yes, well, I spent more time with her than with anyone else in the household."

"It sounds a lonely upbringing," he said quietly.

"Sometimes it was." She walked over to the edge of the balcony and rested her hands on the balustrade as she stared out into the inky night. "Sometimes it wasn't." Then she turned around quite suddenly, her smile bright, and Benedict knew that she would not reveal anything more about her childhood.

"Your upbringing must have been the complete opposite

of lonely," she said, "with so many brothers and sisters about."

"You know who I am," he stated.

She nodded. "I didn't at first."

He walked over to the balustrade and leaned one hip against it, crossing his arms. "What gave me away?"

"It was your brother, actually. You looked so alike—"

"Even with our masks?"

"Even with your masks," she said with an indulgent smile. "Lady Whistledown writes about you quite often, and she never passes up an opportunity to comment upon how alike you look."

"And do you know which brother I am?"

"Benedict," she replied. "If indeed Lady Whistledown is correct when she says that you are tallest among your brothers."

"You're quite the detective."

She looked slightly embarrassed. "I merely read a gossip sheet. It makes me no different from the rest of the people here."

Benedict watched her for a moment, wondering if she realized that she'd revealed another clue to the puzzle of her identity. If she'd recognized him only from *Whistledown*, then she'd not been out in society for long, or perhaps not at all. Either way, she was not one of the many young ladies to whom his mother had introduced him.

"What else do you know about me from *Whistledown*?" he asked, his smile slow and lazy.

"Are you fishing for compliments?" she asked, returning the half smile with the vaguest tilt of her lips. "For you must know that the Bridgertons are almost always spared her rapier quill. Lady Whistledown is nearly always complimentary when writing about your family."

"It's led to quite a bit of speculation about her identity," he admitted. "Some think she must be a Bridgerton."

"Is she?"

He shrugged. "Not that I'm aware of. And you didn't answer my question."

"Which question was that?"

"What you know of me from *Whistledown*."

She looked surprised. "Are you truly interested?"

"If I cannot know anything about *you*, at least I might know what you know about *me*."

She smiled, and touched the tip of her index finger to her lower lip in an endearingly absentminded gesture. "Well, let's see. Last month you won some silly horse race in Hyde Park."

"It wasn't the least bit silly," he said with a grin, "and I'm a hundred quid richer for it."

She shot him an arch look. "Horse races are almost always silly."

"Spoken just like a woman," he muttered.

"Well—"

"Don't point out the obvious," he interrupted.

That made her smile.

"What else do you know?" he asked.

"From *Whistledown*?" She tapped her finger against her cheek. "You once lopped the head off your sister's doll."

"And I'm still trying to figure out how she knew about that," Benedict muttered.

"Maybe Lady Whistledown is a Bridgerton, after all."

"Impossible. Not," he added rather forcefully, "that we're not smart enough to pull it off. Rather, the rest of the family would be too smart not to figure it out."

She laughed out loud at that, and Benedict studied her, wondering if she was aware that she'd given away yet another tiny clue to her identity. Lady Whistledown had written of the doll's unfortunate encounter with a guillotine two years earlier, in one of her very earliest columns. Many people now had the gossip sheet delivered all the way out in the country, but in the beginning, *Whistledown* had been strictly for Londoners.

Which meant that his mystery lady had been in London two years ago. And yet she hadn't known who he was until she'd met Colin.

She'd been in London, but she'd not been out in society. Perhaps she was the youngest in her family, and had been reading *Whistledown* while her older sisters enjoyed their seasons.

It wasn't enough to figure out who she was, but it was a start.

"What else do you know?" he asked, eager to see if she'd inadvertently reveal anything else.

She chuckled, clearly enjoying herself. "Your name has not been seriously linked with any young lady, and your mother despairs of ever seeing you married."

"The pressure has lessened a bit now that my brother's gone and got himself a wife."

"The viscount?"

Benedict nodded.

"Lady Whistledown wrote about that as well."

"In great detail. Although—" He leaned toward her and lowered his voice. "She didn't get all the facts."

"Really?" she asked with great interest. "What did she leave out?"

He tsked-tsked and shook his head at her. "I'm not about to reveal the secrets of my brother's courtship if you won't reveal even your name."

She snorted at that. "*Courtship* might be too strong a word. Why, Lady Whistledown wrote—"

"Lady Whistledown," he interrupted with a vaguely mocking half smile, "is not privy to all that goes on in London."

"She certainly seems privy to *most*."

"Do you think?" he mused. "I tend to disagree. For example, I suspect that if Lady Whistledown were here on the terrace, she would not know your identity."

Her eyes widened under her mask. Benedict took some satisfaction in that.

He crossed his arms. "Is that true?"

She nodded. "But I am so well disguised that no one would recognize me right now."

He raised a brow. "What if you removed your mask? Would she recognize you then?"

She pushed herself away from the railing and took a few steps toward the center of the terrace. "I'm not going to answer that."

He followed her. "I didn't think you would. But I wanted to ask, nonetheless."

Sophie turned around, then caught her breath as she realized he was mere inches away. She'd heard him following her, but she hadn't thought he was quite that close. She parted her lips to speak, but to her great surprise, she hadn't a thing to say. All she could seem to do was stare up at him, at those dark, dark eyes peering at her from behind his mask.

Speech was impossible. Even breathing was difficult.

"You still haven't danced with me," he said.

She didn't move, just stood there as his large hand came to rest at the small of her back. Her skin tingled where he touched her, and the air grew thick and hot.

This was desire, Sophie realized. This was what she'd heard the maids whispering about. This was what no gently bred lady was even supposed to *know* about.

But she was no gently bred lady, she thought defiantly. She was a bastard, a nobleman's by-blow. She was not a member of the *ton* and never would be. Did she really have to abide by their rules?

She'd always sworn that she would never become a man's mistress, that she'd never bring a child into this world to suffer her fate as a bastard. But she wasn't planning anything quite so brazen. This was one dance, one evening, perhaps one kiss.

It was enough to ruin a reputation, but what sort of reputation did she have to begin with? She was outside society, beyond the pale. And she wanted one night of fantasy.

She looked up.

"You're not going to run, then," he murmured, his dark eyes flaring with something hot and exciting.

She shook her head, realizing that once again, he'd known what she was thinking. It should have scared her that he so effortlessly read her thoughts, but in the dark seduction of the night, with the wind tugging at the loose strands of her hair, and the music floating up from below, it was somehow thrilling instead. "Where do I put my hand?" she asked. "I want to dance."

"Right here on my shoulder," he instructed. "No, just a touch lower. There you are."

"You must think me the veriest ninny," she said, "not knowing how to dance."

"I think you're very brave, actually, for admitting it." His free hand found hers and slowly lifted it into the air. "Most women of my acquaintance would have feigned an injury or disinterest."

She looked up into his eyes even though she knew it would leave her breathless. "I haven't the acting skills to feign disinterest," she admitted.

The hand at the small of her back tightened.

"Listen to the music," he instructed, his voice oddly hoarse. "Do you feel it rising and falling?"

She shook her head.

"Listen harder," he whispered, his lips drawing closer to her ear. "*One*, two, three; *one*, two, three."

Sophie closed her eyes and somehow filtered out the endless chatter of the guests below them until all she heard was the soft swell of the music. Her breathing slowed, and she found herself swaying in time with the orchestra, her head rocking back and forth with Benedict's softly uttered numerical instructions.

"*One*, two, three; *one* two three."

"I feel it," she whispered.

He smiled. She wasn't sure how she knew that; her eyes were still closed. But she felt the smile, heard it in the tenor of his breath.

"Good," he said. "Now watch my feet and allow me to lead you."

Sophie opened her eyes and looked down.

"*One*, two, three; *one*, two, three."

Hesitantly, she stepped along with him—right onto his foot.

"Oh! I'm sorry!" she blurted out.

"My sisters have done far worse," he assured her. "Don't give up."

She tried again, and suddenly her feet knew what to do. "Oh!" she breathed in surprise. "This is wonderful!"

"Look up," he ordered gently.

"But I'll stumble."

"You won't," he promised. "I won't let you. Look into my eyes."

Sophie did as he asked, and the moment her eyes touched his, something inside her seemed to lock into place, and she could not look away. He twirled her in circles and spirals around the terrace, slowly at first, then picking up speed, until she was breathless and giddy.

And all the while, her eyes remained locked on his.

"What do you feel?" he asked.

"Everything!" she said, laughing.

"What do you hear?"

"The music." Her eyes widened with excitement. "I hear the music as I've never heard it before."

His hands tightened, and the space between them diminished by several inches. "What do you see?" he asked.

Sophie stumbled, but she never took her eyes off his. "My soul," she whispered. "I see my very soul."

He stopped dancing. "What did you say?" he whispered.

She held silent. The moment seemed too charged, too meaningful, and she was afraid she'd spoil it.

No, that wasn't true. She was afraid she'd make it even better, and that would make it hurt all the more when she returned to reality at midnight.

How on earth was she going to go back to polishing Araminta's shoes after this?

"I know what you said," Benedict said hoarsely. "I heard you, and—"

"Don't say anything," Sophie cut in. She didn't want him to tell her that he felt the same way, didn't want to hear anything that would leave her pining for this man forever.

But it was probably already too late for that.

He stared at her for an agonizingly long moment, then murmured, "I won't speak. I won't say a word." And then, before she even had a second to breathe, his lips were on hers, exquisitely gentle and achingly tender.

With deliberate slowness, he brushed his lips back and forth across hers, the bare hint of friction sending shivers and tingles spiraling through her body.

He touched her lips and she felt it in her toes. It was a singularly odd—and singularly wonderful—sensation.

Then his hand at the small of her back—the one that had guided her so effortlessly in their waltz—started to pull her toward him. The pressure was slow but inexorable, and Sophie grew hot as their bodies grew closer, then positively burned when she suddenly felt the length of him pressing against her.

He seemed very large, and very powerful, and in his arms she felt like she must be the most beautiful woman in the world.

Suddenly anything seemed possible, maybe even a life free of servitude and stigma.

His mouth grew more insistent, and his tongue darted out to tickle the corner of her mouth. His hand, which had still been holding hers in a waltz-pose, slid down the length of her arm and then up her back until it rested at the nape of her neck, his fingers tugging her hair loose from its coiffure.

"Your hair is like silk," he whispered, and Sophie actually giggled, because he was wearing gloves.

He pulled away. "What," he asked with an amused expression, "are you laughing about?"

"How can you know what my hair feels like? You're wearing gloves."

He smiled, a crooked, boyish sort of a smile that sent her stomach into flips and melted her heart. "I don't know how I know," he said, "but I do." His grin grew even more lopsided, and then he added, "But just to be sure, perhaps I'd better test with my bare skin."

He held out his hand before her. "Will you do the honors?"

Sophie stared at his hand for a few seconds before she realized what he meant. With a shaky, nervous breath, she took a step back and brought both of her hands to his. Slowly she pinched the end of each of the glove's fingertips and gave it a little tug, loosening the fine fabric until she could slide the entire glove from his hand.

Glove still dangling from her fingers, she looked up. He had the oddest expression in his eyes. Hunger . . . and something else. Something almost spiritual.

"I want to touch you," he whispered, and then his bare hand cupped her cheek, the pads of his fingers lightly stroking her skin, whispering upward until they touched the hair near her ear. He tugged gently until he pulled one lock loose. Freed from the coiffure, her hair sprang into a light curl, and Sophie could not take her eyes off it, wrapped golden around his index finger.

"I was wrong," he murmured. "It's softer than silk."

Sophie was suddenly gripped by a fierce urge touch him

in the same way, and she held out her hand. "It's my turn," she said softly.

His eyes flared, and then he went to work on her glove, loosening it at the fingers the same way she had done. But then, rather than pulling it off, he brought his lips to the edge of the long glove, all the way above her elbow, and kissed the sensitive skin on the inside of her arm. "Also softer than silk," he murmured.

Sophie used her free hand to grip his shoulder, no longer confident of her ability to stand.

He tugged at the glove, allowing it to slide off her arm with agonizing slowness, his lips following its progress until they reached the inside of her elbow. Barely breaking the kiss, he looked up and said, "You don't mind if I stay here for a bit."

Helplessly, Sophie shook her head.

His tongue darted out and traced the bend of her arm.

"Oh, my," she moaned.

"I thought you might like that," he said, his words hot against her skin.

She nodded. Or rather, she meant to nod. She wasn't sure if she actually did.

His lips continued their trail, sliding sensuously down her forearm until they reached the inside of her wrist. They remained there for a moment before finally coming to rest in the absolute center of her palm.

"Who are you?" he asked, lifting his head but not letting go of her hand.

She shook her head.

"I have to know."

"I can't say." And then, when she saw that he would not take no for an answer, she lied and added, "Yet."

He took one of her fingers and rubbed it gently against his lips. "I want to see you tomorrow," he said softly. "I want to call on you and see where you live."

She said nothing, just held herself steady, trying not to cry.

"I want to meet your parents and pet your damned dog," he continued, somewhat unsteadily. "Do you understand what I mean?"

Music and conversation still drifted up from below, but the only sound on the terrace was the harsh rasp of their breath.

"I want—" His voice dropped to a whisper, and his eyes looked vaguely surprised, as if he couldn't quite believe the truth of his own words. "I want your future. I want every little piece of you."

"Don't say anything more," she begged him. "*Please*. Not another word."

"Then tell me your name. Tell me how to find you tomorrow."

"I—" But then she heard a strange sound, exotic and ringing. "What is that?"

"A gong," he replied. "To signal the unmasking."

Panic rose within her. "What?"

"It must be midnight."

"Midnight?" she gasped.

He nodded. "Time to remove your mask."

One of Sophie's hands flew up to her temple, pressing the mask harshly against her skin, as if she could somehow glue it onto her face through sheer force of will.

"Are you all right?" Benedict asked.

"I have to go," she blurted out, and then, with no further warning, she hitched up her skirts and ran from the terrace.

"Wait!" she heard him call out, felt the rush of air as his arm swiped forward in a futile attempt to grab her dress.

But Sophie was fast, and perhaps more importantly, she was in a state of utter panic, and she tore down the stairs as if the fires of hell were nipping at her heels.

She plunged into the ballroom, knowing that Benedict would prove a determined pursuer, and she'd have the best chance of losing him in a large crowd. All she had to do was make it across the room, and then she could exit via the side door and scoot around the outside of the house to her waiting carriage.

The revelers were still removing their masks, and the party was loud with raucous laughter. Sophie pushed and jostled, anything to beat her way to the other side of the room. She threw one desperate glance over her shoulder. Benedict had entered the ballroom, his face intense as he scanned the crowd. He didn't seem to have seen her yet, but she knew that he would; her silver gown would make her an easy target.

Sophie kept shoving people out of her way. At least half of them didn't seem to notice; probably too drunk. "Excuse me," she muttered, elbowing Julius Caesar in the ribs. "Beg pardon," came out more like a grunt; that was when Cleopatra stepped on her toe.

"Excuse me, I—" And then the breath was quite literally sucked out of her, because she found herself face-to-face with Araminta.

Or rather, face to mask. Sophie was still disguised. But if anyone could recognize her, it would be Araminta. And—

"Watch where you're going," Araminta said haughtily. Then, while Sophie stood openmouthed, she swished her Queen Elizabeth skirts and swept away.

Araminta hadn't recognized her! If Sophie hadn't been so frantic about getting out of Bridgerton House before Benedict caught up with her, she would have laughed with delight.

Sophie glanced desperately behind her. Benedict had spotted her and was pushing his way through the crowd with considerably more efficiency than she had done. With an audible gulp and renewed energy, she pushed forth, almost knocking two Grecian goddesses to the ground before finally reaching the far door.

She looked behind her just long enough to see that Benedict had been waylaid by some elderly lady with a cane, then ran out of the building and around front, where the Penwood carriage was waiting, just as Mrs. Gibbons had said it would.

"Go, go, go!" Sophie shouted frantically to the driver.

And she was gone.

Chapter 4

More than one masquerade attendee has reported to This Author that Benedict Bridgerton was seen in the company of an unknown lady dressed in a silver gown.

Try as she might, This Author has been completely unable to discern the mystery lady's identity. And if This Author cannot uncover the truth, you may be assured that her identity is a well-kept secret indeed.

LADY WHISTLEDOWN'S SOCIETY PAPERS, 7 JUNE 1815

She was gone.

Benedict stood on the pavement in front of Bridgerton House, surveying the street. All of Grosvenor Square was a mad crush of carriages. She could be in any one of them, just sitting there on the cobbles, trying to escape the traffic. Or she could be in one of the three carriages that had just escaped the tangle and rolled around the corner.

Either way, she was gone.

He was half-ready to strangle Lady Danbury, who'd jammed her cane onto his toe and insisted upon giving him her opinion on most of the partygoers' costumes. By the time he'd managed to free himself, his mystery lady had disappeared through the ballroom's side door.

And he knew that she had no intention of letting him see her again.

Benedict let out a low and rather viciously uttered curse. With all the ladies his mother had trotted out before him—and there had been many—he'd never once felt the same soul-searing connection that had burned between him and the lady in silver. From the moment he'd seen her—no, from the moment *before* he'd seen her, when he'd only just felt her presence, the air had been alive, crackling with tension and excitement. And he'd been alive, too—alive in a way he hadn't felt for years, as if everything were suddenly new and sparkling and full of passion and dreams.

And yet . . .

Benedict cursed again, this time with a touch of regret.

And yet he didn't even know the color of her eyes.

They definitely hadn't been brown. Of that much he was positive. But in the dim light of the candled night, he'd been unable to discern whether they were blue or green. Or hazel or gray. And for some reason he found this the most upsetting. It ate at him, leaving a burning, hungry sensation in the pit of his stomach.

They said eyes were the windows to the soul. If he'd truly found the woman of his dreams, the one with whom he could finally imagine a family and a future, then by God he ought to know the color of her eyes.

It wasn't going to be easy to find her. It was never easy to find someone who didn't want to be found, and she'd made it more than clear that her identity was a secret.

His clues were paltry at best. A few dropped comments concerning Lady Whistledown's column and . . .

Benedict looked down at the single glove still clutched in his right hand. He'd quite forgotten that he'd been holding it as he'd dashed through the ballroom. He brought it to his face and inhaled its scent, but much to his surprise, it didn't smell of rosewater and soap, as had his mystery lady. Rather, its scent was a bit musty, as if it had been packed away in an attic trunk for many years.

Odd, that. Why would she be wearing an ancient glove?

He turned it over in his hand, as if the motion would somehow bring her back, and that was when he noticed a tiny bit of stitching at the hem.

SLG. Someone's initials.

Were they hers?

And a family crest. One he did not recognize.

But his mother would. His mother always knew that sort of thing. And chances were, if she knew the crest, she'd know who the initials SLG belonged to.

Benedict felt his first glimmer of hope. He would find her.

He would find her, and he would make her his. It was as simple as that.

It took a mere half hour to return Sophie to her regular, drab state. Gone were the dress, the glittering earbobs, and the fancy coiffure. The jeweled slippers were tucked neatly back in Araminta's closet, and the rouge the maid had used for her lips was resting in its place on Rosamund's dressing table. She'd even taken five minutes to massage the skin on her face, to remove the indentations left by the mask.

Sophie looked as she always looked before bed—plain, simple, and unassuming, her hair pulled into a loose braid, her feet tucked into warm stockings to keep out the chill night air.

She was back to looking what she was in truth—nothing more than a housemaid. Gone were all traces of the fairy princess she'd been for one short evening.

And saddest of all, gone was her fairy prince.

Benedict Bridgerton had been everything she'd read in *Whistledown*. Handsome, strong, debonair. He was the stuff of a young girl's dreams, but not, she thought glumly, of *her* dreams. A man like that didn't marry an earl's by-blow. And he certainly didn't marry a housemaid.

But for one night he'd been hers, and she supposed that would have to be enough.

She picked up a little stuffed dog she'd had since she'd been a small girl. She'd kept it all these years as a reminder of happier times. It usually sat on her dresser, but for some reason she wanted it closer right now. She crawled into bed, the little dog tucked under her arm, and curled up under the covers.

Then she squeezed her eyes shut, biting her lip as silent tears trickled onto her pillow.

It was a long, long night.

"Do you recognize this?"

Benedict Bridgerton was sitting next to his mother in her very feminine rose-and-cream drawing room, holding out his only link to the woman in silver. Violet Bridgerton took the glove and examined the crest. She needed only a second before she announced, "Penwood."

"As in 'Earl of'?"

Violet nodded. "And the G would be for Gunningworth. The title recently passed out of their family, if I recall correctly. The earl died without issue . . . oh, it must have been six or seven years ago. The title went to a distant cousin. And," she added with a disapproving nod of her head, "you forgot to dance with Penelope Featherington last night. You're lucky your brother was there to dance in your stead."

Benedict fought a groan and tried to ignore her scolding. "Who, then, is SLG?"

Violet's blue eyes narrowed. "Why are you interested?"

"I don't suppose," Benedict said on a groan, "that you will simply answer my question without posing one of your own."

She let out a ladylike snort. "You know me far better than that."

Benedict just managed to stop himself from rolling his eyes.

"Who," Violet asked, "does the glove belong to, Benedict?" And then, when he didn't answer quickly enough for her taste, she added, "You might as well tell me everything. You know I will figure it out on my own soon enough, and it will be far less embarrassing for you if I don't have to ask any questions."

Benedict sighed. He was going to have to tell her everything. Or at least, almost everything. There was little he enjoyed less than sharing such details with his mother—she tended to grab hold of any hope that he might actually marry and cling on to it with the tenacity of a barnacle. But he had little choice. Not if he wanted to find *her*.

"I met someone last night at the masquerade," he finally said.

Violet clapped her hands together with delight. "Really?"

"She's the reason I forgot to dance with Penelope."

Violet looked nearly ready to die of rapture. "Who? One of Penwood's daughters?" She frowned. "No, that's impossible. He had no daughters. But he did have two stepdaughters." She frowned again. "Although I must say, having met those two girls . . . well . . ."

"Well, what?"

Violet's brow wrinkled as she fumbled for polite words. "Well, I simply wouldn't have guessed you'd be interested in either of them, that's all. But if you *are*," she added, her face brightening considerably, "then I shall surely invite the dowager countess over for tea. It's the very least I can do."

Benedict started to say something, then stopped when he saw that his mother was frowning yet again. "What now?" he asked.

"Oh, nothing," Violet said. "Just that . . . well . . ."

"Spit it out, Mother."

She smiled weakly. "Just that I don't particularly *like* the dowager countess. I've always found her rather cold and ambitious."

"Some would say you're ambitious as well, Mother," Benedict pointed out.

Violet pulled a face. "Of course I have great ambition that my children marry well and happily, but I am not the sort who'd marry her daughter off to a seventy-year-old man just because he was a duke!"

"Did the dowager countess do that?" Benedict couldn't recall any seventy-year-old dukes making recent trips to the altar.

"No," Violet admitted, "but she would. Whereas I—"

Benedict bit back a smile as his mother pointed to herself with great flourish.

"I would allow my children to marry paupers if it would bring them happiness."

Benedict raised a brow.

"They would be well-principled and hardworking paupers, of course," Violet explained. "No gamblers need apply."

Benedict didn't want to laugh at his mother, so instead he coughed discreetly into his handkerchief.

"But you should not concern yourself with me," Violet said, giving her son a sideways look before punching him lightly in the arm.

"Of course I must," he said quickly.

She smiled serenely. "I shall put aside my feelings for the dowager countess if you care for one of her daughters . . ." She looked up hopefully. "Do you care for one of her daughters?"

"I have no idea," Benedict admitted. "I never got her name. Just her glove."

Violet gave him a stern look. "I'm not even going to ask how you obtained her glove."

"It was all very innocent, I assure you."

Violet's expression was dubious in the extreme. "I have far too many sons to believe *that,*" she muttered.

"The initials?" Benedict reminded her.

Violet examined the glove again. "It's rather old," she said.

Benedict nodded. "I thought so as well. It smelled a bit musty, as if it had been packed away for some time."

"And the stitches show wear," she commented. "I don't know what the L is for, but the S could very well be for Sarah. The late earl's mother, who has also passed on. Which would make sense, given the age of the glove."

Benedict stared down at the glove in his mother's hands for a moment before saying, "As I'm fairly certain I did not converse with a ghost last night, who do you think the glove might belong to?"

"I have no idea. Someone in the Gunningworth family, I imagine."

"Do you know where they live?"

"At Penwood House, actually," Violet replied. "The new earl hasn't given them the boot yet. Don't know why. Perhaps he's afraid they'll want to live with him once he takes up residence. I don't think he's even in town for the season. Never met him myself."

"Do you happen to know—"

"Where Penwood House is?" Violet cut in. "Of course I do. It's not far, only a few blocks away." She gave him directions, and Benedict, in his haste to be on his way, was already on his feet and halfway out the door before she finished.

"Oh, Benedict!" Violet called out, her smile very amused.

He turned around. "Yes?"

"The countess's daughters are named Rosamund and Posy. Just in case you're interested."

Rosamund and Posy. Neither seemed fitting, but what did he know? Perhaps he didn't seem a proper Benedict to people he met. He turned on his heel and tried to exit once again, but his mother stopped him with yet another, "Oh, Benedict!"

He turned around. "Yes, Mother?" he asked, sounding purposefully beleaguered.

"You will tell me what happens, won't you?"

"Of course, Mother."

"You're lying to me," she said with a smile, "but I forgive you. It's so nice to see you in love."

"I'm not—"

"Whatever you say, dear," she said with a wave.

Benedict decided there was little point in replying, so with nothing more than a roll of his eyes, he left the room and hurried out of the house.

"Sophieeeeeeeeeeeeeee!"

Sophie's chin snapped up. Araminta sounded even more irate than usual, if that were possible. Araminta was *always* upset with her.

"Sophie! Drat it, where is that infernal girl?"

"The infernal girl is right here," Sophie muttered, setting down the silver spoon she'd been polishing. As lady's maid to Araminta, Rosamund, and Posy, she shouldn't have had to add the polishing to her list of chores, but Araminta positively reveled in working her to the bone.

"Right here," she called out, rising to her feet and walking out into the hall. The Lord only knew what Araminta was upset about this time. She looked this way and that. "My lady?"

Araminta came storming around the corner. "What," she snapped, holding something up in her right hand, "is the meaning of *this*?"

Sophie's eyes fell to Araminta's hand, and she only just managed to stifle a gasp. Araminta was holding the shoes that Sophie had borrowed the night before. "I—I don't know what you mean," she stammered.

"These shoes are *brand-new*. Brand-new!"

Sophie stood quietly until she realized that Araminta required a reply. "Um, what is the problem?"

"Look at this!" Araminta screeched, jabbing her finger toward one of the heels. "It's scuffed. Scuffed! How could something like this happen?"

"I'm sure I don't know, my lady," Sophie said. "Perhaps—"

"There is no perhaps about it," Araminta huffed. "Someone has been wearing my shoes."

"I assure you no one has been wearing your shoes," Sophie replied, amazed that she was able to keep her voice even. "We all know how particular you are about your footwear."

Araminta narrowed her eyes suspiciously. "Are you being sarcastic?"

Sophie rather thought that if Araminta had to ask, then she was playing her sarcasm very well indeed, but she lied, and said, "No! Of course not. I merely meant that you take very good care of your shoes. They last longer that way."

Araminta said nothing, so Sophie added, "Which means you don't have to buy as many pairs."

Which was, of course, utter ridiculousness, as Araminta already owned more pairs of shoes than any one person could hope to wear in a lifetime.

"This is your fault," Araminta growled.

According to Araminta, everything was always Sophie's fault, but this time she was actually correct, so Sophie just gulped and said, "What would you like me to do about it, my lady?"

"I want to know who wore my shoes."

"Perhaps they were scuffed in your closet," Sophie suggested. "Maybe you accidentally kicked them last time you walked by."

"I never *accidentally* do anything," Araminta snapped.

Sophie silently agreed. Araminta was deliberate in all

things. "I can ask the maids," Sophie said. "Perhaps one of them knows something."

"The maids are a pack of idiots," Araminta replied. "What they know could fit on my littlest fingernail."

Sophie waited for Araminta to say, "Present company excluded," but of course she did not. Finally, Sophie said, "I can try to polish the shoe. I'm sure we can do something about the scuff mark."

"The heels are covered in satin," Araminta sneered. "If you can find a way to polish that, then we should have you admitted to the Royal College of Fabric Scientists."

Sophie badly wanted to ask if there even *existed* a Royal College of Fabric Scientists, but Araminta didn't have much of a sense of humor even when she wasn't in a complete snit. To poke fun now would be a clear invitation for disaster. "I could try to rub it out," Sophie suggested. "Or brush it."

"You do that," Araminta said. "In fact, while you're at it . . ."

Oh, *blast*. All bad things began with Araminta saying, "While you're at it."

". . . you might as well polish all of my shoes."

"All of them?" Sophie gulped. Araminta's collection must have numbered at least eighty pair.

"All of them. And while you're at it . . ."

Not *again*.

"Lady Penwood?"

Araminta blessedly stopped in mid-command to turn and see what the butler wanted.

"A gentleman is here to see you, my lady," he said, handing her a crisp, white card.

Araminta took it from him and read the name. Her eyes widened, and she let out a little, "Oh!" before turning back to the butler, and barking out, "Tea! And biscuits! The best silver. At once."

The butler hurried out, leaving Sophie staring at Araminta

with unfeigned curiosity. "May I be of any help?" Sophie asked.

Araminta blinked twice, staring at Sophie as if she'd forgotten her presence. "No," she snapped. "I'm far too busy to bother with you. Go upstairs at once." She paused, then added, "What are you doing down here, anyway?"

Sophie motioned toward the dining room she'd recently exited. "You asked me to polish—"

"I asked you to see to my shoes," Araminta fairly yelled.

"All—all right," Sophie said slowly. Araminta was acting very odd, even for Araminta. "I'll just put away—"

"Now!"

Sophie hurried to the stairs.

"Wait!"

Sophie turned around. "Yes?" she asked hesitantly.

Araminta's lips tightened into an unattractive frown. "Make sure that Rosamund's and Posy's hair is properly dressed."

"Of course."

"Then you may instruct Rosamund to lock you in my closet."

Sophie stared at her. She actually wanted Sophie to give the order to have herself locked in the closet?

"Do you understand me?"

Sophie couldn't quite bring herself to nod. Some things were simply too demeaning.

Araminta marched over until their faces were quite close. "You didn't answer," she hissed. "Do you understand me?"

Sophie nodded, but just barely. Every day, it seemed, brought more evidence of the depth of Araminta's hatred for her. "Why do you keep me here?" she whispered before she had time to think better of it.

"Because I find you useful," was Araminta's low reply.

Sophie watched as Araminta stalked from the room, then hurried up the stairs. Rosamund's and Posy's hair looked quite acceptable, so she sighed, turned to Posy, and said, "Lock me in the closet, if you will."

Posy blinked in surprise. "I beg your pardon?"

"I was instructed to ask Rosamund, but I can't quite bring myself to do so."

Posy peered in the closet with great interest. "May I ask why?"

"I'm meant to polish your mother's shoes."

Posy swallowed uncomfortably. "I'm sorry."

"So am I," Sophie said with a sigh. "So am I."

Chapter 5

And in other news from the masquerade ball, Miss Posy Reiling's costume as a mermaid was somewhat unfortunate, but not, This Author thinks, as dreadful as that of Mrs. Featherington and her two eldest daughters, who went as a bowl of fruit—Philippa as an orange, Prudence as an apple, and Mrs. Featherington as a bunch of grapes.

Sadly, none of the three looked the least bit appetizing.

LADY WHISTLEDOWN'S SOCIETY PAPERS, 7 JUNE 1815

What had his life come to, Benedict wondered, that he was obsessed with a glove? He'd patted his coat pocket about a dozen times since he'd taken a seat in Lady Penwood's sitting room, silently reassuring himself that it was still there. Uncharacteristically anxious, he wasn't certain what he planned to say to the dowager countess once she arrived, but he was usually fairly glib of tongue; surely he'd figure out something as he went along.

His foot tapping, he glanced over at the mantel clock. He'd given his card to the butler about fifteen minutes earlier, which meant that Lady Penwood ought to be down soon. It seemed an unwritten rule that all ladies of the *ton* must keep their callers waiting for at least fifteen minutes, twenty if they were feeling particularly peevish.

A bloody stupid rule, Benedict thought irritably. Why the rest of the world didn't value punctuality as he did, he would never know, but—

"Mr. Bridgerton!"

He looked up. A rather attractive, extremely fashionable blond woman in her forties glided into the room. She looked vaguely familiar, but that was to be expected. They'd surely attended many of the same society functions, even if they had not been introduced.

"You must be Lady Penwood," he murmured, rising to his feet and offering her a polite bow.

"Indeed," she replied with a gracious incline of her head. "I am so delighted that you have chosen to honor us with a call. I have, of course, informed my daughters of your presence. They shall be down shortly."

Benedict smiled. That was exactly what he'd hoped she'd do. He would have been shocked if she'd behaved otherwise. No mother of marriageable daughters ever ignored a Bridgerton brother. "I look forward to meeting them," he said.

Her brow furrowed slightly. "Then you have not yet met them?"

Blast. Now she'd be wondering why he was there. "I have heard such lovely things about them," he improvised, trying not to groan. If Lady Whistledown caught hold of this—and Lady Whistledown seemed to catch hold of everything—it would soon be all over town that he was looking for a wife, *and* that he'd zeroed in on the countess's daughters. Why else would he call upon two women to whom he had not even been introduced?

Lady Penwood beamed. "My Rosamund is considered one of the loveliest girls of the season."

"And your Posy?" Benedict asked, somewhat perversely.

The corners of her mouth tightened. "Posy is, er, delightful."

He smiled benignly. "I cannot wait to meet Posy."

Lady Penwood blinked, then covered up her surprise with a slightly hard smile. "I'm sure Posy will be delighted to meet you."

A maid entered with an ornate silver tea service, then set it down on a table at Lady Penwood's nod. Before the maid could depart, however, the countess said (somewhat sharply, in Benedict's opinion), "Where are the Penwood spoons?"

The maid bobbed a rather panicked curtsy, then replied, "Sophie was polishing the silver in the dining room, my lady, but she had to go upstairs when you—"

"Silence!" Lady Penwood cut in, even though she'd been the one to ask about the spoons in the first place. "I'm sure Mr. Bridgerton is not so high in the instep that he needs monogrammed spoons for his tea."

"Of course not," Benedict murmured, thinking that Lady Penwood must be a bit too high in the instep herself if she even thought to bring it up.

"Go! Go!" the countess ordered the maid, waving her briskly away. "Begone."

The maid hurried out, and the countess turned back to him, explaining, "Our better silver is engraved with the Penwood crest."

Benedict leaned forward. "Really?" he asked with obvious interest. This would be an excellent way to verify that the crest on the glove was indeed that of the Penwoods. "We don't have anything like that at Bridgerton House," he said, hoping he wasn't lying. In all truth, he'd never even noticed the pattern of the silver. "I should love to see it."

"Really?" Lady Penwood asked, her eyes lighting up. "I knew you were a man of taste and refinement."

Benedict smiled, mostly so he wouldn't groan.

"I shall have to send someone to the dining room to fetch a piece. Assuming, of course, that infernal girl managed to do her job." The corners of her lips turned down in a most unattractive manner, and Benedict noticed that her frown lines were deep indeed.

"Is there a problem?" he asked politely.

She shook her head and waved her hand dismissively. "Merely that it is so difficult to find good help. I'm sure your mother says the same thing all the time."

His mother never said any such thing, but that was probably because all of the Bridgerton servants were treated very well and thus were utterly devoted to the family. But Benedict nodded all the same.

"One of these days I'm going to have to give Sophie the boot," the countess said with a sniff. "She cannot do anything right."

Benedict felt a vague pang of pity for the poor, unseen Sophie. But the last thing he wanted to do was get into a discussion on servants with Lady Penwood, and so he changed the subject by motioning to the teapot, and saying, "I imagine it's well steeped by now."

"Of course, of course." Lady Penwood looked up and smiled. "How do you take yours?"

"Milk, no sugar."

As she prepared his cup, Benedict heard the clatter of feet coming down the stairs, and his heart began to race with excitement. Any minute now the countess's daughters would slip through the door, and surely one of them would be the woman he'd met the night before. It was true that he had not seen most of her face, but he knew her approximate size and height. And he was fairly certain that her hair was a long, light brown.

Surely he'd recognize her when he saw her. How could he not?

But when the two young ladies entered the room, he knew instantly that neither was the woman who'd haunted his every thought. One of them was far too blond, and besides, she held herself with a prissy, rather affected manner. There was no joy in her aspect, no mischief in her smile. The other looked friendly enough, but she was too chubby, and her hair was too dark.

Benedict did his best not to look disappointed. He smiled during the introductions and gallantly kissed each of their hands, murmuring some nonsense about how delighted he was to meet them. He made a point of fawning over the chubby one, if only because her mother so obviously preferred the other.

Mothers like that, he decided, didn't deserve to be mothers.

"And do you have any other children?" Benedict asked Lady Penwood, once the introductions were through.

She gave him an odd look. "Of course not. Else I would have brought them out to meet you."

"I thought you might have children still in the schoolroom," he demurred. "Perhaps from your union with the earl."

She shook her head. "Lord Penwood and I were not blessed with children. Such a pity it was that the title left the Gunningworth family."

Benedict could not help but notice that the countess looked more irritated than saddened by her lack of Penwood progeny. "Did your husband have any brothers or sisters?" he asked. Maybe his mystery lady was a Gunningworth cousin.

The countess shot him a suspicious look, which, Benedict had to admit, was well deserved, considering that his questions were not at all the usual fare for an afternoon call. "Obviously," she replied, "my late husband did not have any brothers, as the title passed out of the family."

Benedict knew he should keep his mouth shut, but something about the woman was so bloody irritating he had to say, "He could have had a brother who predeceased him."

"Well, he did not."

Rosamund and Posy were watching the exchange with great interest, their heads bobbing back and forth like balls at a tennis match.

"And any sisters?" Benedict inquired. "The only reason I ask is that I come from such a large family." He motioned to Rosamund and Posy. "I cannot imagine having only one sibling. I thought perhaps that your daughters might have cousins to keep them company."

It was, he thought, rather paltry as far as explanations went, but it would have to do.

"He did have one sister," the countess replied with a disdainful sniff. "But she lived and died a spinster. She was a woman of great faith," she explained, "and chose to devote her life to charitable works."

So much for *that* theory.

"I very much enjoyed your masquerade ball last night," Rosamund suddenly said.

Benedict looked at her in surprise. The two girls had been so silent he'd forgotten they could even speak. "It was really my mother's ball," he answered. "I had no part in the planning. But I shall convey your compliments."

"Please do," Rosamund said. "Did you enjoy the ball, Mr. Bridgerton?"

Benedict stared at her for a moment before answering. She had a hard look in her eyes, as if she was searching for a specific piece of information. "I did indeed," he finally said.

"I noticed you spent a great deal of time with one lady in particular," Rosamund persisted.

Lady Penwood twisted her head sharply to look at him, but she did not say anything.

"Did you?" Benedict murmured.

"She was wearing silver," Rosamund said. "Who was she?"

"A mystery woman," he said with an enigmatic smile. No need for them to know that she was a mystery to him as well.

"Surely you can share her name with us," Lady Penwood said.

Benedict just smiled and stood. He wasn't going to get any more information here. "I'm afraid I must be going, ladies," he said affably, offering them a smooth bow.

"You never did see the spoons," Lady Penwood reminded him.

"I'll have to save them for another time," Benedict said. It was unlikely that his mother would have incorrectly identified the Penwood crest, and besides, if he spent much more time in the company of the hard and brittle Countess of Penwood, he might retch.

"It has been lovely," he lied.

"Indeed," Lady Penwood said, rising to walk him to the door. "Brief, but lovely."

Benedict didn't bother to smile again.

"What," Araminta said as she heard the front door close behind Benedict Bridgerton, "do you suppose that was about?"

"Well," Posy said, "he might—"

"I didn't ask you," Araminta bit off.

"Well, then, who *did* you ask?" Posy returned with uncharacteristic gumption.

"Perhaps he saw me from afar," Rosamund said, "and—"

"He didn't see you from afar," Araminta snapped as she strode across the room.

Rosamund lurched backward in surprise. Her mother rarely spoke to her in such impatient tones.

Araminta continued, "You yourself said he was besotted with some woman in a silver dress."

"I didn't say 'besotted' precisely . . ."

"Don't argue with me over such trivialities. Besotted or not, he didn't come here looking for either of *you*," Araminta said with a fair amount of derision. "I don't know what he was up to. He . . ."

Her words trailed off as she reached the window. Pulling the sheer curtain back, she saw Mr. Bridgerton standing on the pavement, pulling something from his pocket. "What is he doing?" she whispered.

"I think he's holding a glove," Posy said helpfully.

"It's not a—" Araminta said automatically, too used to contradicting everything Posy had to say. "Why, it *is* a glove."

"I should think I know a glove when I see one," Posy muttered.

"What is he looking at?" Rosamund asked, nudging her sister out of the way.

"There's something on the glove," Posy said. "Perhaps it's a piece of embroidery. We've some gloves with the Penwood crest embroidered on the hem. Maybe that glove has the same."

Araminta went white.

"Are you feeling all right, Mother?" Posy asked. "You look rather pale."

"He came here looking for her," Araminta whispered.

"Who?" Rosamund asked.

"The woman in silver."

"Well, he isn't going to find her here," Posy replied, "as I was a mermaid and Rosamund was Marie Antoinette. And you, of course, were Queen Elizabeth."

"The shoes," Araminta gasped. "The shoes."

"What shoes?" Rosamund asked irritably.

"They were scuffed. Someone wore my shoes." Araminta's face, already impossibly pale, blanched even more. "It was *her*. How did she do it? It had to be her."

"Who?" Rosamund demanded.

"Mother, are you certain you're all right?" Posy asked again. "You're not at all yourself."

But Araminta had already run out of the room.

"Stupid, stupid shoe," Sophie grumbled, scrubbing at the heel of one of Araminta's older pieces of footwear. "She hasn't even worn this one for years."

She finished polishing the toe and put it back in its place

in the neatly ordered row of shoes. But before she could reach for another pair, the door to the closet burst open, slamming against the wall with such force that Sophie nearly screamed with surprise.

"Oh, goodness, you gave me a fright," she said to Araminta. "I didn't hear you coming, and—"

"Pack your things," Araminta said in a low, cruel voice. "I want you out of this house by sunrise."

The rag Sophie had been using to polish the shoes fell from her hand. "What?" she gasped. "Why?"

"Do I really need a reason? We both know I ceased receiving any funds for your care nearly a year ago. It's enough that I don't want you here any longer."

"But where will I go?"

Araminta's eyes narrowed to nasty slits. "That's not my concern, now, is it?"

"But—"

"You're twenty years of age. Certainly old enough to make your way in the world. There will be no more coddling from me."

"You never coddled me," Sophie said in a low voice.

"Don't you dare talk back to me."

"Why not?" Sophie returned, her voice growing shrill. "What have I to lose? You're booting me out of the house, anyway."

"You might treat me with a little respect," Araminta hissed, planting her foot on Sophie's skirt so that she was pinned in her kneeling position, "considering that I have clothed and sheltered you this past year out of the goodness of my heart."

"You do nothing out of the goodness of your heart." Sophie tugged at her skirt, but it was firmly trapped under Araminta's heel. "Why did you really keep me here?"

Araminta cackled. "You're cheaper than a regular maid, and I do enjoy ordering you about."

Sophie hated being Araminta's virtual slave, but at least

Penwood House was home. Mrs. Gibbons was her friend, and Posy was usually sympathetic, and the rest of the world was . . . well . . . rather scary. Where would she go? What would she do? How would she support herself?

"Why now?" Sophie asked.

Araminta shrugged. "You're no longer useful to me."

Sophie looked at the long row of shoes she'd just polished. "I'm not?"

Araminta ground the pointy heel of her shoe into Sophie's skirt, tearing the fabric. "You went to the ball last night, didn't you?"

Sophie felt the blood drain from her face, and she knew that Araminta saw the truth in her eyes. "N-no," she lied. "How would I—"

"I don't know how you did it, but I know you were there." Araminta kicked a pair of shoes in Sophie's direction. "Put these on."

Sophie just stared at the shoes in dismay. They were white satin, stitched in silver. They were the shoes she'd worn the night before.

"Put them on!" Araminta screamed. "I know that Rosamund's and Posy's feet are too large. You're the only one who could have worn my shoes last night."

"And from that you think I went to the ball?" Sophie asked, her voice breathy with panic.

"Put on the shoes, Sophie."

Sophie did as she was told. They were, of course, a perfect fit.

"You have overstepped your bounds," Araminta said in a low voice. "I warned you years ago not to forget your place in this world. You are a bastard, a by-blow, the product of—"

"I *know* what a bastard is," Sophie snapped.

Araminta raised one haughty brow, silently mocking Sophie's outburst. "You are unfit to mingle with polite society," she continued, "and yet you *dared* to pretend you are as good as the rest of us by attending the masquerade."

"Yes, I dared," Sophie cried out, well past caring that Araminta had somehow discovered her secret. "I dared, and I'd dare again. My blood is just as blue as yours, and my heart far kinder, and—"

One minute Sophie was on her feet, screaming at Araminta, and the next she was on the floor, clutching her cheek, made red by Araminta's palm.

"Don't you ever compare yourself to me," Araminta warned.

Sophie remained on the floor. How could her father have done this to her, leaving her in the care of a woman who so obviously detested her? Had he cared so little? Or had he simply been blind?

"You will be gone by morning," Araminta said in a low voice. "I don't ever want to see your face again."

Sophie started to make her way to the door.

"But not," Araminta said, planting the heel of her hand against Sophie's shoulder, "until you finish the job I have assigned you."

"It will take me until morning just to finish," Sophie protested.

"That is your problem, not mine." And with that, Araminta slammed the door shut, turning the lock with a very loud click.

Sophie stared down at the flickering candle she'd brought in to help illuminate the long, dark closet. There was no way the wick would last until morning.

And there was no way—absolutely no way in hell—that she was going to polish the rest of Araminta's shoes.

Sophie sat down on the floor, arms crossed and legs crossed, and stared at the candle flame until her eyes crossed, too. When the sun rose tomorrow, her life would be forever altered. Penwood House might not have been terribly welcoming, but at least it was safe.

She had almost no money. She hadn't received so much as a farthing from Araminta in the past seven years. Luckily, she still had a bit of the pin money she'd received when her father had been alive and she'd been treated as his ward, not his wife's slave. There had been many opportunities to spend it, but Sophie had always known that this day might come, and it had seemed prudent to hold on to what little funds she possessed.

But her paltry few pounds wasn't going to get her very far. She needed a ticket out of London, and that cost money. Probably well over half what she had saved. She supposed she could stay in town for a bit, but the London slums were dirty and dangerous, and Sophie knew that her budget would not place her in any of the better neighborhoods. Besides, if she were going to be on her own, she might as well return to the countryside she loved.

Not to mention that Benedict Bridgerton was here. London was a large city, and Sophie had no doubt that she could successfully avoid him for years, but she was desperately afraid that she wouldn't *want* to avoid him, that she'd find herself gazing at his house, hoping for the merest of glimpses as he came through the front door.

And if he saw her . . . Well, Sophie didn't know what would happen. He might be furious at her deception. He might want to make her his mistress. He might not recognize her at all.

The only thing she was certain he would not do was to throw himself at her feet, declare his undying devotion, and demand her hand in marriage.

Sons of viscounts did not marry baseborn nobodies. Not even in romantic novels.

No, she'd have to leave London. Keep herself far from temptation. But she'd need more money, enough to keep her going until she found employment. Enough to—

Sophie's eyes fell on something sparkly—a pair of shoes

tucked away in the corner. Except she'd cleaned those shoes just an hour earlier, and she knew that those sparklies weren't the shoes but a pair of jeweled shoe clips, easily detachable and small enough to fit in her pocket.

Did she dare?

She thought about all the money that Araminta had received for her upkeep, money Araminta had never seen fit to share.

She thought about all those years she'd toiled as a lady's maid, without drawing a single wage.

She thought about her conscience, then quickly squelched it. In times like these, she didn't have room for a conscience.

She took the shoe clips.

And then, several hours later when Posy came (against her mother's wishes) and let her out, she packed up all of her belongings and left.

Much to her surprise, she didn't look back.

Part Two

Chapter 6

It has now been three years since any of the Bridgerton siblings have wed, and Lady Bridgerton has been heard to declare on several occasions that she is nearing her wit's end. Benedict has not taken a bride (and it is the opinion of This Author that as he has attained the age of thirty, he is far past due), and neither has Colin, although he may be forgiven his tardiness, since he is, after all, merely six-and-twenty.

The dowager viscountess also has two girls about which she must worry. Eloise is nearly one-and-twenty and although she has received several proposals, she has shown no inclination to marry. Francesca is nearly twenty (the girls quite coincidentally share a birthday), and she, too, seems more interested in the season than she does in marriage.

This Author feels that Lady Bridgerton does not need to worry. It is inconceivable that any of the Bridgertons might not eventually make an acceptable match, and besides, her two married children have already given her a total of five grandchildren, and surely that is her heart's desire.

LADY WHISTLEDOWN'S SOCIETY PAPERS, 30 APRIL 1817

Alcohol and cheroots. Card games and lots of hired women. It was just the sort of party Benedict Bridgerton would have enjoyed immensely when he was fresh out of university.

Now he was just bored.

He wasn't even certain why he'd agreed to attend. More boredom, he supposed. The London season of 1817 had thus far been a repeat of the previous year, and he hadn't found 1816 terribly scintillating to begin with. To do the whole thing over again was beyond banal.

He didn't even really know his host, one Phillip Cavender. It was one of those friend of a friend of a friend situations, and now Benedict was fervently wishing he'd remained in London. He'd just gotten over a blistering head cold, and he should have used that as an excuse to cry off, but his friend—whom he hadn't even seen in the past four hours—had prodded and cajoled, and finally Benedict had given in.

Now he heartily regretted it.

He walked down the main hall of Cavender's parents' home. Through the doorway to his left he could see a high-stakes card game in process. One of the players was sweating profusely. "Stupid idiot," Benedict muttered. The poor bloke was probably just a breath away from losing his ancestral home.

The door to his right was closed, but he could hear the sound of feminine giggling, followed by masculine laughter, followed by some rather unattractive grunting and squealing.

This was madness. He didn't want to be here. He hated card games where the stakes were higher than the participants could afford, and he'd never had any interest in copulating in such a public manner. He had no idea what had happened to the friend who had brought him here, and he didn't much like any of the other guests.

"I'm leaving," he declared, even though there was no one in the hall to hear him. He had a small piece of property not so very far away, just an hour's ride, really. It wasn't much more than a cottage, but it was his, and right now it sounded like heaven.

But good manners dictated that he find his host and inform him of his departure, even if Mr. Cavender was so sotted that he wouldn't remember the conversation the next day.

After about ten minutes of fruitless searching, however, Benedict was beginning to wish that his mother had not been so adamant in her quest to instill good manners in all of her children. It would have been a great deal easier just to leave and be done with it. "Three more minutes," he grumbled. "If I don't find the bloody idiot in three more minutes, I'm leaving."

Just then, a pair of young men stumbled by, tripping over their own feet as they exploded in raucous laughter. Alcoholic fumes filled the air, and Benedict took a discreet step back, lest one of them was suddenly compelled to cast up the contents of his stomach.

Benedict had always been fond of his boots.

"Bridgerton!" one of them called out.

Benedict gave them a curt nod in greeting. They were both about five years younger than he was, and he didn't know them well.

"Tha's not a Bridgerton," the other fellow slurred. "Tha's a—why, it *is* a Bridgerton. Got the hair and the nose." His eyes narrowed. "But which Bridgerton?"

Benedict ignored his question. "Have you seen our host?"

"We have a host?"

"Course we have a host," the first man replied. "Cavender. Damned fine fellow, you know, t'let us use his house—"

"Hiss parents' house," the other one corrected. "Hasn't inherited yet, poor bloke."

"Just so! His parents' house. Still jolly of him."

"Have either of you *seen* him?" growled Benedict.

"Just outside," replied the one who previously hadn't recalled that they had a host. "In the front."

"Thank you," Benedict said shortly, then strode past them to the front door of the house. He'd head down the front steps, pay his respects to Cavender, then make his way to the stables to collect his phaeton. He'd barely even have to break his stride.

It was, thought Sophie Beckett, high time she found a new job.

It had been almost two years since she'd left London, two years since she'd finally stopped being Araminta's virtual slave, two years since she'd been completely on her own.

After she'd left Penwood House, she'd pawned Araminta's shoe clips, but the diamonds Araminta had liked to boast about had turned out not to be diamonds at all, but rather simple paste, and they hadn't brought much money. She'd tried to find a job as a governess, but none of the agencies she'd queried was willing to take her on. She was obviously well educated, but she'd had no references, and besides, most women did not like to hire someone quite so young and pretty.

Sophie had eventually purchased a ticket on a coach to Wiltshire, since that was as far as she could go while still reserving the bulk of her pin money for emergencies. Luckily, she'd found employment quickly, as an upstairs maid for Mr. and Mrs. John Cavender. They were an ordinary sort of couple, expecting good work from their servants but not demanding the impossible. After toiling for Araminta for so many years, Sophie found the Cavenders a positive vacation.

But then their son had returned from his tour of Europe, and everything had changed. Phillip was constantly cornering her in the hall, and when his innuendo and suggestions were rebuffed, he'd grown more aggressive. Sophie had just started to think that maybe she ought to find employment elsewhere when Mr. and Mrs. Cavender had left for a week to visit Mrs. Cavender's sister in Brighton, and Phillip had decided to throw a party for two dozen of his closest friends.

It had been difficult to avoid Phillip's advances before, but at least Sophie had felt reasonably protected. Phillip would never dare attack her while his mother was in residence.

But with Mr. and Mrs. Cavender gone, Phillip seemed to think that he could do and take anything he wanted, and his friends were no better.

Sophie knew she should have left the grounds immediately, but Mrs. Cavender had treated her well, and she didn't think it was polite to leave without giving two weeks' notice. After two hours of being chased around the house, however, she decided that good manners were not worth her virtue, and so she'd told the (thankfully sympathetic) housekeeper that she could not stay, packed her meager belongings in one small bag, stolen down the side stairs, and let herself out. It was a two-mile hike into the village, but even in the dead of night, the road to town seemed infinitely safer than remaining at the Cavender home, and besides, she knew of a small inn where she could get a hot meal and a room for a reasonable price.

She'd just come 'round the house and had stepped onto the front drive, however, when she heard a raucous shout.

She looked up. Oh, *blast*. Phillip Cavender, looking even drunker and meaner than usual.

Sophie broke into a run, praying that alcohol had impaired Phillip's coordination because she knew she could not match him for speed.

But her flight must have only served to excite him, because she heard him yell out with glee, then felt his footsteps rumbling on the ground, growing closer and closer until she felt his hand close round the back collar of her coat, jerking her to a halt.

Phillip laughed triumphantly, and Sophie had never been so terrified in her entire life.

"Look what I have here," he cackled. "Little Miss Sophie. I shall have to introduce you to my friends."

Sophie's mouth went dry, and she wasn't sure whether her heart started to beat double time or stopped altogether. "Let me go, Mr. Cavender," she said in her sternest voice. She knew that he liked her helpless and pleading, and she refused to cater to his wishes.

"I don't think so," he said, turning her around so that she was forced to watch his lips stretch into a slippery smile. He turned his head to the side and called out, "Heasley! Fletcher! Look what I have here!"

Sophie watched with horror as two more men emerged from the shadows. From the looks of them, they were just as drunk, or maybe even more so, than Phillip.

"You always host the best parties," one of them said in an oily voice.

Phillip puffed out with pride.

"Let me go!" Sophie said again.

Phillip grinned. "What do you think, boys? Should I do as the lady asks?"

"Hell, no!" came the reply from the younger of the two men.

" 'Lady,' " said the other—the same one who had told Phillip that he hosted the best parties, "might be a bit of a misnomer, don't you think?"

"Quite right!" Phillip replied. "This one's a housemaid, and as we all know, that breed is born to serve." He gave Sophie a shove, pushing her toward one of his friends. "Here. Have a look at the goods."

Sophie cried out as she was propelled forward, and she clutched tightly to her small bag. She was about to be raped; that much was clear. But her panicked mind wanted to hold on to some last shred of dignity, and she refused to allow these men to spill her every last belonging onto the cold ground.

The man who caught her fondled her roughly, then

shoved her toward the third one. He'd just snaked his hand around her waist, when she heard someone yell out, "Cavender!"

Sophie shut her eyes in agony. *A fourth man. Dear God, weren't three enough?*

"Bridgerton!" Phillip called out. "Come join us!"

Sophie's eyes snapped open. Bridgerton?

A tall, powerfully built man emerged from the shadows, moving forward with easy, confident grace.

"What have we here?"

Dear God, she'd recognize that voice anywhere. She heard it often enough in her dreams.

It was Benedict Bridgerton. Her Prince Charming.

The night air was chilly, but Benedict found it refreshing after being forced to breathe the alcohol and tobacco fumes inside. The moon was nearly full, glowing round and fat, and a gentle breeze ruffled the leaves on the trees. All in all, it was an excellent night to leave a boring party and ride home.

But first things first. He had to find his host, go through the motions of thanking him for his hospitality, and inform him of his departure. As he reached the bottom step, he called out, "Cavender!"

"Over here!" came the reply, and Benedict turned his head to the right. Cavender was standing under a stately old elm with two other gentlemen. They appeared to be having a bit of fun with a housemaid, pushing her back and forth between them.

Benedict groaned. He was too far away to determine whether the housemaid was enjoying their attentions, and if she was not, then he was going to have to save her, which was not how he'd planned to spend his evening. He'd never been particularly enamored of playing the hero, but he had far too many younger sisters—four, to be precise—to ignore any female in distress.

"Ho there!" he called out as he ambled over, keeping his posture purposefully casual. It was always better to move slowly and assess the situation than it was to charge in blindly.

"Bridgerton!" Cavender called out. "Come join us!"

Benedict drew close just as one of the men snaked an arm around the young woman's waist and pinned her to him, her back to his front. His other hand was on her bottom, squeezing and kneading.

Benedict brought his gaze to the maid's eyes. They were huge and filled with terror, and she was looking at him as if he'd just dropped fully formed from the sky.

"What have we here?" he asked.

"Just a bit of sport," Cavender chortled. "My parents were kind enough to hire this prime morsel as the upstairs maid."

"She doesn't appear to be enjoying your attentions," Benedict said quietly.

"She likes it just fine," Cavender replied with a grin. "Fine enough for me, anyway."

"But not," Benedict said, stepping forward, "for me."

"You can have your turn with her," Cavender said, ever jovial. "Just as soon as we're through."

"You misunderstand."

There was a hard edge to Benedict's voice, and the three men all froze, looking over at him with wary curiosity.

"Release the girl," he said.

Still stunned by the sudden change of atmosphere, and with reflexes most likely dulled by alcohol, the man holding the girl did nothing.

"I don't want to fight you," Benedict said, crossing his arms, "but I will. And I can assure you that the three-to-one odds don't frighten me."

"Now, see here," Cavender said angrily. "You can't come here and order me about on my own property."

"It's your parents' property," Benedict pointed out, reminding them all that Cavender was still rather wet behind the ears.

"It's my home," Cavender shot back, "and she's my maid. And she'll do what I want."

"I wasn't aware that slavery was legal in this country," Benedict murmured.

"She has to do what I say!"

"Does she?"

"I'll fire her if she doesn't."

"Very well," Benedict said with a tiny quirk of a smile. "Ask her then. Ask the girl if she wants to tup with all three of you. Because that is what you had in mind, isn't it?"

Cavender sputtered as he fought for words.

"Ask her," Benedict said again, grinning now, mostly because he knew his smile would infuriate the younger man. "And if she says no, you can fire her right here on the spot."

"I'm not going to ask her," Cavender whined.

"Well, then, you can't really expect her to do it, can you?" Benedict looked at the girl. She was a fetching thing, with a short bob of light brown curls and eyes that loomed almost too large in her face. "Fine," he said, sparing a brief glance back at Cavender. "I'll ask her."

The girl's lips parted slightly, and Benedict had the oddest sensation that they had met before. But that was impossible, unless she'd worked for some other aristocratic family. And even then, he would have only seen her in passing. His taste in women had never run to housemaids, and in all truth, he tended not to notice them.

"Miss . . ." He frowned. "I say, what's your name?"

"Sophie Beckett," she gasped, sounding as if there were a very large frog caught in her throat.

"Miss Beckett," he continued, "would you be so kind as to answer the following question?"

"No!" she burst out.

"You're not going to answer?" he asked, his eyes amused.

"No, I do *not* want to tup with these three men!" The words practically exploded from her mouth.

"Well, that seems to settle that," Benedict said. He glanced up at the man still holding her. "I suggest you release her so that Cavender here may relieve her of employment."

"And where will she go?" Cavender sneered. "I can assure you she won't work in this district again."

Sophie turned to Benedict, wondering much the same thing.

Benedict gave a careless shrug. "I'll find her a position in my mother's household." He looked over at her and raised a brow. "I assume that's acceptable?"

Sophie's mouth dropped open in horrified surprise. He wanted to take her to his *home*?

"That's not quite the reaction I expected," Benedict said dryly. "It will certainly be more pleasant than your employment here. At the very least, I can assure you you won't be raped. What do you say?"

Sophie glanced frantically at the three men who had intended to rape her. She really didn't have a choice. Benedict Bridgerton was her only means off the Cavender property. She knew she couldn't possibly work for his mother; to be in such close proximity to Benedict and still have to be a servant would be more than she could bear. But she could find a way to avoid that later. For now she just needed to get away from Phillip.

She turned to Benedict and nodded, still afraid to use her voice. She felt as if she were choking inside, although she wasn't certain whether that was from fear or relief.

"Good," he said. "Shall we be off?"

She gave a rather pointed look at the arm that was still holding her hostage.

"Oh, for the love of God," Benedict snarled. "Will you let go of her or will I have to shoot your damned hand off?"

Benedict wasn't even holding a gun, but the tone of his voice was such that the man let go instantly.

"Good," Benedict said, holding his arm out toward the maid. She stepped forward, and with trembling fingers placed her hand on his elbow.

"You can't just take her!" Phillip yelled.

Benedict gave him a supercilious look. "I just did."

"You'll be sorry you did this," Phillip said.

"I doubt it. Now get out of my sight."

Phillip made a huffy sound, then turned his friends and said, "Let's get out of here." Then he turned to Benedict and added, "Don't think you shall ever receive another invitation to one of my parties."

"My heart is breaking," Benedict drawled.

Phillip let out one more outraged snort, and then he and his two friends stalked back to the house.

Sophie watched them walk away, then slowly dragged her gaze back to Benedict. When she'd been trapped by Phillip and his leering friends, she'd known what they wanted to do to her, and she'd almost wanted to die. And then, all of a sudden, there was Benedict Bridgerton, standing before her like a hero from her dreams, and she'd thought maybe she *had* died, because why else would he be here with her unless she was in heaven?

She'd been so completely and utterly stunned, she'd almost forgotten that Phillip's friend still held her pinned against him and was grabbing her behind in a most humiliating manner. For one brief second the world had melted away, and the only thing she could see, the only thing she *knew*, was Benedict Bridgerton.

It had been a moment of perfection.

But then the world had come crashing back, and all she could think was—what on earth was he doing here? It was a disgusting party, full of drunkards and whores. When she'd met him two years ago, he hadn't seemed the sort who would frequent such events. But she'd only known him for a few short hours. Perhaps she'd misjudged him. She closed her eyes in agony. For the past two years, the memory of Benedict Bridgerton had been the brightest light in her drab and dreary life. If she'd misjudged him, if he was little better than Phillip and his friends, then she'd be left with nothing.

Not even a memory of love.

But he *had* saved her. That was irrefutable. Maybe it didn't really matter why he'd come to Phillip's party, only that he had, and he had saved her.

"Are you all right?" he suddenly asked.

Sophie nodded, looking him squarely in the eye, waiting for him to recognize her.

"Are you certain?"

She nodded again, still waiting. It had to happen soon.

"Good. They were handling you roughly."

"I'll be all right." Sophie chewed on her lower lip. She had no idea how he would react once he realized who she was. Would he be delighted? Furious? The suspense was killing her.

"How much time will it take for you to pack your things?"

Sophie blinked rather dumbly, then realized she was still holding her satchel. "It's all right here," she said. "I was trying to leave when they caught me."

"Smart girl," he murmured approvingly.

Sophie just stared at him, unable to believe he hadn't recognized her.

"Let's be off, then," he said. "It makes me ill just to be on Cavender's property."

Sophie said nothing, but her chin jutted slightly forward, and her head tilted to the side as she watched his face.

"Are you certain you're all right?" he asked.

And then Sophie started to think.

Two years ago, when she'd met him, half of her face had been covered by a mask.

Her hair had been lightly powdered, making it seem

blonder than it actually was. Furthermore, she'd since cut it and sold the locks to a wigmaker. Her previous long waves were now short curls.

Without Mrs. Gibbons to feed her, she'd lost nearly a stone.

And when one got right down to it, they'd only been in each other's company a mere hour and a half.

She stared at him, right into his eyes. And that was when she knew.

He wasn't going to recognize her.

He had no idea who she was.

Sophie didn't know whether to laugh or to cry.

Chapter 7

It was clear to all of the guests at the Mottram ball Thursday last that Miss Rosamund Reiling has set her cap for Mr. Phillip Cavender.

It is the opinion of This Author that the two are well matched indeed.

LADY WHISTLEDOWN'S SOCIETY PAPERS, 30 APRIL 1817

Ten minutes later, Sophie was sitting next to Benedict Bridgerton in his phaeton.

"Is there something in your eye?" he asked politely.

That caught her attention. "I-I beg your pardon?"

"You keep blinking," he explained. "I thought perhaps you had something in your eye."

Sophie swallowed hard, trying to suppress a round of nervous laughter. What was she supposed to say to him? The truth? That she was blinking because she kept expecting to wake up from what could only be a dream? Or maybe a nightmare?

"Are you certain you're all right?" he asked.

She nodded.

"Just the aftereffects of shock, I imagine," he said.

She nodded again, letting him think that was all that affected her.

How could he not have recognized her? She'd been dreaming of this moment for years. Her Prince Charming had finally come to rescue her, and he didn't even know who she was.

"What was your name again?" he asked. "I'm terribly sorry. It always takes me twice to remember a name."

"Miss Sophia Beckett." There seemed little reason to lie; she hadn't told him her name at the masquerade.

"I'm pleased to meet you, Miss Beckett," he said, keeping his eyes on the dark road. "I'm Mr. Benedict Bridgerton."

Sophie acknowledged his greeting with a nod even though he wasn't looking at her. She held silent for a moment, mostly because she simply didn't know what to say in such an unbelievable situation. It was, she realized, the introduction that had never taken place two years earlier. Finally, she just said, "That was a very brave thing you did."

He shrugged.

"There were three of them and only one of you. Most men would not have intervened."

This time he did look at her. "I hate bullies," was all he said.

She nodded again. "They would have raped me."

"I know," he replied. And then he added, "I have four sisters."

She almost said "I know," but caught herself just in time. How was a housemaid from Wiltshire supposed to know that? So instead she said, "I expect that is why you were so sensitive to my plight."

"I would like to think another man would come to their aid, should they ever find themselves in a similar situation."

"I pray you never have to find out."

He nodded grimly. "As do I."

They rode on, silence cloaking the night. Sophie remembered the masquerade ball, when they hadn't lacked for conversation, even for a moment. It was different now, she realized. She was a housemaid, not a glorious woman of the *ton*. They had nothing in common.

But still, she kept waiting for him to recognize her, to yank the carriage to a halt, clasp her to his chest, and tell her he'd been looking for her for two years. But that wasn't going to happen, she soon realized. He couldn't recognize the lady in the housemaid, and in all truth, why should he?

People saw what they expected to see. And Benedict Bridgerton surely didn't expect to see a fine lady of the *ton* in the guise of a humble housemaid.

Not a day had gone by that she hadn't thought of him, hadn't remembered his lips on hers, or the heady magic of that costumed night. He had become the centerpiece of her fantasies, dreams in which she was a different person, with different parents. In her dreams, she'd met him at a ball, maybe her own ball, hosted by her devoted mother and father. He courted her sweetly, with fragrant flowers and stolen kisses. And then, on a mellow spring day, while the birds were singing and a gentle breeze ruffled the air, he got down on one knee and asked her to marry him, professing his everlasting love and adoration.

It was a fine daydream, surpassed only by the one in which they lived happily ever after, with three or four splendid children, born safely within the sacrament of marriage.

But even with all her fantasies, she never imagined she'd actually see him again, much less be rescued by him from a trio of licentious attackers.

She wondered if he ever thought of the mysterious woman in silver with whom he'd shared one passionate kiss. She liked to think that he did, but she doubted that it had meant as much to him as it had to her. He was a man, after all, and had most likely kissed dozens of women.

And for him, that one night had been much like any other. Sophie still read *Whistledown* whenever she could get her hands on it. She knew that he attended scores of balls. Why should one masquerade stand out in his memory?

Sophie sighed and looked down at her hands, still clutching the drawstring to her small bag. She wished she owned gloves, but her only pair had worn out earlier that year, and she hadn't been able to afford another. Her hands looked rough and chapped, and her fingers were growing cold.

"Is that everything you own?" Benedict asked, motioning to the bag.

She nodded. "I haven't much, I'm afraid. Just a change of clothing and a few personal mementos."

He was silent for a moment, then said, "You have quite a refined accent for a housemaid."

He was not the first to make that observation, so Sophie gave him her stock answer. "My mother was a housekeeper to a very kind and generous family. They allowed me to share some of their daughters' lessons."

"Why do you not work there?" With an expert twist of his wrists, he guided his team to the left side of the fork in the road. "I assume you do not speak of the Cavenders."

"No," she replied, trying to devise a proper answer. No one had ever bothered to probe deeper than her offered explanation. No one had ever been interested enough to care. "My mother passed on," she finally replied, "and I did not deal well with the new housekeeper."

He seemed to accept that, and they rode on for a few minutes. The night was almost silent, save for the wind and the rhythmic clip-clop of the horses' hooves. Finally, Sophie, unable to contain her curiosity, asked, "Where are we going?"

"I have a cottage not far away," he replied. "We'll stay there a night or two, then I'll take you to my mother's home. I'm certain she'll find a position for you in her household."

Sophie's heart began to pound. "This cottage of yours . . ."

"You will be properly chaperoned," he said with a faint smile. "The caretakers will be in attendance, and I assure you that Mr. and Mrs. Crabtree are not likely to let anything untoward occur in their house."

"I thought it was *your* house."

His smile grew deeper. "I have been trying to get them to think of it as such for years, but I have never been successful."

Sophie felt her lips tug up at the corners. "They sound like people I would like very much."

"I expect you would."

And then there was more silence. Sophie kept her eyes scrupulously straight ahead. She had the most absurd fear that if their eyes met, he would recognize her. But that was mere fancy. He'd already looked her squarely in the eye, more than once even, and he still thought her nothing but a housemaid.

After a few minutes, however, she felt the oddest tingling in her cheek, and as she turned to face him she saw that he kept glancing at her with an odd expression.

"Have we met?" he blurted out.

"No," she said, her voice a touch more choked than she would have preferred. "I don't believe so."

"I'm sure you're right," he muttered, "but still, you do seem rather familiar."

"All housemaids look the same," she said with a wry smile.

"I used to think so," he mumbled.

She turned her face forward, her jaw dropping. Why had she said that? Didn't she *want* him to recognize her? Hadn't she spent the last half hour hoping and wishing and dreaming and—

And that was the problem. She was dreaming. In her dreams he loved her. In her dreams he asked her to marry him. In reality, he might ask her to become his mistress, and that was something she'd sworn she would never do. In reality, he might feel honor bound to return her to Araminta, who would probably turn her straightaways over to the magistrate for stealing her shoe clips (and Sophie didn't for one moment think that Araminta hadn't noticed their disappearance.)

No, it was best if he did not recognize her. It would only complicate her life, and considering that she had no source of income, and in fact very little beyond the clothes on her back, her life did not need complications at this point.

And yet she felt unaccountably disappointed that he had not instantly known who she was.

"Is that a raindrop?" Sophie asked, eager to keep the conversation on more benign topics.

Benedict looked up. The moon was now obscured by clouds. "It didn't look like rain when we left," he murmured. A fat raindrop landed on his thigh. "But I do believe you're correct."

She glanced at the sky. "The wind has picked up quite a bit. I hope it doesn't storm."

"It's sure to storm," he said wryly, "as we are in an open carriage. If I had taken my coach, there wouldn't be a cloud in the sky."

"How close are we to your cottage?"

"About half an hour away, I should think." He frowned. "Provided we are not slowed by the rain."

"Well, I do not mind a bit of rain," she said gamely. "There are far worse things than getting wet."

They both knew exactly what she was talking about.

"I don't think I remembered to thank you," she said, her words quiet.

Benedict turned his head sharply. By all that was holy, there was something damned familiar about her voice. But when his eyes searched her face, all he saw was a simple housemaid. A very attractive housemaid, to be sure, but a housemaid nonetheless. No one with whom he would ever have crossed paths.

"It was nothing," he finally said.

"To you, perhaps. To me it was everything."

Uncomfortable with such appreciation, he just nodded and gave one of those grunts men tended to emit when they didn't know what to say.

"It was a very brave thing you did," she said.

He grunted again.

And then the heavens opened up in earnest.

It took about one minute for Benedict's clothes to be soaked through. "I'll get there as quickly as I can," he yelled, trying to make himself heard over the wind.

"Don't worry about me!" Sophie called back, but when he looked over at her, he saw that she was huddling into herself, her arms wrapped tightly over her chest as she tried to conserve the heat of her body.

"Let me give you my coat."

She shook her head and actually laughed. "It'll probably make me even wetter, soaked as it is."

He nudged the horses into a faster pace, but the road was growing muddy, and the wind was whipping the rain every which way, reducing the already mediocre visibility.

Bloody hell. This was just what he needed. He'd had a head cold all last week, and he probably wasn't completely recovered. A ride in the freezing rain would most likely set him back, and he'd spend the next month with a runny nose, watery eyes . . . all those infuriating, unattractive symptoms.

Of course . . .

Benedict couldn't quite contain a smile. Of course, if he were ill again, his mother couldn't try to cajole him into attending every single party in town, all in the hopes that he would find some suitable young lady and settle down into a quiet and happy marriage.

To his credit, he always kept his eyes open, was always on the lookout for a prospective bride. He certainly wasn't opposed to marriage on principle. His brother Anthony and his sister Daphne had made splendidly happy matches. But

Anthony's and Daphne's marriages were splendidly happy because they'd been smart enough to wed the right people, and Benedict was quite certain he had not yet met the right person.

No, he thought, his mind wandering back a few years, that wasn't entirely true. He'd once met someone . . .

The lady in silver.

When he'd held her in his arms and twirled her around the balcony in her very first waltz, he'd felt something different inside, a fluttering, tingling sensation. It should have scared the hell out of him.

But it hadn't. It had left him breathless, excited . . . and determined to have her.

But then she'd disappeared. It was as if the world were actually flat, and she'd fallen right off the edge. He'd learned nothing in that irritating interview with Lady Penwood, and when he'd queried his friends and family, no one knew anything about a young woman wearing a silver dress.

She hadn't arrived with anyone and she hadn't left with anyone. For all intents and purposes, she hadn't even existed.

He'd watched for her at every ball, party, and musicale he attended. Hell, he attended twice as many functions as usual, just in the hopes that he'd catch a glimpse of her.

But he'd always come home disappointed.

He'd thought he would stop looking for her. He was a practical man, and he'd assumed that eventually he would simply give up. And in some ways, he had. After a few months he found himself back in the habit of turning down more invitations than he accepted. A few months after that, he realized that he was once again able to meet women and not automatically compare them to her.

But he couldn't stop himself from watching for her. He might not feel the same urgency, but whenever he attended a ball or took a seat at a musicale, he found his eyes sweeping across the crowd, his ears straining for the lilt of her laughter.

She was out there somewhere. He'd long since resigned himself to the fact that he wasn't likely to find her, and he hadn't searched actively for over a year, but . . .

He smiled wistfully. He just couldn't stop from looking. It had become, in a very strange way, a part of who he was. His name was Benedict Bridgerton, he had seven brothers and sisters, was rather skilled with both a sword and a sketching crayon, and he always kept his eyes open for the one woman who had touched his soul.

He kept hoping . . . and wishing . . . and watching. And even though he told himself it was probably time to marry, he just couldn't muster the enthusiasm to do so.

Because what if he put his ring on some woman's finger, and the next day he saw *her*?

It would be enough to break his heart.

No, it would be more than that. It would be enough to shatter his soul.

Benedict breathed a sigh of relief as he saw the village of Rosemeade approaching. Rosemeade meant that his cottage was a mere five minutes away, and lud, but he couldn't wait to get inside and throw himself into a steaming tub of water.

He glanced over at Miss Beckett. She, too, was shivering, but, he thought with a touch of admiration, she hadn't let out even a peep of complaint. Benedict tried to think of another woman of his acquaintance who would have stood up to the elements with such fortitude and came up empty-handed. Even his sister Daphne, who was as good a sport as any, would have been howling about the cold by now.

"We're almost there," he assured her.

"I'm all—Oh! Are you all right?"

Benedict was gripped by wave of coughs, the deep, hacking kind that rumble down in one's chest. His lungs felt as if they were on fire, and his throat like someone had taken a razor blade to it.

"I'm fine," he gasped, jerking slightly on the reins to make up for the lack of direction he'd given the horses while he was coughing.

"You don't sound fine."

"Had a head cold last week," he said with a wince. Damn, but his lungs felt sore.

"That didn't sound like your head," she said, giving him what she obviously hoped was a teasing smile. But it didn't look like a teasing smile. In truth, she looked terribly concerned.

"Must've moved," he muttered.

"I don't want you getting sick on my account."

He tried to grin, but his cheekbones ached too much. "I would've been caught in the rain whether I'd taken you along or not."

"Still—"

Whatever she'd intended to say was lost under another stream of deep, chesty coughs.

"Sorry," he mumbled.

"Let me drive," she said, reaching for the reins.

He turned to her in disbelief. "This is a phaeton, not a single-horse wagon."

Sophie fought the urge to throttle him. His nose was running, his eyes were red, he couldn't stop coughing, and still he found the energy to act like an arrogant peacock. "I assure you," she said slowly, "that I know how to drive a team of horses."

"And where did you acquire that skill?"

"The same family that allowed me to share in their daughters' lessons," Sophie lied. "I learned to drive a team when the girls learned."

"The lady of the house must have taken quite a liking to you," he said.

"She did quite," Sophie replied, trying not to laugh. Araminta had been the lady of the house, and she'd fought tooth and nail every time her father had insisted that she be allowed to receive the same instruction as Rosamund and Posy. They'd all three learned how to drive teams the year before the earl had died.

"I'll drive, thank you," Benedict said sharply. Then he ruined the entire effect by launching into yet another coughing fit.

Sophie reached for the reins. "For the love of—"

"Here," he said, thrusting them toward her, as he wiped his eyes. "Take them. But I'll be watching you."

"I would expect no less," she said peevishly. The rain didn't exactly make for ideal driving conditions, and it had been years since she'd held reins in her hands, but she thought she acquitted herself rather nicely. There were some things one didn't forget, she supposed.

It felt rather nice, actually, to do something she hadn't done since her previous life, when she'd been, officially at least, an earl's ward. She'd had fine clothes then, and good food, and interesting lessons, and . . .

She sighed. It hadn't been perfect, but it had been better than anything that had come after.

"What's wrong?" Benedict asked.

"Nothing. Why should you think something is wrong?"

"You sighed."

"You heard me over the wind?" she asked incredulously.

"I've been paying close attention. I'm sick enough"—cough cough—"without you landing us in a ditch."

Sophie decided not even to credit him with a reply.

"Turn right up ahead," he directed. "It'll take us directly to my cottage."

She did as he asked. "Does your cottage have a name?"

"My Cottage."

"I might have known," she muttered.

He smirked. Quite a feat, in her opinion, since he looked sick as a dog. "I'm not kidding," he said.

Sure enough, in another minute they pulled up in front of an elegant country house, complete with a small, unobtrusive sign in front reading, MY COTTAGE.

"The previous owner coined the name," Benedict said as he directed her toward the stables, "but it seemed to fit me as well."

Sophie looked over at the house, which, while fairly small, was no humble dwelling. "You call this a cottage?"

"No, the previous owner did," he replied. "You should have seen his other house."

A moment later they were out of the rain, and Benedict had hopped down and was unhitching the horses. He was wearing gloves, but they were completely sodden and slipping on the bridle, and so he peeled them off and flung them away. Sophie watched him as he went about his work. His fingers were wrinkled like prunes and trembling from the cold. "Let me help," she said, stepping forward.

"I can do it."

"Of course you can," she said placatingly, "but you can do it faster with my help."

He turned, presumably to refuse her again, then doubled over as he was wracked by coughs. Sophie quickly rushed in and led him to a nearby bench. "Sit down, please," she implored him. "I'll finish up the job."

She thought he'd disagree, but this time he gave in. "I'm sorry," he said hoarsely. "I—"

"There's nothing to feel sorry about," she said, making quick work of the job. Or as quick as she could; her fingers were still numb, and bits of her skin had turned white from having been wet for so long.

"Not very . . ." He coughed again, this one lower and deeper than before. ". . . gentlemanly of me."

"Oh, I think I can forgive you this time, considering the

way you saved me earlier this evening." Sophie tried to give him a jaunty smile, but for some reason it wobbled, and without warning she found herself inexplicably near tears. She turned quickly away, not wanting him to see her face.

But he must have seen something, or maybe just sensed that something was wrong, because he called out, "Are you all right?"

"I'm fine!" she replied, but her voice came out strained and choked, and before she knew it, he was next to her, and she was in his arms.

"It's all right," he said soothingly. "You're safe now."

The tears burst forth. She cried for what could have been her fate that evening, and she cried for what had been her fate for the past nine years. She cried for the memory of when he'd held her in his arms at the masquerade, and she cried because she was in his arms right now.

She cried because he was so damned *nice*, and even though he was clearly ill, even though she was, in his eyes, nothing but a housemaid, he still wanted to care for her and protect her.

She cried because she hadn't let herself cry in longer than she could remember, and she cried because she felt so alone.

And she cried because she'd been dreaming of him for so very long, and he hadn't recognized her. It was probably best that he did not, but her heart still ached from it.

Eventually her tears subsided, and he stepped back, touching her chin as he said, "Do you feel better now?"

She nodded, surprised that it was true.

"Good. You had a scare, and—" He jerked away from her, doubling over as he coughed.

"We really need to get you inside," Sophie said, brushing away the last streaks of her tears. "Inside the house, that is."

He nodded. "I'll race you to the door."

Her eyes widened in shock. She couldn't believe that he had the spirit to make a joke of this, when he was obviously feeling so poorly. But she wrapped the drawstring of her bag around her hands, hitched up her skirts, and ran for the front door to the cottage. By the time she reached the steps, she was laughing from the exertion, giggling at the ridiculousness of running wildly to get out of the rain when she was already soaked to the bone.

Benedict had, not surprisingly, beaten her to the small portico. He might have been ill, but his legs were significantly longer and stronger. When she skidded to a halt at his side, he was banging on the front door.

"Don't you have a key?" Sophie yelled. The wind was still howling, making it difficult to be heard.

He shook his head. "I wasn't planning on stopping here."

"Do you think the caretakers will even hear you?"

"I bloody well hope so," he muttered.

Sophie wiped away the rivulets of water running over her eyes and peeked in a nearby window. "It's very dark," she told him. "Do you think they might not be home?"

"I don't know where else they'd be."

"Shouldn't there at least be a maid or a footman?"

Benedict shook his head. "I'm so rarely here it seemed foolish to hire a full staff. The maids only come in for the day."

Sophie grimaced. "I'd suggest we look for an open window, but that's rather unlikely in the rain."

"Not necessary," Benedict said grimly. "I know where the spare key is hidden."

Sophie looked at him in surprise. "Why do you sound so glum about it?"

He coughed several times before answering, "Because it means I have to go back out into the bloody storm."

Sophie knew he was truly reaching the end of his patience. He'd already sworn twice in front of her, and he didn't seem the sort to curse in front of a woman, even a mere housemaid.

"Wait here," he ordered, and then before she could reply, he'd left the shelter of the portico and dashed away.

A few minutes later she heard a key turning in the lock, and the front door swung open to reveal Benedict, holding a candle and dripping all over the floor. "I don't know where Mr. and Mrs. Crabtree are," he said, his voice raspy from all his coughing, "but they're definitely not here."

Sophie gulped. "We're alone?"

He nodded. "Completely."

She edged toward the stairs. "I'd better find the servants' quarters."

"Oh, no you won't," he growled, grabbing hold of her arm.

"I won't?"

He shook his head. "You, dear girl, aren't going anywhere."

Chapter 8

It seems one cannot take two steps at a London ball these days without stumbling across a society matron lamenting the difficulties of finding good help. Indeed, This Author thought that Mrs. Featherington and Lady Penwood were going to come to blows at last week's Smythe-Smith musicale. It seems that Lady Penwood stole Mrs. Featherington's lady's maid right out from under her nose one month ago, promising higher wages and free cast-off clothing. (It should be noted that Mrs. Featherington also gave the poor girl cast-off clothing, but anyone who has ever observed the attire of the Featherington girls would understand why the lady's maid would not view this as a benefit.)

The plot thickened, however, when the lady's maid in question fled back to Mrs. Featherington, begging to be rehired. It seemed that Lady Penwood's idea of a lady's maid included duties more accurately ascribed to the scullery maid, upstairs maid, and cook.

Someone ought to tell the woman that one girl cannot do the work of three.

LADY WHISTLEDOWN'S SOCIETY PAPERS, 2 MAY 1817

"We're going to build a fire," Benedict said, "and get warm before either of us goes off to bed. I didn't save you from Cavender just so you could die of influenza."

Sophie watched him cough anew, the spasms wracking his body and forcing him to bend over at the waist. "Begging your pardon, Mr. Bridgerton," she could not help commenting, "but of the two of us, I should think you're more in danger of contracting influenza."

"Just so," he gasped, "and I assure you I have no desire to be so afflicted, either. So—" He bent over again as he was once again engulfed by coughs.

"Mr. Bridgerton?" Sophie asked, concern in her voice.

He swallowed convulsively and barely managed to say, "Just help me get a fire blazing before I cough myself into oblivion."

Sophie's brow knit with worry. His coughing fits were coming closer and closer together, and each time they were deeper, more rumbly, as if they were coming from the very pit of his chest.

She made easy work of the fire; she'd certainly had enough experience setting them as a housemaid, and soon they were both holding their hands as close to the flames as they dared.

"I don't suppose your change of clothing remained dry," Benedict said, nodding toward Sophie's sodden satchel.

"I doubt it," she said ruefully. "But it's no matter. If I stand here long enough, I'll dry out."

"Don't be silly," he scoffed, turning around so that the fire might heat his back. "I'm sure I can find you a change of clothing."

"You have women's clothing here?" she asked doubtfully.

"You're not so fussy that you can't wear breeches and a shirt for one evening, are you?"

Until that very moment, Sophie had probably been *exactly* that fussy, but put that way, it did seem a little silly. "I suppose not," she said. Dry clothing certainly sounded appealing.

"Good," he said briskly. "Why don't you light the furnaces in two bedrooms, and I'll find us both some clothing?"

"I can stay in the servants' quarters," Sophie said quickly.

"Not necessary," he said, striding out of the room and motioning for her to follow. "I've extra rooms, and you are not a servant here."

"But I *am* a servant," she pointed out, hurrying after him.

"Do whatever you please then." He started to march up the stairs, but had to stop halfway up to cough. "You can find a tiny little room in the servants' quarters with a hard little pallet, or you can avail yourself of a guest bedroom, all of which I assure you come equipped with feather mattresses and goosedown coverlets."

Sophie knew that she should remember her place in the world and march right up the next flight of stairs to the attic, but by God above, a feather mattress and down coverlet sounded like heaven on earth. She hadn't slept in such comfort in years. "I'll just find a small guest bedroom," she acceded. "The, er, smallest you have."

Half of Benedict's mouth quirked up in a dry, I-told-you-so sort of smile. "Pick whichever room you like. But not that one," he said, pointing to the second door on the left. "That's mine."

"I'll get the furnace started in there immediately," she said. He needed the warmth more than she did, and besides, she found herself inordinately curious to see what the inside of his bedroom looked like. One could tell a lot about a person by the décor of his bedchamber. Provided, of course, she thought with a grimace, that one possessed enough funds to decorate in the manner one preferred. Sophie sincerely doubted that anyone could have told anything about her from her little attic turret at the Cavenders'—except for the fact that she had not a penny to her name.

Sophie left her satchel in the hall and scurried into Benedict's bedchamber. It was a lovely room, warm and masculine and very comfortable. Despite the fact that Benedict had said he was rarely in residence, there were all sorts of personal items on the desk and tables—miniatures of what had to be his brothers and sisters, leather-bound books, and even a small glass bowl filled with . . .

Rocks?

"How odd," Sophie murmured, moving forward even though she knew she was being dreadfully invasive and nosy.

"Each one is meaningful in some way," came a deep voice from behind her. "I've collected them since—" He stopped to cough. "Since I was a child."

Sophie's face flushed red at having been caught so shamelessly snooping, but her curiosity was still piqued, so she held one up. It was of a pinkish hue, with a ragged grey vein running straight through the middle. "What about this one?"

"I picked that one up on a hike," Benedict said softly. "It happened to be the day my father died."

"Oh!" Sophie dropped the rock back on the pile as if burned. "I'm so sorry."

"It was long ago."

"I'm still sorry."

He smiled sadly. "As am I." Then he coughed, so hard that he had to lean against the wall.

"You need to get warm," Sophie said quickly. "Let me get to work on that fire."

Benedict tossed a bundle of clothing onto the bed. "For you," he said simply.

"Thank you," she said, keeping her attention focused on the small furnace. It was dangerous to remain in the same room as him. She didn't think he was likely to make an untoward advance; he was far too much of a gentleman to foist himself on a woman he barely knew. No, the danger lay squarely within herself. Frankly, she was terrified that if she spent too much time in his company she might fall head over heels in love.

And what would that get her?

Nothing but a broken heart.

Sophie huddled in front of the small iron furnace for several minutes, stoking the flame until she was confident that it would not flicker out. "There," she announced once she was satisfied. She stood up, arching her back slightly as she stretched and turned around. "That should take care of—Oh my!"

Benedict Bridgerton looked positively green.

"Are you all right?" she asked, hurrying to his side.

"Don' feel too well," he slurred, leaning heavily against the bedpost. He sounded vaguely intoxicated, but Sophie had been in his company for at least two hours, and she knew that he had not been drinking.

"You need to get into bed," she said, stumbling under his weight when he decided to lean against her instead of the bedpost.

He grinned. "You coming?"

She lurched back. "Now I know you're feverish."

He lifted his hand to touch his forehead, but he smacked his nose instead. "Ow!" he yelped.

Sophie winced in sympathy.

His hand crept up to his forehead. "Hmmm, maybe I am a bit hot."

It was horribly familiar of her, but a man's health was at stake, so Sophie reached out and touched her hand to his brow. It wasn't burning, but it certainly wasn't cool. "You need to get out of those wet clothes," she said. "Immediately."

Benedict looked down, blinking as if the sight of his sodden clothing was a surprise. "Yes," he murmured thoughtfully. "Yes, I believe I do." His fingers went to the buttons on his shirt, but they were clammy and numb and kept slipping and sliding. Finally, he just shrugged at her and said helplessly, "I can't do it."

"Oh, dear. Here, I'll . . ." Sophie reached out to undo his buttons, jerked her hands back nervously, then finally gritted her teeth and reached out again. She made quick work of the buttons, doing her best to keep her gaze averted as each undone button revealed another two inches of his skin. "Almost done," she muttered. "Just a moment now."

He didn't say anything in reply, so she looked up. His eyes were closed, and his entire body was swaying slightly. If he weren't standing up, she'd have sworn that he was asleep.

"Mr. Bridgerton?" she asked softly. "Mr. Bridgerton!"

Benedict's head jerked up violently. "What? What?"

"You fell asleep."

He blinked confusedly. "Is there a reason that's bad?"

"You can't fall asleep in your clothing."

He looked down. "How'd my shirt get undone?"

Sophie ignored the question, instead nudging him until his behind was leaning against the mattress. "Sit," she ordered.

She must have sounded suitably bossy, because he did.

"Have you something dry we can change you into?" she asked.

He shrugged the shirt off, letting it land on the floor in a messy heap. "Never sleep with clothes."

Sophie felt her stomach lurch. "Well, tonight I think you should, and—*What* are you doing?"

He looked over at her as if she'd asked the most inane question in the world. "Taking my breeches off."

"Couldn't you at least wait until I'd turned my back?"

He stared at her blankly.

She stared back.

He stared some more. Finally, he said, "Well?"

"Well what?"

"Aren't you going to turn your back?"

"Oh!" she yelped, spinning around as if someone had lit a fire under her feet.

Benedict shook his head wearily as he sat on the edge of the bed and pulled off his stockings. God save him from prudish misses. She was a housemaid, for God's sake. Even if she was a virgin—and given her behavior, he rather suspected she was—she'd surely seen a male form before. Housemaids were always slipping in and out of rooms without knocking, carrying towels and sheets and what have you. It was inconceivable she'd never accidentally barged in on a naked man.

He stripped off his breeches—not an easy task considering they were still more than a little damp and he had quite literally to peel them from his skin. When he was well and truly naked, he quirked a brow in the direction of Sophie's back. She was standing rigidly, her hands fisted tightly at her sides.

With surprise, he realized the sight of her made him smile.

He was starting to feel a bit sluggish, and it took him two tries before he was able to lift his leg high enough to climb into bed. With considerable effort he leaned forward and grabbed the edge of his coverlet, dragging it over his body. Then, completely worn-out, he sagged back against the pillows and groaned.

"Are you all right?" Sophie called.

He made an effort to say, "Fine," but it came out more like, "Fmmph."

He heard her moving about, and when he summoned up the energy to lift one eyelid halfway open, he saw that she'd moved to the side of the bed. She looked concerned.

For some reason that seemed rather sweet. It had been quite a long time since any woman who wasn't related to him had been concerned for his welfare.

"I'm fine," he mumbled, trying to give her a reassuring smile. But his voice sounded like it was coming through a long, narrow tunnel. He reached up and tugged at his ear. His mouth felt like he was talking properly; the problem must be with his ears.

"Mr. Bridgerton? Mr. Bridgerton?"

He pried an eyelid open again. "Go da bed," he grunted. "Get dry."

"Are you certain?"

He nodded. It was getting too difficult to speak.

"Very well. But I'm going to leave your door open. If you need me in the night, just call out."

He nodded again. Or at least he tried to. Then he slept.

It took Sophie barely a quarter of an hour to get ready for bed. A surfeit of nervous energy kept her going as she changed into dry clothing and readied the furnace in her room, but once her head hit her pillow, she felt herself succumbing to an exhaustion so total it seemed to come from her very bones.

It had been a long day, she thought groggily. A really long day, between attending to her morning chores, dashing around the house to escape Cavender and his friends . . . Her eyelids drifted shut. It had been an extraordinarily long day, and . . .

Sophie sat up suddenly, her heart pounding. The fire in the furnace had burned low, so she must have fallen asleep. She'd been dead tired, though, so something must have woken her. Was it Mr. Bridgerton? Had he called out? He'd not looked well when she'd left him, but neither had he seemed at death's door.

Sophie hopped out of bed, grabbed a candle, then dashed toward the door of her room, grabbing hold of the waistband of the too-big breeches Benedict had lent her when they started to slip down her hips. When she reached the hall she heard the sound that must have woken her up.

It was a deep groan, followed by a thrashing noise, followed by what could only be called a whimper.

Sophie dashed into Benedict's room, stopping briefly at the furnace to light her candle. He was lying in his bed, almost preternaturally still. Sophie edged toward him, her eyes focusing on his chest. She knew he couldn't possibly be dead, but she'd feel an awful lot better once she saw his chest rise and fall.

"Mr. Bridgerton?" she whispered. "Mr. Bridgerton?"

No response.

She crept closer, leaning over the edge of the bed. "Mr. Bridgerton?"

His hand shot out and grabbed her shoulder, pulling her off-balance until she fell onto the bed.

"Mr. Bridgerton!" Sophie squealed. "Let go!"

But he'd started to thrash and moan, and there was enough heat coming off his body that Sophie knew he was in the grips of a fever.

She somehow managed to wrench herself free, and she went tumbling off the bed while he continued to toss and turn, mumbling streams of words that made no sense.

Sophie waited for a quiet moment, then darted her hand out to touch his forehead. It was on fire.

She chewed on her lower lip as she tried to decide what to do. She had no experience nursing the feverish, but it seemed to her that the logical thing would be to cool him off. On the other hand, sickrooms always seemed to be kept closed, stuffy, and warm, so maybe . . .

Benedict started to thrash again, and then, out of nowhere, he murmured, "Kiss me."

Sophie lost hold of her breeches; they fell to the floor. She let out a little yelp of surprise as she quickly bent to retrieve them. Clutching the waistband securely with her right hand, she reached out to pat his hand with her left, then thought the better of it. "You're just dreaming, Mr. Bridgerton," she told him.

"Kiss me," he repeated. But he did not open his eyes.

Sophie leaned in closer. Even by the light of one solitary

candle she could see his eyeballs moving quickly under his lids. It was bizarre, she thought, to see another person dream.

"God damn it!" he suddenly yelled. "Kiss me!"

Sophie lurched back in surprise, setting her candle hastily on the bedside table. "Mr. Bridgerton, I—" she began, fully intending to explain why she could not even begin to think about kissing him, but then she thought—*Why not?*

Her heart fluttering wildly, she leaned down and brushed the barest, lightest, most gentle of kisses on his lips.

"I love you," she whispered. "I've always loved you."

To Sophie's everlasting relief, he didn't move. It wasn't the sort of moment she wanted him to remember in the morning. But then, just when she was convinced that he'd settled back into a deep sleep, his head began to toss from side to side, leaving deep indentations in his feather pillow.

"Where'd you go?" he grunted hoarsely. "Where'd you go?"

"I'm right here," Sophie replied.

He opened his eyes, and for the barest of seconds appeared completely lucid, as he said, "Not *you*." Then his eyes rolled back and his head started tossing from side to side again.

"Well, I'm all you've got," Sophie muttered. "Don't go anywhere," she said with a nervous laugh. "I'll be right back."

And then, her heart pounding with fear and nerves, she ran out of the room.

If there was one thing Sophie had learned in her days as a housemaid, it was that most households were run in essentially the same way. It was for that reason that she had no trouble at all finding spare linens to replace Benedict's sweat-soaked sheets. She also scavenged a pitcher full of cool water and a few small towels for dampening his brow.

Upon her return to his bedroom, she found him lying still again, but his breathing was shallow and rapid. Sophie reached out and touched his brow again. She couldn't be certain, but it seemed to her that it was growing warmer.

Oh, dear. This was not good, and she was singularly unqualified to care for a feverish patient. Araminta, Rosamund, and Posy had never had a sick day in their lives, and the Cavenders had all been uncommonly healthy as well. The closest she'd ever come to nursing had been helping Mrs. Cavender's mother, who'd been unable to walk. But she'd never taken care of someone with a fever.

She dunked a cloth in the pitcher of water, then wrung it out until it was no longer dripping from the corners. "This ought to make you feel a little better," she whispered, placing it gingerly on his brow. Then she added, in a rather unconfident voice, "At least I hope it will."

He didn't flinch when she touched him with the cloth. Sophie took that as an excellent sign, and she prepared another cool towel. She had no idea where to put it, though. His chest somehow didn't seem right, and she certainly wasn't going to allow the bedsheet to drift any lower than his waist unless the poor man was at death's door (and even then, she wasn't certain what she could possibly do down there that would resurrect him.) So she finally just dabbed with it behind his ears, and a little on the sides of his neck.

"Does that feel better?" she asked, not expecting any sort of an answer but feeling nonetheless that she ought to continue with her one-sided conversation. "I really don't know very much about caring for the ill, but it just *seems* to me like you'd want something cool on your brow. I know if *I* were sick, that's how I'd feel."

He shifted restlessly, mumbling something utterly incoherent.

"Really?" Sophie replied, trying to smile but failing miserably. "I'm glad you feel that way."

He mumbled something else.

"No," she said, dabbing the cool cloth on his ear, "I'd have to agree with what you said the first time."

He went still again.

"I'd be happy to reconsider," she said worriedly. "Please don't take offense."

He didn't move.

Sophie sighed. One could only converse so long with an unconscious man before one started to feel extremely silly. She lifted up the cloth she'd placed on his forehead and touched his skin. It felt kind of clammy now. Clammy and still warm, which was a combination she wouldn't have thought possible.

She decided to leave the cloth off for now, and she laid it over the top of the pitcher. There seemed little she could do for him at that very moment, so Sophie stretched her legs and walked slowly around his room, shamelessly examining everything that wasn't nailed down, and quite a bit that was.

The collection of miniatures was her first stop. There were nine on the writing desk; Sophie surmised that they were of Benedict's parents and seven brothers and sisters. She started to put the siblings in order according to their ages, but then it occurred to her that the miniatures most likely hadn't been painted all at the same time, so she could be looking at a likeness of his older brother at fifteen and younger brother at twenty.

She was struck by how alike they all were, with the same deep chestnut hair, wide mouths, and elegant bone structure. She looked closely to try to compare eye color but found it impossible in the dim candlelight, and besides, eye color often wasn't easily discerned on a miniature, anyway.

Next to the miniatures was the bowl with Benedict's rock collection. Sophie picked a few of them up in turn, rolling them lightly over her palm. "Why are these so special to you, I wonder?" she whispered, placing them carefully back in the bowl. They just looked like rocks to her, but she supposed that they might appear more interesting and unique to Benedict if they represented special memories for him.

She found a small wooden box that she absolutely could not open; it must have been one of those trick boxes she'd heard about that came from the Orient. And most intriguing, leaning against the side of the desk was a large sketchbook, filled with pencil drawings, mostly of landscapes but with a few portraits as well. Had Benedict drawn them? Sophie squinted at the bottom of each drawing. The small squiggles certainly looked like two Bs.

Sophie sucked in her breath, an unbidden smile lighting her face. She'd never dreamed that Benedict was an artist. There had never even been a peep about it in *Whistledown*, and it seemed like the sort of thing the gossip columnist would have figured out over the years.

Sophie drew the sketchbook closer to her candle and flipped through the pages. She wanted to sit with the book and spend ten minutes perusing each sketch, but it seemed too intrusive to examine his drawings in such detail. She was probably just trying to justify her nosiness, but somehow it didn't seem as bad just to give them a glance.

The landscapes were varied. Some were of My Cottage (or should she call it His Cottage?) and some were of a larger house, which Sophie supposed was the country home of the Bridgerton family. Most of the landscapes featured no architecture at all, just a babbling brook, or a windswept tree, or a rain-dappled meadow. And the amazing thing about his drawings was that they seemed to capture the whole and true moment. Sophie could swear that she could hear that brook babbling or the wind ruffling the leaves on that tree.

The portraits were fewer in number, but Sophie found them infinitely more interesting. There were several of what had to be his littlest sister, and a few of what she thought must be his mother. One of Sophie's favorites was of what appeared to be some kind of outdoor game. At least five

Bridgerton siblings were holding long mallets, and one of the girls was depicted at the forefront, her face screwed up in determination as she tried to aim a ball through a wicket.

Something about the picture almost made Sophie laugh out loud. She could feel the merriment of the day, and it made her long desperately for a family of her own.

She glanced back at Benedict, still sleeping quietly in his bed. Did he realize how lucky he was to have been born into such a large and loving clan?

With a sigh, Sophie flipped through a few more pages until she reached the end of the book. The very last sketch was different from the rest, if only because it appeared to be of a night scene, and the woman in it was holding her skirts above her ankles as she ran across—

Good God! Sophie gasped, thunderstruck. It was her!

She brought the sketch closer to her face. He'd gotten the details of her dress—that wonderful, magical silver concoction that had been hers for only a single evening—perfectly. He'd even remembered her long, elbow-length gloves and the exact manner in which her hair had been styled. Her face was a little less recognizable, but one would have to make allowances for that given that he'd never actually seen it in its entirety.

Well, not until now.

Benedict suddenly groaned, and when Sophie glanced over she saw that he was shifting restlessly in the bed. She closed up the sketchbook and put it back into its place before hurriedly making her way to his side.

"Mr. Bridgerton?" she whispered. She wanted desperately to call him Benedict. That was how she thought of him; that was what she'd called him in her dreams these long two years. But that would be inexcusably familiar and certainly not in keeping with her position as a servant.

"Mr. Bridgerton?" she whispered again. "Are you all right?"

His eyelids fluttered open.

"Do you need anything?"

He blinked several times, and Sophie couldn't be sure whether he'd heard her or not. He looked so unfocused, she couldn't even be sure whether he'd truly seen her.

"Mr. Bridgerton?"

He squinted. "Sophie," he said hoarsely, his throat sounding terribly dry and scratchy. "The housemaid."

She nodded. "I'm here. What do you need?"

"Water," he rasped.

"Right away." Sophie had been dunking the cloths into the water in the pitcher, but she decided that now was no time to be fussy, so she grabbed hold of the glass she'd brought up from the kitchen and filled it. "Here you are," she said, handing it to him.

His fingers were shaky, so she did not let go of the glass as he brought it to his lips. He took a couple of sips, then sagged back against his pillows.

"Thank you," he whispered.

Sophie reached out and touched his brow. It was still quite warm, but he seemed lucid once again, and she decided to take that as a sign that the fever had broken. "I think you'll be better in the morning."

He laughed. Not hard, and not with anything approaching vigor, but he actually laughed. "Not likely," he croaked.

"Well, not recovered," she allowed, "but I think you'll feel better than you do right now."

"It would certainly be hard to feel worse."

Sophie smiled at him. "Do you think you can scoot to one side of your bed so I can change your sheets?"

He nodded and did as she asked, closing his weary eyes as she changed the bed around him. "That's a neat trick," he said when she was done.

"Mrs. Cavender's mother often came to visit," Sophie explained. "She was bedridden, so I had to learn how to change the sheets without her leaving the bed. It's not terribly difficult."

He nodded. “I’m going back to sleep now.”

Sophie gave his shoulder a reassuring pat. She just couldn’t help herself. “You’ll feel better in the morning,” she whispered. “I promise.”

Chapter 9

It has oft been said that physicians make the worst patients, but it is the opinion of This Author that any man makes a terrible patient. One might say it takes patience to be a patient, and heaven knows, the males of our species lack an abundance of patience.

LADY WHISTLEDOWN'S SOCIETY PAPERS, 2 MAY 1817

The first thing Sophie did the following morning was scream.

She'd fallen asleep in the straight-backed chair next to Benedict's bed, her limbs sprawled most inelegantly and her head cocked to the side in a rather uncomfortable position. Her sleep had been light at first, her ears perked to listen for any sign of distress from the sickbed. But after an hour or so of complete, blessed silence, exhaustion claimed her, and she fell into a deeper slumber, the kind from which one ought to awaken in peace, with a restful, easy smile on one's face.

Which may have been why, when she opened her eyes and saw two strange people staring at her, she had such a fright that it took a full five minutes for her heart to stop racing.

"Who are you?" The words tumbled out of Sophie's

mouth before she realized exactly who they must be: Mr. and Mrs. Crabtree, the caretakers of My Cottage.

"Who are *you*?" the man demanded, not a little bit belligerently.

"Sophie Beckett," she said with a gulp. "I . . ." She pointed desperately at Benedict. "He . . ."

"Spit it out, girl!"

"Don't torture her," came a croak from the bed.

Three heads swiveled in Benedict's direction. "You're awake!" Sophie exclaimed.

"Wish to God I weren't," he muttered. "My throat feels like it's on fire."

"Would you like me to fetch you some more water?" Sophie asked solicitously.

He shook his head. "Tea. Please."

She shot to her feet. "I'll go get it."

"*I'll* get it," Mrs. Crabtree said firmly.

"Would you like help?" Sophie asked timidly. Something about this pair made her feel like she were ten years old. They were both short and squat, but they positively exuded authority.

Mrs. Crabtree shook her head. "A fine housekeeper I am if I can't prepare a pot of tea."

Sophie gulped. She couldn't tell whether Mrs. Crabtree was miffed or joking. "I never meant to imply—"

Mrs. Crabtree waved off her apology. "Shall I bring you a cup?"

"You shouldn't fetch anything for me," Sophie said. "I'm a ser—"

"Bring her a cup," Benedict ordered.

"But—"

He jabbed his finger at her, grunting, "Be quiet," before turning to Mrs. Crabtree and bestowing upon her a smile that could have melted an ice cap. "Would you be so kind as to include a cup for Miss Beckett on the tray?"

"Of course, Mr. Bridgerton," she replied, "but may I say—"

"You can say anything you please once you return with the tea," he promised.

She gave him a stern look. "I have a lot to say."

"Of that I have no doubt."

Benedict, Sophie, and Mr. Crabtree waited in silence while Mrs. Crabtree left the room, and then, when she was safely out of earshot, Mr. Crabtree positively chortled, and said, "You're in for it now, Mr. Bridgerton!"

Benedict smiled weakly.

Mr. Crabtree turned to Sophie and explained, "When Mrs. Crabtree has a lot to say, she has a *lot* to say."

"Oh," Sophie replied. She would have liked to have said something slightly more articulate, but "oh" was truly the best she could come up with on such short notice.

"And when she has a lot to say," Mr. Crabtree continued, his smile growing wide and sly, "she likes to say it with great vigor."

"Fortunately," Benedict said in a dry voice, "we'll have our tea to keep us occupied."

Sophie's stomach grumbled loudly.

"And," Benedict continued, shooting her an amused glance, "a fair bit of breakfast, too, if I know Mrs. Crabtree."

Mr. Crabtree nodded. "Already prepared, Mr. Bridgerton. We saw your horses in the stables when we returned from our daughter's house this morning, and Mrs. Crabtree got to work on breakfast straightaway. She knows how you love your eggs."

Benedict turned to Sophie and gave her a conspiratorial sort of smile. "I do love eggs."

Her stomach grumbled again.

"We didn't know there'd be two of you, though," Mr. Crabtree said.

Benedict chuckled, then winced at the pain. "I can't imagine that Mrs. Crabtree didn't make enough to feed a small army."

"Well, she didn't have time to prepare a proper breakfast with beef pie and fish," Mr. Crabtree said, "but I believe she has bacon and ham and eggs and toast."

Sophie's stomach positively growled. She clapped a hand to her belly, just barely resisting the urge to hiss, "Be quiet!"

"You should have told us you were coming," Mr. Crabtree added, shaking a finger at Benedict. "We never would have gone visiting if we'd known to expect you."

"It was a spur-of-the-moment decision," Benedict said, stretching his neck from side to side. "Went to a bad party and decided to leave."

Mr. Crabtree jerked his head toward Sophie. "Where'd she come from?"

"She was at the party."

"I wasn't *at* the party," Sophie corrected. "I just happened to be there."

Mr. Crabtree squinted at her suspiciously. "What's the difference?"

"I wasn't attending the party. I was a servant at the house."

"You're a servant?"

Sophie nodded. "That's what I've been trying to tell you."

"You don't look like a servant." Mr. Crabtree turned to Benedict. "Does she look like a servant to you?"

Benedict shrugged helplessly. "I don't know *what* she looks like."

Sophie scowled at him. It might not have been an insult, but it certainly wasn't a compliment.

"If she's somebody else's servant," Mr. Crabtree persisted, "then what's she doing here?"

"May I save my explanations until Mrs. Crabtree returns?" Benedict asked. "Since I'm certain she'll repeat all of your questions?"

Mr. Crabtree looked at him for a moment, blinked, nodded, then turned back to Sophie. "Why're you dressed like that?"

Sophie looked down and realized with horror that she'd completely forgotten she was wearing men's clothes. Men's clothes so big that she could barely keep the breeches from falling to her feet. "My clothes were wet," she explained, "from the rain."

Mr. Crabtree nodded sympathetically. "Quite a storm last night. That's why we stayed over at our daughter's. We'd planned to come home, you know."

Benedict and Sophie just nodded.

"She doesn't live terribly far away," Mr. Crabtree continued. "Just on the other side of the village." He glanced over at Benedict, who nodded immediately.

"Has a new baby," he added. "A girl."

"Congratulations," Benedict said, and Sophie could see from his face that he was not merely being polite. He truly meant it.

A loud clomping sound came from the stairway; surely Mrs. Crabtree returning with breakfast. "I ought to help," Sophie said, jumping up and dashing for the door.

"Once a servant, always a servant," Mr. Crabtree said sagely.

Benedict wasn't sure, but he thought he saw Sophie wince.

A minute later, Mrs. Crabtree entered, bearing a splendid silver tea service.

"Where's Sophie?" Benedict asked.

"I sent her down to get the rest," Mrs. Crabtree replied. "She should be up in no time. Nice girl," she added in a matter-of-fact tone, "but she needs a belt for those breeches you lent her."

Benedict felt something squeeze suspiciously in his chest at the thought of Sophie-the-housemaid, with her breeches 'round her ankles. He gulped uncomfortably when he realized the tight sensation might very well be desire.

Then he groaned and grabbed at his throat, because uncomfortable gulps were even more uncomfortable after a night of harsh coughing.

"You need one of my tonics," Mrs. Crabtree said.

Benedict shook his head frantically. He'd had one of her tonics before; it had had him retching for three hours.

"I won't take no for an answer," she warned.

"She never does," Mr. Crabtree added.

"The tea will work wonders," Benedict said quickly, "I'm sure."

But Mrs. Crabtree's attention had already been diverted. "Where is that girl?" she muttered, walking back to the door and looking out. "Sophie! Sophie!"

"If you can keep her from bringing me a tonic," Benedict whispered urgently to Mr. Crabtree, "it's a fiver in your pocket."

Mr. Crabtree beamed. "Consider it done!"

"There she is," Mrs. Crabtree declared. "Oh, heaven above."

"What is it, dearie?" Mr. Crabtree asked, ambling toward the door.

"The poor thing can't carry a tray and keep her breeches up at the same time," she replied, clucking sympathetically.

"Aren't you going to help her?" Benedict asked from the bed.

"Oh yes, of course." She hurried out.

"I'll be right back," Mr. Crabtree said over his shoulder. "Don't want to miss this."

"Someone get the bloody girl a belt!" Benedict yelled grumpily. It didn't seem quite fair that everyone got to go out to the hall and watch the sideshow while he was stuck in bed.

And he definitely was stuck there. Just the thought of getting up made him dizzy.

He must have been sicker than he'd realized the night before. He no longer felt the urge to cough every few seconds, but his body felt worn-out, exhausted. His muscles ached, and his throat was damned sore. Even his teeth didn't feel quite right.

He had vague recollections of Sophie taking care of him. She'd put cool compresses on his forehead, watched over him, even sung him a lullaby. But he'd never quite seen her face. Most of the time he hadn't had the energy to open his eyes, and even when he had, the room had been dark, always leaving her in shadows, reminding him of—

Benedict sucked in his breath, his heart thumping crazily in his chest as, in a sudden flash of clarity, he remembered his dream.

He'd dreamed of *her*.

It was not a new dream, although it had been months since he'd been visited by it. It was not a fantasy for the innocent, either. Benedict was no saint, and when he dreamed of the woman from the masquerade, she was not wearing her silver dress.

She was not, he thought with a wicked smile, wearing anything.

But what perplexed him was why this dream would return now, after so many months of dormancy. Was there something about Sophie that had triggered it? He'd thought—he'd hoped—that the disappearance of the dream had meant he was over her.

Obviously not.

Sophie certainly didn't look like the woman he'd danced with two years earlier. Her hair was all wrong, and she was far too thin. He distinctly remembered the lush, curvy feel of the masked woman in his arms; in comparison, Sophie could only be called scrawny. He supposed their voices were a bit similar, but he had to admit to himself that as time passed, his memories of that night grew less vivid, and he could no longer recall his mystery woman's voice with perfect clarity. Besides, Sophie's accent, while exceptionally refined for a housemaid, was not as upper-crust as *hers* had been.

Benedict let out a frustrated snort. How he hated calling

her *her*. That seemed the cruelest of her secrets. She'd kept from him even her name. Part of him wished she'd just lied and given him a false name. At least then he'd have something to think of her by in his mind.

Something to whisper in the night, when he was staring out the window, wondering where in hell she was.

Benedict was saved from further reflection by the sounds of stumbling and bumbling in the hallway. Mr. Crabtree was the first to return, staggering under the weight of the breakfast tray.

"What happened to the rest?" Benedict asked suspiciously, eyeing the door.

"Mrs. Crabtree went off to find Sophie some proper clothing," Mr. Crabtree replied, setting the tray down on Benedict's desk. "Ham or bacon?"

"Both. I'm famished. And what the devil does she mean by 'proper clothing'?"

"A dress, Mr. Bridgerton. That's what women wear."

Benedict seriously considered lobbing a candle stump at him. "I meant," he said with what he considered saintly patience, "where is she going to *find* a dress?"

Mr. Crabtree walked over with a plate of food on a footed tray that would fit over Benedict's lap. "Mrs. Crabtree has several extras. She's always happy to share."

Benedict choked on the bite of egg he'd shoveled into his mouth. "Mrs. Crabtree and Sophie are hardly the same size."

"Neither are you," Mr. Crabtree pointed out, "and she wore your clothes just fine."

"I thought you said the breeches fell off in the hall."

"Well, we don't have to worry about that with the dress, do we? I hardly think her shoulders are going to slip through the neck hole."

Benedict decided it was safer for his sanity to mind his own business, and he turned his full attention to his breakfast. He was on his third plate when Mrs. Crabtree bustled in.

"Here we are!" she announced.

Sophie slunk in, practically drowning in Mrs. Crabtree's voluminous dress. Except, of course, at her ankles. Mrs. Crabtree was a good five inches shorter than Sophie.

Mrs. Crabtree beamed. "Doesn't she look smashing?"

"Oh, yes," Benedict replied, lips twitching.

Sophie glared at him.

"You'll have plenty of room for breakfast," he said gamely.

"It's only until I get her clothing cleaned up," Mrs. Crabtree explained. "But at least it's decent." She waddled over to Benedict. "How is your breakfast, Mr. Bridgerton?"

"Delicious," he replied. "I haven't eaten so well in months."

Mrs. Crabtree leaned forward and whispered, "I like your Sophie. May we keep her?"

Benedict choked. On what, he didn't know, but he choked nonetheless. "I beg your pardon?"

"Mr. Crabtree and I aren't as young as we used to be. We could use another set of hands around here."

"I, ah, well . . ." He cleared his throat. "I'll think about it."

"Excellent." Mrs. Crabtree crossed back to the other side of the room and grabbed Sophie's arm. "You come with me. Your stomach has been growling all morning. When was the last time you ate?"

"Er, sometime yesterday, I should think."

"When yesterday?" Mrs. Crabtree persisted.

Benedict hid a smile under his napkin. Sophie looked utterly overwhelmed. Mrs. Crabtree tended to do that to a person.

"Er, well, actually—"

Mrs. Crabtree planted her hands on her hips. Benedict grinned. Sophie was in for it now.

"Are you going to tell me that you didn't eat yesterday?" Mrs. Crabtree boomed.

Sophie shot a desperate look at Benedict. He replied with

a don't-look-to-*me*-for-help shrug. Besides, he rather enjoyed watching Mrs. Crabtree fuss over her. He'd be willing to bet that the poor girl hadn't been fussed over in years.

"I was very busy yesterday," Sophie hedged.

Benedict frowned. She'd probably been busy running from Phillip Cavender and the pack of idiots he called friends.

Mrs. Crabtree shoved Sophie into the seat behind the desk. "Eat," she ordered.

Benedict watched as Sophie tucked into the food. It was obvious that she was trying to put on her best manners, but eventually hunger must have gotten the best of her, because after a minute she was practically shoveling the food into her mouth.

It was only when Benedict noticed that his jaw was clamped together like a vise that he realized he was absolutely furious. At whom, he wasn't precisely certain. But he did *not* like seeing Sophie so hungry.

They had an odd little bond, he and the housemaid. He'd saved her and she'd saved him. Oh, he doubted his fever from the night before would have killed him; if it had been truly serious, he'd still be battling it now. But she had cared for him and made him comfortable and probably hastened his road to recovery.

"Will you make certain she eats at least another plateful?" Mrs. Crabtree asked Benedict. "I'm going to make up a room for her."

"In the servants' quarters," Sophie said quickly.

"Don't be a silly. Until we hire you on, you're not a servant here."

"But—"

"Nothing more about it," Mrs. Crabtree interrupted.

"Would you like my help, dearie?" Mr. Crabtree asked.

Mrs. Crabtree nodded, and in a moment the couple was gone.

Sophie paused in her quest to consume as much food as

humanly possible to stare at the door through which they'd just disappeared. She supposed they considered her one of their own, because if she'd been anything but a servant, they'd never have left her alone with Benedict. Reputations could be ruined on far less.

"You didn't eat at all yesterday, did you?" Benedict asked quietly.

Sophie shook her head.

"Next time I see Cavender," he growled, "I'm going to beat him to a bloody pulp."

If she were a better person, she would have been horrified, but Sophie couldn't quite prevent a smile at the thought of Benedict further defending her honor. Or of seeing Phillip Cavender with his nose relocated to his forehead.

"Fill up your plate again," Benedict said. "If only for my sake. I assure you that Mrs. Crabtree counted how many eggs and strips of bacon were on the platter when she left, and she'll have my head if the numbers haven't gone down by the time she returns."

"She's a very nice lady," Sophie said, reaching for the eggs. The first plate of food had barely touched upon her hunger; she needed no further urging to eat.

"The best."

Sophie expertly balanced a slice of ham between a serving fork and spoon and moved it to her plate. "How are you feeling this morning, Mr. Bridgerton?"

"Very well, thank you. Or if not well, then at least a damn sight better than I did last night."

"I was very worried about you," she said, spearing a corner of the ham with her fork and then cutting a piece off with her knife.

"It was very kind of you to care for me."

She chewed, swallowed, then said, "It was nothing, really. Anyone would have done it."

"Perhaps," he said, "but not with such grace and good humor."

Sophie's fork froze in midair. "Thank you," she said softly. "That is a lovely compliment."

"I didn't . . . er . . ." He cleared his throat.

Sophie eyed him curiously, waiting for him to finish whatever it was he wanted to say.

"Never mind," he mumbled.

Disappointed, she put a piece of ham in her mouth.

"I didn't do anything for which I ought to apologize, did I?" he suddenly blurted out.

Sophie spat the ham out into her napkin.

"I'll take that as a yes," he muttered.

"No!" she said quickly. "Not at all. You merely startled me."

His eyes narrowed. "You wouldn't lie to me about this, would you?"

Sophie shook her head as she remembered the single, perfect kiss she'd given him. He hadn't done anything that required an apology, but that didn't mean that *she* hadn't.

"You're blushing," he accused.

"No, I'm not."

"Yes," he said, "you are."

"If I'm blushing," she replied pertly, "it's because I'm wondering why *you* would think you had any reason to apologize."

"You have a rather smart mouth for a servant," he said.

"I'm sorry," Sophie said quickly. She had to remember her place. But that was hard to do with this man, the one member of the *ton* who had treated her—if only for a few hours—as an equal.

"I meant it as a compliment," he said. "Do not stifle yourself on my account."

She said nothing.

"I find you rather . . ." He paused, obviously searching for the correct word. "Refreshing."

"Oh." She set her fork down. "Thank you."

"Have you plans for the rest of the day?" he asked.

She looked down at her huge garments and grimaced. "I thought I'd wait for my clothes to be readied, and then I suppose I'll see if any of the nearby houses are in need of housemaids."

Benedict scowled at her. "I told you I would find you a position with my mother."

"And I do appreciate that," she said quickly. "But I would prefer to stay in the country."

He shrugged the shrug of one who has never been thrown one of life's great stumbles. "You can work at Aubrey Hall, then. In Kent."

Sophie chewed on her lower lip. She couldn't exactly come out and say she didn't want to work for his mother because then she'd have to see *him*.

She couldn't think of a torture that would be more exquisitely painful.

"You shouldn't think of me as your responsibility," she finally said.

He gave her a rather superior glance. "I told you I would find you a new position."

"But—"

"What could there possibly be to discuss?"

"Nothing," she grumbled. "Nothing at all." Clearly, it was no use arguing with him just then.

"Good." He leaned back contentedly against his pillows. "I'm glad you see it my way."

Sophie stood. "I should be going."

"To do what?"

She felt rather stupid as she said, "I don't know."

He grinned. "Have fun with it, then."

Her hand tightened around the handle of the serving spoon.

"Don't do it," he warned.

"Do what?"

"Throw the spoon."

"I wouldn't dream of it," she said tightly.

He laughed aloud. "Oh, yes you would. You're dreaming of it right now. You just wouldn't *do* it."

Sophie's hand was gripping the spoon so hard it shook.

Benedict was chuckling so hard his bed shook.

Sophie stood, still holding the spoon.

Benedict smiled. "Are you planning to take that with you?"

Remember your place, Sophie was screaming at herself. *Remember your place.*

"Whatever could you be thinking," Benedict mused, "to look so adorably ferocious? No, don't tell me," he added. "I'm sure it involves my untimely and painful demise."

Slowly and carefully, Sophie turned her back to him and put the spoon down on the table. She didn't want to risk any sudden movements. One false move and she knew she'd be hurling it at his head.

Benedict raised his brows approvingly. "That was very mature of you."

Sophie turned around slowly. "Are you this charming with everyone or only me?"

"Oh, only you." He grinned. "I shall have to make sure you take me up on my offer to find you employment with my mother. You do bring out the best in me, Miss Sophie Beckett."

"This is the best?" she asked with obvious disbelief.

"I'm afraid so."

Sophie just shook her head as she walked to the door. Conversations with Benedict Bridgerton could be exhausting.

"Oh, Sophie!" he called out.

She turned around.

He smiled slyly. "I knew you wouldn't throw the spoon."

What happened next was surely not Sophie's fault. She was, she was convinced, temporarily and fleetingly possessed by a demon. Because she absolutely did not recognize the hand that shot out to the small table next to her and picked up a stump of a candle. True, the hand appeared to be connected quite firmly to her arm, but it didn't look the least bit familiar as it drew back and hurled the stump across the room.

Straight at Benedict Bridgerton's head.

Sophie didn't even wait to see if her aim had been true. But as she stalked out the door, she heard Benedict explode with laughter. Then she heard him shout out, "Well done, Miss Beckett!"

And she realized that for the first time in years, her smile was one of pure, unadulterated joy.

Chapter 10

Although he responded in the affirmative (or so says Lady Covington) Benedict Bridgerton did not make an appearance at the annual Covington Ball. Complaints were heard from young women (and their mamas) across the ballroom.

According to Lady Bridgerton (his mother, not his sister-in-law), Mr. Bridgerton left for the country last week and has not been heard from since. Those who might fear for Mr. Bridgerton's health and well-being should not fret; Lady Bridgerton sounded more annoyed than worried. Last year no less than four couples met their future spouses at the Covington Ball; the previous year, three.

Much to Lady Bridgerton's dismay, if any matches are made at this year's Covington Ball, her son Benedict will not be among the grooms.

LADY WHISTLEDOWN'S SOCIETY PAPERS, 5 MAY 1817

There were advantages, Benedict soon discovered, to a long, drawn-out recovery.

The most obvious was the quantity and variety of most excellent food brought forth from Mrs. Crabtree's kitchen. He'd always been fed well at My Cottage, but Mrs. Crabtree truly rose to the occasion when she had someone tucked away in the sickroom.

And even better, Mr. Crabtree had managed to intercept all of Mrs. Crabtree's tonics and replace them with Benedict's best brandy. Benedict dutifully drank every drop, but the last time he looked out the window, it appeared that three of his rosebushes had died, presumably where Mr. Crabtree had dumped the tonic.

It was a sad sacrifice, but one Benedict was more than willing to make after his last experience with Mrs. Crabtree's tonics.

Another perk of staying abed was the simple fact that, for the first time in years, he could enjoy some quiet time. He read, sketched, and even closed his eyes and just daydreamed—all without feeling guilty for neglecting some other task or chore.

Benedict soon decided that he'd be perfectly happy leading the life of the indolent.

But the best part of his recovery, by far, was Sophie. She popped into his room several times a day, sometimes to fluff his pillows, sometimes to bring him food, sometimes just to read to him. Benedict had a feeling that her industriousness was due to her desire to feel useful, and to thank him with deeds for saving her from Phillip Cavender.

But he didn't much care why she came to visit; he just liked it that she did.

She'd been quiet and reserved at first, obviously trying to adhere to the standard that servants should be neither seen nor heard. But Benedict had had none of that, and he'd purposefully engaged her in conversation, just so she couldn't leave. Or he'd goad and needle her, simply to get a rise out of her, because he liked her far better when she was spitting fire than when she was meek and submissive.

But mostly he just enjoyed being in the same room with her. It didn't seem to matter if they were talking or if she was just sitting in a chair, leafing through a book while he stared out the window. Something about her presence brought him peace.

A sharp knock at the door broke him out of his thoughts, and he looked up eagerly, calling out, "Enter!"

Sophie poked her head in, her shoulder-length curls shaking slightly as they brushed against the edge of the door. "Mrs. Crabtree thought you might like tea."

"Tea? Or tea and biscuits?"

Sophie grinned, pushing the door open with her hip as she balanced the tray. "Oh, the latter, to be sure."

"Excellent. And will you join me?"

She hesitated, as she always did, but then she nodded, as she also always did. She'd long since learned that there was no arguing with Benedict when he had his mind set on something.

Benedict rather liked it that way.

"The color is back in your cheeks," she commented as she set the tray down on a nearby table. "And you don't look nearly so tired. I should think you'll be up and out of bed soon,"

"Oh, soon, I'm sure," he said evasively.

"You're looking healthier every day."

He smiled gamely. "Do you think so?"

She lifted the teapot and paused before she poured. "Yes," she said with an ironic smile. "I wouldn't have said so otherwise."

Benedict watched her hands as she prepared his tea. She moved with an innate sense of grace, and she poured the tea as if she'd been to the manner born. Clearly the art of afternoon tea had been another one of those lessons she'd learned from her mother's generous employers. Or maybe she'd just watched other ladies closely while they'd prepared tea. Benedict had noticed that she was a very observant woman.

They'd enacted this ritual often enough that she didn't have to ask how he liked his tea. She handed him his cup—

milk, no sugar—and then placed a selection of biscuits and scones on a plate.

"Fix yourself a cup," Benedict said, biting into a biscuit, "and come sit by me."

She hesitated again. He knew she'd hesitate, even though she'd already agreed to join him. But he was a patient man, and his patience was rewarded with a soft sigh as she reached out and plucked another cup off the tray.

After she'd fixed her own cup—two lumps of sugar, just the barest splash of milk—she sat in the velvet-covered, straight-backed chair by his bed, regarding him over the rim of her teacup as she took a sip.

"No biscuits for you?" Benedict asked.

She shook her head. "I had a few straight out of the oven."

"Lucky you. They're always best when they're warm." He polished off another biscuit, brushed a few crumbs off of his sleeve, and reached for another. "And how have you spent your day?"

"Since I last saw you two hours earlier?"

Benedict shot her a look that said he recognized her sarcasm but chose not to respond to it.

"I helped Mrs. Crabtree in the kitchen," Sophie said. "She's making a beef stew for supper and needed some potatoes peeled. Then I borrowed a book from your library and read in the garden."

"Really? What did you read?"

"A novel."

"Was it good?"

She shrugged. "Silly, but romantic. I enjoyed it."

"And do you long for romance?"

Her blush was instantaneous. "That's a rather personal question, don't you think?"

Benedict shrugged and started to say something utterly flip, like, "It was worth a try," but as he watched her face, her cheeks turning delightfully pink, her eyes cast down to her lap, the strangest thing happened.

He realized he wanted her.

He really, really wanted her.

He wasn't certain why this so surprised him. Of course he *wanted* her. He was as red-blooded as any man, and one couldn't spend a protracted amount of time around a woman as gamine and adorable as Sophie without wanting her. Hell, he wanted half the women he met, in a purely low-intensity, non-urgent sort of way.

But in that moment, with this woman, it became urgent.

Benedict changed positions. Then he bunched the coverlet up over his lap. Then he changed positions again.

"Is your bed uncomfortable?" Sophie asked. "Do you need me to fluff your pillows?"

Benedict's first urge was to reply in the affirmative, grab her as she leaned across him, and then have his wicked way with her, since they would, rather conveniently, be in bed.

But he had a sneaking suspicion that that particular plan would not go over well with Sophie, so instead he said, "I'm fine," then winced when he realized his voice sounded oddly squeaky.

She smiled as she eyed the biscuits on his plate, saying, "Maybe just one more."

Benedict moved his arm out of the way to allow her easy access to his plate, which was, he realized somewhat belatedly, resting on his lap. The sight of her hand reaching toward his groin—even if she was aiming for a plate of biscuits—did funny things to him, to his groin, to be precise.

Benedict had a sudden vision of things . . . *shifting* down there, and he hastily grabbed the plate, lest it become unbalanced.

"Do you mind if I take the last—"

"Fine!" he croaked.

She plucked a ginger biscuit off the plate and frowned. "You look better," she said, giving the biscuit a little sniff, "but you don't sound better. Is your throat bothering you?"

Benedict took a quick sip of his tea. "Not at all. I must've swallowed a piece of dust."

"Oh. Drink some more tea, then. That shouldn't bother you for long." She set her teacup down. "Would you like me to read to you?"

"Yes!" Benedict said quickly, bunching up his coverlet around his waist. She might try to take away the strategically placed plate, and then where would he be?

"Are you certain you're all right?" she asked, looking far more suspicious than concerned.

He smiled tightly. "Just fine."

"Very well," she said, standing up. "What would you like me to read?"

"Oh, anything," he said with a blithe wave of his hand.

"Poetry?"

"Splendid." He would have said, "Splendid," had she offered to read a dissertation on botany in the arctic tundra.

Sophie wandered over to a recessed bookshelf and idly perused its contents. "Byron?" she asked. "Blake?"

"Blake," he said quite firmly. A hour's worth of Byron's romantic drivel would probably send him quite over the edge.

She slid a slim volume of poetry off the shelf and returned to her chair, swishing her rather unattractive skirts before she sat down.

Benedict frowned. He'd never really noticed before how ugly her dress was. Not as bad as the one Mrs. Crabtree had lent her, but certainly not anything designed to bring out the best in a woman.

He ought to buy her a new dress. She would never accept it, of course, but maybe if her current garments were accidentally *burned* . . .

"Mr. Bridgerton?"

But how could he manage to burn her dress? She'd have to not be wearing it, and that posed a certain challenge in and of itself . . .

"Are you even listening to me?" Sophie demanded.

"Hmmm?"

"You're *not* listening to me."

"Sorry," he admitted. "My apologies. My mind got away from me. Please continue."

She began anew, and in his attempt to show how much attention he was paying her, he focused his eyes on her lips, which proved to be a *big* mistake.

Because suddenly those lips were all he could see, and he couldn't stop thinking about kissing her, and he knew—absolutely knew—that if one of them didn't leave the room in the next thirty seconds, he was going to do something for which he'd owe her a thousand apologies.

Not that he didn't plan to seduce her. Just that he'd rather do it with a bit more finesse.

"Oh, dear," he blurted out.

Sophie gave him an odd look. He didn't blame her. He sounded like a complete idiot. He didn't think he'd uttered the phrase, "Oh, dear," in years. If ever.

Hell, he sounded like his mother.

"Is something wrong?" Sophie asked.

"I just remembered something," he said, rather stupidly, in his opinion.

She raised her brows in question.

"Something that I'd forgotten," Benedict said.

"The things one remembers," she said, looking exceedingly amused, "are most often things one had forgotten."

He scowled at her. "I'll need a bit of privacy."

She stood instantly. "Of course," she murmured.

Benedict fought off a groan. Damn. She looked hurt. He hadn't meant to injure her feelings. He just needed to get her out of the room so that he didn't yank her into the bed. "It's a personal matter," he told her, trying to make her feel better but suspecting that all he was doing was making himself look like a fool.

"Ohhhhh," she said knowingly. "Would you like me to bring you the chamber pot?"

"I can walk to the chamber pot," he retorted, forgetting that he didn't need to use the chamber pot.

She nodded and stood, setting the book of poetry onto a nearby table. "I'll leave you to your business. Just ring the bellpull when you need me."

"I'm not going to summon you like a servant," he growled.

"But I *am* a—"

"Not for me you're not," he said. The words emerged a little more harshly than was necessary, but he'd always detested men who preyed on helpless female servants. The thought that he might be turning into one of those repellent creatures was enough to make him gag.

"Very well," she said, her words meek like a servant. Then she nodded like a servant—he was fairly certain she did it just to annoy him—and left.

The minute she was gone, Benedict leapt out of the bed and ran to the window. Good. No one was in sight. He shrugged off his dressing gown, replaced it with a pair of breeches and a shirt and jacket, and looked out the window again. Good. Still no one.

"Boots, boots," he muttered, glancing around the room. Where the hell were his boots? Not his good boots—the pair for mucking around in the mud . . . ah, there they were. He grabbed the boots and yanked them on.

Back to the window. Still no one. Excellent. Benedict threw one leg over the sill, then another, then grabbed hold of the long, sturdy branch that jutted out from a nearby elm tree. From there it was an easy shimmy, wiggle, and balancing act down to the ground.

And from there it was straight to the lake. To the very cold lake.

To take a very cold swim.

* * *

"If he needed the chamber pot," Sophie muttered to herself, "he could have just said so. It's not as if I haven't fetched chamber pots before."

She stamped down the stairs to the main floor, not entirely certain why she was going downstairs (she had nothing specific to do there) but heading in that direction simply because she couldn't think of anything better to do.

She didn't understand why he had so much trouble treating her like what she was—a servant. He kept insisting that she didn't work for him and didn't have to do anything to earn her keep at My Cottage, and then in the same breath assured her that he would find her a position in his mother's household.

If he would just treat her like a servant, she'd have no trouble remembering that she was an illegitimate nobody and he was a member of one of the *ton*'s wealthiest and most influential families. Every time he treated her like a real person (and it was her experience that most aristocrats did not treat servants like anything remotely approaching a real person) it brought her back to the night of the masquerade, when she'd been, for one perfect evening, a lady of glamour and grace—the sort of woman who had a right to dream about a future with Benedict Bridgerton.

He acted as if he actually liked her and enjoyed her company. And maybe he did. But that was the cruelest twist of all, because he was making her love him, making a small part of her think she had the right to dream about him.

And then, inevitably, she had to remind herself of the truth of the situation, and it hurt so damned much.

"Oh, there you are, Miss Sophie!"

Sophie lifted up her eyes, which had been absently following the cracks in the parquet floor, to see Mrs. Crabtree descending the stairs behind her.

"Good day, Mrs. Crabtree," Sophie said. "How is that beef stew coming along?"

"Fine, fine," Mrs. Crabtree said absently. "We were a bit short on carrots, but I think it will be tasty nonetheless. Have you seen Mr. Bridgerton?"

Sophie blinked in surprise at the question. "In his room. Just a minute ago."

"Well, he's not there now."

"I think he had to use the chamber pot."

Mrs. Crabtree didn't even blush; it was the sort of conversation servants often had about their employers. "Well, if he did use it, he didn't *use* it, if you know what I mean," she said. "The room smelled as fresh as a spring day."

Sophie frowned. "And he wasn't there?"

"Neither hide nor hair."

"I can't imagine where he might have gone."

Mrs. Crabtree planted her hands on her ample hips. "I'll search the downstairs and you search the up. One of us is bound to find him."

"I'm not sure that's such a good idea, Mrs. Crabtree. If he's left his room, he probably had a good reason. Most likely, he doesn't want to be found."

"But he's ill," Mrs. Crabtree protested.

Sophie considered that, then pictured his face in her mind. His skin had held a healthy glow and he hadn't looked the least bit tired. "I'm not so certain about that, Mrs. Crabtree," she finally said. "I think he's malingering on purpose."

"Don't be silly," Mrs. Crabtree scoffed. "Mr. Bridgerton would never do something like that."

Sophie shrugged. "I wouldn't have thought so, but truly, he doesn't look the least bit ill any longer."

"It's my tonics," Mrs. Crabtree said with a confident nod. "I told you they'd speed up his recovery."

Sophie had seen Mr. Crabtree dump the tonics in the rosebushes; she'd also seen the aftermath. It hadn't been a pretty sight. How she managed to smile and nod, she'd never know.

"Well, I for one would like to know where he went," Mrs.

Crabtree continued. "He shouldn't be out of bed, and he knows it."

"I'm sure he'll return soon," Sophie said placatingly. "In the meantime, do you need any help in the kitchen?"

Mrs. Crabtree shook her head. "No, no. All that stew needs to do now is cook. And besides, Mr. Bridgerton has been scolding me for allowing you to work."

"But—"

"No arguments, if you please," Mrs. Crabtree cut in. "He's right, of course. You're a guest here, and you shouldn't have to lift a finger."

"I'm not a guest," Sophie protested.

"Well, then, what are you?"

That gave Sophie pause. "I have no idea," she finally said, "but I'm definitely not a guest. A guest would be . . . A guest would be . . ." She struggled to make sense of her thoughts and feelings. "I suppose a guest would be someone who is of the same social rank, or at least close to it. A guest would be someone who has never had to wait upon another person, or scrub floors, or empty chamber pots. A guest would be—"

"Anyone the master of the house chooses to invite as a guest," Mrs. Crabtree retorted. "That's the beauty of being the master of the house. You can do anything you please. And you should stop belittling yourself. If Mr. Bridgerton chooses to regard you as a houseguest, then you should accept his judgment and enjoy yourself. When was the last time you were able to live in comfort without having to work your fingers to the bone in return?"

"He can't truly regard me as a houseguest," Sophie said quietly. "If he did, he would have installed a chaperone for the protection of my reputation."

"As if *I* would allow anything untoward in my house," Mrs. Crabtree bristled.

"Of course you wouldn't," Sophie assured her. "But where reputations are at stake, appearance is just as important as fact. And in the eyes of society, a housekeeper does not qualify as a chaperone, no matter how strict and pure her morals may be."

"If that's true," Mrs. Crabtree protested, "then you need a chaperone, Miss Sophie."

"Don't be silly. I don't need a chaperone because I'm not of his class. No one cares if a housemaid lives and works in the household of a single man. No one thinks any less of her, and certainly no one who would consider her for marriage would consider her ruined." Sophie shrugged. "It's the way of the world. And obviously it's the way Mr. Bridgerton thinks, whether he'll admit it or not, because he has never once said a word about it being improper for me to be here."

"Well, I don't like it," Mrs. Crabtree announced. "I don't like it one bit."

Sophie just smiled, because it was so sweet of the housekeeper to care. "I think I'm going to take myself off for a walk," she said, "as long as you're certain you don't need any help in the kitchen. And," she added with a sly grin, "as long as I'm in this strange, hazy position. I might not be a guest, but it is the first time in years I'm not a servant, and I'm going to enjoy my free time while it lasts."

Mrs. Crabtree gave her a hearty pat on the shoulder. "You do that, Miss Sophie. And pick a flower for me while you're out there."

Sophie grinned and headed out the front door. It was a lovely day, unseasonably warm and sunny, and the air held the gentle fragrance of the first blooms of spring. She couldn't recall the last time she'd taken a walk for the simple pleasure of enjoying the fresh air.

Benedict had told her about a nearby pond, and she thought she might amble that way, maybe even dip her toes in the water if she was feeling particularly daring.

She smiled up at the sun. The air might be warm, but the water was surely still freezing, so early in May. Still, it would feel good. Anything felt good that represented leisure time and peaceful, solitary moments.

She paused for a moment, frowning thoughtfully at the horizon. Benedict had mentioned that the lake was south of My Cottage, hadn't he? A southward route would take her right through a rather densely wooded patch, but a bit of a hike certainly wouldn't kill her.

Sophie picked her way through the forest, stepping over tree roots, and pushing aside low-lying branches, letting them snap back behind her with reckless abandon. The sun barely squeaked through the canopy of leaves above her, and down at ground level, it felt more like dusk than midday.

Up ahead, she could see a clearing, which she assumed must be the pond. As she drew closer, she saw the glint of sunlight on water, and she breathed a little sigh of satisfaction, happy to know that she'd gone in the correct direction.

But as she drew even closer, she heard the sound of someone splashing about, and she realized with equal parts terror and curiosity that she was not alone.

She was only ten or so feet from the edge of the pond, easily visible to anyone in the water, so she quickly flattened herself behind the trunk of a large oak. If she had a sensible bone in her body, she'd turn right around and run back to the house, but she just couldn't quite keep herself from peeking around the tree and looking to see who might be mad enough to splash about in a lake so early in the season.

With slow, silent movements, she crept out from behind the tree, trying to keep as much of herself concealed as possible.

And she saw a man.

A *naked* man.

A naked . . .

Benedict?

Chapter 11

The housemaid wars rage on in London. Lady Penwood called Mrs. Featherington a conniving, ill-bred thief in front of no less than three society matrons, including the very popular dowager Viscountess Bridgerton!

Mrs. Featherington responded by calling Lady Penwood's home no better than a workhouse, citing the ill treatment of her lady's maid (whose name, This Author has learned, is not Estelle as was originally claimed, and furthermore, she is not remotely French. The girl's name is Bess, and she hails from Liverpool.)

Lady Penwood stalked away from the altercation in quite a huff, followed by her daughter, Miss Rosamund Reiling. Lady Penwood's other daughter, Posy (who was wearing an unfortunate green gown) remained behind with a somewhat apologetic look in her eyes until her mother returned, grabbed her by the sleeve, and dragged her off.

This Author certainly does not make up the guest lists at society parties, but it is difficult to imagine that the Penwoods will be invited to Mrs. Featherington's next soirée.

LADY WHISTLEDOWN'S SOCIETY PAPERS, 7 MAY 1817

It was wrong of her to stay.

So wrong.

So very, very wrong.

And yet she did not move an inch.

She found a large, bald-pated rock, mostly obscured by a short, squat bush, and sat down, never once taking her eyes off of him.

He was *naked*. She still couldn't quite believe it.

He was, of course, partially submerged, with the edge of the water rippling against his rib cage.

The *lower*—she thought giddily—edge of his rib cage.

Or perhaps if she were to be honest with herself, she'd have to rephrase her previous thought to: He was, *unfortunately*, partially submerged.

Sophie was as innocent as the next . . . as, well, the next innocent, but dash it all, she was curious, and she was more than halfway in love with this man. Was it so very wicked to wish for a huge gust of wind, powerful enough to create a small tidal wave that would whip the water away from his body and deposit it somewhere else? Anywhere else?

Very well, it was wicked. *She* was wicked, and she didn't care.

She'd spent her life taking the safe road, the prudent path. Only one night in her short life had she completely thrown caution to the wind. And that night had been the most thrilling, the most magical, the most stupendously wonderful night of her life.

And so she decided to remain right where she was, stay the course, and see what she saw. It wasn't as if she had anything to lose. She had no job, no prospects save for Benedict's promise to find her a position in his mother's household (and she had a feeling that would be a very bad idea, anyway.)

And so she sat back, tried not to move a muscle, and kept her eyes wide, wide open.

* * *

Benedict had never been a superstitious man, and he'd certainly never thought himself the sort with a sixth sense, but once or twice in his life, he'd experienced a strange surge of awareness, a sort of mystical tingling feeling that warned him that something important was afoot.

The first time had been the day his father had died. He'd never told anyone about this, not even his older brother Anthony, who'd been utterly devastated by their father's death, but that afternoon, as he and Anthony had raced across the fields of Kent in some silly horse race, he'd felt an odd, numb feeling in his arms and legs, followed by the strangest pounding in his head. It hadn't hurt, precisely, but it had sucked the air from his lungs and left him with the most intense sensation of terror he could ever imagine.

He'd lost the race, of course; it was difficult to grip reins when one's fingers refused to work properly. And when he'd returned home, he'd discovered that his terror had not been unwarranted. His father was already dead, having collapsed after being stung by a bee. Benedict still had difficulty believing that a man as strong and vital as his father could be felled by a bee, but there had been no other explanation.

The second time it had happened, however, the feeling had been completely different. It had been the night of his mother's masquerade, right before he'd seen the woman in the silver dress. Like the time before, the sensation had started in his arms and legs, but instead of feeling numb, this time he felt an odd tingling, as if he'd just suddenly come alive after years of sleepwalking.

Then he'd turned and seen her, and he'd known she was the reason he was there that night; the reason he lived in England; hell, the very reason he'd been born.

Of course, she had gone and proven him wrong by disappearing into thin air, but at the time he'd believed all that, and if she'd let him, he would have proven it to her as well.

Now, as he stood in the pond, the water lapping at his

midriff, just above his navel, he was struck once again by that odd sense of somehow being more alive than he'd been just seconds earlier. It was a good feeling, an exciting, breathless rush of emotion.

It was like before. When he'd met *her*.

Something was about to happen, or maybe someone was near.

His life was about to change.

And he was, he realized with wry twist of his lips, naked as the day he was born. It didn't exactly put a man at an advantage, at least not unless he was in between a pair of silk sheets with an attractive young woman at his side.

Or underneath.

He took a step into slightly deeper waters, the soft sludge of the pondbottom squishing between his toes. Now the water reached a couple of inches higher. He was bloody well freezing, but at least he was mostly covered up.

He scanned the shore, looking up into trees and down in the bushes. There had to be someone there. Nothing else could account for the strange, tingling feeling that had now spread throughout his body.

And if his body could tingle while submerged in a lake so cold, he was terrified to see his own privates (the poor things felt like they'd shrunk to nothing, which was *not* what a man liked to imagine), then it must be a very strong tingle indeed.

"Who is out there?" he called out.

No answer. He hadn't really expected one, but it had been worth a try.

He squinted as he searched the shore again, turning a full three hundred and sixty degrees as he watched for any sign of movement. He saw nothing but the gentle ruffling of the leaves in the wind, but as he finished his sweep of the area, he somehow *knew*.

"Sophie!"

He heard a gasp, followed by a huge flurry of activity.

"Sophie Beckett," he yelled, "if you run from me right now, I swear I will follow you, and I will not take the time to don my clothing."

The noises coming from the shore slowed.

"I *will* catch up with you," he continued, "because I'm stronger and faster. And I might very well feel compelled to tackle you to the ground, just to be certain you do not escape."

The sounds of her movement ceased.

"Good," he grunted. "Show yourself."

She didn't.

"Sophie," he warned.

There was a beat of silence, followed by the sound of slow, hesitant footsteps, and then he saw her, standing on the shore in one of those awful dresses he'd like to see sunk to the bottom of the Thames.

"What are you doing here?" he demanded.

"I went for a walk. What are *you* doing here?" she countered. "You're supposed to be ill. That"—she waved her arm toward him and, by extension, the pond—"can't possibly be good for you."

He ignored her question and comment. "Were you following me?"

"Of course not," she replied, and he rather believed her. He didn't think she possessed the acting talents to fake that level of righteousness.

"I would never follow you to a swimming hole," she continued. "It would be indecent."

And then her face went completely red, because they both knew she hadn't a leg to stand on with that argument. If she had truly been concerned about decency, she'd have left the pond the second she'd seen him, accidentally or not.

He lifted one hand from the water and pointed toward her, twisting his wrist as he motioned for her to turn around. "Give me your back while you wait for me," he ordered. "It will only take me a moment to pull on my clothing."

"I'll go home right now," she offered. "You'll enjoy greater privacy, and—"

"You'll stay," he said firmly.

"But—"

He crossed his arms. "Do I look like a man in the mood to be argued with?"

She stared at him mutinously.

"If you run," he warned, "I *will* catch you."

Sophie eyed the distance between them, then tried to judge the distance back to My Cottage. If he stopped to pull on his clothing she might have a chance of escaping, but if he *didn't* . . .

"Sophie," he said, "I can practically see the steam coming out of your ears. Stop taxing your brain with useless mathematical computations and do as I asked."

One of her feet twitched. Whether it was itching to run home or merely turn around, she'd never know.

"Now," he ordered.

With a loud sigh and grumble, Sophie crossed her arms and turned around to stare at a knothole in the tree trunk in front of her as if her very life depended on it. The infernal man wasn't being particularly quiet as he went about his business, and she couldn't seem to keep herself from listening to and trying to identify every sound that rustled and splashed behind her. Now he was emerging from the water, now he was reaching for his breeches, now he was . . .

It was no use. She had a dreadfully wicked imagination, and there was no getting around it.

He should have just let her return to the house. Instead she was forced to wait, utterly mortified, while he dressed. Her skin felt like it was on fire, and she was certain her cheeks must be eight different shades of red. A gentleman would have let her weasel out of her embarrassment and hole up in her room back at the house for at least three days in hopes that he'd just forget about the entire affair.

But Benedict Bridgerton was obviously determined not to

be a gentleman this afternoon, because when she moved one of her feet—just to flex her toes, which were falling asleep in her shoes, honest!—barely half a second passed before he growled, "Don't even think about it."

"I wasn't!" she protested. "My foot was falling asleep. And hurry up! It can't possibly take so long to get dressed."

"Oh?" he drawled.

"You're doing this just to torture me," she grumbled.

"You may feel free to face me at any time," he said, his voice laced with quiet amusement. "I assure you that I asked you to turn your back for the sake of *your* sensibilities, not mine."

"I'm just fine where I am," she replied.

After what seemed like an hour but what was probably only three minutes, she heard him say, "You may turn around now."

Sophie was almost afraid to do so. He had just the sort of perverse sense of humor that would compel him to order her around before he'd donned his clothing.

But she decided to trust him—not, she was forced to admit, that she had much choice in the matter—and so she turned around. Much to her relief and, if she was to be honest with herself, a fair bit of disappointment, he was quite decently dressed, save for a smattering of damp spots where the water from his skin had seeped through the fabric of his clothing.

"Why didn't you just let me run home?" she asked.

"I wanted you here," he said simply.

"But why?" she persisted.

He shrugged. "I don't know. Punishment, perhaps, for spying on me."

"I wasn't—" Sophie's denial was automatic, but she cut herself off halfway through, because of course she'd been spying on him.

"Smart girl," he murmured.

She scowled at him. She would have liked to have said

something utterly droll and witty, but she had a feeling that anything emerging from her mouth just then would have been quite the opposite, so she held her tongue. Better to be a silent fool than a talkative one.

"It's very bad form to spy on one's host," he said, planting his hands on his hips and somehow managing to look both authoritative and relaxed at the same time.

"It was an accident," she grumbled.

"Oh, I believe you there," he said. "But even if you didn't intend to spy on me, the fact remains that when the opportunity arose, you took it."

"Do you blame me?"

He grinned. "Not at all. I would have done precisely the same thing."

Her mouth fell open.

"Oh, don't pretend to be offended," he said.

"I'm not pretending."

He leaned a bit closer. "To tell the truth, I'm quite flattered."

"It was academic curiosity," she ground out. "I assure you."

His smile grew sly. "So you're telling me that you would have spied upon any naked man you'd come across?"

"Of course not!"

"As I said," he drawled, leaning back against a tree, "I'm flattered."

"Well, now that we have that settled," Sophie said with a sniff, "I'm going back to Your Cottage."

She made it only two steps before his hand shot out and grabbed a small measure of the fabric of her dress. "I don't think so," he said.

Sophie turned back around with a weary sigh. "You have already embarrassed me beyond repair. What more could you possibly wish to do to me?"

Slowly, he reeled her in. "That's a very interesting question," he murmured.

Sophie tried to plant her heels into the ground, but she was no match for the inexorable tug of his hand. She stumbled slightly, then found herself mere inches away from him. The air suddenly felt hot, very hot, and Sophie had the bizarre sense that she no longer quite knew how to work her hands and feet. Her skin tingled, her heart raced, and the bloody man was just staring at her, not moving a muscle, not pulling her the final few inches against him.

Just staring at her.

"Benedict?" she whispered, forgetting that she still called him Mr. Bridgerton.

He smiled. It was a small, knowing sort of smile, one that sent chills right down her spine to another area altogether. "I like when you say my name," he said.

"I didn't mean to," she admitted.

He touched a finger to her lips. "Shhh," he admonished. "Don't tell me that. Don't you know that's not what a man wishes to hear?"

"I don't have much experience with men," she said.

"Now that's what a man wishes to hear."

"Really?" she asked dubiously. She knew men wanted innocence in their wives, but Benedict wasn't about to marry a girl like her.

He touched her cheek with one fingertip. "It's what I want to hear from *you*."

A soft rush of air crossed Sophie's lips as she gasped. He was going to kiss her.

He was going to kiss her. It was the most wonderful and awful thing that could possibly happen.

But oh, how she wanted this.

She knew she was going to regret this tomorrow. She let out a smothered, choking sort of laugh. Who was she kidding? She'd regret it in ten minutes. But she had spent the last two years remembering what it felt like to be in his arms, and she wasn't sure she'd make it through the rest of her days without at least one more memory to keep her going.

His finger floated across her cheek to her temple, and then from there traced her eyebrow, ruffling the soft hairs as it moved to the bridge of her nose. "So pretty," he said softly, "like a storybook fairy. Sometimes I think you couldn't possibly be real."

Her only reply was a quickening of breath.

"I think I'm going to kiss you," he whispered.

"You think?"

"I think I *have* to kiss you," he said, looking as if he couldn't quite believe his own words. "It's rather like breathing. One doesn't have much choice in the matter."

Benedict's kiss was achingly tender. His lips brushed across hers in a feather-light caress, back and forth with just the barest hint of friction. It was utterly breathtaking, but there was something more, something that made her dizzy and weak. Sophie clutched at his shoulders, wondering why she felt so off-balance and strange, and then it suddenly came to her—

It was just like before.

The way his lips brushed hers so soft and sweet, the way he began with gentle titillation, rather than forcing entry—it was just what he'd done at the masquerade. After two years of dreams, Sophie was finally reliving the single most exquisite moment of her life.

"You're crying," Benedict said, touching her cheek.

Sophie blinked, then reached up to wipe away the tears she hadn't even known were falling.

"Do you want me to stop?" he whispered.

She shook her head. No, she didn't want him to stop. She wanted him to kiss her just as he had at the masquerade, the gentle caress giving way to a more passionate joining. And then she wanted him to kiss her some more, because this time the clock wasn't going to strike midnight, and she wouldn't have to flee.

And she wanted him to know that she was the woman from the masquerade. And she desperately prayed that he would never recognize her. And she was just so bloody confused, and . . .

And he kissed her.

Really kissed her, with fierce lips and probing tongue, and all the passion and desire a woman could ever want. He made her feel beautiful, precious, priceless. He treated her like a woman, not some serving wench, and until that very moment, she hadn't realized just how much she missed being treated like a person. Gentry and aristocrats didn't see their servants, they tried not to hear them, and when they were forced to converse, they kept it as short and perfunctory as possible.

But when Benedict kissed her, she felt real.

And when he kissed her, he did so with his entire body. His lips, which had begun the intimacy with such gentle reverence, were now fierce and demanding on hers. His hands, so large and strong they seemed to cover half her back, held her to him with a strength that left her breathless. And his body—dear God, it ought to be illegal the way it was pressed against hers, the heat of it seeping through her clothing, searing her very soul.

He made her shiver. He made her melt.

He made her want to give herself to him, something she'd sworn she would never do outside the sacrament of marriage.

"Oh, Sophie," he murmured, his voice husky against her lips. "I've never felt—"

Sophie stiffened, because she was fairly certain he'd intended to say he'd never felt that way before, and she had no idea how she felt about that. On the one hand, it was thrilling to be the one woman who could bring him to his knees, make him dizzy with desire and need.

On the other hand, he'd kissed her before. Hadn't he felt the same exquisite torture then, too?

Dear God, was she jealous of herself?

He pulled back a half inch. "What's wrong?"

She gave her head a little shake. "Nothing."

Benedict touched his fingers to the tip of her chin and tilted her face up. "Don't lie to me, Sophie. What's wrong?"

"I'm—I'm only nervous," she stammered. "That's all."

His eyes narrowed with concerned suspicion. "Are you certain?"

"Absolutely certain." She tugged herself from his grasp and took a few steps away from him, her arms hugging over her chest. "I don't do this sort of thing, you know."

Benedict watched her walk away, studying the bleak line of her back. "I know," he said softly. "You're not the sort of girl who would."

She gave a little laugh at that, and even though he could not see her face, he could well imagine its expression. "How do you know that?" she asked.

"It's obvious in everything you do."

She didn't turn around. She didn't say anything.

And then, before he had any idea what he was saying, the most bizarre question tumbled from his mouth. "Who are you, Sophie?" he asked. "Who are you, really?"

She still didn't turn around, and when she spoke, her voice was barely above a whisper. "What do you mean?"

"Something isn't quite right about you," he said. "You speak too well to be a maid."

Her hand was nervously fidgeting with the folds of her skirt as she said, "Is it a crime to wish to speak well? One can't get very far in this country with a lowborn accent."

"One could make the argument," he said with deliberate softness, "that you haven't gotten very far."

Her arms straightened into sticks. Straight rigid sticks with little tight fists at the end. And then, while he waited for her to say something, she started walking away.

"Wait!" he called out, and he caught up with her in under three strides, grabbing hold of her wrist. He tugged at her until she was forced to turn around. "Don't go," he said.

"It is not my habit to remain in the company of people who insult me."

Benedict nearly flinched, and he knew he would be forever haunted by the stricken look in her eyes. "I wasn't insulting you," he said, "and you know it. I was speaking the truth. You're not meant to be a housemaid, Sophie. It's clear to me, and it ought to be clear to you."

She laughed—a hard, brittle sound he'd never thought to hear from her. "And what do you suggest I do, Mr. Bridgerton?" she asked. "Find work as a governess?"

Benedict thought that was a fine idea, and he started to tell her so, but she interrupted him, saying, "And who do you think will hire me?"

"Well . . ."

"No one," she snapped. "No one will hire me. I have no references, and I look far too young."

"And pretty," he said grimly. He'd never given much thought to the hiring of governesses, but he knew that the duty usually fell to the mother of the house. And common sense told him that no mother wanted to bring such a pretty young thing into her household. Just look what Sophie had had to endure at the hands of Phillip Cavender.

"You could be a lady's maid," he suggested. "At least then you wouldn't be cleaning chamber pots."

"You'd be surprised," she muttered.

"A companion to an elderly lady?"

She sighed. It was a sad, weary sound, and it nearly broke his heart. "You're very kind to try to help me," she said, "but I have already explored all of those avenues. Besides, I am not your responsibility."

"You could be."

She looked at him in surprise.

In that moment, Benedict knew that he had to have her. There was a connection between them, a strange, inexplicable bond that he'd felt only one other time in his life, with the mystery lady from the masquerade. And while she was gone, vanished into thin air, Sophie was very real. He was tired of mirages. He wanted someone he could see, someone he could touch.

And she needed him. She might not realize it yet, but she needed him. Benedict took her hand and tugged, catching her off-balance and wrapping her to him when she fell against his body.

"Mr. Bridgerton!" she yelped.

"Benedict," he corrected, his lips at her ear.

"Let me—"

"Say my name," he persisted. He could be very stubborn when it suited his interests, and he wasn't going to let her go until he heard his name cross her lips.

And maybe not even then.

"Benedict," she finally relented. "I—"

"Hush." He silenced her with his mouth, nibbling at the corner of her lips. When she went soft and compliant in his arms, he drew back, just far enough so that he could focus on her eyes. They looked impossibly green in the late-afternoon light, deep enough to drown in.

"I want you to come back to London with me," he whispered, the words tumbling forth before he had a chance to consider them. "Come back and live with me."

She looked at him in surprise.

"Be mine," he said, his voice thick and urgent. "Be mine right now. Be mine forever. I'll give you anything you want. All I want in return is you."

Chapter 12

Speculation continues to abound concerning the disappearance of Benedict Bridgerton. According to Eloise Bridgerton, who as his sister ought to know, he was due back in town several days ago.

But as Eloise must be the first to admit, a man of Mr. Bridgerton's age and stature need hardly report his whereabouts to his younger sister.

LADY WHISTLEDOWN'S SOCIETY PAPERS, 9 MAY 1817

"You want me to be your mistress," she said flatly.

He gave her a confused look, although she couldn't be sure whether that was because her statement was so obvious or because he objected to her choice of words. "I want you to be with me," he persisted.

The moment was so staggeringly painful and yet she found herself almost smiling. "How is that different from being your mistress?"

"Sophie—"

"How is it different?" she repeated, her voice growing strident.

"I don't know, Sophie." He sounded impatient. "Does it matter?"

"It does to me."

"Fine," he said in a short voice. "Fine. Be my mistress, and have *this*."

Sophie had just enough time to gasp before his lips descended on hers with a ferocity that turned her knees to water. It was like no kiss they'd ever shared, harsh with need, and laced with an odd, strange anger.

His mouth devoured hers in a primitive dance of passion. His hands seemed to be everywhere, on her breasts, around her waist, even under her skirt. He touched and squeezed, caressed and stroked.

And all the while, he had her pressed up so tightly against him she was certain she'd melt into his skin.

"I want you," he said roughly, his lips finding the hollow at the base of her throat. "I want you right now. I want you here."

"Benedict—"

"I want you in my bed," he growled. "I want you tomorrow. And I want you the next day."

She was wicked, and she was weak, and she gave in to the moment, arching her neck to allow him greater access. His lips felt so good against her skin, sending shivers and tingles to the very center of her being. He made her long for him, long for all the things she couldn't have, and curse the things she could.

And then somehow she was on the ground, and he was there with her, half-on and half-off of her body. He seemed so large, so powerful, and in that moment, so perfectly *hers*. A very small part of Sophie's mind was still functioning, and she knew that she had to say no, had to put a stop to the madness, but God help her, she couldn't. Not yet.

She'd spent so long dreaming about him, trying desperately to remember the scent of his skin, the sound of his voice. There had been many nights when the fantasy of him had been all that had kept her company.

She had been living on dreams, and she wasn't a woman

for whom many had come true. She didn't want to lose this one just yet.

"Benedict," she murmured, touching the crisp silkiness of his hair and pretending—pretending that he hadn't just asked her to be his mistress, that she was someone else—anyone else.

Anyone but the bastard daughter of a dead earl, with no means of support besides waiting on others.

Her murmurings seemed to embolden him, and his hand, which had been tickling her knee for so long, started to inch upward, squeezing the soft skin of her thigh. Years of hard work had made her lean, not fashionably curvy, but he didn't seem to mind. In fact, she could feel his heart begin to beat even more rapidly, hear his breath coming in hoarser gasps.

"Sophie, Sophie, Sophie," he groaned, his lips moving frantically along her face until they found her mouth again. "I need you." He pressed his hips hotly against hers. "Do you feel how I need you?"

"I need you, too," she whispered. And she did. There was a fire burning within her that had been simmering quietly for years. The sight of him had ignited it anew, and his touch was like kerosene, sending her into a conflagration.

His fingers wrestled with the large, poorly made buttons on back of her dress. "I'm going to burn this," he grunted, his other hand relentlessly stroking the tender skin at the back of her knee. "I'll dress you in silks, in satins." He moved to her ear, nipping at her lobe, then licking the tender skin where her ear met her cheek. "I'll dress you in nothing at all."

Sophie stiffened in his arms. He'd managed to say the one thing that could remind her why she was here, why he was kissing her. It wasn't love, or any of those tender emotions she'd dreamed about, but lust. And he wanted to make her a kept woman.

Just as her mother had been.

Oh, God, it was so tempting. So impossibly tempting. He was offering her a life of ease and luxury, a life with *him.*

At the price of her soul.

No, that wasn't entirely true, or entirely a problem. She might be able to live as a man's mistress. The benefits—and how could she consider life with Benedict anything but a benefit—might outweigh the drawbacks. But while she might be willing to make such decisions with her own life and reputation, she would not do so for a child. And how could there not be a child? All mistresses eventually had children.

With a tortured cry, she gave him a shove and wrenched herself away, rolling to the side until she found herself on her hands and knees, stopping to catch her breath before hauling herself to her feet.

"I can't do this, Benedict," she said, barely able to look at him.

"I don't see why not," he muttered.

"I can't be your mistress."

He rose to his feet. "And why is that?"

Something about him pricked at her. Maybe it was the arrogance of his tone, maybe it was the insolence in his posture. "Because I don't want to," she snapped.

His eyes narrowed, not with suspicion, but with anger. "You wanted to just a few seconds ago."

"You're not being fair," she said in a low voice. "I wasn't thinking."

His chin jutted out belligerently. "You're not supposed to be thinking. That's the point of it."

She blushed as she redid her buttons. He'd done a very good job of making her not think. She'd almost thrown away a lifetime of vows and morals, all at one wicked kiss. "Well, I won't be your mistress," she said again. Maybe if she said it enough, she'd feel more confident that he wouldn't be able to break down her defenses.

"And what are you going to do instead?" he hissed. "Work as a housemaid?"

"If I have to."

"You'd rather wait on people—polish their silver, scrub out their damned chamber pots—than come and live with me."

She said only one word, but it was low and true. "Yes."

His eyes flashed furiously. "I don't believe you. No one would make that choice."

"I did."

"You're a fool."

She said nothing.

"Do you understand what you're giving up?" he persisted, his arm waving wildly as he spoke. She'd hurt him, she realized. She'd hurt him and insulted his pride, and he was lashing out like a wounded bear.

Sophie nodded, even though he wasn't looking at her face.

"I could give you whatever you wanted," he bit off. "Clothes, jewels—Hell, forget about the clothes and jewels, I could give you a bloody roof over your head, which is more than you have now."

"That is true," she said quietly.

He leaned forward, his eyes burning hot into hers. "I could give you everything."

Somehow she managed to stand up straight, and somehow she managed not to cry. And somehow she even managed to keep her voice even as she said, "If you think that's everything, then you probably wouldn't understand why I must refuse."

She took a step back, intending to head to His Cottage and pack her meager bag, but he obviously wasn't through with her yet, because he stopped her with a strident, "Where are you going?"

"Back to the cottage," she said. "To pack my bag."

"And where do you think you're going to go with that bag?"

Her mouth fell open. Surely he didn't expect her to *stay*.

"Do you have a job?" he demanded. "A place to go?"

"No," she replied, "but—"

He planted his hands on his hips and glared at her. "And you think I'm going to just let you leave here, with no money or prospects?"

Sophie was so surprised she started to blink uncontrollably. "W-well," she stammered, "I didn't think—"

"No, you *didn't* think," he snapped.

She just stared at him, eyes wide and lips parted, unable to believe what she was hearing.

"You bloody fool," he swore. "Do you have any idea how dangerous it is in the world for a woman alone?"

"Er, yes," she managed. "Actually, I do."

If he heard her, he gave no indication, just went on about "men who take advantage" and "helpless women" and "fates worse than death." Sophie wasn't positive, but she thought she even heard the phrase, "roast beef and pudding." About halfway through his tirade, she lost all ability to focus on his words. She just kept watching his mouth and hearing the tone of his voice, all the while trying to comprehend the fact that he seemed remarkably concerned for her welfare, considering that she'd just summarily rejected him.

"Are you even listening to a word I'm saying?" Benedict demanded.

Sophie didn't nod or shake her head, instead doing an odd combination of both.

Benedict swore under his breath. "That's it," he announced. "You're coming back to London with me."

That seemed to wake her up. "I just said I'm not!"

"You don't have to be my damned mistress," he bit off. "But I'm not leaving you to fend for yourself."

"I was fending for myself quite adequately before I met you."

"Adequately?" he sputtered. "At the Cavenders'? You call that adequate?"

"You're not being fair!"

"And you're not being intelligent."

Benedict thought that his argument was most reasonable, if a little overbearing, but Sophie obviously did not agree, because, much to his surprise, he found himself lying faceup on the ground, having been felled by a remarkably quick right hook.

"Don't you ever call me stupid," she hissed.

Benedict blinked, trying to get his eyesight back to the point where he only saw one of her. "I wasn't—"

"Yes, you were," she replied in a low, angry voice. Then she turned on her heel, and in the split second before she stalked away, he realized he had only one way to stop her. He certainly wasn't going to make it to his feet with anything resembling speed in his current befuddled state, so he reached out and grabbed one of her ankles with both of his hands, sending her sprawling onto the ground right next to him.

It wasn't a particularly gentlemanly maneuver, but beggars really couldn't be choosers, and besides, she had thrown the first punch.

"You're not going anywhere," he growled.

Sophie slowly lifted her head, spitting out dirt as she glared at him. "I cannot believe," she said scathingly, "that you just did that."

Benedict let go of her foot and hauled himself to a crouching position. "Believe it."

"You—"

He held up a hand. "Don't say anything now. I beg you."

Her eyes bugged out. "You're begging me?"

"I hear your voice," he informed her, "therefore you must be speaking."

"But—"

"And as for begging you," he said, effectively cutting her off again, "I assure you it was merely a figure of speech."

She opened her mouth to say something, then obviously thought the better of it, clamping her lips shut with the petulant look of a three-year-old. Benedict let out a short breath, then offered her his hand. She was, after all, still sitting in the dirt and not looking especially happy about it.

She stared at his hand with remarkable revulsion, then moved her gaze to his face and glared at him with such ferocity that Benedict wondered if he had recently sprouted horns. Still not saying a word, she ignored his offer of help and hefted herself to her feet.

"As you like," he murmured.

"A poor choice of words," she snapped, then started marching away.

As Benedict was on his feet this time, he felt no need to incapacitate her. Instead, he dogged her every step, remaining a mere (and annoying, he was sure) two paces behind her. Finally, after about a minute, she turned around and said, "Please leave me alone."

"I'm afraid I can't," he said.

"Can't or won't?"

He thought about that for a moment. "Can't."

She scowled at him and kept walking.

"I find it as difficult to believe as you do," Benedict called out, keeping pace with her.

She stopped and turned around. "That is impossible."

"I can't help it," he said with a shrug. "I find myself completely unwilling to let you go."

" 'Unwilling' is a far cry from 'can't.' "

"I didn't save you from Cavender just to let you squander your life away."

"That isn't your choice to make."

She had a point there, but he wasn't inclined to give it to her. "Perhaps," he allowed, "but I'm going to make it, anyway. You're coming with me to London. We will discuss it no further."

"You're trying to punish me," she said, "because I refused you."

"No," he said slowly, considering her words even as he answered. "No, I'm not. I'd like to punish you, and in my current state of mind I'd even go so far as to say you deserve to be punished, but that's not why I'm doing it."

"Then why are you?"

"It's for your own good."

"That's the most condescending, patronizing—"

"I'm sure you're right," he allowed, "but nonetheless, in this particular case, at this particular moment, I know what's best for you, and you clearly don't, so—*don't* hit me again," he warned.

Sophie looked down at her fist, which she hadn't even realized was pulled back and ready to fly. He was turning her into a monster. There was no other explanation. She didn't think she'd ever hit anyone in her life, and here she was ready to do it for the second time that day.

Eyes never leaving her hand, she slowly unclenched her fist, stretching her fingers out like a starfish and holding them there for the count of three. "How," she said in a very low voice, "do you intend to stop me from going my way?"

"Does it really matter?" he asked, shrugging nonchalantly. "I'm sure I'll think of something."

Her mouth fell open. "Are you saying you'd tie me up and—"

"*I* didn't say anything of the sort," he cut in with a wicked grin. "But the idea certainly has its charms."

"You are despicable," she spat.

"And you sound like the heroine of a very poorly written novel," he replied. "What did you say you were reading this morning?"

Sophie felt the muscles working frenetically in her cheek, felt her jaw clenching to the point where she was certain her teeth would shatter. How Benedict managed to be the most wonderful and the most awful man in the world at the very same time, she would never understand. Right now, though, the awful side seemed to be winning, and she was quite certain—logic aside—that if she remained in his company one more second, her head would explode.

"I'm leaving!" she said, with, in her opinion, great drama and resolve.

But he just answered her with a sly half smile, and said, "I'm following."

And the bloody man remained two strides behind her the entire way home.

Benedict didn't often go out of his way to annoy people (with the notable exception of his siblings), but Sophie Beckett clearly brought out the devil in him. He stood in the doorway to her room as she packed, casually lounging against the doorframe. His arms were crossed in a manner that he somehow knew would vex her, and his right leg was slightly bent, the toe of his boot stubbed up against the floor.

"Don't forget your dress," he said helpfully.

She glared at him.

"The ugly one," he added, as if clarification were necessary.

"They're both ugly," she spat out.

Ah, a reaction. "I know."

She went back to shoving her belongings into her satchel.

He waved an arm expansively. "Feel free to take a souvenir."

She straightened, her hands planted angrily on her hips. "Does that include the silver tea service? Because I could live for several years on what that would fetch."

"You may certainly take the tea service," he replied genially, "as you will not be out of my company."

"I will not be your mistress," she hissed. "I told you, I won't do it. I *can't* do it."

Something about her use of the word "can't" struck him

as significant. He mulled that over for a few moments while she gathered up the last of her belongings and cinched shut the drawstring to her satchel.

"That's it," he murmured.

She ignored him, instead marching toward the door and giving him a pointed look.

He knew she wanted him to get out of the way so she could depart. He didn't move a muscle, save for one finger that thoughtfully stroked the side of his jaw. "You're illegitimate," he said.

The blood drained from her face.

"You are," he said, more to himself than to her. Strangely, he felt rather relieved by the revelation. It explained her rejection of him, made it into something that had nothing to do with him and everything to do with her.

It took the sting out.

"I don't care if you're illegitimate," he said, trying not to smile. It was a serious moment, but by God, he wanted to break out in a grin because now she'd come to London with him and be his mistress. There were no more obstacles, and—

"You don't understand anything," she said, shaking her head. "It's not about whether I'm good enough to be your mistress."

"I would care for any children we might have," he said solemnly, pushing himself away from the doorframe.

Her stance grew even more rigid, if that were possible. "And what about your wife?"

"I don't have a wife."

"Ever?"

He froze. A vision of the masquerade lady danced through his mind. He'd pictured her many ways. Sometimes she wore her silver ballgown, sometimes nothing at all.

Sometimes she wore a wedding dress.

Sophie's eyes narrowed as she watched his face, then she snorted derisively as she stalked past him.

He followed. "That's not a fair question, Sophie," he said, dogging her heels.

She moved down the hall, not even pausing when she reached the stairs. "I think it's more than fair."

He raced down the stairs until he was below her, halting her progress. "I have to marry someday."

Sophie stopped. She had to; he was blocking her path. "Yes, you do," she said. "But I don't have to be anyone's mistress."

"Who was your father, Sophie?"

"I don't know," she lied.

"Who was your mother?"

"She died at my birth."

"I thought you said she was a housekeeper."

"Clearly I misrepresented the truth," she said, past the point of caring that she'd been caught in a lie.

"Where did you grow up?"

"It's of no interest," she said, trying to squirm her way past him.

One of his hands wrapped itself around her upper arm, holding her firmly in place. "I find it very interesting."

"Let me go!"

Her cry pierced the silence of the hall, loud enough so that the Crabtrees would certainly come running to save her. Except that Mrs. Crabtree had gone to the village, and Mr. Crabtree was outside, out of earshot. There was no one to help her, and she was at his mercy.

"I can't let you go," he whispered. "You're not cut out for a life of servitude. It will kill you."

"If it were going to kill me," she returned, "it would have done so years ago."

"But you don't have to do this any longer," he persisted.

"Don't you dare try to make this about me," she said, nearly shaking with emotion. "You're not doing this out of concern for my welfare. You just don't like being thwarted."

"That is true," he admitted, "but I also won't see you cast adrift."

"I have been adrift all my life," she whispered, and she felt the traitorous sting of tears prick her eyes. God above, she didn't want to cry in front of this man. Not now, not when she felt so off-balance and weak.

He touched her chin. "Let me be your anchor."

Sophie closed her eyes. His touch was painfully sweet, and a not very small part of her was aching to accept his offer, to leave the life she'd been forced to live and cast her lot with him, this marvelous, wonderful, infuriating man who had haunted her dreams for years.

But the pain of her childhood was still too fresh. And the stigma of her illegitimacy felt like a brand on her soul.

She would not do this to another child.

"I can't," she whispered. "I wish—"

"What do you wish?" he asked urgently.

She shook her head. She'd been about to tell him that she wished that she could, but she knew that such words would be unwise. He would only latch on to them, and press his cause anew.

And that would make it all the harder to say no.

"You leave me no choice, then," he stated grimly.

Her eyes met his.

"Either you come with me to London, and—" He held up a silencing hand when she tried to protest. "And I will find you a position in my mother's household," he added pointedly.

"Or?" she asked, her voice sullen.

"Or I will have to inform the magistrate that you have stolen from me."

Her mouth abruptly tasted like acid. "You wouldn't," she whispered.

"I certainly don't want to."

"But you would."

He nodded. "I would."

"They'd hang me," she said. "Or send me to Australia."

"Not if I requested otherwise."

"And what would you request?"

His brown eyes looked strangely flat, and she suddenly realized that he wasn't enjoying the conversation any more than she was.

"I would request," he said, "that you be released into my custody."

"That would be very convenient for you."

His fingers, which had been touching her chin all the while, slid down to her shoulder. "I'm only trying to save you from yourself."

Sophie walked to a nearby window and looked out, surprised that he hadn't tried to stop her. "You're making me hate you, you know," she said.

"I can live with that."

She gave him a curt nod. "I will wait for you in the library, then. I would like to leave today."

Benedict watched her walk away, stood utterly still as the door to the library closed behind her. He knew she would not flee. She was not the sort to go back on her word.

He couldn't let this one go. *She* had left—the great and mysterious "she," he thought with a bitter smile—the one woman who had touched his heart.

The same woman who had not even given him her name.

But now there was Sophie, and she *did* things to him. Things he hadn't felt since *her*. He was sick of pining for a woman who practically didn't exist. Sophie was here, and Sophie would be his.

And, he thought with grim determination, Sophie was *not* going to leave him.

"I can live with you hating me," he said to the closed door. "I just can't live without *you*."

Chapter 13

It was previously reported in this column that This Author predicted a possible match between Miss Rosamund Reiling and Mr. Phillip Cavender. This Author can now say that this is not likely to occur. Lady Penwood (Miss Reiling's mother) has been heard to say that she will not settle for a mere mister, even though Miss Reiling's father, while certainly wellborn, was not a member of the aristocracy.

Not to mention, of course, that Mr. Cavender has begun to show a decided interest in Miss Cressida Cowper.

LADY WHISTLEDOWN'S SOCIETY PAPERS, 9 MAY 1817

Sophie started feeling ill the minute the carriage departed My Cottage. By the time they stopped for the night at an inn in Oxfordshire, she was downright queasy. And when they reached the outskirts of London . . . Well, she was quite convinced she would throw up.

Somehow she managed to keep the contents of her stomach where they belonged, but as their carriage wended farther into the tangled streets of London, she was filled with an intense sense of apprehension.

No, not apprehension. Doom.

It was May, which meant that the season was in full

swing. Which meant that Araminta was in residence.

Which meant that Sophie's arrival was a bad, bad idea.

"Very bad," she muttered.

Benedict looked up. "Did you say something?"

She crossed her arms mutinously. "Just that you're a very bad man."

He chuckled. She'd known he would chuckle, and it still irritated her.

He pulled the curtain away from the window and looked out. "We're nearly there," he said.

He'd said that he was taking her directly to his mother's residence. Sophie remembered the grand house in Grosvenor Square as if she'd been there the night before. The ballroom was huge, with hundreds of sconces on the walls, each adorned by a perfect beeswax candle. The smaller rooms had been decorated in the Adam style, with exquisitely scalloped ceilings and pale, pastel walls.

It had been Sophie's dream house, quite literally. In all her dreams of Benedict and their fictional future together, she'd always seen herself in that house. It was silly, she knew, since he was a second son and thus not in line to inherit the property, but still, it was the most beautiful home she'd ever beheld, and dreams weren't meant to be about reality, anyway. If Sophie had wanted to dream her way right into Kensington Palace, that was her prerogative.

Of course, she thought with a wry smile, she wasn't likely ever to see the interior of Kensington Palace.

"What are you smiling about?" Benedict demanded.

She didn't bother to glance up as she replied, "I'm plotting your demise."

He grinned—not that she was looking at him, but it was one of those smiles she could hear in the way he breathed.

She hated that she was that sensitive to his every nuance. Especially since she had a sneaking suspicion that he was the same way about her.

"At least it sounds entertaining," he said.

"What does?" she asked, finally moving her eyes from the lower hem of the curtain, which she'd been staring at for what seemed like hours.

"My demise," he said, his smile crooked and amused. "If you're going to kill me, you might as well enjoy yourself while you're at it, because Lord knows, I won't."

Her jaw dropped a good inch. "You're mad," she said.

"Probably." He shrugged rather casually before settling back in his seat and propping his feet up on the bench across from him. "I've all but kidnapped you, after all. I should think that would qualify as the maddest thing I've ever done."

"You could let me go now," she said, even though she knew he never would.

"Here in London? Where you could be attacked by footpads at any moment? That would be most irresponsible of me, don't you think?"

"It hardly compares to abducting me against my will!"

"I didn't abduct you," he said, idly examining his fingernails. "I blackmailed you. There's a world of difference."

Sophie was saved from having to reply by the jolt of the carriage as it ground to a halt.

Benedict flipped back the curtains one last time, then let them fall into place. "Ah. Here we are."

Sophie waited while he disembarked, then moved to the doorway. She briefly considered ignoring his outstretched hand and jumping down herself, but the carriage was quite high off the ground, and she really didn't wish to make a fool of herself by tripping and landing in the gutter.

It would be nice to insult him, but not at the cost of a sprained ankle.

With a sigh, she took his hand.

"Very smart of you," Benedict murmured.

Sophie looked at him sharply. How did he know what she'd been thinking?

"I almost always know what you're thinking," he said.

She tripped.

"Whoa!" he called out, catching her expertly before she landed in the gutter.

He held her just a moment longer than was necessary before depositing her on the pavement. Sophie would have said something, except that her teeth were ground together far too tightly for words.

"Doesn't the irony just kill you?" Benedict asked, smiling wickedly.

She pried open her jaw. "No, but it may very well kill *you.*"

He laughed, the blasted man. "Come along," he said. "I'll introduce you to my mother. I'm sure she'll find some position or another for you."

"She may not have any openings," Sophie pointed out.

He shrugged. "She loves me. She'll make an opening."

Sophie held her ground, refusing to take a single step alongside him until she'd made her point. "I'm not going to be your mistress."

His expression was remarkably bland as he murmured, "Yes, you've said as much."

"No, I mean, your plan isn't going to work."

He was all innocence. "I have a plan?"

"Oh, please," she scoffed. "You're going to try to wear me down in hopes that eventually I'll give in."

"I would never dream of it."

"I'm sure you dream of quite a bit more," she muttered.

He must have heard her, because he chuckled. Sophie crossed her arms mutinously, not caring that she looked most undignified in such a position, standing right there on the pavement in full view of the world. No one would pay her half a mind, anyway, dressed as she was in the coarse woolens of a servant. She supposed she ought to adopt a brighter outlook and approach her new position with a more optimistic attitude, but drat it all, she *wanted* to be sullen just then.

Frankly, she thought she'd earned it. If anyone had a right to be sullen and disgruntled, it was she.

"We *could* stand here on the pavement all day," Benedict said, his voice lightly laced with sarcasm.

She started to shoot him an angry glare, but that was when she noticed where they were standing. They weren't in Grosvenor Square. Sophie wasn't even certain where they were. Mayfair, to be sure, but the house before them definitely wasn't the house at which she'd attended the masquerade.

"Er, is this Bridgerton House?" she asked.

He quirked a brow. "How did you know my home is called Bridgerton House?"

"You've mentioned it." Which was, thankfully, true. He'd talked about both Bridgerton House, and the Bridgertons' country residence, Aubrey Hall, several times during their conversations.

"Oh." He seemed to accept that. "Well, no, actually, it's not. My mother moved out of Bridgerton House nearly two years ago. She hosted one last ball—it was a masquerade, actually—and then turned the residence over to my brother and his wife. She'd always said she would leave just as soon as he married and started a family of his own. I believe his first child was born a mere month after she left."

"Was it a boy or a girl?" she asked, even though she knew the answer. Lady Whistledown always reported such things.

"A boy. Edmund. They had another son, Miles, earlier this year."

"How nice for them," Sophie murmured, even though it felt like her heart were strangling. She wasn't likely to have children of her own, and that was one of the saddest realizations she'd ever reached. Children required a husband, and marriage seemed a pipe dream. She hadn't been raised to be a servant, and thus she had very little in common with most of the men she met in her daily life. Not that the other servants weren't good and honorable people, but it was difficult to imagine sharing her life with someone who, for example, couldn't read.

Sophie didn't need to marry someone of particularly high birth, but even the middle class was out of her reach. No self-respecting man in trade would marry a housemaid.

Benedict motioned for her to follow him, and she did, until they reached the front steps.

Sophie shook her head. "I'll use the side entrance."

His lips thinned. "You'll use the front entrance."

"I'll use the side entrance," she said firmly. "No woman of breeding will hire a maid who enters through the front."

"You're with me," he ground out. "You'll use the front entrance."

A bubble of mirth escaped her lips. "Benedict, just yesterday you wanted me to become your mistress. Would you dare bring your mistress to meet your mother through the front door?"

She'd confounded him with that. Sophie grinned as she watched his face twist with frustration.

She felt better than she had in days.

"Would you," she continued, mostly just to torture him further, "bring your mistress to meet her at all?"

"You're not my mistress," he bit off.

"Indeed."

His chin jutted out, and his eyes bored into hers with barely leashed fury. "You're a bloody little housemaid," he said, his voice low, "because you've insisted upon being a housemaid. And as a housemaid, you are, if somewhat low on the social scale, still utterly respectable. Certainly respectable enough for my mother."

Sophie's smile faltered. She might have pushed him too far.

"Good," Benedict grunted, once it was clear that she was not going to argue the point any further. "Come with me."

Sophie followed him up the steps. This might actually

work to her advantage. Benedict's mother surely would not hire a maid who had the effrontery to use the front door. And since she had steadfastly refused to be Benedict's mistress, he would have to accept defeat and allow her to return to the country.

Benedict pushed open the front door, holding it until Sophie entered before him. The butler arrived within seconds.

"Wickham," Benedict said, "kindly inform my mother that I am here."

"I will indeed, Mr. Bridgerton," Wickham replied. "And might I take the liberty of informing you that she has been rather curious as to your whereabouts this past week?"

"I would be shocked if she hadn't been," Benedict replied.

Wickham nodded toward Sophie with an expression that hovered somewhere between curiosity and disdain. "Might I inform her of your guest's arrival?"

"Please do."

"Might I inform her of your guest's identity?"

Sophie looked over at Benedict with great interest, wondering what he'd say.

"Her name is Miss Beckett," Benedict replied. "She is here to seek employment."

One of Wickham's brows rose. Sophie was surprised. She didn't think that butlers were supposed to show any expression whatsoever.

"As a maid?" Wickham inquired.

"As whatever," Benedict said, his tone beginning to show the first traces of impatience.

"Very good, Mr. Bridgerton," Wickham said, and then he disappeared up the staircase.

"I don't think he thought it was very good at all," Sophie whispered to Benedict, careful to hide her smile.

"Wickham is not in charge here."

Sophie let out a little whatever-you-say sort of sigh. "I imagine Wickham would disagree."

He looked at her with disbelief. "He's the butler."

"And I'm a housemaid. I know all about butlers. More, I daresay, than you do."

His eyes narrowed. "You act less like a housemaid than any woman of my acquaintance."

She shrugged and pretended to inspect a still life painting on the wall. "You bring out the worst in me, Mr. Bridgerton."

"Benedict," he hissed. "You've called me by my given name before. Use it now."

"Your mother is about to descend the stairs," she reminded him, "and you are insisting that she hire me as a housemaid. Do many of your servants call you by your given name?"

He glared at her, and she knew he knew she was right. "You can't have it both ways, Mr. Bridgerton," she said, allowing herself a tiny smile.

"I only wanted it *one* way," he growled.

"Benedict!"

Sophie looked up to see an elegant, petite woman descending the stairs. Her coloring was fairer than Benedict's, but her features marked her clearly as his mother.

"Mother," he said, striding to meet her at the bottom of the stairs. "It is good to see you."

"It would be better to see you," she said pertly, "had I known where you were this past week. The last I'd heard you'd gone off to the Cavender party, and then everyone returned without you."

"I left the party early," he replied, "then went off to My Cottage."

His mother sighed. "I suppose I can't expect you to notify me of your every movement now that you're thirty years of age."

Benedict gave her an indulgent smile.

She turned to Sophie. "This must be your Miss Beckett."

"Indeed," Benedict replied. "She saved my life while I was at My Cottage."

Sophie started. "I didn't—"

"She did," Benedict cut in smoothly. "I took ill from driving in the rain, and she nursed me to health."

"You would have recuperated without me," she insisted.

"But not," Benedict said, directing his words at his mother, "with such speed or in such comfort."

"Weren't the Crabtrees at home?" Violet asked.

"Not when we arrived," Benedict replied.

Violet looked at Sophie with such obvious curiosity that Benedict was finally forced to explain, "Miss Beckett had been employed by the Cavenders, but certain circumstances made it impossible for her to stay."

"I . . . see," Violet said unconvincingly.

"Your son saved me from a most unpleasant fate," Sophie said quietly. "I owe him a great deal of thanks."

Benedict looked to her in surprise. Given the level of her hostility toward him, he hadn't expected her to volunteer complimentary information. But he supposed he should have done; Sophie was highly principled, not the sort to let anger interfere with honesty.

It was one of the things he liked best about her.

"I see," Violet said again, this time with considerably more feeling.

"I was hoping you might find her a position in your household," Benedict said.

"But not if it's too much trouble," Sophie hastened to add.

"No," Violet said slowly, her eyes settling on Sophie's face with a curious expression. "No, it wouldn't be any trouble at all, but . . ."

Both Benedict and Sophie leaned forward, awaiting the rest of the sentence.

"Have we met?" Violet suddenly asked.

"I don't think so," Sophie said, stammering slightly. How

could Lady Bridgerton think she knew her? She was positive their paths had not crossed at the masquerade. "I can't imagine how we could have done."

"I'm certain you're right," Lady Bridgerton said with a wave of her hand. "There is something vaguely familiar about you. But I'm sure it's just that I've met someone with similar features. It happens all the time."

"Especially to me," Benedict said with a crooked smile.

Lady Bridgerton looked to her son with obvious affection. "It's not my fault all my children ended up looking remarkably alike."

"If the blame can't be placed with you," Benedict asked, "then where may we place it?"

"Entirely upon your father," Lady Bridgerton replied jauntily. She turned to Sophie. "They all look just like my late husband."

Sophie knew she should remain silent, but the moment was so lovely and comfortable that she said, "I think your son resembles you."

"Do you think?" Lady Bridgerton asked, clasping her hands together with delight. "How lovely. And here I've always just considered myself a vessel for the Bridgerton family."

"Mother!" Benedict said.

She sighed. "Am I speaking too plainly? I do that more and more in my old age."

"You are hardly elderly, Mother."

She smiled. "Benedict, why don't you go visit with your sisters while I take your Miss Bennett—"

"Beckett," he interrupted.

"Yes, of course, Beckett," she murmured. "I shall take her upstairs and get her settled in."

"You need only take me to the housekeeper," Sophie said. It was most odd for a lady of the house to concern herself with the hiring of a housemaid. Granted, the entire situation was unusual, what with Benedict asking that she be hired on, but it was very strange that Lady Bridgerton would take a personal interest in her.

"Mrs. Watkins is busy, I'm sure," Lady Bridgerton said. "Besides, I believe we have need for another lady's maid upstairs. Have you any experience in that area?"

Sophie nodded.

"Excellent. I thought you might. You speak very well."

"My mother was a housekeeper," Sophie said automatically. "She worked for a very generous family and—" She broke off in horror, belatedly remembering that she'd told Benedict the truth—that her mother had died at her birth. She shot him a nervous look, and he answered it with a vaguely mocking tilt of his chin, silently telling her that he wasn't going to expose her lie.

"The family she worked for was very generous," Sophie continued, a relieved rush of air passing across her lips, "and they allowed me to share many lessons with the daughters of the house."

"I see," Lady Bridgerton said. "That explains a great deal. I find it difficult to believe you've been toiling as a housemaid. You are clearly educated enough to pursue loftier positions."

"She reads quite well," Benedict said.

Sophie looked to him in surprise.

He ignored her, instead saying to his mother, "She read to me a great deal during my recuperation."

"Do you write, as well?" Lady Bridgerton asked.

Sophie nodded. "My penmanship is quite neat."

"Excellent. It is always handy to have an extra pair of hands at my disposal when we are addressing invitations. And we do have a ball coming up later in the summer. I have two girls out this year," she explained to Sophie. "I'm hopeful that one of them will choose a husband before the season is through."

"I don't think Eloise wants to marry," Benedict said.

"Quiet your mouth," Lady Bridgerton said.

"Such a statement is sacrilege around here," Benedict said to Sophie.

"Don't listen to him," Lady Bridgerton said, walking toward the stairs. "Here, come with me, Miss Beckett. What did you say your given name was?"

"Sophia. Sophie."

"Come with me, Sophie. I'll introduce you to the girls. And," she added, her nose crinkling with distaste, "we'll find you something new to wear. I cannot have one of our maids dressed so shabbily. A person would think we didn't pay you a fair wage."

It had never been Sophie's experience that members of the *ton* were concerned about paying their servants fairly, and she was touched by Lady Bridgerton's generosity.

"You," Lady Bridgerton said to Benedict. "Wait for me downstairs. We have much to discuss, you and I."

"I'm quaking in my boots," he deadpanned.

"Between him and his brother, I don't know which one of them will kill me first," Lady Bridgerton muttered.

"Which brother?" Sophie asked.

"Either. Both. All three. Scoundrels, the lot of them."

But they were scoundrels she clearly loved. Sophie could hear it in the way she spoke, see it in her eyes when they lit with joy upon seeing her son.

And it made Sophie lonely and wistful and jealous. How different her life might have been had her mother lived through childbirth. They might have been unrespectable, Mrs. Beckett a mistress and Sophie a bastard, but Sophie liked to think that her mother would have loved her.

Which was more than she received from any other adult, her father included.

"Come along, Sophie," Lady Bridgerton said briskly.

Sophie followed her up the stairs, wondering why, if she

were merely about to begin a new job, she felt as if she were entering a new family.

It felt . . . nice.

And it had been a long, long while since her life had felt nice.

Chapter 14

Rosamund Reiling swears that she saw Benedict Bridgerton back in London. This Author is inclined to believe the veracity of the account; Miss Reiling can spot an unmarried bachelor at fifty paces.

Unfortunately for Miss Reiling, she can't seem to land one.

LADY WHISTLEDOWN'S SOCIETY PAPERS, 12 MAY 1817

Benedict had barely taken two steps toward the sitting room when his sister Eloise came dashing down the hall. Like all the Bridgertons, she had thick, chestnut hair and a wide smile. Unlike Benedict, however, her eyes were a clear, crisp gray, a shade quite unlike that possessed by any of her brothers and sisters.

"Benedict!" she called out, throwing her arms rather exuberantly around him. "Where have you been? Mother has been grumbling all week, wondering where you'd gone off to."

"Funny, when I spoke to Mother, not two minutes ago, her grumbles were about *you*, wondering when you were finally planning to marry."

Eloise pulled a face. "When I meet someone worth marrying, that's when. I do wish someone new would move to town. I feel as though I meet the same hundred or so people over and over again."

"You *do* meet the same hundred or so people over and over again."

"Exactly my point," she said. "There are no secrets left in London. I already know everything about everyone."

"Really?" Benedict asked, with no small measure of sarcasm.

"Mock me all you want," she said, jabbing her finger toward him in a manner he was *sure* his mother would deem unladylike, "but I am not exaggerating."

"Not even a little bit?" he grinned.

She scowled at him. "Where *were* you this past week?"

He walked into the sitting room and plopped down on a sofa. He probably should have waited for her to sit, but she was just his sister, after all, and he'd never felt the need to stand on ceremony when they were alone. "Went to the Cavender party," he said, propping his feet up on a low table. "It was abominable."

"Mother will kill you if she catches you with your feet up," Eloise said, sitting down in a chair that was kitty-corner to him. "And why was the party so dreadful?"

"The company." He looked at his feet and decided to leave them where they were. "A more boring bunch of lazy louts, I've never met."

"As long as you don't mince words."

Benedict raised a brow at her sarcasm. "You are hereby forbidden from marrying anyone who was in attendance."

"An order I shall probably have no difficulty obeying." She tapped her hands against the arms of her chair. Benedict had to smile; Eloise had always been a bundle of nervous energy.

"But," she said, looking up with narrowed eyes, "that doesn't explain where you were all *week*."

"Has anyone ever told you that you are exceedingly nosy?"

"Oh, all the time. Where were you?"

"And persistent, too."

"It's the only way to be. Where were you?"

"Have I mentioned I'm considering investing in a company that manufactures human-sized muzzles?"

She threw a pillow at him. "Where *were* you?"

"As it happens," he said, gently tossing the pillow back in her direction, "the answer isn't the least bit interesting. I was at My Cottage, recuperating from a nasty cold."

"I thought you'd already recuperated."

He regarded her with an expression that was an unlikely cross between amazement and distaste. "How do you *know* that?"

"I know everything. You should know that by now." She grinned. "Colds can be so nasty. Did you have a setback?"

He nodded. "After driving in the rain."

"Well, that wasn't very smart of you."

"Is there any reason," he asked, glancing about the room as if he were directing his question at someone other than Eloise, "why I am allowing myself to be insulted by my ninnyhammer of a younger sister?"

"Probably because I do it so well." She kicked at his foot, trying to knock it off the table. "Mother will be here at any second, I'm sure."

"No, she won't," he returned. "She's busy."

"Doing what?"

He waved his hand toward the ceiling. "Orienting the new maid."

She sat up straight. "We have a new maid? Nobody told me about it."

"Heavens," he drawled, "something has happened and Eloise doesn't know about it."

She leaned back in her chair, then kicked his foot again. "Housemaid? Lady's maid? Scullery?"

"Why do you care?"

"It's always good to know what's what."

"Lady's maid, I believe."

Eloise took all of one half second to digest that. "And how do you know?"

Benedict figured he might as well tell her the truth. The Lord knew, she'd know the whole story by sundown, even if he didn't. "Because I brought her here."

"The maid?"

"No, Mother. Of course the maid."

"Since when do you trouble yourself with the hiring of servants?"

"Since this particular young lady nearly saved my life by nursing me while I was ill."

Eloise's mouth fell open. "You were *that* ill?"

Might as well let her believe he'd been at death's door. A little pity and concern might work to his advantage next time he needed to wheedle her into something. "I have felt better," he said mildly. "Where are you going?"

She'd already risen to her feet. "To go find Mother and meet the new maid. She's probably going to wait on Francesca and me, now that Marie is gone."

"You lost your maid?"

Eloise scowled. "She left us for that odious Lady Penwood."

Benedict had to grin at her description. He remembered his one meeting with Lady Penwood quite well; he, too, had found her odious.

"Lady Penwood is notorious for mistreating her servants. She's gone through three lady's maids this year. Stole Mrs. Featherington's right out from under her nose, but the poor girl only lasted a fortnight."

Benedict listened patiently to his sister's tirade, amazed that he was even interested. And yet for some strange reason, he was.

"Marie will come crawling back in a week, asking us to take her back on, you mark my words," Eloise said.

"I always mark your words," he replied, "I just don't always care."

"You," Eloise returned, pointing her finger at him, "are going to regret that you said that."

He shook his head, smiling faintly. "Doubtful."

"Hmmph. I'm going upstairs."

"Do enjoy yourself."

She poked her tongue out at him—surely not appropriate behavior for a woman of twenty-one—and left the room. Benedict managed to enjoy just three minutes of solitude before footsteps once again sounded in the hall, tapping rhythmically in his direction. When he looked up, he saw his mother in the doorway.

He stood immediately. Certain manners could be ignored for one's sister, but never for one's mother.

"I saw your feet on the table," Violet said before he could even open his mouth.

"I was merely polishing the surface with my boots."

She raised her brows, then made her way to the chair so recently vacated by Eloise and sat down. "All right, Benedict," she said in an extremely no-nonsense voice. "Who is she?"

"Miss Beckett, you mean?"

Violet gave him one businesslike nod.

"I have no idea, save that she worked for the Cavenders and was apparently mistreated by their son."

Violet blanched. "Did he . . . Oh dear. Was she . . ."

"I don't think so," Benedict said grimly. "In fact, I'm certain she wasn't. But not for lack of trying on his part."

"The poor thing. How lucky for her that you were there to save her."

Benedict found he didn't like to relive that night on the Cavenders' lawn. Even though the escapade had ended quite favorably, he could not seem to stop himself from racing through the gamut of "what-ifs." What if he hadn't come along in time? What if Cavender and his friends had been a little less drunk and a little more obstinate? Sophie could have been raped. Sophie *would* have been raped.

And now that he knew Sophie, had grown to care about her, the very notion chilled him to the bone.

"Well," Violet said, "she is not who she says she is. Of that I'm certain."

Benedict sat up straight. "Why do you say that?"

"She is far too educated to be a housemaid. Her mother's employers may have allowed her to share in some of their daughters' lessons, but all of them? I doubt it. Benedict, the girl speaks French!"

"She does?"

"Well, I can't be positive," Violet admitted, "but I caught her looking at a book on Francesca's desk that was written in French."

"Looking is not the same as reading, Mother."

She shot him a peevish look. "I'm telling you, I was looking at the way her eyes were moving. She was reading it."

"If you say so, you must be correct."

Violet's eyes narrowed. "Are you being sarcastic?"

"Normally," Benedict said with a smile, "I would say yes, but in this case, I was speaking quite seriously."

"Perhaps she is the cast-off daughter of an aristocratic family," Violet mused.

"Cast-off?"

"For getting herself with child," she explained.

Benedict was not used to his mother speaking quite so frankly. "Er, no," he said, thinking about Sophie's steadfast refusal to become his mistress. "I don't think so."

But then he thought—why not? Maybe she refused to bring an illegitimate child into this world because she had already *had* an illegitimate child and didn't want to repeat the mistake.

Benedict's mouth suddenly tasted quite sour. If Sophie had had a child, then Sophie had had a lover.

"Or maybe," Violet continued, warming to the endeavor, "she's the illegitimate child of a nobleman."

That was considerably more plausible—and more palatable. "One would think he'd have settled enough funds on her so that she didn't have to work as a housemaid."

"A great many men completely ignore their by-blows," Violet said, her face wrinkling with distaste. "It's nothing short of scandalous."

"More scandalous than their having the by-blows in the first place?"

Violet's expression turned quite peevish.

"Besides," Benedict said, leaning back against the sofa and propping one ankle on the other knee, "if she were the bastard of a nobleman, and he'd cared for her enough to make sure she had schooling as a child, then why is she completely penniless now?"

"Hmmm, that's a good point." Violet tapped her index finger against her cheek, pursed her lips, then continued tapping. "But have no fear," she finally said, "I shall discover her identity within a month."

"I'd recommend asking Eloise for help," Benedict said dryly.

Violet nodded thoughtfully. "Good idea. That girl could get Napoleon to spill his secrets."

Benedict stood. "I must be going. I'm weary from the road and would like to get home."

"You can always avail yourself here."

He gave her a half smile. His mother liked nothing better than to have her children close at hand. "I need to get back to my own lodgings," he said, leaning down and dropping a kiss on her cheek. "Thank you for finding a position for Sophie."

"Miss Beckett, you mean?" Violet asked, her lips curving slyly.

"Sophie, Miss Beckett," Benedict said, feigning indifference. "Whatever you wish to call her."

When he left, he did not see his mother smiling broadly at his back.

Sophie knew that she should not allow herself to grow too comfortable at Bridgerton House—she would, after all, be leaving just as soon as she could make the arrangements—but as she looked around her room, surely the nicest any servant had ever been assigned, and she thought about Lady Bridgerton's friendly manner and easy smile . . .

She just couldn't help wishing that she could stay forever.

But that was impossible. She knew that as well as she knew that her name was Sophia Maria Beckett, not Sophia Maria Gunningworth.

First and foremost, there was always the danger that she'd come into contact with Araminta, especially now that Lady Bridgerton had elevated her from housemaid to lady's maid. A lady's maid might, for example, find herself acting as a chaperone or escort on outings outside the house. Outings to places where Araminta and the girls might choose to frequent.

And Sophie had no doubt that Araminta would find a way to make her life a living hell. Araminta hated her in a way that defied reason, went beyond emotion. If she saw Sophie in London, she would not be content simply to ignore her. Sophie had no doubt that Araminta would lie, cheat, and steal just to make Sophie's life more difficult.

She hated Sophie that much.

But if Sophie were to be honest with herself, the true reason she could not remain in London was not Araminta. It was Benedict.

How could she avoid him when she lived in his mother's household? She was furious with him right now—beyond furious, in all truth—but she knew, deep down, that anger could only be short-lived. How could she resist him, day in and day out, when the mere sight of him made her weak with longing? Someday soon he'd smile at her, one of those sideways, crooked sorts of smiles, and she'd find herself clutching on to the furniture, just to keep herself from melting into a pathetic pool on the floor.

She'd fallen in love with the wrong man. She could never have him on her terms, and she refused to go to him on his.

It was hopeless.

Sophie was saved from any further depressing thoughts by a brisk knock on her door. When she called out, "Yes?" the door opened, and Lady Bridgerton entered the room.

Sophie immediately jumped to her feet and bobbed a curtsy. "Was there anything you needed, my lady?" she asked.

"No, not at all," Lady Bridgerton replied. "I was merely checking to see if you were getting settled in. Is there anything I can get for you?"

Sophie blinked. Lady Bridgerton was asking *her* if *she* needed anything? Rather the reverse of the usual lady-servant relationship. "Er, no thank you," Sophie said. "I would be happy to get something for you, though."

Lady Bridgerton waved her offer way. "No need. You shouldn't feel you have to do anything for us today. I'd prefer that you get yourself settled in first so that you do not feel distracted when you begin."

Sophie cast her eyes toward her small bag. "I don't have much to unpack. Truly, I should be happy to begin work immediately."

"Nonsense. It's already nearly the end of the day, and we are not planning to go out this evening, anyway. The girls and I have made do with only one lady's maid for the past week; we shall certainly survive for one more night."

"But—"

Lady Bridgerton smiled. "No arguments, if you please. One last day free is the least I can do after you saved my son."

"I did very little," Sophie said. "He would have been fine without me."

"Nonetheless, you aided him when he needed help, and for that I am in your debt."

"It was my pleasure," Sophie replied. "It was the very least I owed him after what he did for me."

Then, to her great surprise, Lady Bridgerton walked forward and sat down in the chair behind Sophie's writing desk.

Writing desk! Sophie was still trying fathom that. What maid had ever been blessed with a writing desk?

"So tell me, Sophie," Lady Bridgerton said with a winning smile—one that instantly reminded her of Benedict's easy grin. "Where are you from?"

"East Anglia, originally," Sophie replied, seeing no reason to lie. The Bridgertons were from Kent; it was unlikely that Lady Bridgerton would be familiar with Norfolk, where Sophie had grown up. "Not so very far from Sandringham, if you know where that is."

"I do indeed," Lady Bridgerton said. "I haven't been, but I've heard that it is a lovely building."

Sophie nodded. "It is, quite. Of course, I've never been inside. But the exterior is beautiful."

"Where did your mother work?"

"Blackheath Hall," Sophie replied, this lie slipping easily off her tongue. She'd been asked that question often enough; she'd long since settled upon a name for her fictional home. "Are you familiar with it?"

Lady Bridgerton's brow furrowed. "No, I don't believe so."

"A bit north of Swaffham."

Lady Bridgerton shook her head. "No, I do not know it."

Sophie gave her a gentle smile. "Not many people do."

"Do you have any brothers or sisters?"

Sophie was unused to an employer wanting to know so much about her personal background; usually all they cared about were her employment record and references. "No," she said. "There was only me."

"Ah, well, at least you had the company of the girls with whom you shared lessons. That must have been nice for you."

"It was good fun," Sophie lied. In all truth, studying with Rosamund and Posy had been sheer torture. She'd much preferred lessons when she'd been alone with her governess, before they'd come to live at Penwood Park.

"I must say, it was very generous of your mother's employers—I'm sorry," Lady Bridgerton interrupted herself, her brow furrowing, "what did you say their name was?"

"Grenville."

Her forehead wrinkled again. "I'm not familiar with them."

"They don't often come to London."

"Ah, well, that explains it," Lady Bridgerton said. "But as I was saying, it was very generous of them to allow you to share in their daughters' lessons. What did you study?"

Sophie froze, not sure whether she was being interrogated or if Lady Bridgerton were truly interested. No one had ever cared to delve so deeply into the faux background she had created for herself. "Er, the usual subjects," she hedged. "Arithmetic and literature. History, a bit of mythology. French."

"French?" Lady Bridgerton asked, looking quite surprised. "How interesting. French tutors can be very dear."

"The governess spoke French," Sophie explained. "So it didn't cost any extra."

"How *is* your French?"

Sophie wasn't about to tell her the truth and say that it was perfect. Or almost perfect. She'd gotten out of practice these past few years and lost a bit of her fluency. "It's tolerable," she said. "Good enough to pass for a French maid, if that's what you desire."

"Oh, no," Lady Bridgerton said, laughing merrily. "Heavens, no. I know it is all the rage to have French maids, but I would never ask you to go about your chores trying to remember to speak with a French accent."

"That's very thoughtful of you," Sophie said, trying not to let her suspicion show on her face. She was sure that Lady Bridgerton was a nice lady; she'd *have* to be a nice lady to have raised such a nice family. But this was almost *too* nice.

"Well, it's—oh, good day, Eloise. What brings you up here?"

Sophie looked to the doorway and saw what could only be a Bridgerton daughter standing there. Her thick, chestnut hair was coiled elegantly at the back of her neck, and her mouth was wide and expressive, just like Benedict's.

"Benedict told me we have a new maid," Eloise said.

Lady Bridgerton motioned to Sophie. "This is Sophie Beckett. We were just chatting. I think we shall deal famously."

Eloise gave her mother an odd look—or at least Sophie thought it was an odd look. She supposed that it was possible that Eloise always looked at her mother with a slightly suspicious, slightly confused, sideways glance. But somehow Sophie didn't think so.

"My brother tells me you saved his life," Eloise said, turning from her mother to Sophie.

"He exaggerates," Sophie said, a faint smile touching her lips.

Eloise regarded her with an oddly shrewd glance, and Sophie had the distinct impression that Eloise was analyzing her smile, trying to decide whether or not she was poking fun at Benedict, and if so, whether it was in jest or unkindness.

The moment seemed suspended in time, and then Eloise's lips curved in a surprisingly sly manner. "I think my mother is correct," she said. "We shall deal famously."

Sophie rather thought she had just passed some sort of crucial test.

"Have you met Francesca and Hyacinth?" Eloise asked.

Sophie shook her head, just as Lady Bridgerton said, "They are not at home. Francesca is visiting Daphne, and Hyacinth is off at the Featheringtons. She and Felicity seem to be over their row and are once again inseparable."

Eloise chuckled. "Poor Penelope. I think she was enjoying the relative peace and quiet with Hyacinth gone. I know *I* was enjoying the respite from Felicity."

Lady Bridgerton turned to Sophie and explained, "My daughter Hyacinth can more often than not be found at the home of her best friend, Felicity Featherington. And when she is not, then Felicity can be found here."

Sophie smiled and nodded, wondering once again why they were sharing such tidbits with her. They were treating her like family, something even her own family had never done.

It was very odd.

Odd and wonderful.

Odd and wonderful and horrible.

Because it could never last.

But maybe she could stay just a little while. Not long. A few weeks—maybe even a month. Just long enough to get her affairs and thoughts in order. Just long enough to relax and pretend she was more than just a servant.

She knew she could never be a part of the Bridgerton family, but maybe she could be a friend.

And it had been so long since she had been anyone's friend.

"Is something wrong, Sophie?" Lady Bridgerton asked. "You have a tear in your eye."

Sophie shook her head. "Just a speck of dust," she mumbled, pretending to busy herself with the unpacking of her small bag of possessions. She knew that no one believed her, but she didn't much care.

And even though she had no idea where she intended to go from this moment on, she had the oddest feeling that her life had just begun.

Chapter 15

This Author is quite certain that the male half of the population will be uninterested in the following portion of the column, so you are all given leave to skip to the next section. However, for the ladies, let This Author be the first to inform you that the Bridgerton family was recently sucked into the battle of the maids that has been raging all season between Lady Penwood and Mrs. Featherington. It seems that the maid attending to the daughters Bridgerton has defected to the Penwoods, replacing the maid who fled back to the Featherington household after Lady Penwood forced her to polish three hundred pairs of shoes.

And in other Bridgerton news, Benedict Bridgerton is most definitely back in London. It seems he took ill while in the country and extended his stay. One wishes that there were a more interesting explanation (especially when one is, like This Author, dependent upon interesting stories to earn one's living), but sadly, that is all there is to it.

LADY WHISTLEDOWN'S SOCIETY PAPERS, 14 MAY 1817

By the following morning, Sophie had met five of Benedict's seven siblings. Eloise, Francesca, and Hyacinth all still lived with their mother, Anthony had stopped by with his young son for breakfast, and Daphne—who was now the Duchess of Hastings—had been summoned to help Lady Bridgerton plan the end-of-the-season ball. The only Bridgertons Sophie hadn't met were Gregory, who was off at Eton, and Colin, who was off, in Anthony's words, God-knows-where.

Although, if one wanted to put a fine point on it, Sophie already had met Colin—two years earlier at the masquerade. She was rather relieved that he was out of town. She doubted that he would recognize her; Benedict, after all, had not. But somehow the thought of meeting him again was quite stressful and unsettling.

Not that that should matter, she thought ruefully. Everything seemed quite stressful and unsettling these days.

Much to Sophie's extreme *lack* of surprise, Benedict showed up at his mother's home the following morning for breakfast. Sophie should have been able to avoid him completely, except that he was loitering in the hall as she tried to make her way down to the kitchen, where she planned to take her morning meal with the rest of the servants.

"And how was your first night at Number Five, Bruton Street?" he inquired, his smile lazy and masculine.

"Splendid," Sophie replied, stepping aside so that she might make a clean half circle around him.

But as she stepped to her left, he stepped to his right, effectively blocking her path. "I'm so glad you're enjoying yourself," he said smoothly.

Sophie stepped back to her right. "I *was*," she said pointedly.

Benedict was far too debonair to step back to his left, but he somehow managed to turn and lean against a table in just the right way to once again block her movement. "Have you been given a tour of the house?" he asked.

"By the housekeeper."

"And of the grounds?"

"There are no grounds."

He smiled, his brown eyes warm and melting. "There's a garden."

"About the size of a pound note," she retorted.

"Nonetheless . . ."

"Nonetheless," Sophie cut in, "I have to eat breakfast."

He stepped gallantly aside. "Until next time," he murmured.

And Sophie had the sinking feeling that next time would come quickly indeed.

Thirty minutes later, Sophie edged slowly out of the kitchen, half-expecting Benedict to jump out at her from around a corner. Well, maybe not half-expecting. Judging from the way she couldn't quite breathe, she was probably whole-expecting.

But he wasn't there.

She inched forward. Surely he would come bounding down the stairs at any moment, ambushing her with his very presence.

Still no Benedict.

Sophie opened her mouth, then bit her tongue when she realized she'd been about to call out his name.

"Stupid girl," she muttered.

"Who's stupid?" Benedict asked. "Surely not *you*."

Sophie nearly jumped a foot. "Where did you come from?" she demanded, once she'd almost caught her breath.

He pointed to an open doorway. "Right there," he answered, his voice all innocence.

"So now you're jumping out at me from *closets*?"

"Of course not." He looked affronted. "That was a staircase."

Sophie peered around him. It was the side staircase. The *servants'* staircase. Certainly not anyplace a family member would just *happen* to be walking. "Do you often creep down the side staircase?" she asked, crossing her arms.

He leaned forward, just close enough to make her slightly

uncomfortable, and, although she would never admit it to anyone, barely even herself, slightly excited. "Only when I want to sneak up on someone."

She attempted to brush past him. "I have to get to work."

"Now?"

She gritted her teeth. "Yes, now."

"But Hyacinth is eating breakfast. You can hardly dress her hair while she's eating."

"I also attend to Francesca and Eloise."

He shrugged, smiling innocently. "They're eating breakfast, too. Truly, you have nothing to do."

"Which shows how little you know about working for a living," she shot back. "I have ironing, mending, polishing—"

"They make you polish the silver?"

"Shoes!" she fairly yelled. "I have to polish shoes."

"Oh." He leaned back, one shoulder resting against the wall as he crossed his arms. "It sounds dull."

"It *is* dull," she ground out, trying to ignore the tears that suddenly pricked her eyes. *She* knew her life was dull, but it was painful to hear someone else point it out.

One corner of his mouth lifted into a lazy, seductive smile. "Your life doesn't *have* to be dull, you know."

She tried to step past him. "I prefer it dull."

He waved his arm grandly to the side, motioning for her to pass. "If that is how you wish it."

"I do." But the words didn't come out nearly as firmly as she'd intended. "I *do*," she repeated. Oh, very well, no use lying to herself. She didn't. Not entirely. But that was the way it had to be.

"Are you trying to convince yourself, or me?" he asked softly.

"I won't even dignify that with an answer," she replied. But she didn't meet his eyes as she said it.

"You'd best get yourself upstairs, then," he said, raising

one brow when she didn't move. "I'm sure you have a great many shoes to polish."

Sophie ran up the stairs—the servants' stairs—and didn't look back.

He next found her in the garden—that tiny patch of green she'd so recently (and accurately) mocked as the size of a pound note. The Bridgerton sisters had gone off to visit the Featherington sisters, and Lady Bridgerton was taking a nap. Sophie had all of their gowns pressed and ready for that evening's social event, hair ribbons were selected and matched to each dress, and enough shoes had been polished to last a week.

With all her work done, Sophie decided to take a short break and read in the garden. Lady Bridgerton had told her that she might borrow freely from her small library of books, so Sophie selected a recently published novel and settled herself into a wrought-iron chair on the small patio. She'd only read a chapter before she heard footsteps approaching from the house. Somehow she managed not to look up until a shadow fell across her. Predictably, it was Benedict.

"Do you *live* here?" Sophie asked dryly.

"No," he said, plopping down into the chair next to her, "although my mother is constantly telling me to make myself right at home."

She could think of no witty rejoinder, so she merely "hmmphed" and stuck her nose back in her book.

He plunked his feet on the small table in front. "And what are we reading today?"

"That question," she said, snapping the book shut but leaving her finger in to mark her place, "implies that I am actually reading, which I assure you I am unable to do while you are sitting here."

"My presence is that compelling, eh?"

"It's that *disturbing*."

"Better than dull," he pointed out.

"I like my life dull."

"If you like your life dull, then that can only mean that you do not understand the nature of excitement."

The condescension in his tone was appalling. Sophie gripped her book so hard her knuckles turned white. "I have had enough excitement in my life," she said through gritted teeth. "I assure you."

"I would be pleased to participate in this conversation to a greater degree," he drawled, "except that you have not seen fit to share with me *any* of the details of your life."

"It was not an oversight on my part."

He clucked disapprovingly. "So hostile."

Her eyes bugged out. "You abducted me—"

"Coerced," he reminded her.

"Do you *want* me to hit you?"

"I wouldn't mind it," he said mildly. "And besides, now that you're here, was it really so very terrible that I browbeat you into coming? You like my family, don't you?"

"Yes, but—"

"And they treat you fairly, right?"

"Yes, but—"

"Then what," he asked, his tone most supercilious, "is the problem?"

Sophie almost lost her temper. She almost jumped to her feet and grabbed his shoulders and shook and shook and shook, but at the last moment she realized that that was exactly what he wanted her to do. And so instead she merely sniffed and said, "If you cannot recognize the problem, there is no way that I could explain it to you."

He laughed, damn the man. "My goodness," he said, "that was an expert sidestep."

She picked up her book and opened it. "I'm reading."

"Trying, at least," he murmured.

She flipped a page, even though she hadn't read the last

two paragraphs. She was really just trying to make a show of ignoring him, and besides, she could always go back and read them later, after he left.

"Your book is upside down," he pointed out.

Sophie gasped and looked down. "It is not!"

He smiled slyly. "But you still had to look to be sure, didn't you?"

She stood up and announced, "I'm going inside."

He stood immediately. "And leave the splendid spring air?"

"And leave *you*," she retorted, even though his gesture of respect was not lost on her. Gentlemen did not ordinarily stand for mere servants.

"Pity," he murmured. "I was having such fun."

Sophie wondered how much injury he'd sustain if she threw the book at him. Probably not enough to make up for the loss to her dignity.

It amazed her how easily he could infuriate her. She loved him desperately—she'd long since given up lying to herself about that—and yet he could make her entire body shake with anger with one little quip.

"Good-*bye*, Mr. Bridgerton."

He waved her off. "I'll see you later, I'm sure."

Sophie paused, not sure she liked his dismissive demeanor.

"I thought you were leaving," he said, looking faintly amused.

"I am," she insisted.

He cocked his head to the side but didn't say anything. He didn't have to. The vaguely mocking expression in his eyes did the job quite well.

She turned and walked toward the door leading inside, but when she was about halfway to her destination, she heard him call out, "Your new dress is quite fetching."

She stopped and sighed. She might have gone from faux-guardian of an earl to a mere lady's maid, but good manners were good manners, and there was no way she could ignore a compliment. Turning around, she said, "Thank you. It was a gift from your mother. I believe it used to belong to Francesca."

He leaned against the fence, his posture deceptively lazy. "That's a custom, isn't it, to share frocks with one's maid?"

Sophie nodded. "When one is through with them, of course. No one would give a new frock away."

"I see."

Sophie eyed him suspiciously, wondering why on earth he cared about the status of her new dress.

"Didn't you want to go inside?" he inquired.

"What are you up to?" she asked.

"Why would you think I'm up to anything?"

Her lips pursed before she said, "You wouldn't be you if you weren't up to something."

He smiled at that. "I do believe that was a compliment."

"It wasn't necessarily intended as such."

"But nonetheless," he said mildly, "that's how I choose to take it."

She wasn't sure how best to respond, so she said nothing. She also didn't move toward the door. She wasn't sure why, since she'd been quite vocal about her desire to be alone. But what she said and what she felt weren't always one and the same. In her heart she longed for this man, dreamed of a life that could never be.

She shouldn't be so angry with him. He shouldn't have forced her against her wishes to come to London, that was true, but she couldn't fault him for offering her a position as his mistress. He had done what any man in his position would have done. Sophie had no illusions about her place in London society. She was a maid. A servant. And the only thing that separated her from other maids and servants was that she'd had a taste of luxury as a child. She'd been reared gently, if without love, and the experience had shaped her ideals and values. Now she was forever stuck between two worlds, with no clear place in either.

"You look very serious," he said quietly.

Sophie heard him, but she couldn't quite break herself from her thoughts.

Benedict stepped forward. He reached out to touch her chin, then checked himself. There was something untouchable about her just then, something unreachable. "I can't bear it when you look so sad," he said, surprised by his own words. He hadn't intended to say anything; it had just slipped out.

She looked up at that. "I'm not sad."

He gave his head the tiniest shake. "There's a sorrow deep in your eyes. It's rarely gone."

Her hand flew to her face, as if she could actually touch that sorrow, as if it were solid, something that could be massaged away.

Benedict took her hand and raised it to his lips. "I wish you would share your secrets with me."

"I have no—"

"Don't lie," he cut in, his tone harsher than he'd intended. "You have more secrets than any woman I've—" He broke off, a sudden image of the woman from the masquerade flashing through his mind. "More than almost any woman I've known," he finished.

Her eyes met his for the briefest of seconds, and then she looked away. "There is nothing wrong with secrets. If I choose—"

"Your secrets are eating you alive," he said sharply. He didn't want to stand there and listen to her excuses, and his frustration gnawed at his patience. "You have the opportunity to change your life, to reach out and grasp happiness, and yet you won't do it."

"I can't," she said, and the pain in her voice nearly unmanned him.

"Nonsense," he said. "You can do anything you choose. You just don't want to."

"Don't make this harder than it already is," she whispered.

When she said that, something snapped inside of him. He felt it palpably, a strange popping sensation that released a rush of blood, feeding the frustrated anger that had been simmering inside of him for days. "You think it's not hard?" he asked. "You think it's not *hard?*"

"I didn't say that!"

He grabbed her hand and pulled her body against his, so she could see for herself just how hard he was. "I burn for you," he said, his lips touching her ear. "Every night, I lie in bed, thinking of you, wondering why the hell you're here with my mother, of all people, and not with me."

"I didn't want—"

"You don't know what you want," he cut in. It was a cruel statement, condescending in the extreme, but he was beyond caring. She'd wounded him in a way he hadn't even known was possible, with a power he'd never dreamed she possessed. She'd chosen a life of drudgery over a life with him, and now he was doomed to see her almost every day, to see her and taste her and smell her just enough to keep his desire sharp and strong.

It was his own fault, of course. He could have let her stay in the country, could have saved himself this wrenching torture. But he'd surprised even himself by insisting that she come to London. It was odd, and he was almost afraid to analyze what it meant, but he needed to know that she was safe and protected more than he needed her for himself.

She said his name, but her voice was laced with longing, and he knew that she was not indifferent to him. She might not fully understand what it meant to want a man, but she wanted him all the same.

He captured her mouth with his, swearing to himself as he did so that if she said no, if she made any sort of indication that she didn't want this, he'd stop. It'd be the hardest thing he'd ever done, but he would do it.

But she didn't say no, and she didn't push against him or struggle or squirm. Instead, she positively melted into him, her hands twining in his hair as her lips parted beneath his. He didn't know why she'd suddenly decided to let him kiss her—no, to kiss *him*—but he wasn't about to lift his lips from hers to wonder why.

He seized the moment, tasting her, drinking her, *breathing* her. He was no longer quite so confident that he would be able to convince her to become his mistress, and it was suddenly imperative that this kiss be more than just a kiss. It might have to last him a lifetime.

He kissed her with renewed vigor, pushing away the niggling voice in his head, telling him that he'd been here, done this before. Two years earlier he'd danced with a woman, kissed her, and she'd told him that he'd have to pack a lifetime into a single kiss.

He'd been overconfident then; he hadn't believed her. And he'd lost her, maybe lost everything. He certainly hadn't met anyone since with whom he could even imagine building a life.

Until Sophie.

Unlike the lady in silver, she wasn't someone he could hope to marry, but also unlike the lady in silver, she was *here*.

And he wasn't going to let her get away.

She was here, with him, and she felt like heaven. The soft scent of her hair, the slight taste of salt on her skin—she was, he thought, born to rest in the shelter of his arms. And he was born to hold her.

"Come home with me," he whispered in her ear.

She said nothing, but he felt her stiffen.

"Come home with me," he repeated.

"I can't," she said, the breath of each word whispering across his skin.

"You *can*."

She shook her head, but she didn't pull away, so he took advantage of the moment and brought his lips to hers one more time. His tongue darted in, exploring the warm recesses of her mouth, tasting the very essence of her. His hand found the swell of her breast and he squeezed gently, his breath catching as he felt her pucker beneath him. But it wasn't enough. He wanted to feel her skin, not the fabric of her dress.

But this was not the place. They were in his mother's garden, for God's sake. Anyone could come across them, and to be frank, if he hadn't pulled her into the alcove right by the door, anyone could have seen them. It was the sort of thing that could cause Sophie to lose her job.

Maybe he should be pulling her out into the open, where all the world would see, because then she'd be on her own again, and she'd have no choice but to be his mistress.

Which was, he reminded himself, what he wanted.

But it occurred to him—and frankly, he was rather surprised he had the presence of mind at such a moment for *anything* to occur to him—that part of the reason he cared so much for her was her remarkably solid and unflinching sense of herself. She knew who she was, and unfortunately for him, that person didn't stray from the bounds of respectable society.

If he ruined her so publicly, in front of people she admired and respected, he'd break her spirit. And that would be an unforgivable crime.

Slowly, he pulled away. He still wanted her, and he still wanted her to be his mistress, but he wasn't going to force the issue by compromising her in his mother's household. When she came to him—and she *would*, he vowed—it would be of her own free will.

In the meantime, he would woo her, wear her down. In the meantime, he'd—

"You stopped," she whispered, looking surprised.

"This isn't the place," he replied.

For a moment her face showed no change of expression. Then, almost as if someone were pulling a shade over her face, horror dawned. It started in her eyes, which grew impossibly round and somehow even more green than usual, then it reached her mouth, her lips parting as a gasp of air rushed in.

"I didn't think," she whispered, more to herself than to him.

"I know." He smiled. "I know. I hate it when you think. It always ends badly for me."

"We can't do this again."

"We certainly can't do it *here*."

"No, I mean—"

"You're spoiling it."

"But—"

"Humor me," he said, "and let me believe the afternoon ended without your telling me this will never happen again."

"But—"

He pressed a finger to her lips. "You're not humoring me."

"But—"

"Don't I deserve this one little fantasy?"

At last, he broke through. She smiled.

"Good," he said. "That's more like it."

Her lips quivered, then, amazingly, her smile grew.

"Excellent," he murmured. "Now then, I'm going to leave. And you have only one task while I go. You will stay right here, and you will keep smiling. Because it breaks my heart to see any other expression on your face."

"You won't be able to see me," she pointed out.

He touched her chin. "I'll know."

And then, before her expression could change from that enchanting combination of shock and adoration, he left.

Chapter 16

The Featheringtons hosted a small dinner party yesterday eve, and, although This Author was not privileged enough to attend, it has been said that the evening was deemed quite a success. Three Bridgertons attended, but sadly for the Featherington girls, none of the Bridgertons were of the male variety. The always amiable Nigel Berbrooke was there, paying great attention to Miss Philippa Featherington.

This Author is told that both Benedict and Colin Bridgerton were invited, but had to send their regrets.

LADY WHISTLEDOWN'S SOCIETY PAPERS, 19 MAY 1817

As the days melted into a week, Sophie discovered that working for the Bridgertons could keep a girl very busy indeed. Her job was to be maid to all three unmarried girls, and her days were filled with hairdressing, mending, pressing gowns, polishing shoes . . . She hadn't left the house even once—unless one counted time out in the back garden.

But where such a life under Araminta had been dreary and demeaning, the Bridgerton household was filled with laughter and smiles. The girls bickered and teased, but never with the malice Sophie had seen Rosamund show to Posy. And when tea was informal—upstairs, with only Lady Bridgerton and the girls in attendance—Sophie was always invited to partake. She usually brought her basket of mending and darned or sewed buttons while the Bridgertons chattered away, but it was so lovely to be able to sit and sip a fine cup of tea, with fresh milk and warm scones. And after a few days, Sophie even began to feel comfortable enough to occasionally add to the conversation.

It had become Sophie's favorite time of day.

"Where," Eloise asked, one afternoon about a week after what Sophie was now referring to as *the big kiss*, "do you suppose Benedict is?"

"Ow!"

Four Bridgerton faces turned to Sophie. "Are you all right?" Lady Bridgerton asked, her teacup suspended halfway between her saucer and her mouth.

Sophie grimaced. "I pricked my finger."

Lady Bridgerton's lips curved into a small, secret smile.

"Mother has told you," fourteen-year-old Hyacinth said, "at least a *thousand* times—"

"A thousand times?" Francesca asked with arched brows.

"A hundred times," Hyacinth amended, shooting an annoyed look at her older sister, "that you do not have to bring your mending to tea."

Sophie suppressed a smile of her own. "I should feel very lazy if I did not."

"Well, I'm not going to bring my embroidery," Hyacinth announced, not that anyone had asked her to.

"Feeling lazy?" Francesca queried.

"Not in the least," Hyacinth returned.

Francesca turned to Sophie. "You're making Hyacinth feel lazy."

"I do not!" Hyacinth protested.

Lady Bridgerton sipped at her tea. "You *have* been working on the same piece of embroidery for quite some time, Hyacinth. Since February, if my memory serves."

"Her memory always serves," Francesca said to Sophie.

Hyacinth glared at Francesca, who smiled into her teacup.

Sophie coughed to cover a smile of her own. Francesca, who at twenty was merely one year younger than Eloise, had a sly, subversive sense of humor. Someday Hyacinth would be her match, but not yet.

"Nobody answered my question," Eloise announced, letting her teacup clatter into its saucer. "Where is Benedict? I haven't seen him in an age."

"It's been a week," Lady Bridgerton said.

"Ow!"

"Do you need a thimble?" Hyacinth asked Sophie.

"I'm not usually this clumsy," Sophie muttered.

Lady Bridgerton lifted her cup to her lips and held it there for what seemed like a rather long time.

Sophie gritted her teeth together and returned to her mending with a vengeance. Much to her surprise, Benedict had not made even the barest of appearances since *the big kiss* last week. She'd found herself peering out windows, peeking around corners, always expecting to catch a glimpse of him.

And yet he was never there.

Sophie couldn't decide whether she was crushed or relieved. Or both.

She sighed. Definitely both.

"Did you say something, Sophie?" Eloise asked.

Sophie shook her head and murmured, "No," refusing to look up from her poor, abused index finger. Grimacing slightly, she pinched her skin, watching blood slowly bead up on her fingertip.

"Where *is* he?" Eloise persisted.

"Benedict is thirty years of age," Lady Bridgerton said in a mild voice. "He doesn't need to inform us of his every activity."

Eloise snorted loudly. "That's a fine about-face from last week, Mother."

"Whatever do you mean?"

" 'Where is Benedict?' " Eloise mocked, doing a more-than-fair imitation of her mother. " 'How dare he go off without a word? It's as if he's dropped off the face of the earth.' "

"That was different," Lady Bridgerton said.

"How so?" This, from Francesca, who was wearing her usual sly smile.

"He'd said he was going to that awful Cavender boy's party, and then never came back, whereas *this* time . . ." Lady Bridgerton stopped, pursing her lips. "*Why* am I explaining myself to you?"

"I can't imagine," Sophie murmured.

Eloise, who was sitting closest to Sophie, choked on her tea.

Francesca whacked Eloise on the back as she leaned forward to inquire, "Did you say something, Sophie?"

Sophie shook her head as she stabbed her needle into the dress she was mending, completely missing the hem.

Eloise gave her a dubious sideways glance.

Lady Bridgerton cleared her throat. "Well, I think—" She stopped, cocking her head to the side. "I say, is that someone in the hall?"

Sophie stifled a groan and looked over toward the doorway, expecting the butler to enter. Wickham always gave her a disapproving frown before imparting whatever news he was carrying. He didn't approve of the maid taking tea with the ladies of the house, and while he never vocalized his thoughts on the issue in front of the Bridgertons, he rarely took pains to keep his opinions from showing on his face.

But instead of Wickham, Benedict walked through the doorway.

"Benedict!" Eloise called out, rising to her feet. "We were just talking about you."

He looked at Sophie. "Were you?"

"*I* wasn't," Sophie muttered.

"Did you say something, Sophie?" Hyacinth asked.

"Ow!"

"I'm going to have to take that mending away from you," Lady Bridgerton said with an amused smile. "You'll have lost a pint of blood before the day is through."

Sophie lurched to her feet. "I'll get a thimble."

"You don't have a *thimble*?" Hyacinth asked. "I would never *dream* of doing mending without a thimble."

"Have you *ever* dreamed of mending?" Francesca smirked.

Hyacinth kicked her, nearly upsetting the tea service in the process.

"Hyacinth!" Lady Bridgerton scolded.

Sophie stared at the door, trying desperately to keep her eyes focused on anything but Benedict. She'd spent all week hoping for a glimpse, but now that he was here, all she wanted was to escape. If she looked at his face, her eyes inevitably strayed to his lips. And if she looked at his lips, her thoughts immediately went to their kiss. And if she thought about the kiss . . .

"I need that thimble," she blurted out, jumping to her feet. There were some things one just shouldn't think about in public.

"So you said," Benedict murmured, one of his eyebrows quirking up into a perfect—and perfectly arrogant—arch.

"It's downstairs," she muttered. "In my room."

"But your room is upstairs," Hyacinth said.

Sophie could have killed her. "That's what I said," she ground out.

"No," Hyacinth said in a matter-of-fact tone, "you didn't."

"Yes," Lady Bridgerton said, "she did. I heard her."

Sophie twisted her head sharply to look at Lady Bridgerton and knew in an instant that the older woman had lied. "I have to get that thimble," she said, for what seemed like the thirtieth time. She hurried toward the doorway, gulping as she grew close to Benedict.

"Wouldn't want you to hurt yourself," he said, stepping

aside to allow her through the doorway. But as she brushed past him, he leaned forward, whispering, "Coward."

Sophie's cheeks burned, and she was halfway down the stairs before she realized that she'd meant to go back to her room. Dash it all, she didn't want to march back up the stairs and have to walk past Benedict again. He was probably still standing in the doorway, and his lips would tilt upward as she passed—one of those faintly mocking, faintly seductive smiles that never failed to leave her breathless.

This was a disaster. There was no way she was going to be able to stay here. How could she remain with Lady Bridgerton, when every glimpse of Benedict turned her knees to water? She just wasn't strong enough. He was going to wear her down, make her forget all of her principles, all of her vows. She was going to have to leave. There was no other option.

And that was really too bad, because she *liked* working for the Bridgerton sisters. They treated her like a human being, not like some barely paid workhorse. They asked her questions and seemed to care about her answers.

Sophie knew she wasn't one of them, would never be one of them, but they made it so easy to pretend. And in all truth, all that Sophie had ever really wanted out of life was a family.

With the Bridgertons, she could almost pretend that she had one.

"Lost your way?"

Sophie looked up to see Benedict at the top of the stairs, leaning lazily against the wall. She looked down and realized that she was still standing on the stairs. "I'm going out," she said.

"To buy a thimble?"

"Yes," she said defiantly.

"Don't you need money?"

She could lie, and say that she had money in her pocket, or she could tell the truth, and show herself for the pathetic fool she was. Or she could just run down the stairs and out of the house. It was the cowardly thing to do, but . . .

"I have to go," she muttered, and dashed away so quickly that she completely forgot she ought to be using the servants' entrance. She skidded across the foyer and pushed open the heavy door, stumbling her way down the front steps. When her feet hit the pavement, she turned north, not for any particular reason, just because she had to go somewhere, and then she heard a voice.

An awful, horrible, terrible voice.

Dear God, it was Araminta.

Sophie's heart stopped, and she quickly pressed herself back against the wall. Araminta was facing the street, and unless she turned around, she'd never notice Sophie.

At least it was easy to remain silent when one couldn't even breathe.

What was she doing here? Penwood House was at least eight blocks away, closer to—

Then Sophie remembered. She'd read it in *Whistledown* last year, one of the few copies she'd been able to get her hands on while she was working for the Cavenders. The new Earl of Penwood had finally decided to take up residence in London. Araminta, Rosamund, and Posy had been forced to find new accommodations.

Next door to the Bridgertons? Sophie couldn't have imagined a worse nightmare if she tried.

"Where is that insufferable girl?" she heard Araminta said.

Sophie immediately felt sorry for the girl in question. As Araminta's former "insufferable girl," she knew that the position came with few benefits.

"Posy!" Araminta yelled, then marched into a waiting carriage.

Sophie chewed on her lip, her heart sinking. In that moment, she knew exactly what must have happened when she left. Araminta would have hired a new maid, and she was probably just beastly to the poor girl, but she wouldn't have been able to degrade and demean her in quite the same fashion she'd done with Sophie. You had to know a person, really hate them, to be so cruel. Any old servant wouldn't do.

And since Araminta had to put someone down—she didn't know how to feel good about herself without making someone else feel bad—she'd obviously chosen Posy as her whipping boy—or girl, as the case might be.

Posy came dashing out the door, her face pinched and drawn. She looked unhappy, and perhaps a bit heavier than she had been two years earlier. Araminta wouldn't like that, Sophie thought glumly. She'd never been able to accept that Posy wasn't petite and blond and beautiful like Rosamund and herself. If Sophie had been Araminta's nemesis, then Posy had always been her disappointment.

Sophie watched as Posy stopped at the top of the steps, then reached down to fiddle with the laces of her short boots. Rosamund poked her head out of the carriage, yelling, "Posy!" in what Sophie thought was a rather unattractively shrill voice.

Sophie ducked back, turning her head away. She was right in Rosamund's line of sight.

"I'm coming!" Posy called out.

"Hurry up!" Rosamund snapped.

Posy finished tying her laces, then hurried forward, but her foot slipped on the final step, and a moment later she was sprawled on the pavement. Sophie lurched forward, instinctively moving to help Posy, but she jammed herself back against the wall. Posy was unhurt, and there was nothing in life Sophie wanted less than for Araminta to know that she was in London, practically right next door.

Posy picked herself off the pavement, stopping to stretch her neck, first to the right, then to the left, then . . .

Then she saw her. Sophie was sure of it. Posy's eyes widened, and her mouth fell open slightly. Then her lips came together, pursed to make the "S" to begin "Sophie?"

Sophie shook her head frantically.

"Posy!" came Araminta's irate cry.

Sophie shook her head again, her eyes begging, pleading with Posy not to give her away.

"I'm coming, Mother!" Posy called. She gave Sophie a single short nod, then climbed up into the carriage, which thankfully rolled off in the opposite direction.

Sophie sagged against the building. She didn't move for a full minute.

And then she didn't move for another five.

Benedict didn't mean to take anything away from his mother and sisters, but once Sophie ran out of the upstairs sitting room, he lost his interest in tea and scones.

"I was just wondering where you'd been," Eloise was saying.

"Hmmm?" He craned his head slightly to the right, wondering how much of the streetscape he could see through the window from this angle.

"I said," Eloise practically hollered, "I was just wondering—"

"Eloise, lower your voice," Lady Bridgerton interjected.

"But he's not listening."

"If he's not listening," Lady Bridgerton said, "then shouting isn't going to get his attention."

"Throwing a scone might work," Hyacinth suggested.

"Hyacinth, don't you da—"

But Hyacinth had already lobbed the scone. Benedict ducked out of the way, barely a second before it would have bounced off the side of his head. He looked first to the wall, which now bore a slight smudge where the scone had hit, then to the floor, where it had landed, remarkably in one piece.

"I believe that is my cue to leave," he said smoothly, shooting a cheeky smile at his youngest sister. Her airborne scone had given him just the excuse he needed to duck out of the room and see if he couldn't trail Sophie to wherever it was she thought she was going.

"But you just got here," his mother pointed out.

Benedict immediately regarded her with suspicion. Unlike her usual moans of "But you just got here," she didn't sound the least bit upset at his leaving.

Which meant she was up to something.

"I could stay," he said, just to test her.

"Oh, no," she said, lifting her teacup to her lips even though he was fairly certain it was empty. "Don't let us keep you if you're busy."

Benedict fought to school his features into an impassive expression, or at least to hide his shock. The last time he'd informed his mother that he was "busy," she'd answered with, "Too busy for your mother?"

His first urge was to declare, "I'll stay," and park himself in a chair, but he had just enough presence of mind to realize that staying to thwart his mother was rather ridiculous when what he really wanted to do was leave. "I'll go, then," he said slowly, backing toward the door.

"Go," she said, shooing him away. "Enjoy yourself."

Benedict decided to leave the room before she managed to befuddle him any further. He reached down and scooped up the scone, gently tossing it to Hyacinth, who caught it with a grin. He then nodded at his mother and sisters and headed out into the hall, reaching the stairs just as he heard his mother say, "I thought he'd never leave."

Very odd, indeed.

With long, easy strides, he made his way down the steps and out the front door. He doubted that Sophie would still be near the house, but if she'd gone shopping, there was really only one direction in which she would have headed. He turned right, intending to stroll until he reached the small row of shops, but he'd only gone three steps before he saw

Sophie, pressed up against the brick exterior of his mother's house, looking as if she could barely remember how to breathe.

"Sophie?" Benedict rushed toward her. "What happened? Are you all right?"

She started when she saw him, then nodded.

He didn't believe her, of course, but there seemed little point in saying so. "You're shaking," he said, looking at her hands. "Tell me what happened. Did someone bother you?"

"No," she said, her voice uncharacteristically quavery. "I just . . . I, ah . . ." Her gaze fell on the stairs next to them. "I tripped on my way down the stairs and it scared me." She smiled weakly. "I'm sure you know what I mean. When you feel as if your insides have flipped upside down."

Benedict nodded, because of course he knew what she meant. But that didn't mean that he believed her. "Come with me," he said.

She looked up, and something in the green depths of her eyes broke his heart. "Where?" she whispered.

"Anywhere but here."

"I—"

"I live just five houses down," he said.

"You do?" Her eyes widened, then she murmured, "No one told me."

"I promise that your virtue will be safe," he interrupted. And then he added, because he couldn't quite help himself: "Unless *you* want it otherwise."

He had a feeling she would have protested if she weren't so dazed, but she allowed him to lead her down the street. "We'll just sit in my front room," he said, "until you feel better."

She nodded, and he led her up the steps and into his home, a modest town house just a bit south of his mother's.

Once they were comfortably ensconced, and Benedict had shut the door so that they wouldn't be bothered by any of his servants, he turned to her, prepared to say, "Now, why don't you tell me what really happened," but at the very last minute something compelled him to hold his tongue. He could ask, but he knew she wouldn't answer. She'd be put on the defensive, and that wasn't likely to help his cause any.

So instead, he schooled his face into a neutral mask and asked, "How are you enjoying your work for my family?"

"They are very nice," she replied.

"Nice?" he echoed, sure that his disbelief showed clearly on his face. "Maddening, perhaps. Maybe even exhausting, but nice?"

"I think they are very nice," Sophie said firmly.

Benedict started to smile, because he loved his family dearly, and he loved that Sophie was growing to love them, but then he realized that he was cutting off his nose to spite his face, because the more attached Sophie became to his family, the less likely she was to potentially shame herself in their eyes by agreeing to be his mistress.

Damn. He'd made a serious miscalculation last week. But he'd been so focused on getting her to come to London, and a position in his mother's household had seemed the only way to convince her to do it.

That, combined with a fair bit of coercion.

Damn. Damn. Damn. Why hadn't he coerced her into something that would segue a little more easily into his arms?

"You should thank your lucky stars that you have them," Sophie said, her voice more forceful than it had been all afternoon. "I'd give anything for—"

But she didn't finish her sentence.

"You'd give anything for what?" Benedict asked, surprised by how much he wanted to hear her answer.

She gazed soulfully out the window as she replied, "To have a family like yours."

"You have no one," he said, his words a statement, not a question.

"I've never had anyone."

"Not even your—" And then he remembered that she'd slipped and told him that her mother had died at her birth. "Sometimes," he said, keeping his voice purposefully light and gentle, "it's not so easy being a Bridgerton."

Her head slowly turned around. "I can't imagine anything nicer."

"There isn't anything nicer," he replied, "but that doesn't mean it's always easy."

"What do you mean?"

And Benedict found himself giving voice to feelings he'd never shared with any other living soul, not even—no, especially not his family. "To most of the world," he said, "I'm merely a Bridgerton. I'm not Benedict or Ben or even a gentleman of means and hopefully a bit of intelligence. I'm merely"—he smiled ruefully—"a Bridgerton. Specifically, Number Two."

Her lips trembled, then they smiled. "You're much more than that," she said.

"I'd like to think so, but most of the world doesn't see it that way."

"Most of the world are fools."

He laughed at that. There was nothing more fetching than Sophie with a scowl. "You will not find disagreement here," he said.

But then, just when he thought the conversation was over, she surprised him by saying, "You're nothing like the rest of your family."

"How so?" he asked, not quite meeting her gaze. He didn't want her to see just how important her reply was to him.

"Well, your brother Anthony . . ." Her face scrunched in thought. "His whole life has been altered by the fact that he's the eldest. He quite obviously feels a responsibility to your family that you do not."

"Now wait just one—"

"Don't interrupt," she said, placing a calming hand on his

chest. "I didn't say that you didn't love your family, or that you wouldn't give your life for any one of them. But it's different with your brother. He feels responsible, and I truly believe he would consider himself a failure if any of his siblings were unhappy."

"How many times have you met Anthony?" he muttered.

"Just once." The corners of her mouth tightened, as if she were suppressing a smile. "But that was all I needed. As for your younger brother, Colin . . . well, I haven't met him, but I've heard plenty—"

"From whom?"

"Everyone," she said. "Not to mention that he is forever being mentioned in *Whistledown*, which I must confess I've read for years."

"Then you knew about me before you met me," he said.

She nodded. "But I didn't *know* you. You're much more than Lady Whistledown realizes."

"Tell me," he said, placing his hand over hers. "What do you see?"

Sophie brought her eyes to his, gazed into those chocolatey depths, and saw something there she'd never dreamed existed. A tiny spark of vulnerability, of need.

He needed to know what she thought of him, that he was important to her. This man, so self-assured and so confident, needed her approval.

Maybe he needed *her*.

She curled her hand until their palms touched, then used her other index finger to trace circles and swirls on the fine kid of his glove. "You are . . ." she began, taking her time because she knew that every word weighed heavier in such a powerful moment. "You are not quite the man you present to the rest of the world. You'd like to be thought of as debonair and ironic and full of quick wit, and you *are* all those things, but underneath, you're so much more.

"You care," she said, aware that her voice had grown

raspy with emotion. "You care about your family, and you even care about me, although God knows I don't always deserve it."

"Always," he interrupted, raising her hand to his lips and kissing her palm with a fervency that sucked her breath away. "Always."

"And . . . and . . ." It was hard to continue when his eyes were on hers with such single-minded emotion.

"And what?" he whispered.

"Much of who you are comes from your family," she said, the words tumbling forth in a rush. "That much is true. You can't grow up with such love and loyalty and not become a better person because of it. But deep within you, in your heart, in your very soul, is the man you were born to be. *You*, not someone's son, not someone's brother. Just you."

Benedict watched her intently. He opened his mouth to speak, but he discovered that he had no words. There *were* no words for a moment like this.

"Deep inside," she murmured, "you've the soul of an artist."

"No," he said, shaking his head.

"Yes," she insisted. "I've seen your sketches. You're brilliant. I don't think I knew how much until I met your family. You captured them all perfectly, from the sly look in Francesca's smile to the mischief in the very way Hyacinth holds her shoulders."

"I've never shown anyone else my sketches," he admitted.

Her head snapped up. "You can't be serious."

He shook his head. "I haven't."

"But they're brilliant. *You're* brilliant. I'm sure your mother would love to see them."

"I don't know why," he said, feeling sheepish, "but I never wanted to share them."

"You shared them with me," she said softly.

"Somehow," he said, touching his fingers to her chin, "it felt right."

And then his heart skipped a beat, because all of a sudden *everything* felt right.

He loved her. He didn't know how it had happened, only that it was true.

It wasn't just that she was convenient. There had been lots of convenient women. Sophie was different. She made him laugh. She made him want to make *her* laugh. And when he was with her—Well, when he was with her he wanted her like hell, but during those few moments when his body managed to keep itself in check . . .

He was content.

It was strange, to find a woman who could make him happy just with her mere presence. He didn't even have to see her, or hear her voice, or even smell her scent. He just had to know that she was there.

If that wasn't love, he didn't know what was.

He stared down at her, trying to prolong the moment, to hold on to these few moments of complete perfection. Something softened in her eyes, and the color seemed to melt right then and there, from a shiny, glowing emerald to a soft and lilting moss. Her lips parted and softened, and he knew that he had to kiss her. Not that he wanted to, that he had to.

He needed her next to him, below him, on top of him.

He needed her in him, around him, a part of him.

He needed her the way he needed air.

And, he thought in that last rational moment before his lips found hers, he needed her right now.

Chapter 17

This Author has it on the finest authority that two days ago, whilst taking tea at Gunter's, Lady Penwood was hit on the side of her head with a flying biscuit.

This Author is unable to determine who threw the biscuit, but all suspicions point to the establishment's youngest patrons, Miss Felicity Featherington and Miss Hyacinth Bridgerton.

LADY WHISTLEDOWN'S SOCIETY PAPERS, 21 MAY 1817

Sophie had been kissed before—she had been kissed by Benedict before—but nothing, not a single moment of a single kiss, prepared her for this.

It wasn't a kiss. It was heaven.

He kissed her with an intensity she could barely comprehend, his lips teasing hers, stroking, nibbling, caressing. He stoked a fire within her, a desire to be loved, a need to love in return. And God help her, when he kissed her, all she wanted to do was kiss him back.

She heard him murmuring her name, but it barely registered over the roaring in her ears. This was desire. This was need. How foolish of her ever to think that she could deny this. How self-important to think that she could be stronger than passion.

"Sophie, Sophie," he said, over and over, his lips on her cheek, her neck, her ear. He said her name so many times it seemed to soak into her skin.

She felt his hands on the buttons of her dress, could feel the fabric loosening as each slipped through its buttonhole. This was everything she'd always sworn she would never do, and yet when her bodice tumbled to her waist, leaving her shamelessly exposed, she groaned his name and arched her back, offering herself to him like some sort of forbidden fruit.

Benedict stopped breathing when he saw her. He'd pictured this moment in his mind so many times—every night as he lay in bed, and in every dream when he actually slept. But this—reality—was far sweeter than a dream, and far more erotic.

His hand, which had been stroking the warm skin on her back, slowly slid over her rib cage. "You're so beautiful," he whispered, knowing that the words were hopelessly inadequate. As if mere words could describe what he felt. And then, when his trembling fingers finished their journey and cupped her breast, he let out a shuddering groan. Words were impossible now. His need for her was so intense, so primitive. It robbed him of his ability to speak. Hell, he could barely think.

He wasn't certain how this woman had come to mean so much to him. It seemed that one day she was a stranger, and the next she was as indispensable as air. And yet it hadn't happened in a blinding flash. It had been a slow, sneaky process, quietly coloring his emotions until he realized that without her, his life lacked all meaning.

He touched her chin, lifting her face until he could peer into her eyes. They seemed to glow from within, glistening with unshed tears. Her lips were trembling, too, and he knew that she was as affected by the moment as he.

He leaned forward . . . slowly, slowly. He wanted to give her the chance to say no. It would kill him if she did, but it would be far worse to listen to her regrets in the proverbial morning.

But she didn't say no, and when he was but a few inches away, her eyes closed and her head tilted slightly to the side, silently inviting him to kiss her.

It was remarkable, but every time he kissed her, her lips seemed to grow sweeter, her scent more beguiling. And his need grew, too. His blood was racing with desire, and it was taking his every last shred of restraint not to push her back onto the sofa and tear her clothes from her body.

That would come later, he thought with a secret smile. But this—surely her first time—would be slow and tender and everything a young girl dreamed.

Well, maybe not. His smile turned into an outright grin. Half the things he was going to do to her, she wouldn't have even *thought* to dream about.

"What are you smiling about?" she asked.

He drew back a few inches, cupping her face with both hands. "How did you know I was smiling?"

"I could feel it on my lips."

He brought a finger to those lips, tracing the outline, then running the edge of his fingernail along the plump skin. "You make me smile," he whispered. "When you don't make me want to scream, you make me smile."

Her lips trembled, and her breath was hot and moist against his finger. He took her hand and brought it to his mouth, rubbing one finger against his lips in much the same way he had done with hers. But as he watched her eyes widen, he dipped her finger into his mouth, softly sucking at the fingertip, tickling her skin with his teeth and tongue.

She gasped, and the sound was sweet and erotic at the same time.

There were a thousand things that Benedict wanted to ask her— How did she feel? What did she feel? But he was so damned afraid that she'd change her mind if he gave her the opportunity to put any of her thoughts into words. And so instead of questions, he gave her kisses, returning his lips to hers in a searing, barely controlled dance of desire.

He murmured her name like a benediction as he lowered her onto the sofa, her bare back rubbing up against the upholstery. "I want you," he groaned. "You have no idea. No idea."

Her only response was a soft mewling sound that came from deep in her throat. For some reason that was like oil on the fire within him, and his fingers clutched at her even tighter, pressing into her skin, as his lips traveled down the swanlike column of her throat.

He moved lower, lower, burning a hot trail on her skin, pausing only briefly when he reached the gentle swell of her breast. She was completely beneath him now, her eyes glazed with desire, and it was so much better than any of his dreams.

And oh, how he'd dreamed of her.

With a low, possessive growl, Benedict took her nipple into his mouth. She let out a soft squeal, and he was unable to suppress his own low rumble of satisfaction. "Shhh," he crooned, "just let me—"

"But—"

He pressed one of his fingers against her lips, probably a little too roughly, but it was getting harder and harder to control his movements. "Don't think," he murmured. "Just lie back and let me pleasure you."

She looked dubious, but when he moved his mouth to her other breast and renewed his sensual onslaught, her eyes grew dazed, her lips parted, and her head lolled back against the cushions.

"Do you like this?" he whispered, tracing the peak of her breast with his tongue.

Sophie couldn't quite manage to open her eyes, but she nodded.

"Do you like this?" Now his tongue moved to the underside of her breast, and he nibbled the sensitive skin over her rib cage.

Her breath shallow and fast, she nodded again.

"What about this?" He pushed her dress further down, nibbling a trail along her skin until he reached her navel.

This time Sophie couldn't even manage a nod. Dear God, she was practically naked before him, and all she could do was moan and sigh and beg for more.

"I need you," she panted.

His words were murmured into the soft skin of her abdomen. "I know."

Sophie squirmed beneath him, unnerved by this primitive need to move. Something very strange was growing within her, something hot and tingling. It was as if she were growing, getting ready to burst through her skin. It was as if, after twenty-two years of life, she were finally coming alive.

She wanted desperately to feel his skin, and she grabbed at the fine linen of his shirt, bunching it in her hands until it came loose of his breeches. She touched him, skimming her hands along his lower back, surprised and delighted when his muscles quivered beneath her fingers.

"Ah, Sophie," he grunted, shuddering as her hands slipped under his shirt to caress his skin.

His reaction emboldened her, and she stroked him more, moving up until she reached his shoulders, broad and firmly muscled.

He groaned again, then cursed under his breath as he lifted himself off of her. "Damn thing is in the way," he muttered, tearing the shirt off and flinging it across the room. Sophie had just an instant to stare at his bare chest before he was atop her again, and this time they were skin against skin.

It was the most glorious feeling she could ever imagine.

He was so warm, and even though his muscles were hard and powerful, his skin was seductively soft. He even smelled good, a warm masculine mixture of sandalwood and soap.

Sophie touched her fingers to his hair as he moved to nuzzle her neck. It was thick and springy, and it tickled her chin as he tickled her neck. "Oh, Benedict," she sighed. "This is so perfect. I can't imagine anything better."

He looked up, his dark eyes as wicked as his smile. "I can."

She felt her lips part and knew she must look terribly foolish, just lying there staring at him like an idiot.

"Just you wait," he said. "Just you wait."

"But— Oh!" She let out a squeal as he flipped off her shoes. One of his hands wrapped around her ankle, then teased its way up her leg.

"Did you imagine this?" he asked, tracing the crease at the back of her knee.

She shook her head frantically, trying not to squirm.

"Really?" he murmured. "Then I'm sure you didn't imagine *this*." He reached up and unsnapped her garters.

"Oh, Benedict, you mustn't—"

"Oh, no, I *must*." He slid her stockings down her legs with agonizing slowness. "I really must."

Sophie watched with openmouthed delight as he tossed them over his head. Her stockings weren't of the highest quality, but they were nonetheless fairly light, and they floated through the air like dandelion tufts until they landed, one on a lamp and the other on the floor.

Then, while she was still laughing and looking at the stocking, hanging drunkenly from the lampshade, he sneaked up on her, sliding his hands back up her legs until they reached all the way to her thighs.

"I daresay no one has ever touched you here," he said wickedly.

Sophie shook her head.

"And I daresay you never imagined it."

She shook her head again.

"If you didn't imagine this . . ." He squeezed her thighs, causing her to squeal and arch off the sofa. ". . . then I'm sure you won't have imagined *this*." He trailed his fingers ever upward as he spoke, the rounded curves of his nails lightly grazing her skin until he reached the soft thatch of her womanhood.

"Oh, no," she said, more out of reflex than anything else. "You can't—"

"Oh, but I can. I assure you."

"But— Ooooooh." It was suddenly as if her brain had flown right out the window, because it was near impossible to think of anything while his fingers were tickling her. Well, almost anything. She seemed able to think about how utterly naughty this was and how very much she didn't want him to stop.

"What are you doing to me?" she gasped, her every muscle tightening as he moved his fingers in a particularly wicked manner.

"Everything," he returned, capturing her lips with his. "Anything you want."

"I want— Oh!"

"Like that, do you?" His words were murmured against her cheek.

"I don't know what I want," she breathed.

"I do." He moved to her ear, nibbling softly on her lobe. "I know exactly what you want. Trust me."

And it was as easy as that. She gave herself over to him completely—not that she hadn't been nearly to that point already. But when he said, "Trust me," and she realized that she did, something changed slightly inside. She was ready for this. It was still wrong, but she was ready, and she wanted it, and for once in her life she was going to do something wild and crazy and completely out of character.

Just because she wanted to.

As if he'd read her thoughts, he pulled away a few inches and cupped one cheek with his large hand. "If you want me to stop," he said, his voice achingly hoarse, "you need to tell me now. Not in ten minutes, not even in one. It has to be now."

Touched that he would even take the time to ask, she reached up and cupped his cheek in the same way he held hers. But when she opened her mouth to speak, the only word she could manage was, "Please."

His eyes flared with need, and then, as if something snapped within him, he changed in an instant. Gone was the gentle, languorous lover. In his place was a man gripped by desire. His hands were everywhere, on her legs, around her waist, touching her face. And before Sophie knew it, her dress was gone, on the floor next to one of her stockings. She was completely nude, and it felt very odd but somehow also very right as long as he was touching her.

The sofa was narrow, but that didn't seem to matter as Benedict yanked off his boots and breeches. He perched alongside her as his boots went flying, unable to stop touching her, even as he divested himself of his clothing. It took longer to get naked, but on the other hand, he had the oddest notion that he might perish on the spot if he moved from her side.

He'd thought he'd wanted a woman before. He'd thought he'd needed one. But this—this went beyond both. This was spiritual. This was in his soul.

His clothes finally gone, he lay back on top of her, pausing for one shuddering moment to savor the feel of her beneath him, skin to skin, head to toe. He was hard as a rock, harder than he could ever remember, but he fought against his impulses, and tried to move slowly.

This was her first time. It had to be perfect.

Or if not perfect, then damn good.

He snaked a hand between them and touched her. She was ready—more than ready for him. He slipped one finger inside of her, grinning with satisfaction as her entire body jerked and tensed around him.

"That's very—" Her voice was raspy, her breathing labored. "Very—"

"Strange?" he finished for her.

She nodded.

He smiled. Slowly, like a cat. "You'll get used to it," he promised. "I plan to get you very used to it."

Sophie's head lolled back. This was madness. Fever. Something was building inside of her, deep in her gut, coiling, pulsing, making her rigid. It was something that needed release, something that grabbed at her, and yet even with all this pressure, it felt so spectacularly wonderful, as if she'd been born for this very moment.

"Oh, Benedict," she sighed. "Oh, my love."

He froze—just for a fraction of a second, but it was long enough for her to know that he'd heard her. But he didn't say a word, just kissed her neck and squeezed her leg as he positioned himself between her thighs and nudged at her entrance.

Her lips parted with shock.

"Don't worry," he said in an amused voice, reading her mind as always. "It will work."

"But—"

"Trust me," he said, the words murmured against her lips.

Slowly, she felt him entering her. She was being stretched, invaded, and yet she wouldn't say it felt bad, exactly. It was . . . It was . . .

He touched her cheek. "You look serious."

"I'm trying to decide how this feels," she admitted.

"If you have the presence of mind to do that, then I'm certainly not doing a good enough job."

Startled, she looked up. He was smiling at her, that crooked grin that never failed to reduce her to mush.

"Stop thinking so hard," he whispered.

"But it's difficult not to— Oh!" And then her eyes rolled back as she arched beneath him.

Benedict buried his head in her neck so she wouldn't see

his amused expression. It seemed the best way for him to keep her from overanalyzing a moment that should have been pure sensation and emotion was for him to keep moving.

And he did. Inexorably forward, sliding in and out until he reached the fragile barrier of her maidenhead.

He winced. He'd never been with a virgin before. He'd heard it hurt, that there was nothing a man could do to eliminate the pain for the woman, but surely if he was gentle, it would go easier for her.

He looked down. Her face was flushed, and her breath was rapid. Her eyes were glazed, dazed, clearly rapt with passion.

It fueled his own fire. God, he wanted her so badly his bones ached.

"This might hurt," he lied. It *would* hurt. But he was stuck between wanting to give her the truth so that she would be prepared and giving her the softer version so that she would not be nervous.

"I don't care," she gasped. "Please. I need you."

Benedict leaned down for one final, searing kiss as his hips surged forward. He felt her stiffen slightly around him as he broke through her maidenhead, and he bit—he actually *bit* his hand to keep himself from coming at that very second.

It was like he was a green lad of sixteen, not an experienced man of thirty.

She did this to him. Only her. It was a humbling thought.

Gritting his teeth against his baser urges, Benedict began to move within her, slowly stroking when what he really wanted to do was let go completely.

"Sophie, Sophie," he grunted, repeating her name, trying to remind himself that this time was about *her*. He was here to please *her* needs, not his own.

It would be perfect. It had to be perfect. He needed her to love this. He needed her to love *him*.

She was quickening beneath him, and every wiggle, every squirm whipped up his own frenzy of desire. He was trying to be extra gentle for her, but she was making it so damn hard to hold back. Her hands were everywhere—on his hips, on his back, squeezing his shoulders.

"Sophie," he moaned again. He couldn't hold off much longer. He wasn't strong enough. He wasn't noble enough. He wasn't—

"Ohhhhhhhhhhhh!"

She convulsed beneath him, her body arching off the sofa as she screamed. Her fingers bit into his back, nails raking his skin, but he didn't care. All he knew was that she'd found her release, and it was good, and for the love of God, he could finally—

"Ahhhhhhhhhhhh!"

He exploded. There was simply no other word for it.

He couldn't stop moving, couldn't stop shaking, and then, in an instant, he collapsed, dimly aware that he was probably crushing her, but unable to move a single muscle.

He should say something, tell her something about how wonderful it had been. But his tongue felt thick and his lips felt heavy, and on top of all that, he could barely open his eyes. Pretty words would have to wait. He was only a man, and he had to catch his breath.

"Benedict?" she whispered.

He flopped his hand slightly against her. It was the only thing he could manage to indicate that he'd heard.

"Is it always like this?"

He shook his head, hoping that she'd feel the motion and know what it meant.

She sighed and seemed to sink deeper into the cushions. "I didn't think so."

Benedict kissed the side of her head, which was all that he could reach. No, it wasn't always like this. He'd dreamed of her so many times, but this . . . This . . .

This was more than dreams.

* * *

Sophie wouldn't have thought it possible, but she must've dozed off, even with the thrilling weight of Benedict pressing her down against the sofa, making it slightly difficult to breathe. He must've fallen asleep, too, and she woke when he woke, aroused by the sudden rush of cool air when he lifted himself off of her body.

He placed a blanket on top of her before she even had a chance to be embarrassed by her nakedness. She smiled even as she blushed, for there was little that could be done to ease her embarrassment. Not that she regretted her actions. But a woman didn't lose her virginity on a sofa and not feel a little bit embarrassed. It simply wasn't possible.

Still, the blanket had been a thoughtful gesture. Not a surprising one, though. Benedict was a thoughtful man.

He obviously didn't share her modesty, though, because he made no attempt to cover himself as he crossed the room and gathered his carelessly flung garments. Sophie stared shamelessly as he pulled on his breeches. He stood straight and proud, and the smile he gave her when he caught her watching was warm and direct.

God, how she loved this man.

"How do you feel?" he asked.

"Fine," she answered. "Good." She smiled shyly. "Splendid."

He picked up his shirt and stuck one arm into it. "I'll send someone over to collect your belongings."

Sophie blinked. "What do you mean?"

"Don't worry, I'll make sure he's discreet. I know it might be embarrassing for you now that you know my family."

Sophie clutched the blanket to her, wishing that her dress wasn't out of reach. Because she suddenly felt ashamed. She'd done the one thing she'd always sworn she would never do, and now Benedict assumed she would be his mistress. And why shouldn't he? It was a fairly natural assumption.

"Please don't send anyone over," she said, her voice small.

He glanced at her in surprise. "You'd rather go yourself?"

"I'd rather my things stayed where they were," she said softly. It was so much easier saying that than telling him directly that she would not become his mistress.

Once, she could forgive. Once, she could even cherish. But a lifetime with a man who was not her husband—that she knew she could not do.

Sophie looked down at her belly, praying that there would be no child to be brought into the world illegitimately.

"What are you telling me?" he said, his eyes intent upon her face.

Damn. He wasn't going to allow her to take the easy way out. "I'm saying," she said, gulping against the boulder-sized lump that had suddenly developed in her throat, "that I cannot be your mistress."

"What do you call this?" he asked in a tight voice, waving his arm at her.

"I call it a lapse in judgment," she said, not meeting his eyes.

"Oh, so I'm a lapse?" he said, his tone unnaturally pleasant. "How nice. I don't believe I've ever been someone's lapse before."

"You know that's not the way I meant it."

"Do I?" He grabbed one of his boots and perched on the arm of a chair so that he could yank it on. "Frankly, my dear, I have no idea what you mean anymore."

"I shouldn't have done this—"

He whipped his head around to face her, his hot, flashing eyes at odds with his bland smile. "Now I'm a *shouldn't?* Excellent. Even better than a lapse. Shouldn't sounds much naughtier, don't you think? A lapse is merely a mistake."

"There is no need to be so ugly about this."

He cocked his head to the side as if he were truly considering her words. "Is that what I'm being? I rather thought

I was acting in a most friendly and understanding manner. Look, no yelling, no histrionics . . ."

"I'd prefer yelling and histrionics to *this*."

He scooped up her dress and threw it at her, none too gently. "Well, we don't always get what we prefer, do we, Miss Beckett? I can certainly attest to that."

She grabbed her dress and stuffed it under the covers with her, hoping that she'd eventually find a way to don it without moving the blanket.

"It'll be a neat trick if you figure out how to do it," he said, giving her a condescending glance.

She glared at him. "I'm not asking you to apologize."

"Well, that's a relief. I doubt I could find the words."

"Please don't be so sarcastic."

His smile was mocking in the extreme. "You're hardly in a position to ask me anything."

"Benedict . . ."

He loomed over her, leering rudely. "Except, of course, to rejoin you, which I'd gladly do."

She said nothing.

"Do you understand," he said, his eyes softening slightly, "what it feels like to be pushed away? How many times do you expect you can reject me before I stop trying?"

"It's not that I want to—"

"Oh, stop with that old excuse. It's grown tired. If you wanted to be with me, you would be with me. When you say no, it's because you want to say no."

"You don't understand," she said in a low voice. "You've always been in a position where you could do what you wanted. Some of us don't have that luxury."

"Silly me. I thought I was offering you that very luxury."

"The luxury to be your mistress," she said bitterly.

He crossed his arms, his lips twisting as he said, "You won't have to do anything you haven't already done."

"I got carried away," Sophie said slowly, trying to ignore his insult. It was no more than she deserved. She had slept with him. Why shouldn't he think she would be his mistress? "I made a mistake," she continued. "But that doesn't mean I should do it again."

"I can offer you a better life," he said in a low voice.

She shook her head. "I won't be your mistress. I won't be any man's mistress."

Benedict's lips parted with shock as he digested her words. "Sophie," he said incredulously, "you know I cannot *marry* you."

"Of course I know that," she snapped. "I'm a servant, not an idiot."

Benedict tried for a moment to put himself in her shoes. He knew she wanted respectability, but she had to know that he could not give it to her. "It would be hard for you as well," he said softly, "even if I were to marry you. You would not be accepted. The *ton* can be cruel."

Sophie let out a loud, hollow laugh. "I know," she said, her smile utterly humorless. "Believe me, I know."

"Then why—"

"Grant me a favor," she interrupted, turning her face so that she was no longer looking at him. "Find someone to marry. Find someone acceptable, who will make you happy. And then leave me alone."

Her words struck a chord, and Benedict was suddenly reminded of the lady from the masquerade. She had been of his world, his class. She would have been acceptable. And he realized, as he stood there, staring down at Sophie, who was huddled on the sofa, trying not to look at him, that she was the one he'd always pictured in his mind, whenever he thought to the future. Whenever he imagined himself with a wife and children.

He'd spent the last two years with one eye on every door, always waiting for his lady in silver to enter the room. He felt silly sometimes, even stupid, but he'd never been able to erase her from his thoughts.

Or purge the dream—the one in which he pledged his troth to her, and they lived happily ever after.

It was a silly fantasy for a man of his reputation, sickly sweet and sentimental, but he hadn't been able to help himself. That's what came from growing up in a large and loving family—one tended to want the same for oneself.

But the woman from the masquerade had become barely more than a mirage. Hell, he didn't even know her name. And Sophie was *here*.

He couldn't marry her, but that didn't mean they couldn't be together. It would mean compromise, mostly on her part, he admitted. But they could do it. And they'd certainly be happier than if they remained apart.

"Sophie," he began, "I know the situation is not ideal—"

"Don't," she interrupted, her voice low, barely audible.

"If you'd only listen—"

"*Please*. Don't."

"But you're not—"

"Stop!" she said, her voice rising perilously in volume.

She was holding her shoulders so tightly they were practically at her ears, but Benedict forged on, anyway. He loved her. He needed her. He had to make her see reason. "Sophie, I know you'll agree if—"

"I won't have an illegitimate child!" she finally yelled, struggling to keep the blanket around her as she rose to her feet. "I won't do it! I love you, but not that much. I don't love anyone that much."

His eyes fell to her midsection. "It may very well be too late for that, Sophie."

"I know," she said quietly, "and it's already eating me up inside."

"Regrets have a way of doing that."

She looked away. "I don't regret what we did. I wish I could. I know I should. But I can't."

Benedict just stared at her. He wanted to understand her,

but he just couldn't grasp how she could be so adamant about not wanting to be his mistress and have his children and at the same time *not* regret their lovemaking.

How could she say she loved him? It made the pain that much more intense.

"If we don't have a child," she said quietly, "then I shall consider myself very lucky. And I won't tempt the fates again."

"No, you'll merely tempt *me*," he said, hearing the sneer in his voice and hating it.

She ignored him, drawing the blanket closer around her as she stared sightlessly at a painting on the wall. "I'll have a memory I will forever cherish. And that, I suppose, is why I can't regret what we did."

"It won't keep you warm at night."

"No," she agreed sadly, "but it will keep my dreams full."

"You're a coward," he accused. "A coward for not chasing after those dreams."

She turned around. "No," she said, her voice remarkably even considering the way he was glaring at her. "What I am is a bastard. And before you say you don't care, let me assure you that I do. And so does everyone else. Not a day has gone by that I am not in some way reminded of the baseness of my birth."

"Sophie . . ."

"If I have a child," she said, her voice starting to crack, "do you know how much I would love it? More than life, more than breath, more than anything. How could I hurt my own child the way I've been hurt? How could I subject her to the same kind of pain?"

"Would you reject your child?"

"Of course not!"

"Then she wouldn't feel the same sort of pain," Benedict said with a shrug. "Because I wouldn't reject her either."

"You don't understand," she said, the words ending on a whimper.

He pretended he hadn't heard her. "Am I correct in assuming that *you* were rejected by your parents?"

Her smile was tight and ironic. "Not precisely. Ignored would be a better description."

"Sophie," he said, rushing toward her and gathering her in his arms, "you don't have to repeat the mistakes of your parents."

"I know," she said sadly, not struggling in his embrace, but not returning it either. "And that's why I cannot be your mistress. I won't relive my mother's life."

"You wouldn't—"

"They say that a smart person learns from her mistakes," she interrupted, her voice forcefully ending his protest. "But a truly smart person learns from other people's mistakes." She pulled away, then turned to face him. "I'd like to think I'm a truly smart person. Please don't take that away from me."

There was a desperate, almost palpable, pain in her eyes. It hit him in the chest, and he staggered back a step.

"I'd like to get dressed," she said, turning away. "I think you should leave."

He stared at her back for several seconds before saying, "I could make you change your mind. I could kiss you, and you would—"

"You wouldn't," she said, not moving a muscle. "It isn't in you."

"It *is*."

"You would kiss me, and then you would hate yourself. And it would only take a second."

He left without another word, letting the click of the door signal his departure.

Inside the room, Sophie's quivering hands dropped the blanket, and she crumpled onto the sofa, forever staining its delicate fabric with her tears.

Chapter 18

Pickings have been slim this past fortnight for marriage-minded misses and their mamas. The crop of bachelors is low to begin with this season, as two of 1816's most eligible, the Duke of Ashbourne and the Earl of Macclesfield, got themselves leg-shackled last year.

To make matters worse, the two unmarried Bridgerton brothers (discounting Gregory, who is only sixteen and hardly in a position to aid any poor, young misses on the marriage mart) have made themselves very scarce. Colin, This Author is told, is out of town, possibly in Wales or Scotland (although no one seems to know why he would go to Wales or Scotland in the middle of the season). Benedict's story is more puzzling. He is apparently in London, but he eschews all polite social gatherings in favor of less genteel milieus.

Although if truth be told, This Author should not give the impression that the aforementioned Mr. Bridgerton has been spending his every waking hour in debauched abandon. If accounts are correct, he has spent most of the past fortnight in his lodgings on Bruton Street.

As there have been no rumors that he is ill, This Author can only assume that he has finally come to the conclusion that the London season is utterly dull and not worth his time.

Smart man, indeed.

LADY WHISTLEDOWN'S SOCIETY PAPERS, 9 JUNE 1817

Sophie didn't see Benedict for a full fortnight. She didn't know whether to be pleased, surprised, or disappointed. She didn't know whether she *was* pleased, surprised, or disappointed.

She didn't know anything these days. Half the time she felt like she didn't even know herself.

She was certain that she had made the right decision in yet again refusing Benedict's offer. She knew it in her head, and even though she ached for the man she loved, she knew it in her heart. She had suffered too much pain from her bastardy ever to risk imposing the same on a child, especially one of her own.

No, that was not true. She had risked it once. And she couldn't quite make herself regret it. The memory was too precious. But that didn't mean she should do it again.

But if she was so certain that she'd done the right thing, why did it hurt so much? It was as if her heart were perpetually breaking. Every day, it tore some more, and every day, Sophie told herself that it could not get worse, that surely her heart was finished breaking, that it was finally well and fully broken, and yet every night she cried herself to sleep, aching for Benedict.

And every day she felt even worse.

Her tension was intensified by the fact that she was terrified to step outside the house. Posy would surely be looking for her, and Sophie thought it best if Posy didn't find her.

Not that she thought Posy was likely to reveal her presence here in London to Araminta; Sophie knew Posy well enough to trust that Posy would never deliberately break a promise. And Posy's nod when Sophie had been frantically shaking her head could definitely be considered a promise.

But as true of heart as Posy was when it came to keeping promises, the same could not, unfortunately, be said of her lips. And Sophie could easily imagine a scenario—many scenarios as a matter of fact—in which Posy would accidentally blurt out that she'd seen Sophie. Which meant that Sophie's one big advantage was that Posy didn't know where Sophie was staying. For all she knew, Sophie had just been out for a stroll. Or maybe Sophie had come to spy on Araminta.

In all truth, that seemed an awful lot more plausible than the truth, which was that Sophie just happened to have been blackmailed into taking a job as a lady's maid just down the street.

And so, Sophie's emotions kept darting back and forth from melancholy to nervous, brokenhearted to downright fearful.

She'd managed to keep most of this to herself, but she knew she had grown distracted and quiet, and she also knew that Lady Bridgerton and her daughters had noticed it. They looked at her with concerned expressions, spoke with an extra gentleness. And they kept wondering why she did not come to tea.

"Sophie! There you are!"

Sophie had been hurrying to her room, where a small pile of mending awaited, but Lady Bridgerton had caught her in the hall.

She stopped and tried to manage a smile of greeting as she bobbed a curtsy. "Good afternoon, Lady Bridgerton."

"Good afternoon, Sophie. I have been looking all over for you."

Sophie stared at her blankly. She seemed to do a lot of that lately. It was difficult to focus on anything. "You have?" she asked.

"Yes. I was wondering why you haven't been to tea all week. You know that you are always invited when we are taking it informally."

Sophie felt her cheeks grow warm. She'd been avoiding tea because it was just so hard to be in the same room with all those Bridgertons at once and not to think of Benedict.

They all looked so alike, and whenever they were together they were such a family.

It forced Sophie to remember everything that she didn't have, reminded her of what she'd never have: a family of her own.

Someone to love. Someone who'd love her. All within the bounds of respectability and marriage.

She supposed there were women who could throw over respectability for passion and love. A very large part of her wished she were one of those women. But she was not. Love could not conquer all. At least not for her.

"I've been very busy," she finally said to Lady Bridgerton.

Lady Bridgerton just smiled at her—a small, vaguely inquisitive smile, imposing a silence that forced Sophie to say more.

"With the mending," she added.

"How terrible for you. I wasn't aware that we'd poked holes in quite so many stockings."

"Oh, you haven't!" Sophie replied, biting her tongue the minute she said it. There went her excuse. "I have some mending of my own," she improvised, gulping as she realized how bad that sounded. Lady Bridgerton well knew that Sophie had no clothes other than the ones she had given her, which were all, needless to say, in perfect condition. And besides, it was very bad form for Sophie to be doing her own mending during the day, when she was meant to be waiting on the girls. Lady Bridgerton was an understanding employer; she probably wouldn't have minded, but it went against Sophie's own code of ethics. She'd been given a job—a good one, even if it did involve getting her heart broken on a day to day basis—and she took pride in her work.

"I see," Lady Bridgerton said, that enigmatic smile still in place on her face. "You may, of course, bring your own mending to tea."

"Oh, but I could not dream of it."

"But I am telling you that you *can*."

And Sophie could tell by the tone of her voice that what she was really saying was that she *must*.

"Of course," Sophie murmured, and followed her into the upstairs sitting room.

The girls were all there, in their usual places, bickering and smiling and tossing jokes (although thankfully no scones.) The eldest Bridgerton daughter, Daphne—now the Duchess of Hastings—was there as well, with her youngest daughter, Caroline, in her arms.

"Sophie!" Hyacinth said with a beam. "I thought you must have been ill."

"But you just saw me this morning," Sophie reminded her, "when I dressed your hair."

"Yes, but you didn't seem quite yourself."

Sophie had no suitable reply, since she really *hadn't* been quite herself. She couldn't very well contradict the truth. So she just sat in a chair and nodded when Francesca inquired if she wanted some tea.

"Penelope Featherington said she would drop by today," Eloise said to her mother just as Sophie was taking her first sip. Sophie had never met Penelope, but she was frequently written about in *Whistledown*, and she knew that she and Eloise were fast friends.

"Has anyone noticed that Benedict hasn't visited in some time?" Hyacinth asked.

Sophie jabbed her finger but thankfully managed to keep from yelping with pain.

"He hasn't been by to see Simon and me, either," Daphne said.

"Well, he told me he would help me with my arithmetic," Hyacinth grumbled, "and he has most certainly reneged on his word."

"I'm sure it has merely slipped his mind," Lady Bridgerton said diplomatically. "Perhaps if you sent him a note."

"Or simply banged on his door," Francesca said, giving her eyes a slight roll. "It's not as if he lives very far away."

"I am an unmarried female," Hyacinth said with a huff. "I cannot visit bachelor lodgings."

Sophie coughed.

"You're fourteen," Francesca said disdainfully.

"Nevertheless!"

"You should ask Simon for help, anyway," Daphne said. "He's much better with numbers than Benedict."

"You know, she's right," Hyacinth said, looking at her mother after shooting one last glare at Francesca. "Pity for Benedict. He's completely without use to me now."

They all giggled, because they knew she was joking. Except for Sophie, who didn't think she knew how to giggle anymore.

"But in all seriousness," Hyacinth continued, "what *is* he good at? Simon's better at numbers, and Anthony knows more of history. Colin's funnier, of course, and—"

"Art," Sophie interrupted in a sharp voice, a little irritated that Benedict's own family didn't see his individuality and strengths.

Hyacinth looked at her in surprise. "I beg your pardon?"

"He's good at art," Sophie repeated. "Quite a bit better than any of you, I imagine."

That got everyone's attention, because while Sophie had let them see her naturally dry wit, she was generally soft-spoken, and she certainly had never said a sharp word to any of them.

"I didn't even know he drew," Daphne said with quiet interest. "Or does he paint?"

Sophie glanced at her. Of the Bridgerton women, she knew Daphne the least, but it would have been impossible to miss the look of sharp intelligence in her eyes. Daphne was curious about her brother's hidden talent, she wanted to know why she didn't know about it, and most of all, she wanted to know why Sophie *did*.

In less than a second Sophie was able to see all of that in the young duchess's eyes. And in less than a second she decided that she'd made a mistake. If Benedict hadn't told his family about his art, then it wasn't her place to do so.

"He draws," she finally said, in a voice that she hoped was curt enough to prevent further questions.

It was. No one said a word, although five pairs of eyes remained focused quite intently on her face.

"He sketches," Sophie muttered.

She looked from face to face. Eloise's eyes were blinking rapidly. Lady Bridgerton wasn't blinking at all. "He's quite good," Sophie muttered, mentally kicking herself even as she said it. There was something about silence among the Bridgertons that compelled her to fill the void.

Finally, after the longest moment of silence ever to fill the space of a second, Lady Bridgerton cleared her throat and said, "I should like to see one of his sketches." She dabbed a napkin to her lips even though she hadn't taken a sip of her tea. "Provided, of course, that he cares to share it with me."

Sophie stood up. "I think I should go."

Lady Bridgerton speared her with her eyes. "Please," she said, in a voice that was velvet over steel, "stay."

Sophie sat back down.

Eloise jumped to her feet. "I think I hear Penelope."

"You do not," Hyacinth said.

"Why would I lie?"

"I certainly don't know, but—"

The butler appeared in the doorway. "Miss Penelope Featherington," he intoned.

"See," Eloise shot at Hyacinth.

"Is this a bad time?" Penelope asked.

"No," Daphne replied with a small, vaguely amused smile, "just an odd one."

"Oh. Well, I could come back later, I suppose."

"Of course not," Lady Bridgerton said. "Please sit down and have some tea."

Sophie watched as the young woman took a seat on the sofa next to Francesca. Penelope was no sophisticated beauty, but she was rather fetching in her own, uncomplicated way. Her hair was a brownish red, and her cheeks were lightly dusted with freckles. Her complexion was a touch sallow, although Sophie had a suspicion that that had more to do with her unattractive yellow frock than anything else.

Come to think of it, she rather thought that she'd read something in Lady Whistledown's column about Penelope's awful clothes. Pity the poor girl couldn't talk her mother into letting her wear blue.

But as Sophie surreptitiously studied Penelope, she became aware that Penelope was not-so-surreptitiously studying her.

"Have we met?" Penelope suddenly asked.

Sophie was suddenly gripped by an awful, premonition-like feeling. Or maybe it was déjà vu. "I don't think so," she said quickly.

Penelope's gaze didn't waver from her face. "Are you certain?"

"I—I don't see how we could have done."

Penelope let out a little breath and shook her head, as if clearing cobwebs from her mind. "I'm sure you're correct. But there is something terribly familiar about you."

"Sophie is our new lady's maid," Hyacinth said, as if that would explain anything. "She usually joins us for tea when we're only family."

Sophie watched Penelope as she murmured something in response, and then suddenly it hit her. She *had* seen Penelope before! It had been at the masquerade, probably no more than ten seconds before she'd met Benedict.

She'd just made her entrance, and the young men who had quickly surrounded her had still been making their way to her side. Penelope had been standing right there, dressed in some rather strange green costume with a funny hat. For some reason she hadn't been wearing a mask. Sophie had stared at her for a moment, trying to figure out what her costume was meant to be, when a young gentleman had bumped into Penelope, nearly knocking her to the floor.

Sophie had reached out and helped her up, and had just managed to say something like, "There you are," when several more gentlemen had rushed in, separating the two women.

Then Benedict had arrived, and Sophie had had eyes for no one but him. Penelope—and the abominable way she had been treated by the young gentlemen at the masquerade—had been forgotten until this very moment.

And clearly the event had remained buried at the back of Penelope's mind as well.

"I'm sure I must be mistaken," Penelope said as she accepted a cup of tea from Francesca. "It's not your looks, precisely, but rather the way you hold yourself, if that makes any sense."

Sophie decided that a smooth intervention was necessary and so she pasted on her best conversational smile, and said, "I shall take that as a compliment, since I am sure that the ladies of your acquaintance are gracious and kind indeed."

The minute she shut her mouth, however, she realized that that had been overkill. Francesca was looking at her as if she'd sprouted horns, and the corners of Lady Bridgerton's mouth were twitching as she said, "Why, Sophie, I vow that is the longest sentence you have uttered in a fortnight."

Sophie lifted her teacup to her face and mumbled, "I haven't been feeling well."

"Oh!" Hyacinth suddenly blurted out. "I hope you are not feeling too sickly, because I was hoping you could help me this evening."

"Of course," Sophie said, eager for an excuse to turn away from Penelope, who was still studying her as if she were a human puzzle. "What is it you need?"

"I have promised to entertain my cousins this eve."

"Oh, that's right," Lady Bridgerton said, setting her saucer down on the table. "I'd nearly forgotten."

Hyacinth nodded. "Could you help? There are four of them, and I'm sure to be overrun."

"Of course," Sophie said. "How old are they?"

Hyacinth shrugged.

"Between the ages of six and ten," Lady Bridgerton said with a dissaproving expression. "You should know that, Hyacinth."

Sophie said to Hyacinth, "Fetch me when they arrive. I love children and would be happy to help."

"Excellent," Hyacinth said, clasping her hands together. "They are so young and active. They would have worn me out."

"Hyacinth," Francesca said, "you're hardly old and decrepit."

"When was the last time you spent two hours with four children under the age of ten?"

"Stop," Sophie said, laughing for the first time in two weeks. "I'll help. No one will be worn-out. And you should come, too, Francesca. We'll have a lovely time, I'm sure."

"Are you—" Penelope started to say something, then cut herself off. "Never mind."

But when Sophie looked over at her, she was still staring at her face with a most perplexed expression. Penelope opened her mouth, closed it, then opened it again, saying, "I *know* I know you."

"I'm sure she's right," Eloise said with a jaunty grin. "Penelope never forgets a face."

Sophie blanched.

"Are you quite all right?" Lady Bridgerton asked, leaning forward. "You don't look well."

"I think something didn't agree with me," Sophie hastily

lied, clutching her stomach for effect. "Perhaps the milk was off."

"Oh, dear," Daphne said with a concerned frown as she looked down at her baby. "I gave some to Caroline."

"It tasted fine to me," Hyacinth said.

"It might have been something from this morning," Sophie said, not wanting Daphne to worry. "But all the same, I think I had better lie down." She stood and took a step toward the door. "If that is agreeable to you, Lady Bridgerton."

"Of course," she replied. "I hope you feel better soon."

"I'm sure I will," Sophie said, quite truthfully. She'd feel better just as soon as she left Penelope Featherington's line of vision.

"I'll come get you when my cousins arrive," Hyacinth called out.

"If you're feeling better," Lady Bridgerton added.

Sophie nodded and hurried out of the room, but as she left, she caught sight of Penelope Featherington watching her with a most intent expression, leaving Sophie filled with a horrible sense of dread.

Benedict had been in a bad mood for two weeks. And, he thought as he trudged down the pavement toward his mother's house, his bad mood was about to get worse. He'd been avoiding coming here because he didn't want to see Sophie; he didn't want to see his mother, who was sure to sense his bad mood and question him about it; he didn't want to see Eloise, who was sure to sense his mother's interest and try to interrogate him; he didn't want to see—

Hell, he didn't want to see anyone. And considering the way he'd been snapping off the heads of his servants (verbally, to be sure, although occasionally quite literally in his dreams) the rest of the world would do well if they didn't care to see him, either.

But, as luck would have it, right as he placed his foot on

the first step, he heard someone call out his name, and when he turned around, both of his adult brothers were walking toward him along the pavement.

Benedict groaned. No one knew him better than Anthony and Colin, and they weren't likely to let a little thing like a broken heart go unnoticed or unmentioned.

"Haven't seen you in an age," Anthony said. "Where have you been?"

"Here and there," Benedict said evasively. "Mostly at home." He turned to Colin. "Where have *you* been?"

"Wales."

"Wales? Why?"

Colin shrugged. "I felt like it. Never been there before."

"Most people require a slightly more compelling reason to take off in the middle of the season," Benedict said.

"Not I."

Benedict stared at him. Anthony stared at him.

"Oh, very well," Colin said with a scowl. "I needed to get away. Mother has started in on me with this bloody marriage thing."

" 'Bloody marriage thing'?" Anthony asked with an amused smile. "I assure you, the deflowering of one's wife is not quite so gory."

Benedict kept his expression scrupulously impassive. He'd found a small spot of blood on his sofa after he'd made love to Sophie. He'd thrown a pillow over it, hoping that by the time any of the servants noticed, they'd have forgotten that he'd had a woman over. He liked to think that none of the staff had been listening at doors or gossiping, but Sophie herself had once told him that servants generally knew everything that went on in a household, and he tended to think that she was right.

But if he had indeed blushed—and his cheeks did feel a touch warm—neither of his brothers saw it, because they didn't say anything, and if there was anything in life as certain as, say, the sun rising in the east, it was that a Bridgerton never passed up the opportunity to tease and torment another Bridgerton.

"She's been talking about Penelope Featherington non-stop," Colin said with a scowl. "I tell you, I've known the girl since we were both in short pants. Er, since I was in short pants, at least. She was in . . ." He scowled some more, because both his brothers were laughing at him. "She was in whatever it is that young girls wear."

"Frocks?" Anthony supplied helpfully.

"Petticoats?" was Benedict's suggestion.

"The point is," Colin said forcefully, "that I have known her forever, and I can assure you I am not likely to fall in love with her."

Anthony turned to Benedict and said, "They'll be married within a year. Mark my words."

Colin crossed his arms. "Anthony!"

"Maybe two," Benedict said. "He's young yet."

"Unlike *you*," Colin retorted. "Why am I besieged by Mother, I wonder? Good God, you're thirty-one—"

"Thirty," Benedict snapped.

"Regardless, one would think you'd be getting the brunt of it."

Benedict frowned. His mother had been uncharacteristically reserved these past few weeks when it came to her opinions on Benedict and marriage and why the two ought to meet and soon. Of course, Benedict had been avoiding his mother's house like the plague, but even before that, she'd not mentioned a word.

It was most odd.

"At any rate," Colin was still grumbling, "I am not going to marry soon, and I am certainly not going to marry Penelope Featherington!"

"Oh!"

It was a feminine "oh," and without looking up, Benedict

somehow knew that he was about to experience one of life's most awkward moments. Heart filled with dread, he lifted his head and turned toward the front door. There, framed perfectly in the open doorway, was Penelope Featherington, her lips parted with shock, her eyes filled with heartbreak.

And in that moment, Benedict realized what he'd probably been too stupid (and stupidly male) to notice: Penelope Featherington was in love with his brother.

Colin cleared his throat. "Penelope," he squeaked, his voice sounding as if he'd regressed ten years and gone straight back to puberty, "uh . . . good to see you." He looked to his brothers to leap in and save him, but neither chose to intervene.

Benedict winced. It was one of those moments that simply could not be saved.

"I didn't know you were there," Colin said lamely.

"Obviously not," Penelope said, but her words lacked an edge.

Colin swallowed painfully. "Were you visiting Eloise?"

She nodded. "I was invited."

"I'm sure you were!" he said quickly. "Of course you were. You're a great friend of the family."

Silence. Horrible, awkward silence.

"As if you would come uninvited," Colin mumbled.

Penelope said nothing. She tried to smile, but she obviously couldn't quite manage it. Finally, just when Benedict thought she would brush by them all and flee down the street, she looked straight at Colin and said, "I never asked you to marry me."

Colin's cheeks turned a deeper red than Benedict would have thought humanly possible. Colin opened his mouth, but no sound came out.

It was the first—and quite possibly would be the only—moment of Benedict's recollection for which his younger brother was at a complete loss for words.

"And I never—" Penelope added, swallowing convulsively when the words came out a bit tortured and broken. "I never said to anyone that I wanted you to ask me."

"Penelope," Colin finally managed, "I'm so sorry."

"You have nothing to apologize for," she said.

"No," Colin insisted, "I do. I hurt your feelings, and—"

"You didn't know I was there."

"But nevertheless—"

"You are not going to marry me," she said hollowly. "There is nothing wrong with that. I am not going to marry your brother Benedict."

Benedict had been trying not to look, but he snapped to attention at that.

"It doesn't hurt his feeling when I announce that I am not going to marry him." She turned to Benedict, her brown eyes focusing on his. "Does it, Mr. Bridgerton?"

"Of course not," Benedict answered quickly.

"It's settled, then," she said tightly. "No feelings were hurt. Now then, if you will excuse me, gentlemen, I should like to go home."

Benedict, Anthony, and Colin parted as if drops in the Red Sea as she made her way down the steps.

"Don't you have a maid?" Colin asked.

She shook her head. "I live just around the corner."

"I know, but—"

"I'll escort you," Anthony said smoothly.

"That's really not necessary, my lord."

"Humor me," he said.

She nodded, and the two of them took off down the street.

Benedict and Colin watched their retreating forms in silence for a full thirty seconds before Benedict turned to his brother and said, "That was very well done of you."

"I didn't know she was there!"

"Obviously," Benedict drawled.

"Don't. I feel terrible enough already."

"As well you should."

"Oh, and you have never inadvertently hurt a woman's feelings before?" Colin's voice was defensive, just defensive enough so that Benedict knew he felt like an utter heel inside.

Benedict was saved from having to reply by the arrival of his mother, standing at the top of the steps, framed in the doorway much the same way Penelope had been just a few minutes earlier.

"Has your brother arrived yet?" Violet asked.

Benedict jerked his head toward the corner. "He is escorting Miss Featherington home."

"Oh. Well, that's very thoughtful of him. I—Where are you going, Colin?"

Colin paused briefly but didn't even turn his head as he grunted, "I need a drink."

"It's a bit early for—" She stopped mid-sentence when Benedict laid his hand on her arm.

"Let him go," he said.

She opened her mouth as if to protest, then changed her mind and merely nodded. "I'd hoped to gather the family for an announcement," she said with a sigh, "but I suppose that can wait. In the meantime, why don't you join me for tea?"

Benedict glanced at the clock in the hall. "Isn't it a bit late for tea?"

"Skip the tea then," she said with a shrug. "I was merely looking for an excuse to speak with you."

Benedict managed a weak smile. He wasn't in the mood to converse with his mother. To be frank, he wasn't in the mood to converse with any person, a fact to which anyone with whom he'd recently crossed paths would surely attest.

"It's nothing serious," Violet said. "Heavens, you look as if you're ready to go to the gallows."

It probably would have been rude to point out that that was exactly how he felt, so instead he just leaned down and kissed her on the cheek.

"Well, that's a nice surprise," she said, beaming up at him.

"Now come with me," she added, motioning toward the downstairs sitting room. "I have someone I want to tell you about."

"Mother!"

"Just hear me out. She's a lovely girl . . ."

The gallows indeed.

Chapter 19

Miss Posy Reiling (younger step-daughter to the late Earl of Penwood) isn't a frequent subject of this column (nor, This Author is sad to say, a frequent subject of attention at social functions) but one could not help but notice that she was acting very strangely at her mother's musicale on Tuesday eve. She insisted upon sitting by the window, and she spent most of the performance staring at the streetscape, as if looking for something . . . or perhaps someone?

LADY WHISTLEDOWN'S SOCIETY PAPERS, 11 JUNE 1817

Forty-five minutes later, Benedict was slouching in his chair, his eyes glazed. Every now and then he had to stop and makc sure his mouth wasn't hanging open.

His mother's conversation was *that* boring.

The young lady she had wanted to discuss with him had actually turned out to be seven young ladies, each of which she *assured* him was better than the last.

Benedict thought he might go mad. Right there in his mother's sitting room he was going to go stark, raving mad. He'd suddenly pop out of his chair, fall to the floor in a frenzy, his arms and legs waving, mouth frothing—

"Benedict, are you even *listening* to me?"

He looked up and blinked. Damn. Now he would have to focus on his mother's list of possible brides. The prospect of losing his sanity had been infinitely more appealing.

"I was trying to tell you about Mary Edgeware," Violet said, looking more amused than frustrated.

Benedict was instantly suspicious. When it came to her children dragging their feet to the altar, his mother was never amused. "Mary who?"

"Edge—Oh, never mind. I can see that I cannot compete with whatever is plaguing you just now."

"Mother," Benedict said abruptly.

She cocked her head slightly to the side, her eyes intrigued and perhaps a bit surprised. "Yes?"

"When you met Father—"

"It happened in an instant," she said softly, somehow knowing what he'd meant to ask.

"So you knew that he was the one?"

She smiled, and her eyes took on a faraway, misty look. "Oh, I wouldn't have admitted it," she said. "At least not right away. I fancied myself a practical sort. I'd always scoffed at the notion of love at first sight." She paused for a moment, and Benedict knew she was no longer in the room with him, but at some long-ago ball, meeting his father for the first time. Finally, just when he thought she'd completely forgotten the conversation, she looked back up and said, "But I knew."

"From the first moment you saw him?"

"Well, from the first time we spoke, at least." She took his offered handkerchief and dabbed at her eyes, smiling sheepishly, as if embarrassed by her tears.

Benedict felt a lump forming in his throat, and he looked away, not wanting her to see the moisture forming in his own eyes. Would anyone cry for him more than a decade after he died? It was a humbling thing to be in the presence of true love, and Benedict suddenly felt so damned jealous—of his own *parents*.

They'd found love and had the good sense to recognize and cherish it. Few people were so fortunate.

"There was something about his voice that was so soothing, so warm," Violet continued. "When he spoke, you felt like you were the only person in the room."

"I remember," Benedict said with a warm, nostalgic smile. "It was quite a feat, to be able to do that with eight children."

His mother swallowed convulsively, then said, her voice once again brisk, "Yes, well, he never knew Hyacinth, so I suppose it was only seven."

"Still . . ."

She nodded. "Still."

Benedict reached out and patted her on the hand. He didn't know why; he hadn't planned to. But somehow it seemed the right thing to do.

"Yes, well," she said, giving his hand a little squeeze before returning hers to her lap. "Was there any particular reason you asked about your father?"

"No," he lied. "At least not . . . Well . . ."

She waited patiently, with that mildly expectant expression that made it impossible to keep one's feelings to oneself.

"What happens," he asked, as surprised by the words tumbling forth as she undoubtedly was, "when one falls in love with someone unsuitable?"

"Someone unsuitable," she repeated.

Benedict nodded painfully, immediately regretting his words. He should never have said anything to his mother, and yet . . .

He sighed. His mother had always been a remarkably good listener. And truly, for all her annoying matchmaking ways, she was more qualified to give advice on matters of the heart than anyone he knew.

When she spoke, she appeared to be choosing her words carefully. "What do you mean by unsuitable?"

"Someone . . ." He stopped, paused. "Someone someone like me probably shouldn't marry."

"Someone perhaps who is not of our social class?"

He glanced at a painting on the wall. "Someone like that."

"I see. Well . . ." Violet's brow scrunched a bit, then she said, "I suppose it would depend on how far out of our social class this person is."

"Far."

"A little bit far or quite a lot far?"

Benedict was convinced that no man of his age and reputation had ever had such a conversation with his mother, but he nonetheless answered, "Quite a lot."

"I see. Well, I would have to say . . ." She chewed on her lower lip for a moment before continuing. "I would have to say," she said, slightly more forcefully (although not, if one was judging in absolute terms, forceful at all).

"I would have to say," she said for a third time, "that I love you very much and will support you in all things." She cleared her throat. "If indeed we are talking about *you*."

It seemed useless to deny it, so Benedict just nodded.

"But," Violet added, "I would caution you to consider what you are doing. Love is, of course, the most important element in any union, but outside influences can put a strain on a marriage. And if you marry someone of, say"—she cleared her throat—"the servant class, then you will find yourself the subject of a great deal of gossip and no small amount of ostracism. And that will be difficult for one such as you to bear."

"One such as me?" he asked, bristling at her choice of words.

"You must know I mean no insult. But you and your brothers do lead charmed lives. You're handsome, intelligent, personable. Everyone likes you. I cannot tell you how happy that makes me." She smiled, but it was a wistful, slightly sad smile. "It is not easy to be a wallflower."

And suddenly Benedict understood why his mother was always forcing him to dance with the girls like Penelope Featherington. The ones who stood at the fringes of the ballroom, the ones who always pretended they didn't actually *want* to dance.

She had been a wallflower herself.

It was difficult to imagine. His mother was hugely popular now, with an easy smile and piles of friends. And if Benedict had heard the story correctly, his father had been considered the catch of the season.

"Only you will be able to make this decision," Violet continued, bringing Benedict's thoughts back to the here and now, "and I'm afraid it won't be an easy one."

He stared out the window, his silence his agreement.

"But," she added, "should you decide to join your life with someone not of our class, I will of course support you in every possible manner."

Benedict looked up sharply. There were few women of the *ton* who would say the same to their sons.

"You are my son," she said simply. "I would give my life for you."

He opened his mouth to speak but was surprised to find that he couldn't make a sound.

"I certainly wouldn't banish you for marrying someone unsuitable."

"Thank you," he said. It was all he could manage to say.

Violet sighed, loudly enough to regain his full attention. She looked tired, wistful. "I wish your father were here," she said.

"You don't say that very often," he said quietly.

"I always wish your father were here." She closed her eyes for a brief moment. "Always."

And then somehow it became clear. As he watched his mother's face, finally realizing—no, finally *understanding*—the depth of his parents' love for one another, it all became clear.

Love. He loved Sophie. That was all that should have mattered.

He'd thought he'd loved the woman from the masquerade. He'd thought he'd wanted to marry her. But he understood now that that had been nothing but a dream, a fleeting fantasy of a woman he barely knew.

But Sophie was . . .

Sophie was Sophie. And that was everything he needed.

Sophie wasn't a great believer in destiny or fate, but after one hour with Nicholas, Elizabeth, John, and Alice Wentworth, young cousins to the Bridgerton clan, she was beginning to think that maybe there was a reason she had never managed to obtain a position as a governess.

She was exhausted.

No, no, she thought, with more than a touch of desperation. Exhaustion didn't really provide an adequate description for the current state of her existence. Exhaustion didn't quite capture the slight edge of insanity the foursome had brought to her mind.

"No, no, no, that's *my* doll," Elizabeth said to Alice.

"It's mine," Alice returned.

"It is not!"

"Is too!"

"I'll settle this," ten-year-old Nicholas said, swaggering over with his hands on his hips.

Sophie groaned. She had a feeling that it was not a terribly good idea to allow the dispute to be settled by a ten-year-old boy who happened to think he was a pirate.

"Neither of you will want the doll," he said, with a devious gleam in his eye, "if I simply *lop* off its—"

Sophie leapt to intervene. "You will not lop off its head, Nicholas Wentworth."

"But then they'll stop—"

"No," Sophie said forcefully.

He looked at her, obviously assessing her commitment to

that particular course of action, then grumbled and walked away.

"I think we need a new game," Hyacinth whispered to Sophie.

"I *know* we need a new game," Sophie muttered.

"Let go of my soldier!" John screeched. "Let go let go let go!"

"I'm never having children," Hyacinth announced. "In fact, I may never get married."

Sophie forbore to point out that when Hyacinth married and had children, she would certainly have a flotilla of nurses and nannies to aid her with their keeping and care.

Hyacinth winced as John pulled Alice's hair, then swallowed uncomfortably as Alice slugged John in the stomach. "The situation is growing desperate," she whispered to Sophie.

"Blind man's bluff!" Sophie suddenly exclaimed. "What do you think, everyone? How about a game of blind man's bluff?"

Alice and John nodded enthusiastically, and Elizabeth gave a reluctant, "All right," after carefully considering the issue.

"What do you say, Nicholas?" Sophie asked, addressing the last remaining holdout.

"It could be fun," he said slowly, terrifying Sophie with the devilish gleam in his eye.

"Excellent," she said, trying to keep the wariness out of her voice.

"But *you* must be the blind man," he added.

Sophie opened her mouth to protest, but at that moment, the other three children started jumping up and down and squealing with delight. Then her fate was sealed when Hyacinth turned to her with a sly smile and said, "Oh, you must."

Sophie knew that protest was useless, so she let out a long-suffering sigh—exaggerated, just to delight the children—

and turned around so that Hyacinth could fasten a scarf over her eyes.

"Can you see?" Nicholas demanded.

"No," Sophie lied.

He turned to Hyacinth with a grimace. "She can see."

How could he tell?

"Add a second scarf," he said. "This one is too sheer."

"The indignity," Sophie muttered, but nonetheless, she leaned down slightly so that Hyacinth could tie another scarf over her eyes.

"She's blind now!" John hooted.

Sophie gave them all a sickly-sweet smile.

"All right now," Nicholas said, clearly in charge. "You wait ten seconds so that we can take our places."

Sophie nodded, then tried not to wince as she heard the sounds of a mad scramble around the room. "Try not to break anything!" she yelled, as if that would make any difference to an overexcited six-year-old.

"Are you ready?" she asked.

No response. That meant yes.

"Blind Man!" she called out.

"Bluff!" came five voices in unison.

Sophie frowned in concentration. One of the girls was definitely behind the sofa. She took a few baby steps to the right.

"Blind Man!"

"Bluff!" Followed, of course, by a few titters and chuckles.

"Blind M— OW!"

More hoots and squeals of laughter. Sophie grunted as she rubbed her bruised shin.

"Blind Man!" she called, with considerably less enthusiasm.

"Bluff!"

"Bluff!"

"BLUFF!"

"BLUFF!"

"BLUFF!"

"You are all mine, Alice," she muttered under her breath, deciding to go for the smallest and presumably weakest of the bunch. "All mine."

Benedict had nearly made a clean escape. After his mother had left the sitting room, he'd downed a much-needed glass of brandy and headed out toward the door, only to be caught by Eloise, who informed him that he absolutely *couldn't* leave yet, that Mother was trying *very* hard to assemble all of her children in one place because Daphne had an *important* announcement to make.

"With child again?" Benedict asked.

"Act surprised. You weren't supposed to know."

"I'm not going to act anything. I'm leaving."

She made a desperate leap forward and somehow managed to grab his sleeve. "You can't."

Benedict let out a long breath and tried to pry her fingers off of his arm, but she had his shirt in a death grip. "I am going to pick up one foot," he said in slow, tedious tones, "and step forward. Then I will pick up the next foot—"

"You promised Hyacinth you would help her with her arithmetic," Eloise blurted out. "She hasn't seen hide nor hair of you in two weeks."

"It's not as if she has a school to flunk out of," Benedict muttered.

"Benedict, that is a terrible thing to say!" Eloise exclaimed.

"I know," he groaned, hoping to stave off a lecture.

"Just because we of the female gender are not allowed to study at places like Eton and Cambridge doesn't mean our educations are any less precious," Eloise ranted, completely ignoring her brother's weak "I know."

"Furthermore—" she carried on.

Benedict sagged against the wall.

"—I am of the opinion that the reason we are *not* allowed access is that if we *were*, we would trounce you men in all subjects!"

"I'm sure you're right," he sighed.

"Don't patronize me."

"Believe me, Eloise, the last thing I would dream of doing is patronizing you."

She eyed him suspiciously before crossing her arms and saying, "Well, don't disappoint Hyacinth."

"I won't," he said wearily.

"I believe she's in the nursery."

Benedict gave her a distracted nod, turning toward the stairs.

But as he trudged on up, he didn't see Eloise turn toward his mother, who was peeking out of the music room, and give her a big wink and a smile.

The nursery was located on the second floor. Benedict didn't often come up that high; most of his siblings' bedrooms were on the first floor. Only Gregory and Hyacinth still lived adjacent to the nursery, and with Gregory off at Eton most of the year and Hyacinth usually terrorizing someone in some other section of the house, Benedict simply didn't have much reason to visit.

It didn't escape him that aside from the nursery, the second floor was home to bedrooms for the higher servants. Including the lady's maids.

Sophie.

She was probably off in some corner somewhere with her mending—certainly not in the nursery, which was the domain of nurses and nannies. A lady's maid would have no reason to—

"Heeheeheehahaha!"

Benedict raised his brows. That was most definitely the sound of childish laughter, not something likely to come out of fourteen-year-old Hyacinth's mouth.

Oh, right. His Wentworth cousins were visiting. His mother had mentioned something about that. Well, that would be a bonus. He hadn't seen them in a few months, and they were nice enough children, if a little high-spirited.

As he approached the nursery door, the laughter increased, with a few squeals thrown in for good measure. The sounds brought a smile to Benedict's face, and he turned when he reached the open doorway, and then—

He saw her.

Her.

Not Sophie.

Her.

And yet it *was* Sophie.

She was blindfolded, smiling as she groped her hands toward the giggling children. He could see only the bottom half of her face, and that's when he knew.

There was only one other woman in the world for whom he'd seen only the bottom half of her face.

The smile was the same. The gamine little point at the end of her chin was the same. It was *all* the same.

She was the woman in silver, the woman from the masquerade ball.

It suddenly made sense. Only twice in his life had he felt this inexplicable, almost mystical attraction to a woman. He'd thought it remarkable, to have found two, when in his heart he'd always believed there was only one perfect woman out there for him.

His heart had been right. There *was* only one.

He'd searched for her for months. He'd pined for her even longer. And here she'd been right under his nose.

And she hadn't told him.

Did she understand what she'd put him through? How many hours he'd lain awake, feeling that he was betraying the lady in silver—the woman he'd dreamed of marrying—all because he was falling in love with a housemaid?

Dear God, it bordered on the absurd. He'd finally decided

to let the lady in silver go. He was going to ask Sophie to marry him, social consequences be damned.

And they were one and the same.

A strange roaring filled his head, as if two enormous seashells had been clapped to his ears, whistling, whirring, humming; and the air suddenly smelled a bit acrid and everything looked a little bit red, and—

Benedict could not take his eyes off of her.

"Is something wrong?" Sophie asked. All the children had gone silent, staring at Benedict with open mouths and large, large eyes.

"Hyacinth," he bit off, "will you please evacuate the room?"

"But—"

"Now!" he roared.

"Nicholas, Elizabeth, John, Alice, come along now," Hyacinth said quickly, her voice cracking. "There are biscuits in the kitchen, and I know that . . ."

But Benedict didn't hear the rest. Hyacinth had managed to clear the room out in record time and her voice was disappearing down the hall as she ushered the children away.

"Benedict?" Sophie was saying, fumbling with the knot at the back of her head. "Benedict?"

He shut the door. The click was so loud she jumped. "What's wrong?" she whispered.

He said nothing, just watched her as she tore at the scarf. He liked it that she was helpless. He didn't feel terribly kind and charitable at the moment.

"Do you have something you need to tell me?" he asked. His voice was controlled, but his hands were shaking.

She went still, so still that he would have sworn that he could see the heat rise from her body. Then she cleared her throat—an uncomfortable, awkward sort of sound—and went back to work on the knot. Her movements tightened her dress around her breasts, but Benedict felt not one speck of desire.

It was, he thought ironically, the first time he *hadn't* felt desire for this woman, in either of her incarnations.

"Can you help me with this?" she asked. But her voice was hesitant.

Benedict didn't move.

"Benedict?"

"It's interesting to see you with a scarf tied around your head, Sophie," he said softly.

Her hands dropped slowly to her sides.

"It's almost like a demi-mask, wouldn't you say?"

Her lips parted, and the soft rush of air that crossed them was the room's only noise.

He walked toward her, slowly, inexorably, his footsteps just loud enough so that she had to know he was stalking her. "I haven't been to a masquerade in many years," he said.

She knew. He could see it in her face, the way she held her mouth, tight at the corners, and yet still slightly open. She knew that he knew.

He hoped she was terrified.

He took another two steps toward her, then abruptly turned to the right, his arm brushing past her sleeve. "Were you ever going to tell me that we'd met before?"

Her mouth moved, but she didn't speak.

"Were you?" he asked, his voice low and controlled.

"No," she said, her voice wavering.

"Really?"

She didn't make a sound.

"Any particular reason?"

"It—it didn't seem pertinent."

He whirled around. "It didn't seem *pertinent*?" he snapped. "I fell in love with you two years ago, and it didn't seem pertinent?"

"Can I please remove the scarf?" she whispered.

"You can remain blind."

"Benedict, I—"

"Like *I* was blind this past month," he continued angrily. "Why don't you see how you like it?"

"You didn't fall in love with me two years ago," she said, yanking at the too-tight scarf.

"How would you know? *You* disappeared."

"I *had* to disappear," she cried out. "I didn't have a choice."

"We always have choices," he said condescendingly. "We call it free will."

"That's easy for you to say," she snapped, tugging frantically at the blindfold. "You, who have everything! I had to—Oh!" With one wrenching movement, she somehow managed to yank down the scarves until they hung loosely around her neck.

Sophie blinked against the sudden onslaught of light. Then she caught sight of Benedict's face and stumbled back a step.

His eyes were on fire, burning with a rage, and yes, a hurt that she could barely comprehend. "It's good to see you, Sophie," he said in a dangerously low voice. "If indeed that is your real name."

She nodded.

"It occurs to me," he said, a little too casually, "if you were at the masquerade, then you are not exactly of the servant class, are you?"

"I didn't have an invitation," she said hastily. "I was a fraud. A pretender. I had no right to be there."

"You lied to me. Through everything, all this, you lied to me."

"I had to," she whispered.

"Oh, please. What could possibly be so terrible that you must conceal your identity from *me*?"

Sophie gulped. Here in the Bridgerton nursery, with him looming over her, she couldn't quite remember why she'd decided not to tell him that she was the lady at the masquerade.

Maybe she'd feared that he would want her to become his mistress.

Which had happened anyway.

Or maybe she hadn't said anything because by the time she'd realized that this wasn't going to be a chance meeting, that he wasn't about to let Sophie-the-housemaid out of his life, it was too late. She'd gone too long without telling him, and she feared his rage.

Which was exactly what had happened.

Proving her point. Of course, that was cold consolation as she stood across from him, watching his eyes go hot with anger and cold with disdain—all at the same time.

Maybe the truth—as unflattering as it might be—was that her pride had been stung. She'd been disappointed that he hadn't recognized her himself. If the night of the masquerade had been as magical for him as it had been for her, shouldn't he have known instantly who she was?

Two years she'd spent dreaming about him. Two years she'd seen his face every night in her mind. And yet when he'd seen hers, he'd seen a stranger.

Or maybe, just maybe, it hadn't been any of those things. Maybe it was simpler than that. Maybe she'd just wanted to protect her heart. She didn't know why, but she'd felt a little safer, a little less exposed as an anonymous housemaid. If Benedict had known who she was—or at least known that she'd been the woman at the masquerade—then he would have pursued her. Relentlessly.

Oh, he had certainly pursued her when he'd thought she'd been a maid. But it would have been different if he'd known the truth. Sophie was sure of it. He wouldn't have perceived the class differences as being quite so great, and Sophie would have lost an important barrier between them. Her social status, or lack thereof, had been a protective wall around her heart. She *couldn't* get too close because, quite honestly, she couldn't get too close. A man such as Benedict—son of and brother to viscounts—would never marry a servant.

But an earl's by-blow—now that was a much trickier situation. Unlike a servant, an aristocratic bastard could dream.

But like those of a servant, the dreams weren't likely to come true. Making the dreaming all that much more painful. And she'd known—every time it had been on the tip of her tongue to blurt out her secret she had known—that telling him the truth would lead straight to a broken heart.

It almost made Sophie want to laugh. Her heart couldn't possibly feel worse than it did now.

"I searched for you," he said, his low, intense voice cutting into her thoughts.

Her eyes widened, grew wet. "You did?" she whispered.

"For six bloody months," he cursed. "It was as if you fell right off the face of the earth."

"I had nowhere to go," she said, not sure why she was telling him that.

"You had *me*."

The words hung in the air, heavy and dark. Finally, Sophie, propelled by some perverse sense of belated honesty, said, "I didn't know you searched for me. But—but—" She choked on the word, closing her eyes tightly against the pain of the moment.

"But what?"

She swallowed convulsively, and when she did open her eyes, she did not look at his face. "Even if I'd known you were looking," she said, hugging her arms to her body, "I wouldn't have let you find me."

"Was I that repulsive to you?"

"No!" she cried out, her eyes flying to his face. There was hurt there. He hid it well, but she knew him well. There was hurt in his eyes.

"No," she said, trying to make her voice calm and even. "It wasn't that. It could never be that."

"Then what?"

"We're from different worlds, Benedict. Even then I knew that there could be no future for us. And it would have been torture. To tease myself with a dream that couldn't come true? I couldn't do that."

"Who are you?" he asked suddenly.

She just stared at him, frozen into inaction.

"Tell me," he bit off. "Tell me who you are. Because you're no damned lady's maid, that's for certain."

"I'm exactly who I said I was," she said, then, at his murderous glare, hastily added, "Almost."

He advanced on her. "Who *are* you?"

She backed up another step. "Sophia Beckett."

"Who are you?"

"I've been a servant since I was fourteen."

"And who were you before that?"

Her voice dropped to a whisper. "A bastard."

"Whose bastard?"

"Does it matter?"

His stance grew more belligerent. "It matters to me."

Sophie felt herself deflate. She hadn't expected him to ignore the duties of his birth and actually *marry* someone like her, but she'd hoped he wouldn't care quite that much.

"Who were your parents?" Benedict persisted.

"No one you know."

"Who were your parents?" he roared.

"The Earl of Penwood," she cried out.

He stood utterly still, not a muscle moving. He didn't even blink.

"I am a nobleman's bastard," she said harshly, years of anger and resentment pouring forth. "My father was the Earl of Penwood and my mother was a maid. Yes," she spat out when she saw his face grow pale, "my mother was a lady's maid. Just as I am a lady's maid."

A heavy pause filled the air, and then Sophie said in a low voice, "I won't be like my mother."

"And yet, if she'd behaved otherwise," he said, "you wouldn't be here to tell me about it."

"That's not the point."

Benedict's hands, which had been fisted at his sides, began to twitch. "You lied to me," he said in a low voice.

"There was no need to tell you the truth."

"Who the hell are you to decide?" he exploded. "Poor little Benedict, he can't handle the truth. He can't make up his own mind. He—"

He broke off, disgusted by the whiny edge to his voice. She was turning him into someone he didn't know, someone he didn't like.

He had to get out of there. He had to—

"Benedict?" She was looking at him oddly. Her eyes were concerned.

"I have to go," he muttered. "I can't see you right now."

"Why?" she asked, and he could see from her face that she instantly regretted the question.

"I am so angry right now," he said, each word a slow, staccato beat in the sentence, "that I don't know myself. I—" He looked down at his hands. They were shaking. He wanted to hurt her, he realized. No, he didn't want to hurt her. He would never want to hurt her. And yet . . .

And yet . . .

It was the first time in his life he'd felt so out of control. It scared him.

"I have to go," he said again, and he brushed roughly past her as he strode out the door.

Chapter 20

While we are on the topic, Miss Reiling's mother, the Countess of Penwood, has also been acting very strange of late. According to servants' gossip (which we all know is always the most reliable sort), the countess threw quite the tantrum last night, hurling no fewer than seventeen shoes at her servants.

One footman sports a bruised eye, but other than that, all remain in good health.

LADY WHISTLEDOWN'S SOCIETY PAPERS, 11 JUNE 1817

Within an hour, Sophie had her bag packed. She didn't know what else to do. She was gripped—painfully gripped—by nervous energy, and she could not sit still. Her feet kept moving and her hands were shaking, and every few minutes, she found herself taking a big spontaneous gulp of air, as if the extra breath could somehow calm her inside.

She could not imagine that she would be allowed to remain here in Lady Bridgerton's household after such a horrible falling-out with Benedict. Lady Bridgerton was fond of Sophie, it was true, but Benedict was her son. Blood really was thicker than just about anything else, especially when it was Bridgerton blood.

It was sad, really, she thought as she sat down on her bed, her hands still torturing a hopelessly mangled handkerchief. For all her inner turmoil over Benedict, she'd *liked* living in the Bridgerton household. Sophie had never before had the honor of living amongst a group of people who truly understood the meaning of the word family.

She would miss them.

She would miss Benedict.

And she would mourn the life she could not have.

Unable to sit still, she jumped back to her feet and walked to the window. "Damn you, Papa," she said, looking up at the skies. "There. I've called you Papa. You never let me do that. You never wanted to *be* that." She gasped convulsively, using the back of her hand to wipe at her nose. "I've called you Papa. How does it feel?"

But there was no sudden clap of thunder, no gray cloud appearing out of nowhere to cover up the sun. Her father would never know how angry she was with him for leaving her penniless, leaving her with Araminta. Most likely, he wouldn't have cared.

She felt rather weary, and she leaned against the window frame, rubbing her eyes with her hand. "You gave me a taste of another life," she whispered, "and then left me in the wind. It would have been so much easier if I'd been raised a servant.

"I wouldn't have wanted so much. It would have been easier."

She turned back around, her eyes falling upon her single, meager bag. She hadn't wanted to take any of the dresses that Lady Bridgerton and her daughters had given her, but she'd had little choice in the matter, as her old dresses had already been relegated to the rag bin. So she'd chosen only two, the same number with which she'd arrived—the one she happened to be wearing when Benedict had discovered her identity, and a spare, which she'd tucked in the bag. The rest had been left hanging, neatly pressed, in the wardrobe.

Sophie sighed, closing her eyes for a moment. It was time to go. Where, she didn't know, but she couldn't stay here.

She leaned down and picked up the bag. She had a little money saved. Not much, but if she worked and was frugal, she'd have enough funds for passage to America within a year. She'd heard that things were easier there for those of less-than-respectable birth, that the boundaries of class weren't quite as strict as they were here in England.

She poked her head out into the hall, which was blessedly vacant. She knew she was a coward, but she didn't want to have to say good-bye to the Bridgerton daughters. She might do something *really* stupid, like cry, and then she'd feel even worse. Never in her life had she had the chance to spend time with women of her own age who treated her with respect and affection. She'd once hoped that Rosamund and Posy would be her sisters, but that had never come to pass. Posy might have tried, but Araminta wouldn't allow it, and Posy, for all her sweetness, had never been strong enough to stand up to her mother.

But she did have to bid farewell to Lady Bridgerton. There was no getting around that. Lady Bridgerton had been kind to her far beyond any expectations, and Sophie would not thank her by sneaking out and disappearing like some criminal. If she was lucky, Lady Bridgerton would not yet have heard of her altercation with Benedict. Sophie could give her notice, bid her farewell, and be off.

It was late afternoon, well past tea time, so Sophie decided to take a chance and see if Lady Bridgerton was in the small office she kept off of her bedchamber. It was a warm and cozy little room, with a writing desk and several bookshelves—a place where Lady Bridgerton penned her correspondence and settled the household accounts.

The door was ajar, so Sophie knocked softly, allowing the door to swing open a few inches as her knuckles connected with the wood.

"Enter!" came Lady Bridgerton's bidding.

Sophie pushed the door open and poked her head in. "Am I interrupting?" she asked quietly.

Lady Bridgerton set down her quill. "Yes, but it's a welcome interruption. I've never enjoyed balancing the household accounts."

"I would—" Sophie bit her tongue. She had been about to say that she would have been happy to take over the task; she'd always been good with numbers.

"You were saying?" Lady Bridgerton asked, her eyes warm.

Sophie gave her head a little shake. "Nothing."

The room lapsed into silence until Lady Bridgerton gave Sophie a slightly amused smile, and asked, "Was there a specific reason you knocked on my door?"

Sophie took a deep breath that was meant to settle her nerves (but didn't) and said, "Yes."

Lady Bridgerton looked at her expectantly but didn't say anything.

"I'm afraid I must resign my position here," Sophie said.

Lady Bridgerton actually rose out of her seat. "But why? Aren't you happy? Have any of the girls been mistreating you?"

"No, no," Sophie hastened to assure her. "That could not be further from the truth. Your daughters are so lovely—in heart as well as in appearance. I've never— That is to say, no one has ever—"

"What is it, Sophie?"

Sophie clutched at the doorframe, desperately trying to find her balance. Her legs felt unsteady, her heart felt unsteady. Any moment now she was going to burst into tears, and why? Because the man she loved would never marry her? Because he hated her for lying to him? Because he'd broken her heart twice—once by asking her to be his mistress, and once by making her love his family and then forcing her to leave?

He might not have demanded that she go, but it couldn't have been more obvious that she could not stay.

"It's Benedict, isn't it?"

Sophie's head snapped up.

Lady Bridgerton smiled sadly. "It's obvious that there is some feeling between you," she said gently, answering the question that Sophie knew must show in her eyes.

"Why didn't you fire me?" Sophie whispered. She didn't think that Lady Bridgerton knew that Sophie and Benedict had been intimate, but no one of Lady Bridgerton's position would want her son pining for a housemaid.

"I don't know," Lady Bridgerton replied, looking more conflicted than Sophie could ever have imagined. "I probably should have done." She shrugged, her eyes strangely helpless. "But I like you."

The tears Sophie had been working so hard to keep in check began to roll down her face, but beyond that, she somehow managed to keep her composure. She didn't shake, and she didn't make a sound. She just stood there, utterly still, as the tears came forth.

When Lady Bridgerton spoke again, her words held a very careful and measured quality, as if she were choosing them with great care, searching for a specific reply. "You are," she said, her eyes never leaving Sophie's face, "the sort of woman I would like for my son. Our acquaintance has not been a long one, but I know your character and I know your heart. And I wish—"

A small, choked sob burst forth from Sophie's mouth, but she swallowed it down as quickly as she could.

"I wish that you were of a different background," Lady Bridgerton continued, acknowledging Sophie's cry with a sympathetic tilt of her head and a sad, slow blink of her eyes. "Not that I hold such a thing against you, or think the less of you, but it makes things very difficult."

"Impossible," Sophie whispered.

Lady Bridgerton didn't say anything, and Sophie knew

that in her heart she agreed—if not completely, then ninety-eight percent—with her assessment.

"Is it possible," Lady Bridgerton asked, her words even more measured and careful than before, "that your background is not quite what it seems?"

Sophie said nothing.

"There are things about you that don't add up, Sophie."

Sophie knew that she expected her to ask what, but she had a fair idea what Lady Bridgerton meant.

"Your accent is impeccable," Lady Bridgerton said. "I know you told me that you had lessons with the children your mother worked for, but that doesn't seem like enough of an explanation to me. Those lessons wouldn't have started until you were a bit older, six at the very earliest, and your speech patterns would have already been rather set by that point."

Sophie felt her eyes widen. She'd never seen that particular hole in her story, and she was rather surprised that no one else had until now. But then again, Lady Bridgerton was a good deal smarter than most of the people to whom she had told her fabricated history.

"And you know Latin," Lady Bridgerton said. "Don't try to deny it. I heard you muttering under your breath the other day when Hyacinth vexed you."

Sophie kept her gaze fixed firmly on the window just to Lady Bridgerton's left. She couldn't quite bring herself to meet her eyes.

"Thank you for not denying it," Lady Bridgerton said. And then she waited for Sophie to say something, waited so long that finally Sophie had to fill the interminable silence.

"I'm not a suitable match for your son," was all she said.

"I see."

"I really have to go." She had to get the words out quickly, before she changed her mind.

Lady Bridgerton nodded. "If that is your wish, there is

nothing I can do to stop you. Where is it you plan to go?"

"I have relatives in the north," Sophie lied.

Lady Bridgerton clearly didn't believe her, but she answered, "You will, of course, use one of our carriages."

"No, I couldn't possibly."

"You can't think I would permit you to do otherwise. I consider you to be my responsibility—at least for the next few days—and it is far too dangerous for you to leave unescorted. It's not safe for women alone in this world."

Sophie couldn't quite suppress a rueful smile. Lady Bridgerton's tone might be different, but her words were almost exactly those uttered by Benedict a few weeks earlier. And look where that had gotten her. She would never say that she and Lady Bridgerton were close friends, but she knew her well enough to know that she would not be budged on this issue.

"Very well," Sophie acceded. "Thank you." She could have the carriage drop her off somewhere, preferably not too far from a port where she could eventually book passage to America, and then decide where to go from there.

Lady Bridgerton offered her a small, sad smile. "I assume you already have your bags packed?"

Sophie nodded. It didn't seem necessary to point out that she only had one bag, singular.

"Have you made all of your good-byes?"

Sophie shook her head. "I'd rather not," she admitted.

Lady Bridgerton stood and nodded. "Sometimes that is best," she agreed. "Why don't you await me in the front hall? I will see to having a coach brought 'round."

Sophie turned and started to walk out, but when she reached the doorway, she stopped and turned around. "Lady Bridgerton, I—"

The older lady's eyes lit up, as if she were expecting some good news. Or if not good, then at least something different. "Yes?"

Sophie swallowed. "I just wanted to thank you."

The light in Lady Bridgerton's eyes dimmed a little. "Whatever for?"

"For having me here, for accepting me, and allowing me to pretend I was a part of your family."

"Don't be sil—"

"You didn't have to let me take tea with you and the girls," Sophie interrupted. If she didn't get this all out now, she'd lose her courage. "Most women wouldn't have done. It was lovely . . . and new . . . and . . ." She gulped. "I will miss you all."

"You don't have to go," Lady Bridgerton said softly.

Sophie tried to smile, but it came out all wobbly, and it tasted like tears. "Yes," she said, almost choking on the word. "I do."

Lady Bridgerton stared at her for a very long moment, her pale blue eyes filled with compassion and then maybe a touch of realization. "I see," she said quietly.

And Sophie feared that she did see.

"I'll meet you downstairs," Lady Bridgerton said.

Sophie nodded as she stood aside to let the dowager viscountess pass. Lady Bridgerton paused in the hallway, looking down at Sophie's well-worn bag. "Is that all you have?" she asked.

"Everything in the world."

Lady Bridgerton swallowed uncomfortably, and her cheeks took on the slightest hue of pink, almost as if she were actually embarrassed by her riches—and Sophie's lack thereof.

"But that . . ." Sophie said, motioning to the bag, "that's not what's important. What you have . . ." She stopped and swallowed, doing battle with the lump in her throat. "I don't mean what you own . . ."

"I know what you mean, Sophie." Lady Bridgerton dabbed at her eyes with her fingers. "Thank you."

Sophie's shoulders rose and fell in a tiny shrug. "It's the truth."

"Let me give you some money before you go, Sophie," Lady Bridgerton blurted out.

Sophie shook her head. "I couldn't. I've already taken two of the dresses you gave me. I didn't want to, but—"

"It's all right," Lady Bridgerton assured her. "What else could you do? The ones you came with are gone." She cleared her throat. "But please, let me give you some money." She saw Sophie open her mouth to protest and said, "*Please.* It would make me feel better."

Lady Bridgerton had a way of looking at a person that truly made one want to do as she asked, and besides that, Sophie really did need the money. Lady Bridgerton was a generous lady; she might even give Sophie enough to book third-class passage across the ocean. Sophie found herself saying, "Thank you," before her conscience had a chance to grapple with the offer.

Lady Bridgerton gave her a brief nod and disappeared down the hall.

Sophie took a long, shaky breath, then picked up her bag and walked slowly down the stairs. She waited in the foyer for a moment, then decided she might as well wait outside. It was a fine spring day, and Sophie thought that a bit of sun on her nose might be just the thing to make her feel better. Well, at least a little bit better. Besides, she'd be less likely to run into one of the Bridgerton daughters, and much as she was going to miss them, she just didn't want to have to say good-bye.

Still clutching her bag in one hand, she pushed open the front door and descended the steps.

It shouldn't take too long for the coach to be brought around. Five minutes, maybe ten, maybe—

"Sophie Beckett!"

Sophie's stomach dropped right down to her ankles. Araminta. How could she have forgotten?

Frozen into inaction, she looked around and up the stairs, trying to figure out which way to flee. If she ran back into the Bridgerton house, Araminta would know where to find her, and if she took off on foot—

"Constable!" Araminta shrieked. "I want a constable!"

Sophie dropped her bag and took off running.

"Someone stop her!" Araminta screamed. "Stop thief! Stop thief!"

Sophie kept running, even though she knew it would make her look guilty. She ran with every last fiber in her muscles, with every gulp of air she could force into her lungs. She ran and she ran and she ran . . .

Until someone tackled her, thumping into her back and knocking her to the ground.

"I got her!" the man yelled. "I got her for you!"

Sophie blinked and gasped at the pain. Her head had hit the pavement with a stunning blow, and the man who had caught her was practically sitting on her abdomen.

"There you are!" Araminta crowed as she hurried over. "Sophie Beckett. The nerve!"

Sophie glared at her. Words didn't exist to express the loathing in her heart. Not to mention that she was in too much pain to speak.

"I've been looking for you," Araminta said, smiling evilly. "Posy told me she'd seen you."

Sophie closed her eyes for a longer than the usual blink. *Oh, Posy*. She doubted that she'd meant to give her away, but Posy's tongue had a way of getting ahead of her mind.

Araminta planted her foot very close to Sophie's hand—the one that was being held immobile by her captor's fingers around her wrist—then smiled as she moved her foot *onto* Sophie's hand. "You shouldn't have stolen from me," Araminta said, her blue eyes glinting.

Sophie just grunted. It was all she could manage.

"You see," Araminta continued gleefully, "now I can have you thrown in jail. I suppose I could have done so before, but now I have the truth on my side."

Just then, a man ran up, skidding to a halt before Araminta. "The authorities are on the way, milady. We'll have this thief taken away in no time."

Sophie caught her lower lip between her teeth, torn between praying that the authorities would be delayed until Lady Bridgerton came outside, and praying that they'd come right away, so that the Bridgertons would never see her shame.

And in the end, she got her wish. The latter one, that was. Not two minutes later the authorities arrived, threw her into a wagon, and carted her off to jail.

And all Sophie could think of as she rode away was that the Bridgertons would never know what had happened to her, and maybe that was for the best.

Chapter 21

La, but such excitement yesterday on the front steps of Lady Bridgerton's residence on Bruton Street!

First, Penelope Featherington was seen in the company of not one, not two, but THREE Bridgerton brothers, surely a heretofore impossible feat for the poor girl, who is rather infamous for her wallflower ways. Sadly (but perhaps predictably) for Miss Featherington, when she finally departed, it was on the arm of the viscount, the only married man in the bunch.

If Miss Featherington were to somehow manage to drag a Bridgerton brother to the altar, it would surely mean the end of the world as we know it, and This Author, who freely admits she would not know heads from tails in such a world, would be forced to resign her post on the spot.

If Miss Featherington's gathering weren't enough gossip, not three hours later, a woman was accosted right in front of the town house by the Countess of Penwood, who lives three doors down. It seems the woman, who This Author suspects was working in the Bridgerton household, used to work for Lady Penwood. Lady Penwood alleges that the unidentified woman stole from her two years ago and immediately had the poor thing carted off to jail.

This Author is not certain what the punishment is these days for theft, but one has to suspect that if one has the au-

dacity to steal from a countess, the punishment is quite strict. The poor girl in question is likely to be hanged, or at the very least, find herself transported.

The previous housemaid wars (reported last month in This Column) seem rather trivial now.

LADY WHISTLEDOWN'S SOCIETY PAPERS, 13 JUNE 1817

Benedict's first inclination the following morning was to pour himself a good, stiff drink. Or maybe three. It might have been scandalously early in the day for spirits, but alcoholic oblivion sounded rather appealing after the emotional skewering he'd received the previous evening at the hands of Sophie Beckett.

But then he remembered that he'd made a date that morning for a fencing match with his brother Colin. Suddenly, skewering his brother sounded rather appealing, no matter that he'd had nothing to do with Benedict's wretched mood.

That, Benedict thought with a grim smile as he pulled on his gear, was what brothers were for.

"I've only an hour," Colin said as he attached the safety tip to his foil. "I have an appointment this afternoon."

"No matter," Benedict replied, lunging forward a few times to loosen up the muscles in his leg. He hadn't fenced in some time; the sword felt good in his hand. He drew back and touched the tip to the floor, letting the blade bend slightly. "It won't take more than an hour to best you."

Colin rolled his eyes before he drew down his mask.

Benedict walked to the center of the room. "Are you ready?"

"Not quite," Colin replied, following him.

Benedict lunged again.

"I said I wasn't ready!" Colin hollered as he jumped out of the way.

"You're too slow," Benedict snapped.

Colin cursed under his breath, then added a louder, "Bloody hell," for good measure. "What's gotten into you?"

"Nothing," Benedict nearly snarled. "Why would you say so?"

Colin took a step backward until they were a suitable distance apart to start the match. "Oh, I don't know," he intoned, sarcasm evident. "I suppose it could be because you nearly took my head off."

"I've a tip on my blade."

"And you were slashing like you were using a sabre," Colin shot back.

Benedict gave a hard smile. "It's more fun that way."

"Not for my neck." Colin passed his sword from hand to hand as he flexed and stretched his fingers. He paused and frowned. "You sure you have a foil there?"

Benedict scowled. "For the love of God, Colin, I would never use a real weapon."

"Just making sure," Colin muttered, touching his neck lightly. "Are you ready?"

Benedict nodded and bent his knees.

"Regular rules," Colin said, assuming a fencer's crouch. "*No* slashing."

Benedict gave him a curt nod.

"En garde!"

Both men raised their right arms, twisting their wrists until their palms were up, foils gripped in their fingers.

"Is that new?" Colin suddenly asked, eyeing the handle of Benedict's foil with interest.

Benedict cursed at the loss of his concentration. "Yes, it's new," he bit off. "I prefer an Italian grip."

Colin stepped back, completely losing his fencing posture as he looked at his own foil, with a less elaborate French grip. "Might I borrow it some time? I wouldn't mind seeing if—"

"Yes!" Benedict snapped, barely resisting the urge to advance and lunge that very second. "Will you get back *en garde*?"

Colin gave him a lopsided smile, and Benedict just *knew* that he had asked about his grip simply to annoy him. "As you wish," Colin murmured, assuming position again.

They held still for one moment, and then Colin said, "Fence!"

Benedict advanced immediately, lunging and attacking, but Colin had always been particularly fleet of foot, and he retreated carefully, meeting Benedict's attack with an expert parry.

"You're in a bloody bad mood today," Colin said, lunging forward and just nearly catching Benedict on the shoulder.

Benedict stepped out of his way, lifting his blade to block the attack. "Yes, well, I had a bad"—he advanced again, his foil stretched straight forward—"*day*."

Colin sidestepped his attack neatly. "Nice riposte," he said, touching his forehead with the handle of his foil in a mock salute.

"Shut up and fence," Benedict snapped.

Colin chuckled and advanced, swishing his blade this way and that, keeping Benedict on the retreat. "It must be a woman," he said.

Benedict blocked Colin's attack and quickly began his own advance. "None of your damned business."

"It's a woman," Colin said, smirking.

Benedict lunged forward, the tip of his foil catching Colin on the collarbone. "Point," he grunted.

Colin gave a curt nod. "Touch for you." They walked back to the center of the room. "Are you ready?" he asked.

Benedict nodded.

"*En garde*. Fence!"

This time Colin was the first to take the attack. "If you need some advice about women . . ." he said, driving Benedict back to the corner.

Benedict raised his foil, blocking Colin's attack with

enough force to send his younger brother stumbling backward. "If I need advice about women," he returned, "the last person I'd go to would be *you*."

"You wound me," Colin said, regaining his balance.

"No," Benedict drawled. "That's what the safety tip is for."

"I certainly have a better record with women than *you*."

"Oh really?" Benedict said sarcastically. He stuck his nose in the air, and in a fair imitation of Colin said, " 'I am certainly *not* going to marry Penelope Featherington!' "

Colin winced.

"You," Benedict said, "shouldn't be giving advice to anyone."

"I didn't know she was there."

Benedict lunged forward, just barely missing Colin's shoulder. "That's no excuse. You were in public, in broad daylight. Even if she hadn't been there, someone would have heard and the bloody thing would have ended up in *Whistledown*."

Colin met his lunge with a parry, then riposted with blinding speed, catching Benedict neatly in the belly. "My touch," he grunted.

Benedict gave him a nod, acknowledging the point.

"I was foolish," Colin said as they walked back to the center of the room. "You, on the other hand, are stupid."

"What the hell does that mean?"

Colin sighed as he pushed up his mask. "Why don't you just do us all a favor and marry the girl?"

Benedict just stared at him, his hand going limp around the handle of his sword. Was there any possibility that Colin didn't know who they were talking about?

He removed his mask and looked into his brother's dark green eyes and nearly groaned. Colin knew. He didn't know how Colin knew, but he definitely knew. He supposed he shouldn't have been surprised. Colin always knew everything. In fact, the only person who ever seemed to know more gossip than Colin was Eloise, and it never took her more than a few hours to impart all of her dubious wisdom to Colin.

"How did you know?" Benedict finally asked.

One corner of Colin's mouth tilted up into a crooked smile. "About Sophie? It's rather obvious."

"Colin, she's—"

"A maid? Who cares? What is going to happen to you if you marry her?" Colin asked with a devil-may-care shrug of his shoulders. "People you couldn't care less about will ostracize you? Hell, I wouldn't mind being ostracized by some of the people with whom I'm forced to socialize."

Benedict shrugged dismissively. "I'd already decided I didn't care about all that," he said.

"Then what in bloody hell is the problem?" Colin demanded.

"It's complicated."

"Nothing is ever as complicated as it is in one's mind."

Benedict mulled that over, planting the tip of his foil against the floor and allowing the flexible blade to wiggle back and forth. "Do you remember Mother's masquerade?" he asked.

Colin blinked at the unexpected question. "A few years ago? Right before she moved out of Bridgerton House?"

Benedict nodded. "That's the one. Do you remember meeting a woman dressed in silver? You came upon us in the hall."

"Of course. You were rather taken with—" Colin's eyes suddenly bugged out. "That wasn't *Sophie*?"

"Remarkable, isn't it?" Benedict murmured, his every inflection screaming understatement.

"But . . . How . . ."

"I don't know how she got there, but she's not a maid."

"She's not?"

"Well, she is a maid," Benedict clarified, "but she's also the bastard daughter of the Earl of Penwood."

"Not the current—"

"No, the one who died several years back."

"And you knew all this?"

"No," Benedict said, the word short and staccato on his tongue, "I did not."

"Oh." Colin caught his lower lip between his teeth as he digested the meaning of his brother's short sentence. "I see." He stared at Benedict. "What are you going to do?"

Benedict's sword, whose blade had been wiggling back and forth as he pressed the tip against the floor, suddenly sprang straight and skittered out of his hand. He watched it dispassionately as it slid across the floor, and didn't look back up as he said, "That's a very good question."

He was still furious with Sophie for her deception, but neither was he without blame. He shouldn't have demanded that Sophie be his mistress. It had certainly been his right to ask, but it had also been her right to refuse. And once she had done so, he should have let her be.

Benedict hadn't been brought up a bastard, and if her experience had been sufficiently wretched so that she refused to risk bearing a bastard herself—well, then, he should have respected that.

If he respected *her*, then he had to respect her beliefs.

He shouldn't have been so flip with her, insisting that anything was possible, that she was free to make any choice her heart desired. His mother was right; he *did* live a charmed life. He had wealth, family, happiness . . . and nothing was truly out of his reach. The only awful thing that had ever happened in his life was the sudden and untimely death of his father, and even then, he'd had his family to help him through. It was difficult for him to imagine certain pains and hurts because he'd never experienced them.

And unlike Sophie, he'd never been alone.

What now? He had already decided that he was prepared to brave social ostracism and marry her. The unrecognized bastard daughter of an earl was a slightly more acceptable match than a servant, but only slightly. London society might accept her if he forced them to, but they wouldn't go out of their way to be kind. He and Sophie would most likely have to live quietly in the country, eschewing the London society that would almost certainly shun them.

But it took his heart less than a second to know that a quiet life with Sophie was by far preferable to a public life without her.

Did it matter that she was the woman from the masquerade? She'd lied to him about her identity, but he knew her soul. When they kissed, when they laughed, when they simply sat and talked—she had never feigned a moment.

The woman who could make his heart sing with a simple smile, the woman who could fill him with contentment just through the simple act of sitting by him while he sketched—that was the real Sophie.

And he loved her.

"You look as if you've reached a decision," Colin said quietly.

Benedict eyed his brother thoughtfully. When had he grown so perceptive? Come to think of it, when had he grown up? Benedict had always thought of Colin as a youthful rascal, charming and debonair, but not one who had ever had to assume any sort of responsibility.

But when he regarded his brother now, he saw someone else. His shoulders were a little broader, his posture a little more steady and subdued. And his eyes looked wiser. That was the biggest change. If eyes truly were windows to the soul, then Colin's soul had gone and grown up on him when Benedict hadn't been paying attention.

"I owe her a few apologies," Benedict said.

"I'm sure she'll forgive you."

"She owes me several as well. More than several."

Benedict could tell that his brother wanted to ask, "What

for?" but to his credit, all Colin said was, "Are you willing to forgive her?"

Benedict nodded.

Colin reached out and plucked Benedict's foil from his hands. "I'll put this away for you."

Benedict stared at his brother's fingers for a rather stupidly long moment before snapping to attention. "I have to go," he blurted out.

Colin barely suppressed a grin. "I surmised as much."

Benedict stared at his brother and then, for no other reason than an overwhelming urge, he reached out and pulled him into a quick hug. "I don't say this often," he said, his voice starting to sound gruff in his ears, "but I love you."

"I love you, too, big brother." Colin's smile, always a little bit lopsided, grew. "Now get the hell out of here."

Benedict tossed his mask at his brother and strode out of the room.

"What do you mean, she's gone?"

"Just that, I'm afraid," Lady Bridgerton said, her eyes sad and sympathetic. "She's gone."

The pressure behind Benedict's temples began to build; it was a wonder his head didn't explode. "And you just let her *go*?"

"It would hardly have been legal for me to force her to stay."

Benedict nearly groaned. It had hardly been legal for him to force her to come to London, but he'd done it, anyway.

"Where did she go?" he demanded.

His mother seemed to deflate in her chair. "I don't know. I had insisted that she take one of our coaches, partly because I feared for her safety but also because I wanted to know where she went."

Benedict slammed his hands on the desk. "Well, then, what happened?"

"As I was *trying* to say, I attempted to get her to take one of our coaches, but it was obvious she didn't want to, and she disappeared before I could have the carriage brought 'round."

Benedict cursed under his breath. Sophie was probably still in London, but London was huge and hugely populated. It would be damn near impossible to find someone who didn't want to be found.

"I had assumed," Violet said delicately, "that the two of you had had a falling-out."

Benedict raked his hand through his hair, then caught sight of his white sleeve. "Oh, Jesus," he muttered. He'd run over here in his fencing clothes. He looked up at his mother with a roll of his eyes. "No lectures on blasphemy just now, Mother. Please."

Her lips twitched. "I wouldn't dream of it."

"Where am I going to find her?"

The levity left Violet's eyes. "I don't know, Benedict. I wish I did. I quite liked Sophie."

"She's Penwood's daughter," he said.

Violet frowned. "I suspected something like that. Illegitimate, I assume?"

Benedict nodded.

His mother opened her mouth to say something, but he never did find out what, because at that moment, the door to her office came flying open, slamming against the wall with an amazing crash. Francesca, who had obviously been running across the house, smashed into her mother's desk, followed by Hyacinth, who smashed into Francesca.

"What is wrong?" Violet asked, rising to her feet.

"It's Sophie," Francesca panted.

"I know," Violet said. "She's gone. We—"

"No!" Hyacinth cut in, slapping a piece of paper down on the desk. "Look."

Benedict tried to grab the paper, which he immediately

recognized as an issue of *Whistledown*, but his mother got there first. "What is it?" he asked, his stomach sinking as he watched her face pale.

She handed him the paper. He scanned it quickly, passing by bits about the Duke of Ashbourne, the Earl of Macclesfield, and Penelope Featherington before he reached the section about what had to be Sophie.

"Jail?" he said, the word mere breath on his lips.

"We must see her released," his mother said, throwing her shoulders back like a general girding for battle.

But Benedict was already out the door.

"Wait!" Violet yelled, dashing after him. "I'm coming, too."

Benedict stopped short just before he reached the stairs. "You are not coming," he ordered. "I will not have you exposed to—"

"Oh, please," Violet returned. "I'm hardly a wilting flower. And I can vouch for Sophie's honesty and integrity."

"I'm coming, too," Hyacinth said, skidding to a halt alongside Francesca, who had also followed them out into the upstairs hall.

"No!" came the simultaneous reply from her mother and brother.

"But—"

"I said *no*," Violet said again, her voice sharp.

Francesca let out a sullen snort. "I suppose it would be fruitless for me to insist upon—"

"Don't even finish that sentence," Benedict warned.

"As if you would let me even try."

Benedict ignored her and turned to his mother. "If you want to go, we leave immediately."

She nodded. "Have the carriage brought 'round, and I'll be waiting out front."

Ten minutes later, they were on their way.

Chapter 22

Such a scurry on Bruton Street. The dowager Viscountess Bridgerton and her son, Benedict Bridgerton, were seen dashing out of her house Friday morning. Mr. Bridgerton practically threw his mother into a carriage, and they took off at breakneck speed. Francesca and Hyacinth Bridgerton were seen standing in the doorway, and This Author has it on the best authority that Francesca was heard to utter a very unladylike word.

But the Bridgerton household was not the only one to see such excitement. The Penwoods also experienced a great deal of activity, culminating in a public row right on the front steps between the countess and her daughter, Miss Posy Reiling.

As This Author has never liked Lady Penwood, she can only say, "Huzzah for Posy!"

LADY WHISTLEDOWN'S SOCIETY PAPERS, 16 JUNE 1817

It was cold. Really cold. And there was an awful scurrying noise that definitely belonged to a small, four-legged creature. Or even worse, a large, four-legged creature. Or to be more precise, a large version of a small, four-legged creature.

Rats.

"Oh, God," Sophie moaned. She didn't often take the Lord's name in vain, but now seemed as good a time as any to start. Maybe He would hear, and maybe He would smite the rats. Yes, that would do very nicely. A big jolt of lightning. Huge. Of biblical proportions. It could hit the earth, spread little electrical tentacles around the globe, and sizzle all the rats dead.

It was a lovely dream. Right up there with the ones in which she found herself living happily ever after as Mrs. Benedict Bridgerton.

Sophie took a quick gasp as a sudden stab of pain pierced her heart. Of the two dreams, she feared that the genocide of the rats might be the more likely to come true.

She was on her own now. Well and truly on her own. She didn't know why this was so upsetting. In all truth, she'd always been on her own. Not since her grandmother had deposited her on the front steps of Penwood Park had she had a champion, someone who put her interests above—or even at the same level—as their own.

Her stomach growled, reminding her that she could add hunger to her growing list of miseries.

And thirst. They hadn't even brought her so much as a sip of water. She was starting to have very strange fantasies about tea.

Sophie let out a long, slow breath, trying to remember to breathe through her mouth when it came time to inhale. The stench was overwhelming. She'd been given a crude chamber pot to use for her bodily functions, but so far she'd been holding it in, trying to relieve herself with as little frequency as possible. The chamber pot had been emptied before it had been tossed into her cell, but it hadn't been cleaned, and in fact when Sophie had picked it up it had been wet, causing her to drop it immediately as her entire body shuddered with revulsion.

She had, of course, emptied many chamber pots in her

time, but the people she'd worked for had generally managed to hit their mark, so to speak. Not to mention that Sophie had always been able to wash her hands afterward.

Now, in addition to the cold and the hunger, she didn't feel clean in her own skin.

It was a horrible sensation.

"You have a visitor."

Sophie jumped to her feet at the warden's gruff, unfriendly voice. Could Benedict have found out where she was? Would he even wish to come to her aid? Did he—

"Well, well, well."

Araminta. Sophie's heart sank.

"Sophie Beckett," she clucked, approaching the cell and then holding a handkerchief to her nose, as if Sophie were the sole cause of the stench. "I would never have guessed that you would have the audacity to show your face in London."

Sophie clamped her mouth together in a mutinous line. She knew that Araminta wanted to get a rise out of her, and she refused to give her the satisfaction.

"Things aren't going well for you, I'm afraid," Araminta continued, shaking her head in a parody of sympathy. She leaned forward and whispered, "The magistrate doesn't take very kindly to thieves."

Sophie crossed her arms and stared stubbornly at the wall. If she so much as looked at Araminta, she probably wouldn't be able to restrain herself from lunging at her, and the metal bars of her cell were likely to do serious damage to her face.

"The shoe clips were bad enough," Araminta said, tapping her chin with her forefinger, "but he grew so very angry when I informed him of the theft of my wedding ring."

"I didn't—" Sophie caught herself before she yelled any more. That was exactly what Araminta wanted.

"Didn't you?" she returned, smiling slyly. She waggled her fingers in the air. "I don't appear to be wearing it, and it's your word against mine."

Sophie's lips parted, but not a sound emerged. Araminta was right. And no judge would take her word over the Countess of Penwood's.

Araminta smiled slightly, her expression vaguely feline. "The man in front—I think he said he was the warden—said you're not likely to be hanged, so you needn't worry on that score. Transportation is a much more likely outcome."

Sophie almost laughed. Just the day before she'd been considering emigrating to America. Now it seemed she'd be leaving for certain—except her destination would be Australia. And she'd be in chains.

"I'll plead for clemency on your behalf," Araminta said. "I don't want you killed, only . . . gone."

"A model of Christian charity," Sophie muttered. "I'm sure the justice will be touched."

Araminta brushed her fingers against her temple, idly pushing back her hair. "Won't he, though?" She looked directly at Sophie and smiled. It was a hard and hollow expression, and suddenly Sophie had to know—

"Why do you hate me?" she whispered.

Araminta did nothing but stare at her for a moment, and then she whispered, "Because he loved you."

Sophie was stunned into silence.

Araminta's eyes grew impossibly brittle. "I will never forgive him for that."

Sophie shook her head in disbelief. "He never loved me."

"He clothed you, he fed you." Araminta's mouth tightened. "He forced me to live with you."

"That wasn't love," Sophie said. "That was guilt. If he loved me he wouldn't have left me with *you*. He wasn't stupid; he had to have known how much you hated me. If he loved me he wouldn't have forgotten me in his will. If he loved me—" She broke off, choking on her own voice.

Araminta crossed her arms.

"If he loved me," Sophie continued, "he might have taken the time to talk to me. He might have asked me how my day went, or what I was studying, or did I enjoy my breakfast." She swallowed convulsively, turning away. It was too hard to look at Araminta just then. "He never loved me," she said quietly. "He didn't know how to love."

No words passed between the two women for many moments, and then Araminta said, "He was punishing me."

Slowly, Sophie turned back around.

"For not giving him an heir." Araminta's hands began to shake. "He hated me for that."

Sophie didn't know what to say. She didn't know if there was anything to say.

After a long moment, Araminta said, "At first I hated you because you were an insult to me. No woman should have to shelter her husband's bastard."

Sophie said nothing.

"But then . . . But then . . ."

To Sophie's great surprise, Araminta sagged against the wall, as if the memories were sucking away her very strength.

"But then it changed," Araminta finally said. "How could he have had you with some whore, and I could not give him a child?"

There seemed little point in Sophie's defending her mother.

"I didn't just hate *you,* you know," Araminta whispered. "I hated seeing you."

Somehow, that didn't surprise Sophie.

"I hated hearing your voice. I hated the fact that your eyes were his. I hated knowing that you were in my house."

"It was my house, too," Sophie said quietly.

"Yes," Araminta replied. "I know. I hated that, too."

Sophie turned quite sharply, looking Araminta in the eye. "Why are you here?" she asked. "Haven't you done enough? You've already ensured my transportation to Australia."

Araminta shrugged. "I can't seem to stay away. There's something so lovely about seeing you in jail. I shall have to bathe for three hours straight to rid myself of the stench, but it's worth it."

"Then excuse me if I go sit in the corner and pretend to read a book," Sophie spat out. "There is nothing lovely about seeing *you*." She marched over to the wobbly three-legged stool that was her cell's only piece of furniture and sat down, trying not to look as miserable as she felt. Araminta had bested her, it was true, but her spirit had not been broken, and she refused to let Araminta think otherwise.

She sat, arms crossed, her back to the cell opening, listening for signs that Araminta was leaving.

But Araminta stayed.

Finally, after about ten minutes of this nonsense, Sophie jumped to her feet and yelled, "Would you *go?*"

Araminta cocked her head slightly to the side. "I'm thinking."

Sophie would have asked, "About what?" but she was rather afraid of the answer.

"I wonder what it is like in Australia," Araminta mused. "I've never been, of course; no civilized person of my acquaintance would even consider it. But I hear it is dreadfully warm. And you with your fair skin. That lovely complexion of yours isn't likely to survive the hot sun. In fact—"

But whatever Araminta had been about to say was cut off (*thankfully*—because Sophie feared she might be moved to attempt murder if she had to listen to another word) by a commotion erupting around the corner.

"What the devil . . . ?" Araminta said, taking a few steps back and craning her neck for a better view.

And then Sophie heard a very familiar voice.

"Benedict?" she whispered.

"What did you say?" Araminta demanded.

But Sophie had already jumped to her feet and had her face pressed up against the bars of her cell.

"I said," Benedict boomed, *"let us pass!"*

"Benedict!" Sophie yelled. She forgot that she didn't particularly want the Bridgertons to see her in such demeaning surroundings. She forgot that she had no future with him. All she could think was that he had come for her, and he was *here*.

If Sophie could have fit her head through the bars, she would have.

A rather sickening smack, obviously that of flesh against bone, echoed through the air, followed by a duller thud, most probably that of body against floor.

Running steps, and then . . .

"Benedict!"

"Sophie! My God, are you well?" His hands reached through the bars, cupping her cheeks. His lips found hers; the kiss was not one of passion but of terror and relief.

"Mr. Bridgerton?" Araminta squeaked.

Sophie somehow managed to pull her eyes off of Benedict and onto Araminta's shocked face. In the flurry of excitement, she'd quite forgotten that Araminta was still unaware of her ties to the Bridgerton family.

It was one of life's most perfect moments. Maybe it meant she was a shallow person. Maybe it meant that she didn't have her priorities in the proper order. But Sophie just *loved* that Araminta, for whom position and power were everything, had just witnessed Sophie being kissed by one of London's most eligible bachelors.

Of course, Sophie was also rather glad to see Benedict.

Benedict pulled away, his reluctant hands trailing lightly across Sophie's face as he drew back out of her cell. As he crossed his arms, he gave Araminta a glare that Sophie was convinced would scorch earth.

"What are your charges against her?" Benedict demanded.

Sophie's feelings for Araminta could best be categorized as "extreme dislike," but even so, she never would have described the older woman as stupid. She was now, however, prepared to reassess that judgment because Araminta, instead of quaking and cowering as any sane person might do under such fire, instead planted her hands on her hips and belted out, "Theft!"

At that very moment, Lady Bridgerton came scurrying around the corner. "I can't believe Sophie would do any such thing," she said, rushing to her son's side. Her eyes narrowed as she regarded Araminta. "And," she added rather peevishly, "I never liked you, Lady Penwood."

Araminta drew back and planted an affronted hand on her chest. "This is not about me," she huffed. "It is about that girl"—(said with a scathing glance toward Sophie)—"who had the audacity to steal my wedding band!"

"I never stole your wedding band, and you know it!" Sophie protested. "The last thing I would want of yours—"

"You stole my shoe clips!"

Sophie's mouth shut into a belligerent line.

"Ha! See!" Araminta looked about, trying to gauge how many people had seen. "A clear admission of guilt."

"She is your stepdaughter," Benedict ground out. "She should never have been in a position where she felt she had to—"

Araminta's face twisted and grew red. "Don't you *ever*," she warned, "call her my stepdaughter. She is nothing to me. Nothing!"

"I beg your pardon," Lady Bridgerton said in a remarkably polite voice, "but if she truly meant nothing to you, you'd hardly be here in this filthy jail, attempting to have her hanged for theft."

Araminta was saved from having to reply by the arrival of the magistrate, who was followed by an extremely grumpy-looking warden, who also happened to be sporting a rather stunning black eye.

As the warden had spanked her on the bottom while shoving her into her cell, Sophie really couldn't help but smile.

"What is going on here?" the magistrate demanded.

"This woman," Benedict said, his loud, deep voice effectively blotting out all other attempts at an answer, "has accused my fiancée of theft."

Fiancée?

Sophie just managed to snap her mouth closed, but even so, she had to clutch tightly on to the bars of her cell, because her legs had turned to instant water.

"Fiancée?" Araminta gasped.

The magistrate straightened. "And precisely who are you, sir?" he asked, clearly aware that Benedict was someone important, even if he wasn't positive who.

Benedict crossed his arms as he said his name.

The magistrate paled. "Er, any relation to the viscount?"

"He's my brother."

"And she's"—he gulped as he pointed to Sophie—"your fiancée?"

Sophie waited for some sort of supernatural sign to stir the air, branding Benedict as a liar, but to her surprise, nothing happened. Lady Bridgerton was even nodding.

"You can't marry her," Araminta insisted.

Benedict turned to his mother. "Is there any reason I need to consult Lady Penwood about this?"

"None that I can think of," Lady Bridgerton replied.

"She is nothing but a whore," Araminta hissed. "Her mother was a whore, and blood runs—urp!"

Benedict had her by the throat before anyone was even aware that he had moved. "Don't," he warned, "make me hit you."

The magistrate tapped Benedict on the shoulder. "You really ought to let her go."

"Might I muzzle her?"

The magistrate looked torn, but eventually he shook his head.

With obvious reluctance, Benedict released Araminta.

"If you marry her," Araminta said, rubbing her throat, "I shall make sure everyone knows *exactly* what she is—the bastard daughter of a whore."

The magistrate turned to Araminta with a stern expression. "I don't think we need that sort of language."

"I can assure you I am not in the habit of speaking in such a manner," she replied, sniffing disdainfully, "but the occasion warrants strong speech."

Sophie actually bit her knuckle as she stared at Benedict, who was flexing and unflexing his fingers in a most menacing manner. Clearly *he* felt the occasion warranted strong fists.

The magistrate cleared his throat. "You accuse her of a very serious crime." He gulped. "And she's going to be married to a Bridgerton."

"I am the Countess of Penwood," she shrilled. "Countess!"

The magistrate looked back and forth between the occupants of the room. As a countess, Araminta outranked everyone, but at the same time, she was only one Penwood against two Bridgertons, one of whom was very large, visibly angry, and had already planted his fist in the warden's eye.

"She stole from me!"

"No, you stole from her!" Benedict roared.

The room fell into instant silence.

"You stole her very childhood," Benedict said, his body shaking with rage. There were huge gaps in his knowledge of Sophie's life, but somehow he knew that this woman had caused much of the pain that lurked behind her green eyes. And he'd have been willing to bet that her dear, departed papa was responsible for the rest.

Benedict turned to the magistrate and said, "My fiancée is the bastard daughter of the late Earl of Penwood. And that is why the dowager countess has falsely accused her of theft. It is revenge and hate, pure and simple."

The magistrate looked from Benedict to Araminta and

then finally to Sophie. "Is this true?" he asked her. "Have you been falsely accused?"

"She took the shoe clips!" Araminta shrieked. "I swear on my husband's grave, she took the shoe clips!"

"Oh, for the love of God, Mother, *I* took the shoe clips."

Sophie's mouth fell open. "Posy?"

Benedict looked at the newcomer, a short, slightly pudgy young woman who was obviously the countess's daughter, then glanced back to Sophie, who had gone white as a sheet.

"Get out of here," Araminta hissed. "You have no place in these proceedings."

"Obviously she does," the magistrate said, turning to Araminta, "if she took the shoe clips. Do you want to have her charged?"

"She's my daughter!"

"Put me in the cell with Sophie!" Posy said dramatically, clasping one of her hands to her breast with great effect. "If she is transported for theft, then I must be as well."

For the first time in several days, Benedict found himself smiling.

The warden took out his keys. "Sir?" he said hesitantly, nudging the magistrate.

"Put those away," the magistrate snapped. "We're not incarcerating the countess's daughter."

"Do not put those away," Lady Bridgerton cut in. "I want my future daughter-in-law released immediately."

The warden looked helplessly at the magistrate.

"Oh, very well," the magistrate said, jabbing his finger in Sophie's direction. "Let that one free. But no one is going anywhere until I have this sorted out."

Araminta bristled in protest, but Sophie was duly released. She started to run to Benedict, but the magistrate held out a restraining arm. "Not so fast," he warned. "We'll be having no lovey-dovey reunions until I figure out who is to be arrested."

"No one is to be arrested," Benedict growled.

"She is going to Australia!" Araminta cried out, pointing toward Sophie.

"Put me in the cell!" Posy sighed, placing the back of her hand against her brow. "I did it!"

"Posy, will you be quiet?" Sophie whispered. "Trust me, you do not want to be in that cell. It's dreadful. And there are rats."

Posy started inching away from the cell.

"You will never see another invitation again in this town," Lady Bridgerton said to Araminta.

"I am a countess!" Araminta hissed.

"And I am more popular," Lady Bridgerton returned, the snide words so out of character that both Benedict's and Sophie's mouths dropped open.

"Enough!" the magistrate said. He turned to Posy, pointing to Araminta as he said, "Is she your mother?"

Posy nodded.

"And you said you stole the shoe clips?"

Posy nodded again. "And no one stole her wedding ring. It's in her jewelry box at home."

No one gasped, because no one was terribly surprised.

But Araminta said, nonetheless, "It is not!"

"Your other jewelry box," Posy clarified. "The one you keep in the third drawer from the left."

Araminta paled.

The magistrate said, "You don't seem to have a very good case against Miss Beckett, Lady Penwood."

Araminta began to shake with rage, her outstretched arm quivering as she pointed one long finger at Sophie. "She stole from me," she said in a deadly low voice before turning furious eyes on Posy. "My daughter is lying. I do not know why, and I certainly do not know what she hopes to gain, but she is lying."

Something very uncomfortable began to churn in Sophie's stomach. Posy was going to be in horrible trouble when she went home. There was no telling what Araminta would do in retaliation for such public humiliation. She couldn't let Posy take the blame for her. She had to—

"Posy didn't—" The words burst forth from her mouth before she had a chance to think, but she didn't manage to finish her sentence because Posy elbowed her in the belly.

Hard.

"Did you say something?" the magistrate inquired.

Sophie shook her head, completely unable to speak. Posy had knocked her breath clear to Scotland.

The magistrate let out a weary sigh and raked his hand through his thinning blond hair. He looked at Posy, then at Sophie, then Araminta, then Benedict. Lady Bridgerton cleared her throat, forcing him to look at her, too.

"Clearly," the magistrate said, looking very much as if he'd rather be anywhere other than where he was, "this is about a great deal more than a stolen shoe clip."

"Shoe *clips*," Araminta sniffed. "There were two of them."

"Regardless," the magistrate ground out, "you all obviously detest one another, and I would like to know why before I go ahead and charge anyone."

For a second, no one spoke. Then everyone spoke.

"Silence!" the magistrate roared. "You," he said, pointing at Sophie, "start."

"Uhhhh . . ." Now that Sophie actually had the floor, she felt terribly self-conscious.

The magistrate cleared his throat. Loudly.

"What he said was correct," Sophie said quickly, pointing to Benedict. "I am the daughter of the Earl of Penwood, although I was never acknowledged as such."

Araminta opened her mouth to say something, but the magistrate sent her such a withering glare that she kept quiet.

"I lived at Penwood Park for seven years before she married the earl," she continued, motioning to Araminta. "The earl said that he was my guardian, but everyone knew the truth." She paused, remembering her father's face, and thinking that she ought not be so surprised that she couldn't picture him with a smile. "I look a great deal like him," she said.

"I knew your father," Lady Bridgerton said softly. "And your aunt. It explains why I've always thought you looked so familiar."

Sophie flashed her a small, grateful smile. Something in Lady Bridgerton's tone was very reassuring, and it made her feel a little warmer inside, a little more secure.

"Please continue," the magistrate said.

Sophie gave him a nod, then added, "When the earl married the countess, she didn't want me living there, but the earl insisted. I rarely saw him, and I don't think he thought very much of me, but he did see me as his responsibility, and he wouldn't allow her to boot me out. But when he died . . ."

Sophie stopped and swallowed, trying to get past the lump in her throat. She'd never actually told her story to anyone before; the words seemed strange and foreign coming from her mouth. "When he died," she continued, "his will specified that Lady Penwood's portion would be trebled if she kept me in her household until I turned twenty. So she did. But my position changed dramatically. I became a servant. Well, not really a servant." Sophie smiled wryly. "A servant is paid. So I was really more like a slave."

Sophie looked over at Araminta. She was standing with her arms crossed and her nose tipped in the air. Her lips were pursed tightly, and it suddenly struck Sophie how very many times before she had seen that exact same expression on Araminta's face. More times than she could dare to count. Enough times to have broken her soul.

Yet here she was, dirty and penniless to be sure, but with her mind and spirit still strong.

"Sophie?" Benedict asked, gazing at her with a concerned expression. "Is everything all right?"

She nodded slowly, because she was just coming to realize that everything *was* all right. The man she loved had (in a rather roundabout way) just asked her to marry him, Araminta was finally about to receive the drubbing she deserved—at the hands of the Bridgertons, no less, who would leave her in shreds by the time they were through, and Posy . . . now that might have been the loveliest of all. Posy, who had always wanted to be a sister to her, who had never quite had the courage to be herself, had stood up to her mother and quite possibly saved the day. Sophie was one hundred percent certain that if Benedict had not come and declared her his fiancée, Posy's testimony would have been the only thing to save her from transportation—or maybe even execution. And Sophie knew better than anyone that Posy would pay dearly for her courage. Araminta was probably already plotting how to make her life a living hell.

Yes, everything *was* all right, and Sophie suddenly found herself standing a little straighter as she said, "Allow me to finish my story. After the earl died, Lady Penwood kept me on as her unpaid lady's maid. Although in truth I was made to do the work of three maids."

"You know, Lady Whistledown said that very thing just last month!" Posy said excitedly. "I told Mother that she—"

"Posy, shut *up*!" Araminta snapped.

"When I turned twenty," Sophie continued, "she didn't turn me out. To this day I don't know why."

"I think we've heard enough," Araminta said.

"I don't think we've heard nearly enough," Benedict snapped.

Sophie looked to the magistrate for guidance. At his nod she continued. "I can only deduce that she rather enjoyed having someone to order about. Or maybe she just liked having a maid she didn't have to pay. There was nothing left from his will."

"That's not true," Posy blurted out.

Sophie turned to her in shock.

"He did leave you money," Posy insisted.

Sophie felt her jaw go slack. "That's not possible. I had nothing. My father saw to my welfare up to age twenty, but after that—"

"After that," Posy said rather forcefully, "you had a dowry."

"A dowry?" Sophie whispered.

"That's not true!" Araminta shrilled.

"It *is* true," Posy insisted. "You ought not leave incriminating evidence about, Mother. I read a copy of the earl's will last year." She turned to the rest of the room and said, "It was in the same box where she put her wedding band."

"You stole my dowry?" Sophie said, her voice barely more than breath. All these years she'd thought her father had left her with nothing. She'd known that he'd never loved her, that he saw her as little more than his responsibility, but it had stung that he'd left dowries for Rosamund and Posy—who were not even his blood daughters—and not for her.

She'd never really thought that he'd ignored her on purpose; in all truth, she'd mostly felt . . . forgotten.

Which had felt worse than a deliberate snub would have done.

"He left me a dowry," she said dazedly. Then to Benedict, "I have a dowry."

"I don't care if you have a dowry," Benedict replied. "I don't need it."

"I care," Sophie said. "I thought he'd forgotten me. All these years I'd thought he'd written up his will and simply forgotten about me. I know he couldn't really leave money to his bastard daughter, but he'd told all the world I was his ward. There was no reason he couldn't provide for his ward." For some reason she looked to Lady Bridgerton. "He could have provided for a ward. People do that all the time."

The magistrate cleared his throat and turned on Araminta, "And what has happened to her dowry?"

Araminta said nothing.

Lady Bridgerton cleared her throat. "I don't think it's terribly legal," she said, "to embezzle a young woman's dowry." She smiled—a slow, satisfied sort of smile. "Eh, Araminta?"

Chapter 23

Lady Penwood appears to have left town. So does Lady Bridgerton. Interesting . . .

LADY WHISTLEDOWN'S SOCIETY PAPERS, 18 JUNE 1817

Benedict decided he had never loved his mother more than he did at that very minute. He was trying not to grin, but it was exceedingly difficult with Lady Penwood gasping like a fish on land.

The magistrate's eyes bugged out. "You're not suggesting I arrest the *countess*?"

"No, of course not," Violet demurred. "She'd likely go free. The aristocracy rarely pays for its crimes. But," she added, tilting her head slightly to the side as she gave Lady Penwood a very pointed glance, "if you *were* to arrest her, it would be terribly embarrassing while she defended the charges."

"What are you trying to say?" Lady Penwood asked through decidedly clenched teeth.

Violet turned to the magistrate. "Might I have a few moments alone with Lady Penwood?"

"Of course, my lady." He gave her a gruff nod, then barked, "Everyone! Out!"

"No, no," Violet said with a sweet smile as she pressed something that looked suspiciously like a pound note into his palm. "My family may stay."

The magistrate blushed slightly, then grabbed the warden's arm and yanked him out of the room.

"There now," Violet murmured. "Where were we?"

Benedict beamed with pride as he watched his mother march right up to Lady Penwood and stare her down. He stole a glance at Sophie. Her mouth was hanging open.

"My son is going to marry Sophie," Violet said, "and you are going to tell anyone who will listen that she was the ward of your late husband."

"I will never lie for her," Lady Penwood shot back.

Violet shrugged. "Fine. Then you can expect my solicitors to begin looking for Sophie's dowry immediately. After all, Benedict will be entitled to it once he marries her."

Benedict slipped his arm around Sophie's waist and gave her a light squeeze.

"If someone asks me," Lady Penwood ground out, "I will confirm whatever story you bandy about. But do not expect me to go out of my way to help her."

Violet pretended to mull that over, then said, "Excellent. I do believe that will do nicely." She turned to her son. "Benedict?"

He gave her a sharp nod.

His mother turned back to Lady Penwood. "Sophie's father was named Charles Beckett and he was a distant cousin of the earl's, no?"

Lady Penwood looked as if she'd swallowed a bad clam, but she nodded nonetheless.

Violet pointedly turned her back on the countess, and said, "I'm sure some members of the *ton* will consider her a bit shabby, since obviously nobody will be familiar with her family, but at least she will be respectable. After all"—she turned back around and flashed a wide smile at Araminta—"there is that connection with the Penwoods."

Araminta let out a strange, growling sound. It was all Benedict could do not to laugh.

"Oh, magistrate!" Violet called out, and when he bustled back into the room, she smiled gamely at him and said, "I believe my work here is done."

He let out a sigh of relief, saying, "Then I don't have to arrest anyone?"

"It seems not."

He practically sagged against the wall.

"Well, I am leaving!" Lady Penwood announced, as if anyone might possibly miss her. She turned to her daughter with furious eyes. "Come along, Posy."

Benedict watched as the blood quite literally drained from Posy's face. But before he could intervene, Sophie jumped forward, blurting out, "Lady Bridgerton!" just as Araminta roared, *"Now!"*

"Yes, dear?"

Sophie grabbed Violet's arm and pulled her close enough to whisper something in her ear.

"Quite right," Violet said. She turned to Posy. "Miss Gunningworth?"

"Actually, it's Miss Reiling," Posy corrected. "The earl never adopted me."

"Of course. Miss Reiling. How old are you?"

"One-and-twenty, my lady."

"Well, that's certainly old enough to make your own decisions. Would you like to come to my home for a visit?"

"Oh, *yes*!"

"Posy, you may *not* go live with the Bridgertons!" Araminta ordered.

Violet ignored her completely as she said to Posy, "I believe I will quit London early this season. Would you care to join us for an extended stay in Kent?"

Posy nodded quickly. "I would be much obliged."

"That settles it, then."

"That does not settle it," Araminta snapped. "She is my daughter, and—"

"Benedict," Lady Bridgerton said in a rather bored voice, "what was the name of my solicitor?"

"Go!" Araminta spat at Posy. "And don't ever darken my door again."

For the first time that afternoon, Posy began to look a little scared. It didn't help when her mother stalked right up to her and hissed straight in her face, "If you go with them now, you are dead to me. Do you understand? *Dead!*"

Posy threw a panicked look at Violet, who immediately stepped forward and linked their arms together.

"It's all right, Posy," Violet said softly. "You may stay with us as long as you wish."

Sophie stepped forward and slid her arm through Posy's free one. "Now we will be sisters truly," she said, leaning forward and giving her a kiss on the cheek.

"Oh, Sophie," Posy cried out, a well of tears bursting forth. "I'm so sorry! I never stood up for you. I should have said something. I should have done something, but—"

Sophie shook her head. "You were young. I was young. And I know better than anyone how difficult it is to defy *her*." She threw a scathing glare at Araminta.

"Don't you speak to me that way," Araminta seethed, raising her hand as if to strike.

"Ah ah ah!" Violet cut in. "The solicitors, Lady Penwood. Don't forget the solicitors."

Araminta dropped her hand, but she looked as if she might spontaneously burst into flame at any moment.

"Benedict?" Violet called out. "How quickly could we be at the solicitors' office?"

Grinning inside, he gave his chin a thoughtful stroke. "They're not too terribly far away. Twenty minutes? Thirty if the roads are full."

Araminta shook with rage as she directed her words at Violet. "Take her then. She's never been anything to me but a disappointment. And you can expect to be stuck with her until your dying day, as no one is likely to offer for her. I have to bribe men just to ask her to dance."

And then the strangest thing occurred. Sophie began to shake. Her skin turned red, her teeth clenched, and the most amazing roar burst forth from her mouth. And before anyone could even think to intervene, she had planted her fist squarely into Araminta's left eye and sent the older woman sprawling.

Benedict had thought that nothing could have surprised him more than his mother's heretofore undetected Machiavellian streak.

He was wrong.

"That," Sophie hissed, "is *not* for stealing my dowry. It's not for all the times you tried to boot me out of my house before my father died. And it's not even for turning me into your personal slave."

"Er, Sophie," Benedict said mildly, "what, then, is it for?"

Sophie's eyes never wavered off of Araminta's face as she said, "*That* was for not loving your daughters equally."

Posy began to bawl.

"There's a special place in hell for mothers like you," Sophie said, her voice dangerously low.

"You know," the magistrate squeaked, "we really do need to clear this cell out for the next occupant."

"He's right," Violet said quickly, stepping in front of Sophie before she decided to start kicking Araminta. She turned to Posy. "Have you any belongings you wish to retrieve?"

Posy shook her head.

Violet's eyes turned sad as she gave Posy's hand a little squeeze. "We shall make new memories for you, my dear."

Araminta rose to her feet, gave Posy one last horrific glare, then stalked away.

"Well," Violet declared, planting her hands on her hips. "I thought she would never leave."

Benedict disengaged his arm from Sophie's waist with a murmur of, "Don't move a muscle," then walked quickly to his mother's side.

"Have I told you lately," he whispered in her ear, "how much I love you?"

"No," she said with a jaunty smile, "but I know, anyway."

"Have I mentioned that you're the best of mothers?"

"No, but I know that, too."

"Good." He leaned down and dropped a kiss on her cheek. "Thank you. It's a privilege to be your son."

His mother, who had held her own throughout the day, and indeed proven herself the most hardheaded and quick-witted of them all, burst into tears.

"What did you say to her?" Sophie demanded.

"It's all right," Violet said, sniffling mightily. "It's . . ." She threw her arms around Benedict. "I love you, too!"

Posy turned to Sophie and said, "This is a nice family."

Sophie turned to Posy and said, "I know."

One hour later Sophie was in Benedict's sitting room, perched on the very same sofa on which she had lost her innocence just a few weeks earlier. Lady Bridgerton had questioned the wisdom (and propriety) of Sophie's going to Benedict's home by herself, but he had given her such a look that she had quickly backed down, saying only, "Just have her home by seven."

Which gave them one hour together.

"I'm sorry," Sophie blurted out, the instant her bottom touched the sofa. For some reason they hadn't said anything during the carriage ride home. They'd held hands, and Benedict had brought her fingers to his lips, but they hadn't said anything.

Sophie had been relieved. She hadn't been ready for

words. It had been easy at the jail, with all the commotion and so many people, but now that they were alone . . .

She didn't know what to say.

Except, she supposed, "I'm sorry."

"No, I'm sorry," Benedict replied, sitting beside her and taking her hands in his.

"No, I'm—" She suddenly smiled. "This is very silly."

"I love you," he said.

Her lips parted.

"I want to marry you," he said.

She stopped breathing.

"And I don't care about your parents or my mother's bargain with Lady Penwood to make you respectable." He stared down at her, his dark eyes meltingly in love. "I would have married you no matter what."

Sophie blinked. The tears in her eyes were growing fat and hot, and she had a sneaking suspicion that she was about to make a fool of herself by blubbering all over him. She managed to say his name, then found herself completely lost from there.

Benedict squeezed her hands. "We couldn't have lived in London, I know, but we don't need to live in London. When I thought about what it was in life I really needed—not what I wanted, but what I needed—the only thing that kept coming up was you."

"I—"

"No, let me finish," he said, his voice suspiciously hoarse. "I shouldn't have asked you to be my mistress. It wasn't right of me."

"Benedict," she said softly, "what else would you have done? You thought me a servant. In a perfect world we could have married, but this isn't a perfect world. Men like you don't marry—"

"Fine. I wasn't wrong to ask, then." He tried to smile. It came out lopsided. "I would have been a fool not to ask. I wanted you so badly, and I think I already loved you, and—"

"Benedict, you don't have to—"

"Explain? Yes, I do. I should never have pressed the issue once you refused my offer. It was unfair of me to ask, especially when we both knew that I would eventually be expected to marry. I would die before sharing you. How could I ask you to do the same?"

She reached out and brushed something off of his cheek. Jesus, was he crying? He couldn't remember the last time he'd cried. When his father had died, perhaps? Even then, his tears had fallen in private.

"There are so many reasons I love you," he said, each word emerging with careful precision. He knew that he had won her. She wasn't going to run away; she *would* be his wife. But he still wanted this to be perfect. A man only got one shot at declaring himself to his true love; he didn't want to muck it up completely.

"But one of the things I love best," he continued, "is the fact that you know yourself. You know who you are, and what you value. You have principles, Sophie, and you stick by them." He took her hand and brought it to his lips. "That is so rare."

Her eyes were filling with tears, and all he wanted to do was hold her, but he knew he had to finish. So many words had been welling up inside of him, and they all had to be said.

"And," he said, his voice dropping in volume, "you took the time to see *me*. To know me. Benedict. Not Mr. Bridgerton, not 'Number Two.' Benedict."

She touched his cheek. "You're the finest person I know. I adore your family, but I love *you*."

He crushed her to him. He couldn't help it. He had to feel her in his arms, to reassure himself that she was there and that she would always be there. With him, by his side, until death did they part. It was strange, but he was driven by the oddest compulsion to hold her . . . just hold her.

He wanted her, of course. He always wanted her. But more than that, he wanted to hold her. To smell her, to feel her.

He was, he realized, comforted by her presence. They didn't need to talk. They didn't even need to touch (although he wasn't about to let go just then). Simply put, he was a happier man—and quite possibly a better man—when she was near.

He buried his face in her hair, inhaling her scent, smelling . . .

Smelling . . .

He drew back. "Would you care for a bath?"

Her face turned an instant scarlet. "Oh, no," she moaned, the words muffled into the hand she'd clapped over her mouth. "It was so filthy in jail, and I was forced to sleep on the ground, and—"

"Don't tell me any more," he said.

"But—"

"Please." If he heard more he might have to kill someone. As long as there had been no permanent damage, he didn't want to know the details.

"I think," he said, the first hint of a smile tugging at the left corner of his mouth, "that you should take a bath."

"Right." She nodded as she rose to her feet. "I'll go straight to your mother's—"

"Here."

"Here?"

The smile spread to the right corner of his mouth. "Here."

"But we told your mother—"

"That you'd be home by nine."

"I think she said seven."

"Did she? Funny, I heard nine."

"Benedict . . ."

He took her hand and pulled her toward the door. "Seven sounds an *awful* lot like nine."

"Benedict . . ."

"Actually, it sounds even more like eleven."

"Benedict!"

He deposited her right by the door. "Stay here."

"I beg your pardon?"

"Don't move a muscle," he said, touching his fingertip to her nose.

Sophie watched helplessly as he slipped out into the hall, only to return two minutes later. "Where did you go?" she asked.

"To order a bath."

"But—"

His eyes grew very, very wicked. "For two."

She gulped.

He leaned forward. "They happened to have water heating already."

"They did?"

He nodded. "It'll only take a few minutes to fill the tub."

She glanced toward the front door. "It's nearly seven."

"But I'm allowed to keep you until twelve."

"Benedict!"

He pulled her close. "You want to stay."

"I never said that."

"You don't have to. If you really disagreed with me, you'd have something more to say than, 'Benedict'!"

She had to smile; he did *that* good an imitation of her voice.

His mouth curved into a devilish grin. "Am I wrong?"

She looked away, but she knew her lips were twitching.

"I thought not," he murmured. He motioned with his head toward the stairs. "Come with me."

She went.

To Sophie's great surprise, Benedict vacated the room while she undressed for her bath. She held her breath as she pulled her dress over her head. He was right; she did smell rank.

The maid who had drawn the bath had scented it with oil and a sudsy soap that left bubbles floating on the surface.

Once Sophie had shed all of her clothing, she dipped her toe into the steaming water. The rest of her soon followed.

Heaven. It was hard to believe it had only been two days since she'd had a bath. One night in jail made it feel more like a year.

Sophie tried to clear her mind and enjoy the hedonism of the moment, but it was difficult to enjoy with the anticipation growing within her veins. She knew when she'd decided to stay that Benedict planned on joining her. She could have refused; for all his wheedling and cajoling, he would have taken her back home to his mother's.

But she had decided to stay. Somewhere between the sitting-room doorway and the base of the stairs she'd realized she *wanted* to stay. It had been such a long road to this moment, and she wasn't quite ready to relinquish him, even if it would only be until the following morning, when he was sure to come by his mother's for breakfast.

He would be here soon. And when he was . . .

She shivered. Even in the steaming hot tub, she shivered. And then, as she was sinking deeper into the water, allowing it to rise above her shoulders and neck, even right up to her nose, she heard the click of the door opening.

Benedict. He was wearing a dark green dressing gown, tied with a sash at his waist. His feet were bare, as were his legs from the knees down.

"I hope you don't mind if I have this destroyed," he said, glancing down at her dress.

She smiled at him and shook her head. It wasn't what she'd been expecting him to say, and she knew that he'd done it to set her at ease.

"I'll send someone to fetch you another," he said.

"Thank you." She shifted slightly in the water to make room for him, but he surprised her by walking to her end of the tub.

"Lean forward," he murmured.

She did, and sighed with pleasure as he began to wash her back.

"I've dreamed of doing this for years."

"Years?" she asked, amused.

"Mmm-hmm. I had *many* dreams about you after the masquerade."

Sophie was glad she was leaning forward, her forehead resting on her bent knees, because she blushed.

"Dunk your head so I can wash your hair," he ordered.

She slid under the water, then quickly came back up.

Benedict rubbed the bar of soap in his hands and then began to work the lather through her hair. "It was longer before," he commented.

"I had to cut it," she said. "I sold it to a wigmaker."

She wasn't sure, but she thought she might have heard him growl.

"It used to be much shorter," she added.

"Ready to rinse."

She dunked back in the tub, swishing her head this way and that under the water before coming back up for air.

Benedict cupped his hands and filled them with water. "You've still got some in the back," he said, letting the water pour over her hair.

Sophie let him repeat that process a few times, then finally asked, "Aren't you coming in?" It was dreadfully brazen of her, and she knew she must be blushing like a raspberry, but she simply had to know.

He shook his head. "I'd planned to, but this is too much fun."

"Washing me?" she asked doubtfully.

One corner of his mouth quirked into the faintest of half smiles. "I'm rather looking forward to drying you off as well." He reached down and picked up a large white towel. "Up you go."

Sophie chewed on her lower lip in indecision. She had, of

course, already been as close to him as two people could be, but she wasn't so sophisticated that she could rise naked from the tub without a large degree of embarrassment.

Benedict smiled faintly as he stood and unfolded the towel. Holding it wide, he averted his gaze and said, "I'll have you all wrapped up before I can see a thing."

Sophie took a deep breath and stood, somehow feeling that that one action might mark the beginning of the rest of her life.

Benedict gently wrapped the towel around her, his hands bringing the corners to her face when he was done. He dabbed at her cheeks, where light droplets of water were still clinging to her skin, then leaned down and kissed her nose. "I'm glad you're here," he murmured.

"I'm glad, too."

He touched her chin. His eyes never left hers, and she almost felt as if he'd touched those as well. And then, with the softest, most tender caress imaginable, he kissed her. Sophie didn't just feel loved; she felt revered.

"I should wait until Monday," he said, "but I don't want to."

"I don't want you to wait," she whispered.

He kissed her again, this time with a bit more urgency. "You're so beautiful," he murmured. "Everything I ever dreamed of."

His lips found her cheek, her chin, her neck, and every kiss, every nibble robbed her of balance and breath. She was sure her legs would give out, sure her strength would fail her under his tender onslaught, and just when she was convinced she'd crumple to the floor, he scooped her into his arms and carried her to the bed.

"In my heart," he vowed, settling her against the quilts and pillows, "you are my wife."

Sophie's breath caught.

"After our wedding it will be legal," he said, stretching out alongside her, "blessed by God and country, but right now—" His voice grew hoarse as he propped himself up on one elbow so that he could gaze into her eyes. "Right now it is *true*."

Sophie reached up and touched his face. "I love you," she whispered. "I have always loved you. I think I loved you before I even knew you."

He leaned down to kiss her anew, but she stopped him with a breathy, "No, wait."

He paused, mere inches from her lips.

"At the masquerade," she said, her voicc uncharacteristically shaky, "even before I saw you, I *felt* you. Anticipation. Magic. There was something in the air. And when I turned, and you were there, it was as if you'd been waiting for me, and I knew that you were the reason I'd stolen into the ball."

Something wet hit her cheek. A single tear, fallen from his eye.

"You are the reason I exist," she said softly, "the very reason I was born."

He opened his mouth, and for a moment she was certain he would say something, but the only sound that emerged was a rough, halting noise, and she realized that he was overcome, that he could not speak.

She was undone.

Benedict kissed her again, trying to show in deeds what he could not say in words. He hadn't thought he could love her any more than he did just five seconds earlier, but when she'd said . . . when she'd told him . . .

His heart had grown, and he'd thought it might burst.

He loved her. Suddenly the world was a very simple place. He loved her, and that was all that mattered.

His robe and her towel melted away, and when they were skin to skin he worshipped her with his hands and lips. He wanted her to realize the extent of his need for her, and he wanted her to know the same desire.

"Oh, Sophie," he groaned, her name the only word he could manage to say. "Sophie, Sophie, Sophie."

She smiled up at him, and he was struck by the most remarkable desire to laugh. He was happy, he realized. So damned happy.

And it felt good.

He positioned himself over her, ready to enter her, ready to make her his. This was different from the last time, when they'd both been swept away by emotion. This time they had been deliberate. They had chosen more than passion; they had chosen each other.

"You're mine," he said, his eyes never leaving hers as he slid inside. "You're mine."

And much later, when they were exhausted and spent, lying in each other's arms, he brought his lips to her ear and whispered, "And I'm yours."

Several hours later, Sophie yawned and blinked herself awake, wondering why she felt so lovely and warm, and—

"Benedict!" she gasped. "What time is it?"

He didn't respond, so she clutched at his shoulder and shook hard. "Benedict! Benedict!"

He grunted as he rolled over. "I'm sleeping."

"What time is it?"

He buried his face in the pillow. "Haven't the foggiest."

"I'm supposed to be at your mother's by seven."

"Eleven," he mumbled.

"Seven!"

He opened one eye. It looked like it took a great deal of effort. "You knew you weren't going to make it back by seven when you decided to take a bath."

"I know, but I didn't think I'd be much past nine."

Benedict blinked a few times as he looked around the room. "I don't think you're going to make it—"

But she'd already caught sight of the mantel clock and was presently choking frantically.

"Are you all right?" he inquired.

"It's three in the morning!"

He smiled. "You might as well spend the night, then."

"Benedict!"

"You wouldn't want to put out any of the servants, would you? They're all quite asleep, I'm sure."

"But I—"

"Have mercy, woman," he finally declared. "I'm marrying you next week."

That got her attention. "Next week?" she squeaked.

He tried to assume a serious mien. "It's best to take care of these things quickly."

"Why?"

"Why?" he echoed.

"Yes, why?"

"Er, ah, stemming gossip and all that."

Her lips parted and her eyes grew round. "Do you think Lady Whistledown will write about me?"

"God, I hope not," he muttered.

Her face fell.

"Well, I suppose she *might*. Why on earth would you want her to?"

"I've been reading her column for years. I always dreamed of seeing my name there."

He shook his head. "You have very strange dreams."

"Benedict!"

"Very well, yes, I imagine Lady Whistledown will report our marriage, if not before the ceremony, then certainly very quickly after the fact. She's diabolical that way."

"I wish I knew who she was."

"You and half of London."

"Me and *all* of London, I should think." She sighed, then said, not very convincingly, "I really should go. Your mother is surely worried about me."

He shrugged. "She knows where you are."

"But she'll think less of me."

"I doubt it. She'll give you a bit of latitude, I'm sure, considering we're to be married in three days."

"Three days?" she yelped. "I thought you said next week."

"Three days *is* next week."

Sophie frowned. "Oh. You're right. Monday, then?"

He nodded, looking very satisfied.

"Imagine that," she said. "I'll be in *Whistledown*."

He propped himself up on one elbow, eyeing her suspiciously. "Are you looking forward to marrying me," he asked in an amused voice, "or is it merely the *Whistledown* mention that has you so excited?"

She gave him a playful swat on the shoulder.

"Actually," he said thoughtfully, "you've already been in *Whistledown*."

"I have? When?"

"After the masquerade. Lady Whistledown remarked that I'd been rather taken with a mystery woman in silver. Try as she might, she couldn't deduce your identity." He grinned. "It very well may be the only secret in London she *hasn't* uncovered."

Sophie's face went instantly serious and she scooted a foot or so away from him on the bed. "Oh, Benedict. I have to . . . I want to . . . That is to say . . ." She stopped, looking away for a few seconds before turning back. "I'm sorry."

He considered yanking her back into his arms, but she looked so damned earnest he had no choice but to take her seriously. "What for?"

"For not telling you who I was. It was wrong of me." She bit her lip. "Well, not *wrong* precisely."

He drew back slightly. "If it wasn't wrong, then what was it?"

"I don't know. I can't explain exactly why I did what I did, but it just . . ." She chewed on her lips some more. He started to think that she might do herself permanent harm.

She sighed. "I didn't tell you right away because it didn't seem to make any sense to do so. I was so sure we'd part ways just as soon as we left the Cavenders. But then you grew ill, and I had to care for you, and you didn't recognize me, and . . ."

He lifted a finger to her lips. "It doesn't matter."

Her brows rose. "It seemed to matter a great deal the other night."

He didn't know why, but he just didn't want to get into a serious discussion at that moment. "A lot has changed since then."

"Don't you want to know why I didn't tell you who I was?"

He touched her cheeks. "I know who you are."

She chewed on her lip.

"And do you want to hear the funniest part?" he continued. "Do you know one of the reasons I was so hesitant to give my heart completely to you? I'd been saving a piece of it for the lady from the masquerade, always hoping that one day I'd find her."

"Oh, Benedict," she sighed, thrilled by his words, and at the same time miserable that she had hurt him so.

"Deciding to marry you meant I had to abandon my dream of marrying *her*," he said quietly. "Ironic, isn't it?"

"I'm sorry I hurt you by not revealing my identity," she said, not quite looking at his face, "but I'm not sure that I'm sorry I did it. Does that make any sense?"

He didn't say anything.

"I think I would do the same thing again."

He still didn't say anything. Sophie started to feel very uneasy inside.

"It just seemed like the right thing to do at the time," she persisted. "Telling you that I'd been at the masquerade would have served no purpose."

"I would have known the truth," he said softly.

"Yes, and what would you have done with that truth?" She sat up, pulling the covers until they were tucked under her arms. "You would have wanted your mystery woman to be your mistress, just as you wanted the housemaid to be your mistress."

He said nothing, just stared at her face.

"I guess what I'm saying," Sophie said quickly, "is that if I'd known at the beginning what I know now, I would have said something. But I didn't know, and I thought I'd just be positioning myself for heartbreak, and—" She choked on her final words, frantically searching his face for some kind of clue to his feelings. "*Please* say something."

"I love you," he said.

It was all she needed.

Epilogue

Sunday's bash at Bridgerton House is sure to be the event of the season. The entire family will gather, along with a hundred or so of their closest friends, to celebrate the dowager vis countess's birthday.

It is considered crass to mention a lady's age, and so This Author will not reveal which birthday Lady Bridgerton is celebrating.

But have no fear . . . This Author knows!

LADY WHISTLEDOWN'S SOCIETY PAPERS, 9 APRIL 1824

"Stop! Stop!"

Sophie shrieked with laughter as she ran down the stone steps that led to the garden behind Bridgerton House. After three children and seven years of marriage, Benedict could still make her smile, still make her laugh . . . and he still chased her around the house any chance he could get.

"Where are the children?" she gasped, once he'd caught her at the base of the steps.

"Francesca is watching them."

"And your mother?"

He grinned. "I daresay Francesca is watching her, too."

"Anyone could stumble upon us out here," she said, looking this way and that.

His smile turned wicked. "Maybe," he said, catching hold of her green-velvet skirt and reeling her in, "we should adjourn to the *private* terrace."

The words were oh-so-familiar, and it was only a second before she was transported back nine years to the masquerade ball. "The private terrace, you say?" she asked, amusement dancing in her eyes. "And how, pray tell, would you know of a *private* terrace?"

His lips brushed against hers. "I have my ways," he murmured.

"And I," she returned, smiling slyly, "have my secrets."

He drew back. "Oh? And will you share?"

"We five," she said with a nod, "are about to be six."

He looked at her face, then looked at her belly. "Are you sure?"

"As sure as I was last time."

He took her hand and raised it to lips. "This one will be a girl."

"That's what you said last time."

"I know, but—"

"And the time before."

"All the more reason for the odds to favor me *this* time."

She shook her head. "I'm glad you're not a gambler."

He smiled at that. "Let's not tell anyone yet."

"I think a few people already suspect," Sophie admitted.

"I want to see how long it takes that Whistledown woman to figure it out," Benedict said.

"Are you serious?"

"The blasted woman knew about Charles, and she knew about Alexander, and she knew about William."

Sophie smiled as she let him pull her into the shadows. "Do you realize that I have been mentioned in Whistledown *two hundred* and thirty-two times?"

That stopped him cold. "You've been counting?"

"Two hundred and thirty-three if you include the time after the masquerade."

"I can't believe you've been counting."

She gave him a nonchalant shrug. "It's exciting to be mentioned."

Benedict thought it was a bloody nuisance to be mentioned, but he wasn't about to spoil her delight, so instead he just said, "At least she always writes nice things about you. If she didn't, I might have to hunt her down and run her out of the country."

Sophie couldn't help but smile. "Oh, *please*. I hardly think you could discover her identity when no one else in the *ton* has managed it."

He raised one arrogant brow. "That doesn't sound like wifely devotion and confidence to me."

She pretended to examine her glove. "You needn't expend the energy. She's obviously very good at what she does."

"Well, she won't know about Violet," Benedict vowed. "At least not until it's obvious to the world."

"Violet?" Sophie asked softly.

"It's time my mother had a grandchild named after her, don't you think?"

Sophie leaned against him, letting her cheek rest against the crisp linen of his shirt. "I think Violet is a lovely name," she murmured, nestling deeper into the shelter of his arms. "I just hope it's a girl. Because if it's a boy, he's never going to forgive us . . ."

Later that night, in a town house in the very best part of London, a woman picked up her quill and wrote:

Lady Whistledown's Society Papers
12 April 1824

Ah, Gentle Reader, This Author has learned that the Bridgerton grandchildren will soon number eleven . . .

But when she tried to write more, all she could do was close her eyes and sigh. She'd been doing this for so very long now. Could it have possibly been eleven years already?

Maybe it was time to move on. She was tired of writing about everyone else. It was time to live her own life.

And so Lady Whistledown set down her quill and walked to her window, pushing aside her sage green curtains and looking out into the inky night.

"Time for something new," she whispered. "Time to finally be me."

Dear Reader,

Have you ever wondered what happened to your favorite characters after you closed the final page? Wanted just a little bit more of a favorite novel? I have, and if the questions from my readers are any indication, I'm not the only one. So after countless requests from Bridgerton fans, I decided to try something a little different, and I wrote a "2nd Epilogue" for each of the novels. These are the stories that come after *the stories.*

At first, the Bridgerton 2nd Epilogues were available exclusively online; later they were published (along with a novella about Violet Bridgerton) in a collection called The Bridgertons: Happily Ever After. *Now, for the first time, each 2nd Epilogue is being included with the novel it follows. I hope you enjoy Benedict and Sophie as they continue their journey.*

Warmly,
Julia Quinn

An Offer From a Gentleman: The 2nd Epilogue

At five and twenty, Miss Posy Reiling was considered *nearly* a spinster. There were those who might have considered her past the cutoff from young miss to hopeless ape leader; three and twenty was often cited as the unkind chronological border. But Posy was, as Lady Bridgerton (her unofficial guardian) often remarked, a unique case.

In debutante years, Lady Bridgerton insisted, Posy was only twenty, *maybe* twenty-one.

Eloise Bridgerton, the eldest unmarried daughter of the house, put it a little more bluntly: Posy's first few years out in society had been worthless and should not be counted against her.

Eloise's youngest sister, Hyacinth, never one to be verbally outdone, simply stated that Posy's years between the ages of seventeen and twenty-two had been "utter rot."

It was at this point that Lady Bridgerton had sighed, poured herself a stiff drink, and sunk into a chair. Eloise, whose mouth was as sharp as Hyacinth's (though thankfully tempered by some discretion), had remarked that they had best get Hyacinth married off quickly or their mother was going to become an alcoholic. Lady Bridgerton had not appreciated the comment, although she privately thought it might be true.

Hyacinth was like that.

But this is a story about Posy. And as Hyacinth has a tendency to take over anything in which she is involved . . . please do forget about her for the remainder of the tale.

The truth was, Posy's first few years on the Marriage Mart *had* been utter rot. It was true that she'd made her debut at a proper age of seventeen. And, indeed, she was the stepdaughter of the late Earl of Penwood, who had so prudently made arrangements for her dowry before his untimely death several years prior.

She was perfectly pleasant to look at, if perhaps a little plump, she had all of her teeth, and it had been remarked upon more than once that she had uncommonly kind eyes.

Anyone assessing her on paper would not understand why she'd gone so long without even a single proposal.

But anyone assessing her on paper might not have known about Posy's mother, Araminta Gunningworth, the dowager Countess of Penwood.

Araminta was splendidly beautiful, even more so than Posy's elder sister, Rosamund, who had been blessed with fair hair, a rosebud mouth, and eyes of cerulean blue.

Araminta was ambitious, too, and enormously proud of her ascension from the gentry to the aristocracy. She'd gone from Miss Wincheslea to Mrs. Reiling to Lady Penwood, although to hear her speak of it, her mouth had been dripping silver spoons since the day of her birth.

But Araminta had failed in one regard; she had not been able to provide the earl with an heir. Which meant that despite the *Lady* before her name, she did not wield a terribly large amount of power. Nor did she have access to the type of fortune she felt was her due.

And so she pinned her hopes on Rosamund. Rosamund, she was sure, would make a splendid match. Rosamund was achingly beautiful. Rosamund could sing and play the pianoforte, and if she wasn't talented with a needle, then she knew exactly how to poke Posy, who was. And since Posy did not enjoy repeated needle-sized skin punctures, it was Rosamund's embroidery that always looked exquisite.

Posy's, on the other hand, generally went unfinished.

And since money was not as plentiful as Araminta would have her peers believe, she lavished what they had on Rosamund's wardrobe, and Rosamund's lessons, and Rosamund's *everything*.

She wasn't about to let Posy look embarrassingly shabby, but really, there was no point in spending more than she had to on her. You couldn't turn a sow's ear into a silk purse, and you certainly couldn't turn a Posy into a Rosamund.

But.

(And this is a rather large but.)

Things didn't turn out so well for Araminta. It's a terribly long story, and one probably deserving of a book of its own, but suffice it to say that Araminta cheated another young girl of her inheritance, one Sophia Beckett, who happened to be the earl's illegitimate daughter. She would have got away with it completely, because who cares about a bastard, except that Sophie had had the temerity to fall in love with Benedict Bridgerton, second son in the aforementioned (and extremely well-connected) Bridgerton family.

This would not have been enough to seal Araminta's fate, except that Benedict decided he loved Sophie back. Quite madly. And while he might have overlooked embezzlement, he certainly could not do the same for having Sophie hauled off to jail (on mostly fraudulent charges).

Things were looking grim for dear Sophie, even with intervention on the part of Benedict and his mother, the also aforementioned Lady Bridgerton. But then who should show up to save the day but Posy?

Posy, who had been ignored for most of her life.

Posy, who had spent years feeling guilty for not standing up to her mother.

Posy, who was still a little bit plump and never would be as beautiful as her sister, but who would always have the *kindest* eyes.

Araminta had disowned her on the spot, but before Posy had even a moment to wonder if this constituted good or bad fortune, Lady Bridgerton had invited her to live in her home, for as long as she wished.

Posy might have spent twenty-two years being poked and pricked by her sister, but she was no fool. She accepted gladly, and did not even bother to return home to collect her belongings.

As for Araminta, well, she'd quickly ascertained that it was in her best interest not to make any public comment about the soon-to-be Sophia

Bridgerton unless it was to declare her an absolute joy and delight.

Which she didn't do. But she didn't go around calling her a bastard, either, which was all anyone could have expected.

All of this explains (in an admittedly roundabout way) why Lady Bridgerton was Posy's unofficial guardian, and why she considered her a unique case. To her mind, Posy had not truly debuted until she came to live with her. Penwood dowry or no, who on earth would have looked twice at a girl in ill-fitting clothes, always stuck off in the corner, trying her best not to be noticed by her own mother?

And if she was still unmarried at twenty-five, why, that was certainly equal to a mere twenty for anyone else. Or so Lady Bridgerton said.

And no one really wanted to contradict her.

As for *Posy*, she often said that her life had not really begun until she went to jail.

This tended to require some explaining, but most of Posy's statements did.

Posy didn't mind. The Bridgertons actually *liked* her explanations. They liked *her*.

Even better, she rather liked herself.

Which was more important than she'd ever realized.

Sophie Bridgerton considered her life to be almost perfect. She adored her husband, loved her cozy home, and was quite certain that her two little boys were the most handsome, brilliant creatures ever to be born anywhere, anytime, any . . . well, any *any* one could come up with.

It was true that they *had* to live in the country because even with the sizable influence of the Bridgerton family, Sophie was, on account of her birth, not likely to be accepted by some of the more particular London hostesses.

(Sophie called them particular. Benedict called them something else entirely.)

But that didn't matter. Not really. She and Benedict preferred life in the country, so it was no great loss. And even though it would always be whispered that Sophie's birth was not what it should be, the official story was that she was a distant—and completely legitimate—relative of the late Earl of Penwood. And even though no one *really* believed Araminta when she'd confirmed the story, confirmed it she had.

Sophie knew that by the time her children were grown, the rumors would be old enough so that no doors would be closed to them, should they wish to take their spots in London society.

All was well. All was perfect.

Almost. Really, all she needed to do was find a husband for Posy. Not just any husband, of course. Posy deserved the best.

"She is not for everyone," Sophie had admitted to Benedict the previous day, "but that does not mean she is not a brilliant catch."

"Of course not," he murmured. He was trying to read the newspaper. It was three days old, but to his mind it was all still news to him.

She looked at him sharply.

"I mean, of course," he said quickly. And

then, when she did not immediately carry on, he amended, "I mean whichever one means that she will make someone a splendid wife."

Sophie let out a sigh. "The problem is that most people don't seem to realize how lovely she is."

Benedict gave a dutiful nod. He understood his role in this particular tableau. It was the sort of conversation that wasn't really a conversation. Sophie was thinking aloud, and he was there to provide the occasional verbal prompt or gesture.

"Or at least that's what your mother reports," Sophie continued.

"Mmm-hmm."

"She doesn't get asked to dance nearly as often as she ought."

"Men are beasts," Benedict agreed, flipping to the next page.

"It's true," Sophie said with some emotion. "Present company excluded, of course."

"Oh, of course."

"Most of the time," she added, a little waspishly.

He gave her a wave. "Think nothing of it."

"Are you listening to me?" she asked, her eyes narrowing.

"Every word," he assured her, actually lowering the paper enough to see her above the top edge. He hadn't actually *seen* her eyes narrow, but he knew her well enough to hear it in her voice.

"We need to find a husband for Posy."

He considered that. "Perhaps she doesn't want one."

"Of course she wants one!"

"I have been told," Benedict opined, "that every

woman wants a husband, but in my experience, this is not precisely true."

Sophie just stared at him, which he did not find surprising. It was a fairly lengthy statement, coming from a man with a newspaper.

"Consider Eloise," he said. He shook his head, which was his usual inclination while thinking of his sister. "How many men has she refused now?"

"At least three," Sophie said, "but that's not the point."

"What *is* the point, then?"

"Posy."

"Right," he said slowly.

Sophie leaned forward, her eyes taking on an odd mix of bewilderment and determination. "I don't know why the gentlemen don't see how wonderful she is."

"She's an acquired taste," Benedict said, momentarily forgetting that he wasn't supposed to offer a real opinion.

"What?"

"*You* said she's not for everyone."

"But you're not supposed to—" She slumped a bit in her seat. "Never mind."

"What were you going to say?"

"Nothing."

"*Sophie,*" he prodded.

"Just that you weren't supposed to agree with me," she muttered. "But even I can recognize how ridiculous that is."

It was a splendid thing, Benedict had long since realized, to have a sensible wife.

Sophie didn't speak for some time, and Benedict would have resumed his perusal of the newspaper, except that it was too interesting watching her face. She'd chew on her lip, then let out a weary sigh, then straighten a bit, as if she'd got a good thought, then frown.

Really, he could have watched her all afternoon.

"Can *you* think of anyone?" she suddenly asked.

"For Posy?"

She gave him a look. A whom-else-might-I-be-speaking-of look.

He let out a breath. He should have anticipated the question, but he'd begun to think of the painting he was working on his studio. It was a portrait of Sophie, the fourth he'd done in their three years of marriage. He was beginning to think that he'd not got her mouth quite right. It wasn't the lips so much as the corners of her mouth. A good portraitist needed to understand the muscles of the human body, even those on the face, and—

"Benedict!"

"What about Mr. Folsom?" he said quickly.

"The solicitor?"

He nodded.

"He looks shifty."

She was right, he realized, now that he thought on it. "Sir Reginald?"

Sophie gave him another look, visibly disappointed with his selection. "He's *fat*."

"So is—"

"She is *not*," Sophie cut in. "She is pleasantly plump."

"I was going to say that so is Mr. Folsom," Benedict said, feeling the need to defend himself, "but that you had chosen to comment upon his shiftiness."

"Oh."

He allowed himself the smallest of smiles.

"Shiftiness is far worse than excess weight," she mumbled.

"I could not agree more," Benedict said. "What about Mr. Woodson?"

"Who?"

"The new vicar. The one you said—"

"—has a brilliant smile!" Sophie finished excitedly. "Oh, Benedict, that's perfect! Oh, I love you love you love you!" At that, she practically leapt across the low table between them and into his arms.

"Well, I love you, too," he said, and he congratulated himself on having had the foresight to shut the door to the drawing room earlier.

The newspaper flew over his shoulder, and all was right with the world.

The season drew to a close a few weeks later, and so Posy decided to accept Sophie's invitation for an extended visit. London was hot and sticky and rather smelly in the summer, and a sojourn in the country seemed just the thing. Besides, she had not seen either of her godsons in several months, and she had been *aghast* when Sophie had written to say that Alexander had already begun to lose some of his baby fat.

Oh, he was just the most squeezable, adorable thing. She had to go see him before he grew too thin. She simply had to.

And it would be nice to see Sophie, too. She'd

written that she was still feeling a bit weak, and Posy did like to be a help.

A few days into the visit, she and Sophie were taking tea, and talk turned, as it occasionally did, to Araminta and Rosamund, whom Posy occasionally bumped into in London. After over a year of silence, her mother finally had begun to acknowledge her, but even so, conversation was brief and stilted. Which, Posy had decided, was for the best. Her mother might have had nothing to say to her, but she didn't have anything to say to her mother, either.

As far as epiphanies went, it had been rather liberating.

"I saw her outside the milliner," Posy said, fixing her tea just the way she liked it, with extra milk and no sugar. "She'd just come down the steps, and I couldn't avoid her, and then I realized I didn't want to avoid her. Not that I wished to speak with her, of course." She took a sip. "Rather, I didn't wish to expend the energy needed to hide."

Sophie nodded approvingly.

"And then we spoke, and said nothing, really, although she did manage to get in one of her clever little insults."

"I hate that."

"I know. She's *so* good at it."

"It's a talent," Sophie remarked. "Not a good one, but a talent nonetheless."

"Well," Posy continued, "I must say, I was rather mature about the entire encounter. I let her say what she wished, and then I bid her goodbye. And then I had the most amazing realization."

"What is that?"

Posy gave a smile. "I like myself."

"Well, of course you do," Sophie said, blinking with confusion.

"No, no, you don't understand," Posy said. It was strange, because Sophie ought to have understood perfectly. She was the only person in the world who knew what it meant to live as Araminta's unfavored child. But there was something so sunny about Sophie. There always had been. Even when Araminta treated her as a virtual slave, Sophie had never seemed beaten. There had always been a singular spirit to her, a sparkle. It wasn't defiance; Sophie was the least defiant person Posy knew, except perhaps for herself.

Not defiance . . . resilience. Yes, that was it exactly.

At any rate, Sophie ought to have understood what Posy had meant, but she didn't, so Posy said, "I didn't always like myself. And why should I have done? My own mother didn't like me."

"Oh, Posy," Sophie said, her eyes brimming with tears, "you mustn't—"

"No, no," Posy said good-naturedly. "Don't think anything of it. It doesn't bother me."

Sophie just looked at her.

"Well, not anymore," Posy amended. She eyed the plate of biscuits sitting on the table between them. She really oughtn't to eat one. She'd had three, and she *wanted* three more, so maybe that meant that if she had one, she was really abstaining from two . . .

She twiddled her fingers against her leg. Probably she shouldn't have one. Probably she should leave them for Sophie, who had just had a baby and needed to regain her strength. Although

Sophie did look perfectly recovered, and little Alexander was already four months old . . .

"Posy?"

She looked up.

"Is something amiss?"

Posy gave a little shrug. "I can't decide whether I wish to eat a biscuit."

Sophie blinked. "A biscuit? Really?"

"There are at least two reasons why I should not, and probably more than that." She paused, frowning.

"You looked quite serious," Sophie remarked. "Almost as if you were conjugating Latin."

"Oh, no, I should look far more at peace if I were conjugating Latin," Posy declared. "That would be quite simple, as I know nothing about it. Biscuits, on the other hand, I ponder endlessly." She sighed and looked down at her middle. "Much to my dismay."

"Don't be silly, Posy," Sophie scolded. "You are the loveliest woman of my acquaintance."

Posy smiled and took the biscuit. The marvelous thing about Sophie was that she wasn't lying. Sophie really did think her the loveliest woman of her acquaintance. But then again, Sophie had always been that sort of person. She saw kindness where others saw . . . Well, where others didn't even bother to look, to be frank.

Posy took a bite and chewed, deciding that it was absolutely worth it. Butter, sugar, and flour. What could be better?

"I received a letter from Lady Bridgerton today," Sophie remarked.

Posy looked up in interest. Technically, Lady

Bridgerton could mean Sophie's sister-in-law, the wife of the current viscount. But they both knew she referred to Benedict's mother. To them, she would always be Lady Bridgerton. The other one was Kate. Which was just as well, as that was Kate's preference within the family.

"She said that Mr. Fibberly called." When Posy did not comment, Sophie added, "He was looking for you."

"Well, of course he was," Posy said, deciding to have that fourth biscuit after all. "Hyacinth is too young and Eloise terrifies him."

"Eloise terrifies me," Sophie admitted. "Or at least she used to. Hyacinth I'm quite sure will terrify me to the grave."

"You just need to know how to manage her," Posy said with a wave. It was true, Hyacinth Bridgerton *was* terrifying, but the two of them had always got on quite well. It was probably due to Hyacinth's firm (some might say unyielding) sense of justice. When she'd found out that Posy's mother had never loved her as well as Rosamund . . .

Well, Posy had never told tales, and she wasn't going to begin now, but let it be said that Araminta had never again eaten fish.

Or chicken.

Posy had got this from the servants, and they always had the most accurate gossip.

"But you were about to tell me about Mr. Fibberly," Sophie said, still sipping at her tea.

Posy shrugged, even though she hadn't been about to do any such thing. "He's so dull."

"Handsome?"

Posy shrugged again. "I can't tell."

"One generally need only look at the face."

"I can't get past his dullness. I don't think he laughs."

"It can't be that bad."

"Oh, it can, I assure you." She reached out and took another biscuit before she realized she hadn't meant to. Oh well, it was already in her hand now, she couldn't very well put it back. She waved it in the air as she spoke, trying to make her point. "He sometimes makes this dreadful noise like, 'Ehrm ehrm ehrm,' and I think he thinks he's laughing, but he's clearly not."

Sophie giggled even though she looked as if she thought she shouldn't.

"And he doesn't even look at my bosom!"

"Posy!"

"It's my *only* good feature."

"It is not!" Sophie glanced about the drawing room, even though there was precisely no one about. "I can't believe you said that."

Posy let out a frustrated exhale. "I can't say *bosom* in London and now I can't do so in Wiltshire, either?"

"Not when I'm expecting the new vicar," Sophie said.

A chunk of Posy's biscuit fell off and fell into her lap. "What?"

"I didn't tell you?"

Posy eyed her suspiciously. Most people thought Sophie was a poor liar, but that was only because she had such an angelic look about her. And she rarely lied. So everyone assumed that if she did, she'd be dreadful at it.

Posy, however, knew better. "No," she said, brushing off her skirts, "you did not tell me."

"How very unlike me," Sophie murmured. She picked up a biscuit and took a bite.

Posy stared at her. "Do you know what I'm not doing now?"

Sophie shook her head.

"I am not rolling my eyes, because I am trying to act in a fashion that befits my age and maturity."

"You do look very grave."

Posy stared her down a bit more. "He is unmarried, I assume."

"Er, yes."

Posy lifted her left brow, the arch expression possibly the only useful gift she'd received from her mother. "How old is this vicar?"

"I do not know," Sophie admitted, "but he has all of his hair."

"And it has come to this," Posy murmured.

"I thought of you when I met him," Sophie said, "because he smiles."

Because he *smiled*? Posy was beginning to think that Sophie was a bit cracked. "I beg your pardon?"

"He smiles so often. And so well." At that *Sophie* smiled. "I couldn't help but think of you."

Posy did roll her eyes this time, then followed it with an immediate "I have decided to forsake maturity."

"By all means."

"I shall meet your vicar," Posy said, "but you should know I have decided to aspire to eccentricity."

"I wish you the best with that," Sophie said, not without sarcasm.

"You don't think I can?"

"You're the least eccentric person I know."

It was true, of course, but if Posy had to spend her life as an old maid, she wanted to be the eccentric one with the large hat, not the desperate one with the pinched mouth.

"What is his name?" she asked.

But before Sophie could answer, they heard the front door opening, and then it was the butler giving her her answer as he announced, "Mr. Woodson is here to see you, Mrs. Bridgerton."

Posy stashed her half-eaten biscuit under a serviette and folded her hands prettily in her lap. She was a little miffed with Sophie for inviting a bachelor for tea without warning her, but still, there seemed little reason not to make a good impression. She looked expectantly at the doorway, waiting patiently as Mr. Woodson's footsteps drew near.

And then . . .

And then . . .

Honestly, it wouldn't do to try to recount it, because she remembered almost nothing of what followed.

She saw him, and it was as if, after twenty-five years of life, her heart finally began to beat.

Hugh Woodson had never been the most admired boy at school. He had never been the most handsome, or the most athletic. He had never been the cleverest, or the snobbiest, or the most foolish. What he had been, and what he had been all of his life, was the most well liked.

People liked him. They always had. He supposed it was because he liked most everybody in return. His mother swore he'd emerged from the womb smiling. She said so with great frequency, although Hugh suspected she did so only to give her father the lead-in for: "Oh, Georgette, you know it was just gas."

Which never failed to set the both of them into fits of giggles.

It was a testament to Hugh's love for them both, and his general ease with himself, that he usually laughed as well.

Nonetheless, for all his likeability, he'd never seemed to attract the females. They adored him, of course, and confided their most desperate secrets, but they always did so in a way that led Hugh to believe he was viewed as a jolly, dependable sort of creature.

The worst part of it was that every woman of his acquaintance was absolutely positive that she knew the *perfect* woman for him, or if not, then she was quite sure that a perfect woman did indeed exist.

That no woman ever thought *herself* the perfect woman had not gone unnoticed. Well, by Hugh, at least. Everyone else was oblivious.

But he carried on, because there could be no point in doing otherwise. And as he had always suspected that women were the cleverer sex, he still held out hope that the perfect woman was indeed out there.

After all, no fewer than four dozen women had said so. They couldn't *all* be wrong.

But Hugh was nearing thirty, and Miss Perfection had not yet seen fit to reveal herself. Hugh was beginning to think that he should take matters into his own hands, except that he hadn't the slightest idea how to do such a thing, especially as he'd just taken a living in a rather quiet corner of Wiltshire, and there didn't seem to be a single appropriately-aged unmarried female in his parish.

Remarkable but true.

Maybe he should wander over to Gloucestershire Sunday next. There was a vacancy there, and he'd been asked to pitch in and deliver a sermon or two until they found a new vicar. There had to be at least one unattached female. The whole of the Cotswolds couldn't be bereft.

But this wasn't the time to dwell on such things. He was just arriving for tea with Mrs. Bridgerton, an invitation for which he was enormously grateful. He was still familiarizing himself with the area and its inhabitants, but it had taken but one church service to know that Mrs. Bridgerton was universally liked and admired. She seemed quite clever and kind as well.

He hoped she liked to gossip. He really needed someone to fill him in on the neighborhood lore. One really couldn't tend to one's flock without knowing its history.

He'd also heard that her cook laid a very fine tea. The biscuits had been mentioned in particular.

"Mr. Woodson to see you, Mrs. Bridgerton."

Hugh stepped into the drawing room as the butler stated his name. He was rather glad he'd forgotten to eat lunch, because the house smelled heavenly and—

And then he quite forgot everything.

Why he'd come.

Who he was.

The color of the sky, even, and the smell of the grass.

Indeed, as he stood there in the arched doorway of the Bridgertons' drawing room, he knew one thing, and one thing only.

The woman on the sofa, the one with the extraordinary eyes who was not Mrs. Bridgerton, was Miss Perfection.

Sophie Bridgerton knew a thing or two about love at first sight. She had, once upon a time, been hit by its proverbial lightning bolt, struck dumb with breathless passion, heady bliss, and an odd tingling sensation across her entire body.

Or at least, that was how she remembered it.

She also remembered that while Cupid's arrow had, in her case, proven remarkably accurate, it had taken quite a while for her and Benedict to reach their happily ever after. So even though she wanted to bounce in her seat with glee as she watched Posy and Mr. Woodson stare at each other like a pair of lovesick puppies, another part of her—the extremely practical, born-on-the-wrong-side-of-the-blanket, I-am-well-aware-that-the-world-is-not-made-up-of-rainbows-and-angels part of her—was trying to hold back her excitement.

But the thing about Sophie was, no matter how awful her childhood had been (and parts of it had been quite dreadfully awful), no matter what cruelties and indignities she'd faced in her life (and there, too, she'd not been fortunate), she was, at heart, an incurable romantic.

Which brought her to Posy.

It was true that Posy visited several times each year, and it was also true that one of those visits almost always coincided with the end of the season, but Sophie *might* have added a little extra entreaty to her recently tendered invitation. She might have exaggerated a bit when describing how quickly the children were growing, and there was a chance that she had actually lied when she said that she was feeling poorly.

But in this case, the ends absolutely justified the means. Oh, Posy had told her that she would be perfectly content to remain unmarried, but Sophie did not believe her for a second. Or to be more precise, Sophie believed that Posy believed that she would be perfectly content. But one had only to look at Posy snuggling little William and Alexander to know that she was a born mother, and that the world would be a much poorer place if Posy did not have a passel of children to call her own.

It was true that Sophie had, one time or twelve, made a point of introducing Posy to whichever unattached gentleman was to be found at the moment in Wiltshire, but *this time* . . .

This time Sophie knew.

This time it was love.

"Mr. Woodson," she said, trying not to grin like a madwoman, "may I introduce you to my dear sister, Miss Posy Reiling?"

Mr. Woodson looked as if he thought he was saying something, but the truth was, he was staring at Posy as if he'd just met Aphrodite.

"Posy," Sophie continued, "this is Mr. Woodson, our new vicar. He is only recently arrived, what was it, three weeks ago?"

He had been in residence for nearly two months. Sophie knew this perfectly well, but she was eager to see if he'd been listening well enough to correct her.

He just nodded, never taking his eyes off Posy.

"Please, Mr. Woodson," Sophie murmured, "do sit down."

He managed to understand her meaning, and he lowered himself into a chair.

"Tea, Mr. Woodson?" Sophie inquired.

He nodded.

"Posy, will you pour?"

Posy nodded.

Sophie waited, and then when it became apparent that Posy wasn't going to do much of anything besides smile at Mr. Woodson, she said, *"Posy."*

Posy turned to look at her, but her head moved so slowly and with such reluctance, it was as if a giant magnet had turned its force onto her.

"Will you pour Mr. Woodson's tea?" Sophie murmured, trying to restrict her smile to her eyes.

"Oh. Of course." Posy turned back to the vicar, that silly smile returning to her face. "Would you like some tea?"

Normally Sophie might have mentioned that she had already asked Mr. Woodson if he wanted tea, but there was nothing normal about this encounter, so she decided to simply sit back and observe.

"I would love some," Mr. Woodson said to Posy. "Above all else."

Really, Sophie thought, it was as if she weren't even there.

"How do you take it?" Posy asked.

"However you wish."

Oh now, this was too much. No man fell so blindingly into love that he no longer held a preference for his tea. This was England, for heaven's sake. More to the point, this was *tea*.

"We have both milk and sugar," Sophie said, unable to help herself. She'd intended to sit and watch, but really, even the most hopeless romantic couldn't have remained silent.

Mr. Woodson didn't hear her.

"Either of them would be appropriate in your cup," she added.

"You have the most extraordinary eyes," he said, and his voice was full of wonder, as if he couldn't quite believe that he was right there in this room, with Posy.

"Your smile," Posy said in return. "It's . . . lovely."

He leaned forward. "Do you like roses, Miss Reiling?"

Posy nodded.

"I must bring you some."

Sophie gave up trying to appear serene and finally let herself grin. It wasn't as if either of them was looking at her, anyway. "We have roses," she said.

No response.

"In the back garden."

Again, nothing.

"Where the two of you might go for a stroll."

It was as if someone had just stuck a pin in both of them.

"Oh, shall we?"

"I would be delighted."

"Please, allow me to—"

"Take my arm."

"I would—"

"You must—"

By the time Posy and Mr. Woodson were at the door, Sophie could hardly tell who was saying what. And not a drop of tea had entered Mr. Woodson's cup.

Sophie waited for a full minute, and then burst out laughing, clapping her hand over her mouth to stifle the sound, although she wasn't sure why she needed to. It was a laugh of pure delight. Pride, too, at having orchestrated the whole thing.

"What are you laughing about?" It was Benedict, wandering into the room, his fingers stained with paint. "Ah, biscuits. Excellent. I'm famished. Forgot to eat this morning." He took the last one and frowned. "You might have left more for me."

"It's Posy," Sophie said, grinning. "And Mr. Woodson. I predict a very short engagement."

Benedict's eyes widened. He turned to the door, then to the window. "Where are they?"

"In the back. We can't see them from here."

He chewed thoughtfully. "But we could from my studio."

For about two seconds neither moved. But only two seconds.

They ran for the door, pushing and shoving their way down the hall to Benedict's studio, which jutted out of the back of the house, giving it light from three directions. Sophie got there first, although not by entirely fair means, and let out a shocked gasp.

"What is it?" Benedict said from the doorway.

"They're kissing!"

He strode forward. "They are not."

"Oh, they are."

He drew up beside her, and his mouth fell open. "Well, I'll be damned."

And Sophie, who never cursed, responded, "I know. I *know*."

"And they only just met? Really?"

"You kissed me the first night we met," she pointed out.

"That was different."

Sophie managed to pull her attention from the kissing couple on the lawn for just long enough to demand, "How?"

He thought about that for a moment, then answered, "It was a masquerade."

"Oh, so it's all right to kiss someone if you don't know who they are?"

"Not fair, Sophie," he said, clucking as he shook his head. "I asked you, and you wouldn't tell me."

That was true enough to put an end to that particular branch of the conversation, and they stood there for another moment, shamelessly watching Posy and the vicar. They'd stopped kissing and were now talking—from the looks of it, a mile a minute. Posy would speak, and then Mr. Woodson would nod vigorously and interrupt her, and then she would interrupt him, and then he looked like he was giggling, of all things, and then Posy began to speak with such animation that her arms waved all about her head.

"What on earth could they be saying?" Sophie wondered.

"Probably everything they should have said

before he kissed her." Benedict frowned, crossing his arms. "How long have they been at this, anyway?"

"You've been watching just as long as I have."

"No, I meant, when did he arrive? Did they even speak before . . ." He waved his hand toward the window, gesturing to the couple, who looked about ready to kiss again.

"Yes, of course, but . . ." Sophie paused, thinking. Both Posy and Mr. Woodson had been rather tongue-tied at their meeting. In fact, she couldn't recall a single substantive word that was spoken. "Well, not very much, I'm afraid."

Benedict nodded slowly. "Do you think I should go out there?"

Sophie looked at him, then at the window, and then back. "Are you mad?"

He shrugged. "She is my sister now, and it *is* my house . . ."

"Don't you dare!"

"So I'm not supposed to protect her honor?"

"It's her first kiss!"

He quirked a brow. "And here we are, spying on it."

"It's my right," Sophie said indignantly. "I arranged the whole thing."

"Oh you did, did you? I seem to recall that *I* was the one to suggest Mr. Woodson."

"But you didn't *do* anything about it."

"That's your job, darling."

Sophie considered a retort, because his tone was rather annoying, but he did have a point. She did rather enjoy trying to find a match for Posy, and she was *definitely* enjoying her obvious success.

"You know," Benedict said thoughtfully, "we might have a daughter someday."

Sophie turned to him. He wasn't normally one for such non sequiturs. "I beg your pardon?"

He gestured to the lovebirds on the lawn. "Just that this could be excellent practice for me. I'm quite certain I wish to be an overbearingly protective father. I could storm out and tear him apart from limb to limb."

Sophie winced. Poor Mr. Woodson wouldn't stand a chance.

"Challenge him to a duel?"

She shook her head.

"Very well, but if he lowers her to the ground, I am interceding."

"He won't— Oh dear heavens!" Sophie leaned forward, her face nearly to the glass. "Oh my God."

And she didn't even cover her mouth in horror at having blasphemed.

Benedict sighed, then flexed his fingers. "I really don't want to injure my hands. I'm halfway through your portrait, and it's going so well."

Sophie had one hand on his arm, holding him back even though he wasn't really moving anywhere. "No," she said, "don't—" She gasped. "Oh, my. Maybe we should do something."

"They're not on the ground yet."

"Benedict!"

"Normally I'd say to call the priest," he remarked, "except that seems to be what got us into this mess in the first place."

Sophie swallowed. "Perhaps you can procure a special license for them? As a wedding gift?"

He grinned. "Consider it done."

It was a splendid wedding. And that kiss at the end . . .

No one was surprised when Posy produced a baby nine months later, and then at yearly intervals after that. She took great care in the naming of her brood, and Mr. Woodson, who was as beloved a vicar as he'd been in every other stage of his life, adored her too much to argue with any of her choices.

First there was Sophia, for obvious reasons, and then Benedict. The next would have been Violet, except that Sophie begged her not to. She'd always wanted the name for her daughter, and it would be far too confusing with the families living so close. So Posy went with Georgette, after Hugh's mother, whom she thought had just the *nicest* smile.

After that was John, after Hugh's father. For quite some time it appeared that he would remain the baby of the family. After giving birth every June for four years in a row, Posy stopped getting pregnant. She wasn't doing anything differently, she confided in Sophie; she and Hugh were still very much in love. It just seemed that her body had decided it was through with childbearing.

Which was just as well. With two girls and two boys, all in the single digits, she had her hands full.

But then, when John was five, Posy rose from bed one morning and threw up on the floor. It could only mean one thing, and the following autumn, she delivered a girl.

Sophie was present at the birth, as she always was. "What shall you name her?" she asked.

Posy looked down at the perfect little creature in her arms. It was sleeping quite soundly, and even though she knew that newborns did not smile, the baby really did look as if it were rather pleased about something.

Maybe about being born. Maybe this one was going to attack life with a smile. Good humor would be her weapon of choice.

What a splendid human being she would be.

"Araminta," Posy said suddenly.

Sophie nearly fell over from the shock of it. "*What?*"

"I want to name her Araminta. I'm quite certain." Posy stroked the baby's cheek, then touched her gently under the chin.

Sophie could not seem to stop shaking her head. "But your mother . . . I can't believe you would—"

"I'm not naming her *for* my mother," Posy cut in gently. "I'm naming her *because* of my mother. It's different."

Sophie looked dubious, but she leaned over to get a closer peek at the baby. "She's really quite sweet," she murmured.

Posy smiled, never once taking her eyes off the baby's face. "I know."

"I suppose I could grow accustomed to it," Sophie said, her head bobbing from side to side in acquiescence. She wiggled her finger between the baby's hand and body, giving the palm a little tickle until the tiny fingers wrapped instinctively around her own. "Good evening, Araminta," she said. "Very nice to meet you."

"Minty," Posy said.

Sophie looked up. "What?"

"I'm calling her Minty. Araminta will do well in the family Bible, but I do believe she's a Minty."

Sophie pressed her lips together in an effort not to smile. "Your mother would hate that."

"Yes," Posy murmured, "she would, wouldn't she?"

"Minty," Sophie said, testing the sound on her tongue. "I like it. No, I think I love it. It suits her."

Posy kissed the top of Minty's head. "What kind of girl will you be?" she whispered. "Sweet and docile?"

Sophie chuckled at that. She had been present at twelve birthings—four of her own, five of Posy's, and three of Benedict's sister Eloise. Never had she heard a baby enter this world with as loud a cry as little Minty. "This one," she said firmly, "is going to lead you a merry chase."

And she did. But that, dear reader, is another story . . .

Meet the Bridgerton family . . .

The Bridgertons are by far the most prolific family in the upper echelons of society. Such industriousness on the part of the viscountess and the late viscount is commendable, although one can find only banality in their choice of names for their children. Anthony, Benedict, Colin, Daphne, Eloise, Francesca, Gregory, and Hyacinth (orderliness is, of course, beneficial in all things, but one would think that intelligent parents would be able to keep their children straight without needing to alphabetize their names).

It has been said that Lady Bridgerton's dearest goal is to see all of her offspring happily married, but truly, one can only wonder if this is an impossible feat. Eight children? Eight happy marriages? It boggles the mind.

LADY WHISTLEDOWN'S SOCIETY PAPERS,
SUMMER 1813

The Duke and I

WHO: Daphne Bridgerton and the Duke of Hastings.
WHAT: A sham courtship.
WHERE: London, of course. Where else could one pull off such a thing?
WHY: They each have their reasons, neither of which includes falling in love . . .

The Viscount Who Loved Me

The season has opened for the year of 1814, and there is little reason to hope that we will see any noticeable change from 1813. The ranks of society are once again filled with Ambitious Mamas, whose only aim is to see their Darling Daughters married off to Determined Bachelors. Discussion amongst the Mamas fingers Viscount Bridgerton as this year's most eligible catch, and indeed, if the poor man's hair looks ruffled and windblown, it is because he cannot go anywhere without some young miss batting her eyelashes with such vigor and speed as to create a breeze of hurricane force. Perhaps the only young lady not interested in Bridgerton is Miss Katharine Sheffield, and in fact, her demeanor toward the viscount occasionally borders on the hostile.

And that is why, Dear Reader, This Author feels that a match between Bridgerton and Miss Sheffield would be just the thing to enliven an otherwise ordinary season.

LADY WHISTLEDOWN'S SOCIETY PAPERS, 13 APRIL 1814

An Offer From a Gentleman

The 1815 season is well under way, and while one would think that all talk would be of Wellington and Waterloo, in truth, there is little change from the conversations of 1814, which centered around that most eternal of society topics—marriage.

As usual, the matrimonial hopes among the debutante set center upon the Bridgerton family, most specifically the eldest of the available brothers, Benedict. He might not possess a title, but his handsome face, pleasing form, and heavy purse appear to have made up for that lack handily. Indeed, This Author has heard, on more than one occasion, an Ambitious Mama saying of her daughter: "She'll marry a duke . . . or a Bridgerton."

For his part, Mr. Bridgerton seems most uninterested in the young ladies who frequent society events. He attends almost every party, yet he does nothing but watch the doors, presumably waiting for some special person.

Perhaps . . .

A potential bride?

LADY WHISTLEDOWN'S SOCIETY PAPERS, 12 JULY 1815

Romancing Mister Bridgerton

April is nearly upon us, and with it a new social season here in London. Ambitious Mamas can be found at dress-shops all across town with their Darling Debutantes, eager to purchase that one magical evening gown that they simply know will mean the difference between marriage and spinsterhood.

As for their prey—the Determined Bachelors—Mr. Colin Bridgerton once again tops the list of desirable husbands, even though he is not yet back from his recent trip abroad. He has no title, that is true, but he is in abundant possession of looks, fortune, and, as anyone who has ever spent even a minute in London knows, charm.

But Mr. Bridgerton has reached the somewhat advanced age of three-and-thirty without ever showing an interest in any particular young lady, and there is little reason to anticipate that 1824 will be any different from 1823 in this respect.

Perhaps the Darling Debutantes—and perhaps more importantly their Ambitious Mamas—would do well to look elsewhere. If Mr. Bridgerton is looking for a wife, he hides that desire well.

On the other hand, is that not just the sort of challenge a debutante likes best?

LADY WHISTLEDOWN'S SOCIETY PAPERS

To Sir Phillip, With Love

. . . I know you say I shall someday like boys, but I say never! NEVER!!! With three exclamation points!!!

—from Eloise Bridgerton to her mother,
shoved under Violet Bridgerton's door
during Eloise's eighth year

. . . I never dreamed that a season could be so exciting! The men are so handsome and charming. I know I shall fall in love straightaway. How could I not?

—from Eloise Bridgerton to her brother Colin,
upon the occasion of her London debut

. . . I am quite certain I shall never marry. If there was someone out there for me, don't you think I should have found him by now?

—from Eloise Bridgerton to her
dear friend Penelope Featherington,
during her sixth season as a debutante

. . . this is my last chance. I am grabbing destiny with both my hands and throwing caution to the wind. Sir Phillip, please, *please,* be all that I have imagined you to be. Because if you are the man your letters portray you to be, I think I could love you. And if you felt the same . . .

—from Eloise Bridgerton, jotted on a scrap of paper
on her way to meet Sir Phillip Crane
for the very first time

When He Was Wicked

WHAT DOES IT MEAN TO BE WICKED?

For Michael Stirling, it was a hidden love, an insatiable longing for the one woman who could never be his.

WHAT DOES IT MEAN TO BE WANTON?

For Francesca Bridgerton, it started with a single kiss, placed on her lips by the one man she never thought she'd desire.

WHAT HAPPENS WHEN THERE ARE NO MORE SECRETS?

Find out in Julia Quinn's most breathtaking and passionate romance yet . . .

It's In His Kiss

Our Cast of Characters

Hyacinth Bridgerton: The youngest of the famed Bridgerton siblings, she's a little too smart, a little too outspoken, and certainly not your average romance heroine. She's also, much to her dismay, falling in love with . . .

Gareth St. Clair: There are some men in London with wicked reputations, and there are others who are handsome as sin. But Gareth is the only one who manages to combine the two with such devilish success. He'd be a complete rogue, if not for . . .

Lady Danbury: Grandmother to Gareth, mentor to Hyacinth, she has an opinion on everything, especially love and marriage. And she'd like nothing better than to see Gareth and Hyacinth joined in holy matrimony. Luckily, she's to have help from . . .

One meddling mother, one overprotective brother, one very bad string quartet, one (thankfully fictional) mad baron, and of course, let us not forget the shepherdess, the unicorn, and Henry the Eighth.

Join them all in the most memorable
love story of the year . . .

On the Way to the Wedding

In which:

Firstly, Gregory Bridgerton falls in love with the wrong woman, and

Secondly, she falls in love with someone else, but

Thirdly, Lucy Abernathy decides to meddle; however,

Fourthly, she falls in love with Gregory, which is highly inconvenient because

Fifthly, she is practically engaged to Lord Haselby, but

Sixthly, Gregory falls in love with Lucy.

Which leaves everyone in a bit of a pickle.

Watch them all find their happy endings in:

The stunning conclusion
to the Bridgerton series
Available now

THE SMYTHE-SMITH QUARTET BY #1 *NEW YORK TIMES* BESTSELLING AUTHOR

JUST LIKE HEAVEN

978-0-06-149190-0

Honoria Smythe-Smith is to play the violin (badly) in the annual musicale performed by the Smythe-Smith quartet. But first she's determined to marry by the end of the season. When her advances are spurned, can Marcus Holroyd, her brother Daniel's best friend, swoop in and steal her heart in time for the musicale?

A NIGHT LIKE THIS

978-0-06-207290-0

Anne Wynter is not who she says she is, but she's managing quite well as a governess to three highborn young ladies. Daniel Smythe-Smith might be in mortal danger, but that's not going to stop the young earl from falling in love. And when he spies a mysterious woman at his family's annual musicale, he vows to pursue her.

THE SUM OF ALL KISSES

978-0-06-207292-4

Hugh Prentice has never had patience for dramatic females, and Lady Sarah Pleinsworth has never been acquainted with the words *shy* or *retiring*. Besides, a reckless duel has left Hugh with a ruined leg, and now he could never court a woman like Sarah, much less dream of marrying her.

THE SECRETS OF SIR RICHARD KENWORTHY

978-0-06-207294-8

Sir Richard Kenworthy has less than a month to find a bride, and when he sees Iris Smythe-Smith hiding behind her cello at her family's infamous musicale, he thinks he might have struck gold. Iris is used to blending into the background, so when Richard courts her, she can't quite believe it's true.

Don't miss the Bridgerton 2nd Epilogues . . .
where you get the story *after* the story.

Because when you're a Bridgerton, Happily Ever After is a whole lot of fun.

Available as a collection in
The Bridgertons: Happily Ever After,
wherever books are sold.

Visit **www.juliaquinn.com** for Bridgerton FAQs and the interactive Bridgerton family tree.

How to Marry a Marquis

978-0-380-80081-0

When Elizabeth Hotchkiss stumbles upon a guidebook to seduction, she thinks what harm can there be in taking a little peek?

To Catch an Heiress

978-0-380-78935-1

When Caroline Trent is kidnapped by Blake Ravenscroft, she doesn't even try to elude this dangerously handsome agent of the crown.

And Don't Miss

Brighter Than the Sun

978-0-380-78934-4

Everything and the Moon

978-0-380-78933-7

Minx

978-0-380-78562-9

Dancing at Midnight

978-0-380-78075-4

Splendid

978-0-380-78074-7

Available wherever books are sold or please call 1-800-331-3761 to order.

JQ1 0415

#1 New York Times Bestselling Author

Julia Quinn

The Secret Diaries of Miss Miranda Cheever

978-0-06-123083-7

When Miranda Cheever was ten, Nigel Bevelstoke, the dashing Viscount Turner, kissed her hand and promised her one day she would be as beautiful as she was already smart. And even at ten, Miranda knew she would love him forever.

The Lost Duke of Wyndham

978-0-06-087610-4

Grace Eversleigh has spent the last five years toiling as the companion to the dowager Duchess of Wyndham. It is a thankless job...until Jack Audley, the long-lost son of the House of Wyndham, lands in her life, all rakish smiles and debonair charm.

Mr. Cavendish, I Presume

978-0-06-087611-1

A mere six months old when she's contractually engaged to Thomas Cavendish, the Duke of Wyndham, Amelia Willoughby has spent her life waiting to be married. But their worlds are rocked by the arrival of his long-lost cousin, who may be the true Duke of Wyndham...and Amelia's intended.

What Happens In London

978-0-06-149188-7

When Olivia Bevelstoke is told her new neighbor may have killed his fiancée, she doesn't believe it, but, still, how can she help spying on him, just to be sure? She stakes out a spot near her bedroom window and discovers a most intriguing man, who is definitely up to something...